Slot-Machine Kelly

Slot-Machine Kelly

The Collected Private Eye Cases
of the "One-Armed Bandit"

Dennis Lynds

writing as

Michael Collins

With an introduction by Robert J. Randisi

Crippen & Landru   Norfolk, VA   2005

ISBN (clothbound edition): 1-932009-40-X
ISBN (trade softcover edition): 1-932009-41-8

FIRST EDITION

Printed in the United States of America on acid-free paper

Crippen & Landru Publishers
P. O. Box 9315
Norfolk, VA 23505
USA

Email: Info@crippenlandru.com
Web: www.crippenlandru.com

CONTENTS

False Pretenses: An Introduction
by Robert J. Randisi

I have known Dennis Lynds for about twenty-six years. Before we even met I'd been reading him, ever since 1967, when *Act of Fear* was published under the pseudonym "Michael Collins." It won the Edgar for Best First Mystery Novel, that year. The book introduced one-armed private detective Dan Fortune, who went on to appear in eighteen novels, and who became one of the most enduring P.I.'s in the genre. (Four Dan Fortune stories were published in 2004, so the character has appeared in five different decades. Dennis, himself, has been published in six.) Later, Dennis served as President of the Private Eye Writers of America, and later still won that organization's Life Achievement Award, "The Eye." (In 1982, when we gave our first Life Achievement Award to Ross Macdonald, it was Dennis who stepped up and accepted that award on behalf of his good friend, who was too ill to attend.) One wonders why the Mystery Writers of America have not yet awarded him the Grand Master?

And perhaps, for me, that is more the point of this introduction. Maybe someone in MWA will read this and make the suggestion. So you'll forgive me if I don't cover the stories that appear in this collection individually, one by one. I'm hoping readers of this introduction will—if they do not already—realize all that Dennis Lynds has meant to the mystery genre in general, and to the P.I. sub-genre in particular.

A collection of Dan Fortune stories was published as *Fortune's World*. (I was not asked to do the introduction for that book and later discovered the book was dedicated to me. That was my honor, but led me to seek out the right to do this introduction, and have my say.) Those stories were published under the name Michael Collins. Another collection, of non-P.I. and "literary" stories, was published under the title *Talking to the World*, using his own name. Under either name, however, Lynds or Collins—or even Mark Sadler or John Crowe, two more of his better known *nom de plumes*—Dennis has been writing in this genre for a very long time. As a writer myself, I have named him as one of my earliest influences. It was then my privilege to have him move from influence to friend. But in spite of all that I claim objectivity. I claim that my opinions are not influenced by friendship, because of the simple fact that the man can write. These Slot-Machine Kelly stories could be dismissed by some as pulp fiction, but I venture beyond that opinion. If this is true then they are pulp writing at its best, but they are also the early work of a man whose social conscience peers over his shoulder at every word he writes. It did so 50 years ago and it does so today. His work not only entertains, it informs and it provokes. For me, that's the description of the perfect writer.

7

So he's a talented and thoroughly professional writer, has been a major influence on my work, a colleague, and a friend.

That said I'd like to point out the fact that you cannot draw a line from Ross Macdonald to Robert B. Parker without having it go right through the name "Michael Collins." It was Dennis who, under the Collins byline, beginning in 1967—along with his colleague in crime, Bill Pronzini—kept the P.I. genre alive by coming out with a book a year about Dan Fortune. This was during a time when New York editors were claiming that "private eye" novels did not sell. It was not until the early 80's that the resurgence of the P.I. truly began in earnest with the regular appearance of work by such authors as Valin, Greenleaf, Lewin, Lutz, Lyons, Muller, Grafton, Paretsky, Healy and another M. Collins—this one Max Allan—all of whom followed Robert B. Parker's lead into the fray. (Max and "Michael" had a discussion about this at one time, with Michael pointing out that he was there first, and Max pointing out that Collins was his real name. They agreed to coexist.)

However, since it was Dennis who kept the genre alive until the others could arrive, this established "Michael Collins" as a major figure in the development of the American P.I. And while the stories in this collection may not reflect that—they are probably too raw for that distinction—this was an opportunity for me to point that out. So you may accuse me of being here under false pretenses, but this collection is still an opportunity for you, the reader, to experience the early talents of a "major figure in the development of the American P.I." (Quoting myself, here.)

Where else could you get such a opportunity?

IF THE WHISKY DON'T,
THE WOMEN WILL

Sometime in early 1959 in New York, with one unsold novel in the drawer, I holed up in my fourth-floor walkup on West Seventy-Third Street on a two week vacation from the magazine where I worked, finished my second novel, and in February 1960 sold it to New American Library. I sold my third to NAL in September 1960. I was unattached at the time, so on the strength of those two advances I quit my job, and went to Santa Barbara to finish my next novel.

But I met a new lady between the time I gave notice, and the time I actually left for California. One thing led to another, I returned to New York, married her, and the fourth novel was bad. I worked on rewriting it, started other mainstream novels, realized I hadn't found the kind of novel I wanted to write yet, and needed money. New York was always expensive.

I had published many short stories in the literary monthlies and quarterlies, even one in New World Writing, *the literary showcase of NAL-Signet, but they paid from nothing to next-to-nothing. So I decided to try my hand at commercial fiction. I'd always loved detective stories, had met a tacky two-bit P.I. named Harry down in the Village some years before, and, using him as a basis for an anti-hero, came up with an appropriately sleazy plot, and wrote this story. I sent it to* Mike Shayne Mystery Magazine, *they bought it for $40.00—a penny a word. It was my first detective fiction publication, and Slot-Machine Kelly was born.*

SLOT-MACHINE KELLY is a private eye with a two-by-four office down by the docks. His weakness is whisky and women. This time it was a woman. More dames go for Slot-Machine than go for any two other guys I ever met, and it ain't his money. He ain't got money most of the time. And that is a testimonial.

I've known Slot for twenty years, and I can tell it. Slot-Machine, he's my best friend. Which means he lets me buy him booze, he gives me some leg work once in a while, and he don't steal from me too much. I'm Joe Harris, I'm bartender days at Eddie Tomasian's *Mona Lisa Tavern* on Tenth Avenue and 25th Street. At least, I was until that night.

Slot-Machine he ain't a big guy. About five-foot-eight, 160 pounds, and his face ain't exactly a school-kid's dream even around Tenth Avenue. He looks poor, and dumb, and too beat-up to hurt a fly. He's poor all right, but he ain't dumb, so as you'd notice, and he can move that arm to catch a fly so quick you don't even see his hand move. I said hand 'cause that's why we calls him Slot-Machine. He got only one arm and he'll do just about anything for a buck. Patrick X. Kelly, the one-armed bandit. Only don't call him that to his face, he's sensitive. About the bandit part, not the arm.

9

"The dames like me," Slot-Machine says. "It's the flipper I lost does it. Ever tell you how I lost it in the war, Joe?"

"You told me," I said.

He tells everyone how he lost that arm in the war. He tells it real nice, with actions and all. The only trouble is he's told it maybe ten different ways to the same guys. It can be a real pretty story when he's had too much of Eddie's bar whisky. Nobody reminds him he told it before different. He's fast and he learned a lot of tricks with his good arm and his two good feet. Only I like to think they don't spoil it because they like him, and if telling it that way about the war makes him feel good, it's okay with them.

I guess that missing wing is the big thing in Slot-Machine's life, and down by the docks everybody got his troubles and don't go around knocking another guy's way out. Some guys use whisky, and some guys uses junk, and some guys chases girl kids up dark alleys. Slot-Machine he just makes up stories about how he lost the arm in the war.

Slot-Machine never made the war. The wing was gone already, and maybe that's it. He wanted to make that war. He lost the wing in an industrial accident. At least that's what the cops and the company got down on the records. We was both just punk kids then, working on the docks. Slot fell into a hold on a Dutchman ship at 2:00 A.M. on a dark night with about $50 worth of loot in a bag and me waitin' outside the ship. Busted the arm up bad, complications set in, and he lost the wing.

We both got fired from the job and no more 'cause all they could prove was trespassing seeing as how Slot got the stuff out a porthole busted arm or no busted arm. Only the real story got around then, and that's how he got the name. Sometimes I figure he tells those war stories 'cause he's ashamed how he lost it now that he's been almost legal for twenty years.

He's got a one room office on 28th Street over by Eighth Avenue, and he lives in a six flight walk-up hole I pays for most of the time. He ain't never learned a trade, never had the chance, and who's gonna hire a one-armed guy with no talent except for makin' deals right close to the line of the law? Deals, and the fact no one takes much notice of a cripple or kicks up a fuss when he's serving a summons, is what made Slot-Machine a private eye.

It don't pay so good. Summonses and divorces and a lot of deals mighty thin this side of the law is Slot's trade. His trouble is women. And whisky. And the fact he don't like work much at all.

This time it was a broad. It's a quiet Monday about 4:00 P.M. and I'm behind the bar in the *Mona Lisa* and Slot-Machine's on the other side building up a tab. No loot at all.

"Go to work," I said.

"I'm servin' summonses, ain't I"

"You'll get it in a ditch."

"Who's gonna take on a cripple?"

And this dame comes in. Now we got some pretty nice dames around Tenth

Avenue. We got the kind with faces that says they live on their knees in church, but eyes that says they're liars. We got dames you don't mind looking at all day. And we got big blondes who walk by the pool hall and the guys forget to rack their cues on the way out. But this one had something more.

Slot-Machine was staring like he just seen $5,000 cold cash handed him for free, and in the back Eddie Tomasian's forgetting to count the take. She wasn't big and she wasn't lush and she didn't have a face like Elizabeth Taylor. But she had it. From the long red hair that shined like it had a built-in sun, to the green sheath dress, and down to the legs so tanned only technicolor could do them justice. You know how it is, you can't explain it.

About five foot five and a hundred and fifteen pounds I'd say. Nothing special. But she had it. Maybe it was the way she stood there, sort of proud and bored but a real small smile like she was thinking of something a little funny. Just stood there inside the door with the sun following her like it didn't want to lose a minute of her. Then Slot-Machine and me see she's heading toward us.

"You're Kelly?" she says. She says it, she doesn't ask. "Slot-Machine Kelly, the one-armed bandit?"

Now, like I said, Slot-Machine he's sensitive, but the dame is smiling and it's like he don't hear her.

"I've got a proposition," she says.

Now Slot-Machine goes for the dames, I told you about that, but dames he's got, and proposition means loot to him so he comes down to earth fast. The world's full of dames so he comes down off the cloud in one second flat and eyes the redhead all business-like.

"Everybody got a proposition," Slot-Machine says. "Yours personal or business? Legal, or is there money in it?"

"Business," she says, "and there's money in it."

Slot-Machine says, "There's business and there's business, I'm listening."

She goes into her spiel. She tells it straight with no fancy riffs on the violins. I listen, and she don't look the part she talkin' about—maybe that's why she does good enough to wear the real fine rags she got on her back. Seems she's got a racket. She runs a peep show. Now maybe that don't sound much of a job for a doll like her, but down on the docks we knows that there's a whole lot of beautiful dolls, and beautiful don't pay the rent as easy as most squares think.

She's got the looks and the talent, and peeping ain't as hard on the nerves as some jobs dolls got to take. She's new in town, and she needs a little muscle to collect the dough and keep the peepers in line in case they get ideas, and she needs a guy to keep the cops happy enough to let her alone.

She's all business. "I have the rooms lined up, I just need some protection."

"What kind of peeping?" Slot-Machine wants to know. But I can see it's strictly for the record that question, so he don't look too anxious. The dollar signs are already marking up in his eyes. Mine, too, I admit. Times was bad.

She shrugs, "Usual routine. I'm the dame next door, and you're the smart guy who has the room next to me cut with peep-holes. I don't know they're even looking. I go through the getting ready for bed routine. That's all, but they get their money's worth."

I'm thinking I'll bet they sure as hell do when I feel Eddie Tomasian standing next to me. Eddie's a big shot, he's going way up top if you hear him tell it, and he don't like Slot-Machine. Slot-Machine's the independent type, and Eddie don't figure a guy with one arm got anything to feel proud about.

I seen a lot of guys like Eddie in my time. They always figure a guy without an arm or a leg or all his marbles upstairs ain't got no rights. Like Eddie didn't think Slot-Machine had a right breathing the same air as him. There was that Susy O'Hara dame, too. Eddie don't forget losing a dame to a one-armed guy.

Eddie says, "Peddle your trade, somewhere else, sister."

"She's my cousin," Slot-Machine says. "I'm giving her the grocery list."

"Kelly, you got two months tab in this place, keep your yap shut or blow."

"I likes your decoration," Slot-Machine says, "it's restful like."

The dame says, "Who's your oily friend, Kelly?"

"He comes in a bottle, Red," Slot-Machine says. "He's half grease and half water."

Eddie turns blue. Then he turns red. "You got a big mouth for a cripple, Kelly."

I held Slot-Machine. If I lost the job we both starve. Slot is mad, but he ain't so mad he's going to tackle Eddie in his own place. So Slot just says, "Let's blow, Red, we're in business. I'll get my heap out front and go pay a call on the law."

"Well use mine," the dame said. "The law knows your heap like it's a calling card, right? The law don't always stay paid."

"You got a head," Slot-Machine says.

"I got more," the dame said.

She gives Eddie a real mean eye and goes up to Slot and kisses him. I hear warning bells in my head. The dame is holding that kiss a hell of a long time, and there's an alarm ringing in my head. Slot likes a dame like this, and that makes him careless.

I heard a doc say once it was Slot looking for his mother, and I heard guys say he was just provin' he was as good as anyone with two arms, but me I figured he just likes dames. And now I'm worrying. We need that bread. But the dame pulls away now. She turns to give Eddie the stare. Eddie looks like he could murder Slot right there. The dame sort of grins, and walks right up to Eddie.

"Take it slow, two-arms," she says to Eddie, and she puts her hand inside that hundred buck jacket he's wearing.

Eddie turns purple and grabs her hand. The dame laughed like hell. "You ain't so hard, two arms. Give my friends and me drinks all around and maybe I'll throw you a bone."

"Joe," Eddie said, "Give 'em what they want. Take one yourself."

And Eddie walks off into the street like he needs air. Well, any dame can make Eddie spring for a round has to have talent. I didn't ask any questions, not when Eddie is buying, and we had double Scotches on the rocks all around. It tasted good all the way down. Slot and the redhead are nose to nose. They're discussing business. With their mouths anyway. With her eyes the dame is not talking business to Slot.

Eddie is still out for the air, so I served another round. When Eddie gets back, he gives me the fish eye, but I've got the glasses in the water by then. Eddie slides up to the dame, sort of holds her the way Eddie always holds a dame, like she was a door prize.

The dame says, "Hands off, big man, one drink gets you a quick look. Let's blow, one arm."

It's quittin' time so I went out with them, and we're in business. Slot-Machine goes to do his part with the precinct fuzz, the dame goes to set up the peep, and I start to cruise for customers. You know: the bars and alleys and pool rooms where the suckers hang out. Guys who got so little to be happy about they'll pay to peep at a dame through a hole in the wall. I guess it's better than nothing.

So I cruise, and then it's 7:00 P.M., and dark, and I head for rooms the dame has set up. They're in a dump on 27th Street. Three flights up, knock four long and two short, say Harris sent you.

Slot is in the corner on a stool. Five guys're lined up at the peep holes, and five more're waiting. Slot waves me over. He's got his own private peep hole cut with his blade. He says I can be his guest a while. I am.

When the third show's over, it's maybe eleven. Slot has to pry their eyeballs loose from the peepholes. They left hard every time. But the bread is piling up, and I'm just about to start out for another cruise, when Slot bangs on the wall and the dame comes in from the next room. She's got those rich rags on again, but I can remember. I smile at her. Her eyes looks right through me at Slot-Machine.

She says, "Ready?"

"Since I was weaned," Slot said.

"We'll count the take at my place," the dame says all sweet. "If you're nice maybe there's a bonus."

"We got hours!" I protest.

"You work, bartender, I'm tired," the dame says. "Whistle up a cab, One Arm."

I'm hurt, you know? I mean, Slot's my best friend, and besides it's too early to quit such a sweet racket. But out they go. So I was alone in that room with the peep-holes and nothin' to peep at. It was discouraging. It was so bad I went over to the *Mona Lisa* for a drink. If I know Slot, the dame won't feel like business tomorrow, and that bread was rolling in.

I walked slow, the *Mona Lisa* ain't the best place to drink, and anyway I was seeing all that lost bread. When I see that Slot's car ain't out front no more, I'm really worried. With a dame in a car he won't even have gas in the tank tomorrow. The way it turned out, I should have been thinking about somethin' besides that money, and I should have been really worried.

Slot-Machine got back to the *Mona Lisa* about 2:00 A.M. The cops had been there since 1:00 A.M. by that time. They came in slow the way they always do when they mean business. When a fuzz is friendly he walks quick and heads for the bar with a smile. When they come in slow, sort of looking the place over, there's trouble.

And it don't look like peep show trouble. Captain Gazzo ain't a funny man, and when he smiles it's a bad one. Gazzo don't like Slot much more'n Eddie Tomasian does, only the Captain's honest, you got to give him credit for that.

Gazzo said, "Where's Eddie?"

"He crawls in a hole at night," I said.

"You oughta know better than to drink your own whisky, Harris," Sergeant Jonas said.

"I got a death wish," I said. "What's the scene, Cap'n?"

Gazzo said, "I'd like a few words with Kelly. You maybe expecting him soon?"

"Me?" I said. I mean, Slot-Machine's my best friend, but I don't even know what the rap is, and who needs a friend Gazzo's looking for? "He don't tell me his plans."

"We'll wait," Gazzo said.

And they do. All four of them. Patrolman Riley, the pride of the block, is on the door. The rest just hang around. I mean, they don't take a beer. I got one chance to go into the back room. There ain't a back door, Eddie Tomasian feels uneasy like when there's a back door.

I sent Sheik, the dishwasher, for the shyster. Sheik had polio, he likes Slot, so he goes. An hour later Sheik's back, the shyster ain't shown, and Slot comes walking right into their arms.

"Don't talk," I said, "the shyster's comin'."

"I got an alibi," Slot said. "What did I do?"

Jonas said, "Where was you the last couple of hours?"

"Joe was with me," Slot said.

"Since when is Joe an alibi?" Jonas said.

"Not for four hours Joe ain't with you," Gazzo said. "That heap out front, it's yours? Give it to me straight and clean, Kelly, this is a bad one. Where you been, say, twelve o'clock on?"

It was that line about Slot's car that rang the bell. They ain't worried about me, so I go and take a look. The heap's right there all right. It's a frame, and it's the dame's frame, only how does Slot prove it? It's got to be that dame. Slot hears the same message. When I go back he's telling it straight and fast. Peep show, redhead, and all. I figure Slot's really scared this time. Peeping's a crime, like, and he's confessing for both of us.

"... so the dame takes me up to her pad. Was quite a pad, Park Avenue and all. When I says peeping looks like it pays good, she says she got other lines, and that figures. Well we divides up the money, she's nice and easy, no fuss over the cut, and we get cosy after. Then it slows down. She starts holding out. That I don't dig. I mean, she got me up there like she's seen we got it in the stars, and then she starts holding out and talking about how she likes it slow, and won't breakfast together be grand. We horse around, and then she wants a massage. Never had a one-arm massage.

"Something wasn't kosher, but I gives her the massage. I was sort of clumsy, I spilled the alcohol, I had to mop it off her clear to her sweet little rear, all over her back. Then I make like the alcohol ruined the cigarettes, and I better go get more. I cut out and here I am."

Now me, I believed him. Only who else would, you know? Those cops don't even believe the peep-show bit. They're homicide, it figures the precinct fuzz didn't bother to fill them in on the peep. They'll check it out, sure, but that don't help Slot after eleven o'clock.

Gazzo said, "Doorman see you, maybe?"

"No doorman."

"Elevator operator?"

"Self-service."

"Janitor? Super? Clean-up man?"

"There was a little guy hanging on a poodle."

"You're in trouble," Gazzo says. "Your car was used in the job, one watchman got the license plain as day. The other watchmen got a slug. We found some of the junk in your heap, the motor's still warm, we got the gun did the job, and it's yours. A half a million in heroin, Kelly, where'd you stash it?"

"I did all that by myself?" Slot says. "I'm good."

"You can name your friends later," Sergeant Jonas said.

I said, "It's too good, Gazzo, it's a frame!"

"Captain Gazzo, Harris. Sure it's too good. It's so good it could be true. It's so good it got to be a frame, or the real thing, that much coincidence couldn't be. Can you give me one witness, Kelly? Just one."

"Let's travel," Slot said.

When we get to the Park Avenue pad, the dame herself lets us in. She ain't wearing that green low-cut now. She's got on some kind of purple robe that covers her up like completely. She ain't alone, and the whole thing's as clear as a brand-new picture window.

Eddie Tomasian's sitting on the couch, dress suit, cool martini, his tie off, the works. Eddie smiles at the cops. The dame looks right through Slot and me. The fuzz don't waste time, they go right into Slot's story. Now it even sounds phony to me. Eddie laughs like hell, and the dame acts mad. What would she be doing with a crum like Slot-Machine, she wants to know.

It all figures, and if I know Eddie, his story is going to check out fine. There're a lot of ways to make a story check better than if it was true. I am wondering if that shyster knows his way to the Tombs.

Eddie says, "The gimp got some imagination, Gazzo. Me and Sheila been to a show, I got the stubs, six guys saw us. We went dancing, you can check the doorman. We had some food, the waiter'll remember. Got home about an hour ago. Two neighbors caught that part."

The fuzz are trying to tie the elegant pad into Slot's yarn about peeping. It don't tie. That pad was no peep show dame's pad.

Gazzo said, "If it's a fix, Kelly, it's a good one. You got any ideas?"

Slot-Machine, he grinned. "Like I said, Gazzo, me and this dame been together since maybe four P.M. I ain't seen my car since then. The old cannon's always in the heap, it ain't never loaded unless I'm on a live one, which ain't often. Now, the way I see it, the dame got the key when she made up to me in the *Mona Lisa*. She passed it to Eddie, he got it back to her when he came back, she got it to me, and then she kept me busy. Now the one thing …"

"Keep talking gimp, it's a comic book," Eddie said.

The dame said, "Now look, Captain, I'm not going to stand here and let that gimpy bum try to …" And that was as far as she got.

Slot grabs her with his one good arm. She yells and tries to bust loose. But, like I said before, Slot knows how to use that one arm. He's got her arm twisted good. She hollers. The cops jump. Eddie Tomasian jumps. I jump. Slot has the dame between him and us. He's behind her, and for one bad minute I think he's trying for a break-out.

Slot says, "If I can prove I was with this dame just one minute, you buy the story, Gazzo?"

Slot can break her arm with one twist. I know it. The cops know it. I hope the dame knows it.

"I'll buy," Gazzo said.

"Right," Slot said, and he let go of the dame, ripped that robe right down to the navel, and grabbed her again before she could even blink. He turned her around with her back to us.

On her back, right down in the middle where she'd never see it, printed in small letters in some kind of purple ink, is: PATRICK X. KELLY, *Confidential Investigator.*

Slot-Machine grins. I grin. Gazzo laughs. Eddie is sort of white, you know, pale. Sergeant Jonas has one eye looking at the dame's back, and the other looking at Eddie Tomasian. The third cop has both eyes watching Eddie. I always did say the fuzz gets the point pretty quick when they see it clear.

Slot said, "I gives a real good massage. Like I said, it wasn't kosher. I figure they had me pegged for all night with the dame, so I cut early, and left my card, you might say. That ink's hard to get off, ask my Chinaman with the soap."

The dame is swearing and struggling to get out of Slot's grip. He let her go, and she started twisting to see what she had on her back. Slot gives her a hand mirror. Eddie looks very sick. And you know, I don't think it was the chair that was botherin' him right then, it was gettin' hooked cold by a cripple.

After Jonas and the other fuzz had taken Eddie and the dame down to the room and board with bars, Slot shows me and Gazzo the rubber stamp. It was one of those small ones in a case. They advertise them in all the papers, like old-time seals.

Slot-Machine said, "I figured it'd give me some class when I sent off for it. It cost me two bucks."

Gazzo said, "You're lucky, Kelly.

"I guess I am, Gazzo. Well, nice to have seen you."

We made it to a saloon on Eleventh Avenue. I wasn't exactly sleepy, and Slot was thirsty. Slot looks at himself in the mirror, and says, "Trouble with guys like Eddie is they think 'cause I got one arm I got half a brain."

I said, "Dames stalled you all night before. What put you wise?"

Slot pulled out a pile of bills and laid them on the bar. "The cut of the bread, Joe, the cut of the take. It was too easy. She split right down the middle as sweet as you please, and she even tossed in half of your ten percent. Now, tell me, you ever see a hustling dame who don't beef blue murder about the split no matter what?"

I looked at the loot. "You come close that time."

Slot shrugged. "If the women don't, the whisky will, Joe boy." And he started to laugh. "She should of stuck to peep shows, she could of made a fortune."

Like I said, with Slot it's whisky or dames. It was a dame this time. Probably a dame next time, too. It figures.

THE DREAMER

Having sold my first effort, and created a character, I plunged right into a second story. I took a concept I'd carried for many years, probably since my experiences in the war, combined it with a personal trauma of a few years earlier, and the cynical world-view of my new detective, and produced this story.

I must have liked the result of the combination of these elements, at least the first two, because quite a few years later I turned it into my sixth Dan Fortune novel, The Silent Scream, *with a great many new elements, different and fully fleshed out characters, and Slot-Machine's cynicism replaced by the observing eye and essential compassion of Dan Fortune.*

SLOT-MACHINE KELLY was in his office sleeping off a hard night when they walked in. There were four of them and they knew their trade. Their trade was muscle. When they decided the fun and games was over, Slot had just about enough left in him to pull the phone off the hook, dial me, and grunt. I'm working in a saloon on 24th Street now so I didn't waste time on a taxi. I picked up the doc on the way.

"Pretty, Kelly, mighty pretty work," The doc admired the artistry of the four callers. "You got a bruise everywhere and not one bone broken. A lovely job."

"I'll give 'em your testimonial one at a time," Slot said.

"Be glad they didn't bust that lonesome flipper, Slot-Machine," the doc said.

The doc knew Slot was too weak to object. He's sensitive about having one arm. Slot-Machine Kelly, the one-armed bandit. It's the bandit part he objects to, he says he's been almost legal for twenty years. I'm his best friend, so I can call him Slot-Machine to his face.

After the doc's patched him up, and gone, we sat in the office trying to figure who and why.

"First time in ten years I got three jobs in a bunch. It got to be one of 'em."

"You got friends would do it for an afternoon's happy time," I said. "On boyish impulse."

"They were pros, cash on the line. It got to be one of the jobs. There's the pilfering down by the docks, but that's penny-ante and those boys was gilt-edged. There's the tail on that kid's wife, and the Mancuso divorce."

"Mancuso don't believe in divorce, he's religious. And his shop's in his wife's name."

"Mancuso ain't got four friends," Slot said.

"He's got cash."

"Not that much. It don't figure, but it got to be the kid's tail job."

"What you got on it?"

"She's cheatin', but I ain't spotted the john yet."

"So spot him."

18

"Joe Harris the philosopher," Slot said.

"Fill me in," I said. I'm Joe Harris.

It was about a week before the hard boys worked him over that Slot had the kid come up to the office. A nice kid, Slot said, big and blond but skinny. Maybe six foot three and 180. Slot's only five-eight, 160, so the kid looked big.

"A nice kid," Slot said. "That's the worst part of the business. You get used to the bums and the shysters, the killers and the hustlers, the cheats and the guys who chases little girls. You never get used to the nice ones. They sit there and sort of smile and look around like they wonders what the hell they're doing in my crummy office. None of 'em ever done this before, you know? And I can see the kid sitting in the crummy hole-in-the-wall, sort of nervous, and saying, 'I never did this before, Mr. Kelly. I just want to find out the price and—'"

Slot named the fee. "Plus expenses. And, kid, you never got married before, this place goes with the deal."

"Does it have to be that way, Mr. Kelly?"

"I don't know, kid, I only gets the smelly side."

"It must be discouraging for you," the kid said.

What do you say to that? Slot just looked at the kid. A kid about twenty-three, and nice. Like Slot says, nice guys always get a wrong woman. Especially if they got an eye for a good-looking woman. The picture the kid gave Slot made Slot want to try for the broad himself.

SLOT GOES FOR the dames, and this one was 24-karat. Good-looking women get restless, and nice guys make it easy. When a guy's good to a hot-shot woman she gets the idea he'll forgive her no matter what. Maybe she tells herself she's no good, she's a tramp, she can't help herself, and she means it, but deep down she knows he'll forgive her, the nice guy.

So she gets restless, and the nice husband ends up in a crummy office with a guy like Slot.

"I just want to know," the kid says, "nothing else. I'd follow her myself, but I work evenings and go to college in the afternoon. She'd recognize me anyway. I don't want to embarrass her."

"That's real thoughtful," Slot said.

He took the kid's retainer. A routine job, and Slot don't work too hard. He strings the kid along for the loot. He's got those other two jobs, and, besides, the dame's a real live blonde so he's enjoying the tailing. He tails her a week before the hard guys bust him up. After that it ain't routine.

He went at it hard after that. I wasn't there when he cornered one of those four hard guys down by a pier. We got to eat, so I got to work some, you know? The hard guy wasn't so hard after Slot finished working him with that one flipper he knows how to use with every trick in the book, and some he invented himself.

The hard guy don't exactly talk, but he gives Slot enough to make a stake-out at the right place. That hard boy was still traveling north the last time an Eskimo saw him. I don't blame that boy. He told Slot where to find the blonde's boyfriend, and the boyfriend is Pete Maxwell. If I was that hood I'd volunteer for the moon.

I said, "Maxwell? Holy—"

"Yeh," Slot said, "the little blonde is moving high."

"Or low," I said. "Maxwell ain't a nice guy."

"They meets in a beauty parlor." Slot said. "They go out the back way. That got to be the dame's idea. Maxwell never worried about a husband's feelings."

"Where they go?"

"You figure I tails Maxwell? I got a message. Now I tell the kid and fade out."

He does. The kid don't like it. I don't blame the kid. He's probably been telling himself the little woman is playing checkers with the girls, and he's a heel to suspect her.

The kid said, "Who's Pete Maxwell?"

The kid says it like it hurts to say the name. Those nice ones with imagination suffer the most 'cause they can see their woman right there in bed with the new guy.

Slot said, "He don't run the town, just the West Side. Numbers, junk, book, robbery, you name it. Find yourself another wife, kid."

The kid ain't sure. I seen the picture of his wife, and I wouldn't be sure either. Only I know Pete Maxwell. I'd be sure. But the kid said, "It's not so much her, I wouldn't stand in her way. It's that she's sort of a dream, you know? I mean, she's a dream of living I had even before I met her. Just me and her against the world. In the Army, while we were hiding there behind the lines all alone, everyone the enemy, I used to dream of her before I knew her."

Slot said, "The war's over, everybody dreams."

"If she wants a punk like Maxwell," I said, "you don't want her."

"I suppose you're right," the kid said.

"You're whistling a happy tune," Slot said. "You owe me another twenty bucks, kid."

That, Slot figured, was the end of that. It wasn't. I was dogging it behind the bar a week or so later, when some bum brings in a paper he's fished out of a can and sells it to me.

I never got past the headlines. Pete Maxwell ain't a hard man anymore. He ain't even a man, he's an exhibit on a slab in the cold, white place—with the blonde. She's not dancing anymore. Seems they was blasted in his pad. Slot tells me to cool it, and I do. But the fuzz find two more corpses floating in three inches of water in the Jersey swamps, and the paper is screaming gang war, and that doesn't please the city fathers. The fuzz really began to dig, and they came up with Slot.

When I got the call I made it to the office on an IRT jet. Slot wasn't alone. I put on the brakes. One of the faces is Mickey Bonner, one of the late Maxwell's best boys. That was bad enough, but it's the other two in the office that starts me thinking of one-way tickets to Siberia. Just the other two standing there.

I think they calls it unholy company, because the other two with Bonner are Captain Gazzo and Sergeant Jonas fresh from the sweet fields of homicide.

Gazzo said, "In a hurry, Harris?"

"They're runnin' down at Tropical. I come for my toothbrush. See you around."

Slot said, "Drop anchor, Joe, I need a character witness."

When Gazzo stops laughing at that one, he said, "Take a seat, Harris, it's cold this time."

Bonner was just looking at Slot with ideas that don't exactly call for the presence of the fuzz. Like he was having a hard time waiting for Slot to walk up a reasonably dark alley.

Gazzo said, "You're sure, Bonner?"

Bonner said, "He was tailing Pete, we had to have some boys work him over. I don't figure it stopped him, he's a hardhead. I told Pete we oughta use—"

"You fingering me, Bonner? Him?"

Jonas said, "Believe it or not, Bonner's clean this week."

"It gives you faith in mankind," Slot said. "Where are the hard guys, Mickey, one way to Outer Mongolia?"

"Shut up, Kelly," Gazzo said. "I've rousted every hood in town. There's a gang of visitors from Philly, for the Flower Show the way they tell it. You working for them, Kelly? Or maybe some friends from Florida? Tanorio maybe coming out of retirement? Come on, Kelly, when a punk like Bonner hollers copper it got to be big talent."

"Or no talent and he can't figure it," Slot said. Then he floors them. "I'll tell it straight, Gazzo. I wasn't tailing Maxwell, you think I got half a brain as well as one arm? I was tailing that broad."

Bonner almost strangles, and Gazzo don't know how loud to laugh. Jonas looked at Slot like he really admired a guy who could come up with a story as bad as that.

Slot said, "You can look at my records. Her husband hired me, a nice kid. When I saw it was Maxwell she was playing musical beds with I cut out fast. Check that with Bonner."

Bonner said, "Ain't seen him in two weeks, that's right. I figured we maybe had scared him."

"You did," Slot said.

Gazzo said, "We'll check it. Don't visit your maiden Aunt in Duluth, Kelly."

Gazzo checked it. He figured it made the kid the prime prospect for burning. Only he checked out sweet. The kid had to identify her body. I heard later that the morgue boys almost fainted themselves when the kid had to look at her. She wasn't pretty, the killer had used a .45. The kid went down like a tree in a tall wind. Gazzo went over the kid like a plucked chicken. An all night session under the hot lights brought the kid out clean. He was in his lab class at the college when it happened, there was no gun anywhere.

I never saw Slot so relieved when the kid came out clear. Gazzo looked pleased too, as much as any cop can look pleased when his only suspect checks out and leaves him with a blank wall to stare at. That was what Gazzo had, nothing. Every hood came out like a rose.

A COUPLE OF weeks passed, and nothing happened, and then Bonner and his friends started making noises of an unfriendly nature in Slot's direction. Bonner has heard that Slot has been known to work for more than one client on the same job, it cuts down the overhead. This gives Bonner ideas, we can hear the weapons being oiled. Now Gazzo don't want anymore talk of gang wars. Slot wants to live a while. So Slot talked Gazzo into letting Slot help out.

"Okay, Kelly, I guess you've a right to live too. Here's the file and pictures. They were both shot at close range, same weapon, an Army forty-five. It blasted excavations. The funny part is we dug two other slugs out of the wall. He must have missed twice, and the range don't make that easy to believe."

"A nervous boy," Slot said. "Maybe one of Maxwell's own? Bonner's making a lot of noise, could be a screen."

"I thought of that," Gazzo said, "we're still looking for some missing talent."

"Keep looking," Slot said.

Gazzo said, "The bed had been used, if you know what I mean. Only they weren't in bed, they were across the room up against a wall. He was stark naked, she was wearing a slip. Time of death: four P.M. Door locked from inside, no prints in or out except Maxwell's."

I said, "Pete shot her, and then killed himself. He was the type."

"Yeh," Slot said. "So how'd the killer get in, Gazzo?"

"Window. The lock wasn't busted, but one pane near it was smashed from the outside. Kelly, that room is six stories up, the building's ten stories high, no fire escape. The day Maxwell slept in a pad with a fire escape ain't been invented yet. Bonner swears he was in the lobby and no one came in."

"Bonner would swear to anything," Slot said. "I'll check it. Where was Maxwell's gun?"

"Hanging on the bed, he never touched it."

"Where was the bed?"

"Maybe six feet from the window."

Slot said, "So the guy came in a window six stories up and four down. He busted a pane to open the window, he opened the window, climbed in, and all the time Maxwell left his gun on his hip when he could of got it in three seconds flat. The guy don't blast through the window like any smart hood. He comes in, gets them out of bed, lines them up, fires four blasts close up, misses with two. Gazzo, it's out of the Wizard of Oz."

"You tell me?" Gazzo said.

"A human fly," I said.

Slot said, "Somehow the guy had them covered from outside all the way, in mid air."

"You tailed her," Gazzo said. "Maybe another lover boy?"

"She was the faithful type."

"An old broad of Maxwell's?"

"I'll work on it, but the entry don't sound like no broad. Damn it, Gazzo, it got to be that kid husband."

"I've sweated him every three days regular. He was in that lab, five people swear to it. And he shoots like he invented the forty-five, at that range he couldn't miss once in a thousand."

"It got to be him," Slot said.

So we started around again from the top. In the kid's lab class they remember him working all afternoon, even went on smoking breaks at 3:00 and 4:00 P.M. It's a long class, but they say he was there. Slot checks out Pete's old girl friends. Nothing. Slot has to muss up a few of Pete's friends. Nothing.

So we end up on that roof looking down. It's a back window. On the parapet we found the marks. Sort of scrapes like something bad been hanging there.

"Hooks," Slot said, "scaling hooks. The guy went down here on a rope."

"And still covered Pete from the outside? How many hands he got?"

"He had to be good at it."

"A mountain climbing hood," I said. "Find him and we're in."

Slot said, "I'm hearing something. It's buzzing in my head like a rattlesnake. Let's take a look at those pictures of the room again."

We looked at the pictures. We looked and looked. Then Slot yells, "The clothes!"

I look. In the picture he's holding, the death scene as we writers say, I can see Maxwell's clothes hanging in the open closet. A neat boy, Pete. The broad's clothes are on a chair near the door. They're kind of mussed up like someone had grabbed at them. I mean, they look like they had been stacked neat on the chair. All in order, you know? Skirt on the bottom, then blouse, stockings, bra, panties, and garter belt.

The skirt and blouse are still on the chair, flat and neat. The pants, bra, and garter belt are on the floor. The stockings are hanging off the chair. I looked at that picture while Slot was on the phone. He called Gazzo first. Then he made another call.

We grabbed a cab to the kid husband's apartment. He was waiting for us in his doorway. "Hello, Mr. Kelly. You have news?"

Slot said, "Sure, kid. Have a seat."

We all sat. The kid was calm as ice. Slot sort of smiles. It's a nice smile, but maybe sad, I know Slot likes the kid.

Slot said, "Kid, why don't you tell me? Maybe we can find a shyster can get you off with a plea. Insanity, maybe, or crime of passion manslaughter while of unsound mind, you know the bit."

The kid said, "But why, Mr. Kelly, the police—"

"Gazzo's down at that lab now. He'll break your alibi, you know he will, kid. You had to make it back there awful fast. You either tossed the gun, and it'll be found easy, or you stashed it in that lab somewhere, and that'll be easy now Gazzo knows what he's looking for."

"You work very hard, Mr. Kelly," the kid said.

"You had to buy the ammunition, kid, we'll find out." The kid just smiles. Slot said, "All right tell me what you was in the Army, kid."

"The Army?"

"Yeh. I remembered. You said you used to dream about a woman while 'we were hiding there behind the lines.' Behind the lines, their lines, kid. What were you?"

The kid said, "Rangers, you can check my record. I was good. We always went in first, we were a well-trained unit."

"I'll bet you can scale a wall great, kid."

"A wall?" The kid was not smiling.

"I figure the rope and stuff is in that lab somewhere, too. It had to be a man who could handle a rope and a gun at the same time, like a Commando or a Ranger, check? How come you missed twice."

"Now you listen, Kelly—"

Slot said, "It was the clothes, kid. That and the Army bit and not shooting through the window. Her clothes was piled neat as a pin on a chair thirty feet from the bed, see? The slip had been pulled from the pile and handed to her. I mean, the way they was piled you had to know she wasn't wearing that slip in bed. Now who would make her cover herself except a husband? I mean when he's got a killing in mind? She couldn't have grabbed the slip herself. You know?"

In a way it's sort of nice to think that a punk kid who was a soldier was a better man with a gun than big-shot Pete Maxwell. The kid showed us later how he could handle a rope and a gun. Maxwell never had a chance. But right then after Slot said it about the clothes, the kid sort of collapsed, sat there so damned sad and thin.

"Her eyes, the way she looked at me," the kid said. He was hunched over in his chair like he had a pain deep down. "Not even pleading, sort of smiling at me as if she knew I was right, had the right. My hand shook. That's when I missed—twice. She started to scream then, and that Maxwell tried for his gun. I wish he hadn't done that. I think I wanted to miss, maybe after I missed twice I'd have left. But that bastard went toward his gun, and my hand steadied, and I shot them both. I'm well-trained, you know. It was like a reflex when he moved for his gun."

The kid looked up and I never saw so much sadness in two eyes. "It hasn't helped any. I still dream. I suppose I could take a plea, temporary insanity, but it doesn't matter much. It wasn't her, really, it was the dream. She was just a girl. I made her more. A woman dies easy, I suppose, but a dream goes on and on. She wasn't a bad girl, just a careless one. I think she really was hurt when I couldn't shrug it off and find another woman the way she found another guy. But that was part of the dream, you see?

"I had a sensitive girl, a very deep and feeling girl, in my dream. She wasn't any of that and I couldn't admit it. Just careless and not very deep. When she was happy she didn't think about anyone else, and a man made her happy. I suppose it's my fault, I don't think of a woman as a woman, I think of my woman as something very special, that was my dream.

"She never meant to hurt me, but she was the kind of girl who hurt people just by living. I wish to God I'd never met her! No, that's not true. Funny, she picked me up, chased me, broke me down, loved and married me, and when it was over all that didn't matter at all. Not to her. But it did to me.

"I was a reasonably happy man, then she found me, chased me, loved me, and I built a dream on her love Two people against the world, perfect, and I tried to live that dream. And all she wanted was to get in bed with a man. Any man! She wasn't very special, but I couldn't face knowing that. I couldn't accept it, she had to be special! I don't know, it hasn't helped at all, killing her. I still dream, and I still remember."

After Gazzo picked him up, we cut out for my saloon. The fuzz had found the gun, and the rope and stuff, buried just outside the door of that lab building. The witnesses admitted the kid was maybe gone for an hour. In the saloon we stood at the bar looking into the long mirror.

Slot said, "You just never get used to the nice ones in this racket, what the hell."

I said, "He's a nice kid, maybe they'll get him off on that insanity bit. I figure he was nuts, all for one two-bit cheatin' broad. He was sure a nice kid."

"He was a dreamer," Slot said, "a lousy dreamer."

THE BODYGUARD

In "If The Whisky Don't ..." I'd established Slot-Machine as strictly a small-timer, and mentioned his typical grunt jobs. In that story, he was "protection" for the illegal peep show, more scene decoration for the sake of the clients than anything else. Such a small operator he could not afford printed stationery so used a rubber ink stamp for his return address.

In the second story I'd turned to the lifeblood of most real life private detectives, tailing an errant wife to catch her in adultery for a possible divorce case. (The only grounds for divorce in New York at the time, although lawyers actually hated a "real" adultery case. It was far too messy, and the financial settlement open to the whims of a trial. Most "adulteries" were carefully arranged by settlement between both parties, usually by the husband having a "tryst" in Atlantic City, where he and his "lover" took a room and probably played gin rummy until time for the investigator to "break in" and catch them.)

For the third, I decided to do an official bodyguard job. At the same time I'd always wanted to try an impossible crime-locked room style mystery, and this one is what I came up with.

SLOT-MACHINE KELLY is the best blackjack player on the East Coast. I oughta know, he skins me regular. This time we're playing a two-handed game in Slot-Machine's office and I'm losing like always.

It's ten o'clock in the morning on a Thursday but Slot ain't had a job in three weeks, if you don't count the summons Slot served on Max Moylan's mother to get her evicted from Max's tenement on Ninth Avenue, so he got to make money some way. He's making it off me. Thursday's my day off from the steak house where I'm tending bar now.

"Hit me," I said.

I got a nine total on my two cards, Slot hits me with a King. I figure the two bucks I got on the line is all mine, with two just like them out of Slot's pocket. Slot hits himself with a nine.

"I pay twenty-one," Slot-Machine says, already reaching for the money like he can see right through my cards, and turning up the nine and deuce he got to go with his nine showing.

"They oughta call you Black Jack instead o' Slot-Machine," I said.

"It's all in the wrist," Slot-Machine said, "besides, I go to church regular."

"Why work so hard, it all goes in the kitty anyhow."

I guess I'm the only guy this side o' Mars could tell Slot he lives off me and get away with it. He's almost as sensitive about that as he is about his one arm.

"It tastes better I steal it legal from you," he said. "Anyhow, I got another summons tomorrow."

"That and fifty bucks pays the rent," I said. "Who's the old lady this time?"

Slot-Machine don't have time to answer. The door opened like it was kicked, and this guy walks in. No, he didn't exactly walk in, he sort of stalks in like one of them old time straw-bosses walking into the slave quarters on the old plantation.

He's a little guy, sort of skinny, and he's got a mustache so small you got to look hard to see it ain't dirt on his upper lip. He's small, the guy, only his eyes is real big. I mean, he looks at me and Slot-Machine like he already bought us cheap, like he owns us.

I figured he could do it, too. The price of the clothes he's wearing would buy me, and Slot-Machine, and the office, and have change left over. The guy don't waste time. He sits down like the chair was dirty, which it is. Slot-Machine's no housekeeper.

"Mr. Kelly? Patrick X. Kelly, Confidential Investigator?"

"You been reading signs," Slot-Machine said.

"We can talk privately, I think?" the guy says, and even I can tell the guy's got a accent.

"Joe's deaf and dumb, so go ahead and talk," Slot-Machine says.

The little guy don't like it, but he goes into his spiel anyway. "You have been told to me for good at a job I am having. But I do not know you are cripple."

I start to get out of the way because I figure in about one second flat the little guy is going to be on his way out the door horizontal for talking that way to Slot-Machine.

But the guy says, "Perhaps I take the chance. It is dangerous job I have—will pay one thousand dollar American."

"Get up, friend, I'll dust off that chair," Slot-Machine says.

I relax, the little guy is safe as in church now. I can hear Slot counting the loot already. Maybe there's something Slot Machine won't do for a dollar, but I ain't seen it yet.

"I work for His Excellency Presidente Gonzalez Puerto, the job is to guard his body, I think is what you say." The guy rolls the name off his smooth tongue like he was talking about the Angel Gabriel and John D. Rockefeller rolled in one.

"Good for you," Slot said. "Who does His Excellency work for?"

I said, "I know about him, Slot, he's President of one of them Latin countries. The way I heard it he owns the country. Sort of a bush-league Hitler."

The little guy jumps up. "You say to me he deaf and dumb! I go!"

"You get two for the price of one, Joe works for me," Slot-Machine said. "How'd you get to me? I ain't exactly got an international clientele?"

"We have the ways," the little guy said.

"Why do you need me? A big-shot like your Presidente gets New York's Finest for breakfast."

The little guy shrugs. "A policeman he is easy to know."

"They got plain clothes."

"And you yourself know who they are, these men in the plain clothes, yes?"

"Every last one," Slot said.

"So perhaps our enemies they know, yes? They are not the stupid men, our enemies."

"Okay, you got a boy. What's your name, by the way?"

"Perez. Señor Perez, you need no more to know."

"I need to know five hundred now, five hundred after the job, and where do I find the great man?"

"I tell you hotel the name," Perez said.

And then they started talking details. From the way the little guy talks the great man is as scared as a one-eyed cat in a dog pound. The list of His Excellency's enemies isn't exactly as long as the Manhattan telephone book.

I can tell Slot-Machine don't like the look of it, but loot is loot. The little guy, Perez, leaves us counting the five hundred like we ain't seen that much in a long time. We ain't.

I DROVE Slot-Machine to the hotel in my car. We park across the street and there's cops everywhere. Slot he figures this'll be about the easiest ten bills he ever made, the cops'll just about do the job for him.

Before he goes he says to me, "You just watch the door. You see any Latin types heading in beep the horn. I'll be at that window up there. It's the men's room. With the door open I can watch the whole hall and the finest can't spot me."

"Leave the bottle here," I said, "and if the Latin type is a dame remember you're working."

"I'm insulted," Slot says.

"These guys play for keeps," I says. "Dames can shoot."

"You've got a dirty mind."

"We need the dough. Whisky and dames can get you killed."

"Who wants to live forever?"

And Slot is gone. He ain't a big guy, Slot-Machine, but he ain't small either, and the way he can just vanish like he was swallowed up down some man-hole always surprises me. I settled down behind the wheel of my heap, my hat down low so it looks like I'm sleeping.

I can see the hotel entrance real good, and the only thing I'm worried about is the cops chasing me. I mean, they get nervous if they spot a parked car hanging around while they're guarding a big shot with bad friends. Maybe an hour goes by, and then that's just what happens. This beefy cop comes over and he ain't friendly.

"Lemme see your license, buddy?"

"My brother's a doctor, I'm waitin' for him," I say.

"Your license, creep," the cop says.

I see now he's got Sergeants stripes and a couple of those medal strips. I give him my license.

"I was tired," I said, "you wouldn't want a guy to drive asleep, would you? That makes accidents, messy."

"Okay, Harris, just see if you remember how to drive that jalopy."

I figure I'm going to have to tell the cop about Slot, not that I think that'll do much good, when all hell breaks loose. The cop is half way back to the hotel with his gun out almost before I heard the shots. They're coming from the hotel all right, and I can tell they're from the floor where Slot is.

I forgot to mention I used to be a track man at P.S. 3, and I caught that cop at the elevator. The cop didn't even notice me he was yelling so loud. The place is full of cops running. I headed for the stairs. By the time I made it to the floor it's all over.

I'll say one thing for the great man, he wasn't a coward. He was standing out in that hallway with a gun a little smaller than a cannon in his meaty fist. He's about five feet tall, and five feet wide.

They eat good down in South America. At least they do if they're dictators. The Dictator's eyes are about as hard as armor plate steel, and he's looking down at what is left of a young guy who looked like he hadn't had a square meal since the Spanish went to Peru.

Slot-Machine is standing right next to the great man. The kid on the floor has company. Down the hall two more guys are lying around, and one cop looks like he won't get up. One of the Latin types is still alive, only his arm don't fit right. I can see Slot-Machine worked over the guy, and that arm is broken in two places.

"You okay?" I said to Slot-Machine.

"Right as rain. Meet His Excellency, he ain't bad with a gun."

But His Excellency is busy with the cops now. They're howling like stuck pigs and telling him to get inside. He doesn't like it, I can tell. I guess he's not used to taking orders. He never met a New York cop before.

"Amateurs," Slot-Machine said to me. "They put most of their shots in the ceiling. The one got the cop must have been a ricochet. Two got away."

"How?"

"Back stairs. Next time I'll get them."

The Dictator turned to Slot-Machine. "No, my friend, you will not."

"Your friends hired me, I work for my dough," Slot-Machine said.

"They will pay you," the squat little Dictator said. "I do not ask them to hire you, but they think of me, that is good. You do a good job, I thank you. But you have now no more job. Two got away, yes? They now know you. A secret body-guard is useless when he is known, yes my friend?"

"You got a point," Slot-Machine said. "They'll pay me?"

"I will order it."

Slot-Machine didn't argue. We gave the cops our names, and the Dictator verified Slot's working for him, and we got out of there. With the loot already burning a hole in his pocket, Slot-Machine made me drive him to Brooklyn where his current chick lives. That's one thing you can say for Slot-Machine. He's not tight with a buck, his or mine.

I left him there and took a cruise down around Coney Island. After a couple of Nathan's hot dogs, some of those french fries that's half grease and half smell, a little chili, and some steamed clams, I made it home just in time to take some bicarb and sleep off the heartburn.

It was dark when the telephone woke me up. It was Slot-Machine. He wasn't in Brooklyn.

"That little joker just called, I'm back on the job, get over to the hotel and meet me."

"The great man gave you your walking papers."

"The little man says no jobbee no green stuff," Slot says, "so I'm on the job again."

"It figures," I said.

"You want to analyze me or eat?"

"I'm on my way," I said.

But I was too late. I left the car across the street, and walked into the hotel. I was half way to the elevators when I saw Gazzo. Now I don't say I don't like Captain Gazzo, I just say we ain't exactly like brothers.

So I saw Gazzo and made a fast left toward the newspaper stand trying to look like a man who really needed a newspaper bad. It didn't work. Two large boys in blue had me by each arm before I got five steps. Gazzo was not friendly.

"Coming or going, Harris?"

"I live here, Captain, my grandfather died and left me the dough."

"If you're coming you're late, if you're going you're late," Captain Gazzo said. "Take your pick, bartender."

That's what I like about homicide boys, they got a fine sense of humor. I said, "I been in Coney Island. I got the heartburn to prove it."

"You and Kelly," Gazzo says.

"Me and Slot-Machine," I said. Now I know something's wrong, so when something's wrong, and it's got to be trouble for Slot, I lie, naturally. "We was in Coney all the time while it was happening."

"While what was happening, Harris?"

And that's the trouble with the boys from homicide, they hear real good. So I said, "How do I know, I just got here."

I figure it's a good rule that cops ain't allowed to hit a man, at least not in a hotel lobby with everyone watching, because I can see Gazzo is losing his temper. And I guess I didn't have to have been there to know what had happened. The lobby looks like Grand Central on the day before Christmas. There's a hell of a lot of Spanish shouting around.

"They got the great man," I said.

"Dead center," Gazzo said. "Where's Kelly?"

"I figured he was with you."

Gazzo didn't even snicker. "He ran out, Harris."

So then I know how bad it is. I go sort of cold. You know the way you go cold when you reach into your pocket for your money and it ain't there? I said, "Maybe he had an appointment."

"With the chair he's got an appointment," Gazzo said, and the Captain almost grins this time, he don't like Slot-Machine too much. Then Gazzo tells me. "We got a tip there was going to be trouble. When we got here and got up to His Excellency's suite the patrolmen on duty were outside the door right where they were supposed to be. Only the door was locked. We knocked, no one answered, so we kicked it in."

"The President, Puerto, was still falling when we got the door down. Kelly was right behind him. You got that, Harris? Puerto couldn't have been stabbed more than a second before we kicked the door down, and Kelly was the only one in the room. He took one look and took a brodie out the window and down the fire escape."

"Someone else had to be in there!" I said.

Gazzo turned to a patrolman. "Read the list."

The patrolman read from a small book. "Two of the President's assistants, known to me, went in. They came out an hour later, both of them. Ten minutes later Sergeants Paulson and Malone walked past to the men's room. Returned five minutes later. A Police Captain went past to the men's room. Private Detective Patrick X. Kelly went in. Captain Gazzo and squad came to break in the door."

Gazzo said, "Are you satisfied, Harris?"

"Slot-Machine was working for Puerto. He saved his skin this afternoon, it's on your record. We figured the job was over until the guy that hired us told Slot to get down here again tonight."

Gazzo said, "You mean Señor Perez? This man?"

And there was the little guy, three-hundred dollar suit, thin mustache, and all. The little guy said, "I did not tell Mr. Kelly to come here again. His Excellency gave orders to pay Mr. Kelly and let him go, I did so that. I did not call to Mr. Kelly. I think he has work for the enemies of His Excellency, yes?"

Gazzo said, "Kelly would do anything for a buck, you know that, Harris. It looks like when he got fired he just went over to the other side."

They couldn't be right, of course, but even I had to admit Slot-Machine would do anything for a dollar. They were all grinning at me. They figured Slot-Machine was finished this time. Maybe they were right.

THE COPS LET me go, with a warning. I figured they'd put a tail on me, so I made like a snake and lost him. When I got home, the message was there. Two coke bottles, one lying on its side. The message me and Slot-Machine always used for emergencies, It meant that Slot-Machine was holed up in the building on Perry Street.

I made it over there fast, but careful. Gazzo was no fool, and I knew I was out walking around as bait to lead them to Slot. He was in a room in the back on the second floor where he could see the stairs.

"You hit the jackpot," I said.

"Through the window," Slot-Machine said. "He never knew what hit him."

"Someone threw the shiv?"

"Yeh. The cops knocked, Puerto heads for the door, the cops kicked it in, the shiv comes through the window. I'm caught with my pants hanging. They didn't have to read me a book, so I made it out that window."

"You're in trouble."

Slot-Machine lights up a cigarette. I always liked the way he can do it with his one hand, using his thumbnail to light the match. "One thing's bothering me, Joe. There wasn't no one on that fire escape. Where'd the guy go?"

"How he get there in the first place? I mean, the cops had the alley watched, those two was outside the door watching the hall. Come to think of it, how'd you get out of the alley?"

"I bruised my knuckles," Slot-Machine said. "They oughta teach those cops better Judo. Gazzo can send me the hospital bills."

"He'll send you an electric bill, and you'll get free voltage."

"Cheer me up."

"I'll get you on a boat," I said. "How far can you get for a thousand?"

"Five hundred," Slot-Machine said. "I never got paid the rest. And for five hundred you couldn't buy me as far as Staten Island."

"You're in trouble."

"You said that."

"Okay," I said, "what do we do?"

"We get out of here and look up the boys who missed this morning."

"You know where to find them?"

"I ain't been sitting here countin' the take."

"I got my heap," I said.

"And every cop as far as Pittsburgh knows it. We walk."

We walked. It was a long walk, and slow. Slot was as shy of cops as an old maid school teacher looking at a man with his muscles showing. But we made it. I don't know how Slot-Machine pegged them, but they were there.

It was an old warehouse up around 56th Street near the river. They were real amateurs, they were all shooting crap under a light in the old office. There was one guy on lookout. He didn't even make a gurgle when Slot-Machine gave him the Judo on the neck.

We sort of crawled up and came out of the shadows like we'd come up from the floor. The guy rolling didn't even get to see if he'd made his point. They sounded like a barnyard full of chickens. Slot-Machine shut them up with a couple of waves of his .45 Army Special.

"Okay, patriots, give me one guy who did it, I let the rest off the hook."

A big, skinny guy with a face that looked like the chickens had walked on it grinned. "We hear about it, we thank our American friend."

When they all stopped laughing, Slot-Machine didn't even blink. "One guy to throw to the cops, and I don't muss you up."

"They are want you, not for us," the skinny guy said.

"And I've got you, sonny," Slot-Machine said. "One hero of the people, that's the price."

From the rear of the mob of them a short, dark man with a long scar on his thick face stepped toward Slot-Machine. The scarface was serious.

"Today you killed two of us," he says, "you hurt another. For that we plan we kill you. Now the Dictator is dead, we are happy. We hold no bitterness. Why you have kill him, we do not know, but we thank you. We will try to help. We have friends, we will try to get you from the country."

Sometimes, Slot-Machine says, you know right away when a guy is telling the truth. I could see by the look on Slot's face that this was one of the times. These kids were telling the truth. I looked at Slot-Machine and he was about as low as I've ever seen him.

"I didn't kill him," Slot says. "You didn't kill him. Who killed him?"

The scarface was surprised. "You don't kill?"

"Who you kid, man?" the big, skinny one with the pimples said.

"You don't kill, who kill?" one of the others said.

It was pretty clear now that Scarface was the leader. He said something in Spanish, short and sharp, and the kids shut up.

Scarface said to Slot, "If you do not kill him, who then can say? I know five, maybe six hundred want to kill the pig. So many he hurt, families die, country not free, you see? Maybe year ago five, six thousand want to kill. The pig make promises, there will be reforms, he has plan for make country free. But he say it take time and the money from Yankees. Some believe, we do not believe."

And it's right then I see the wheels going in Slot-Machine's head. I mean, I could see it turning there behind Slot's eyes like a barrel of wheels with no place to go. "You know, he didn't seem such a bad guy. Maybe you got him wrong?"

"We no believe," Scarface said.

"That plan," Slot-Machine said, "read me chapter and verse!"

Scarface shrugged. "He say he will get money from Yankee Presidente, give people work, make the elections very soon. He lie."

Slot-Machine's eyes was running fast. "That call, the one put me back on the job, you made it to set me up?"

"Call?" Scarface said. "We make you no call. We not know your name, yes?"

"You not know my name, no!" Slot says. "Sit tight on your tamales, patriots, maybe we're all off the hook."

Slot-Machine is out of that warehouse so fast the wind drags me right behind him. Outside Slot skids to a fast halt.

"Joe, go get Gazzo," he says.

"You gonna strap yourself in the chair, too?"

"I'm allergic to electricity. Go to Gazzo, keep him busy as long as you can, wait for a call. If it's what I think, I'll call, and you bring Gazzo running."

"Something tells me I won't have to pay him to run."

"Get going," Slot-Machine says, and he's gone. I make it fast over to homicide.

CAPTAIN GAZZO IS a suspicious man. When I walked in he didn't kiss me. For an hour I fed him the pure white snow, and he's getting colder and colder. I start to wonder, how long I can keep it going. Slot-Machine hasn't called and I'm sweating. Gazzo hasn't cracked a smile.

"Let's try it again, Harris," Gazzo says. "You lost my boys, you made like the Invisible Man, just so you could take another drive to Coney for one of Nathan's hot dogs."

"I like Nathan," I said. "He serves good food!"

"He's a brother to you," Gazzo says. "Where's Kelly?"

"Honest, Captain," I said, "I ain't seen him. He does bad things, I don't keep bad company."

"You love your mother," Gazzo says.

"Doesn't everybody?" I said.

"You're stalling, Harris, what's the pitch?"

"I heard you was looking for me again so I come in, I'm a good citizen."

"All right," Gazzo says, "from the top again. You ducked our tail so you could meet Kelly. Now where is he, and what fairy tale did he feed you?"

I was beginning to think if I sweated much more I'd be skinny enough to be carried off by the homicide cockroaches, when the telephone began to make sweet music.

Gazzo picked it up and turned a nice shade of purple. The purple on the Captain's face changed to blue, and green, and by the time it got back to purple, and the Captain had stopped shouting, I figured it was Slot on the telephone all right.

The Captain handed me the telephone. "He wants to talk to you. Bring him in, Harris. It'll go easier maybe."

"You'll just give him a small hot chair," I said.

I took the telephone. Slot-Machine gave it quick. I was to bring Gazzo to the hotel where Puerto was killed. The Captain was to bring four men. Gazzo was to let me walk in alone, into the cellar, and if I said there wasn't a trap out there, Slot-Machine would come out far enough to talk.

Gazzo almost blew a gasket, but he finally agreed to go along.

When we got to the hotel, Gazzo and his boys waited in the back hall while I went down to talk to Slot. I told Slot it looked okay to me. Slot put me between him and the cops, just in case they started shooting. I mean, I'm Slot-Machine's best friend, but a guy has to take care of his own skin first.

Gazzo stands in the door and looks at me and Slot grinning behind me. "Why all the cloak and dagger, Kelly, you can't get out?"

Slot-Machine laughs. "I figured if I just called you myself you might try to get fancy. Some of your boys might get trigger-happy."

"Okay, start the fiction," Gazzo says.

Slot-Machine says, "I made a call. It worked. Your killers are up in the late great man's suite right now. All you got to do is walk up and take them."

"I got my killer, Kelly," Gazzo says.

"You got no imagination, Gazzo," Slot-Machine says. "One question?"

"Take two," Gazzo says.

"One'll do. Fingerprints—was mine on that shiv?"

"No."

"Whose then?"

"No prints," Gazzo says.

"Was I wearin' gloves?"

"No," Gazzo says. "You never had the price of a glove. It was a rough handle, Kelly."

"There would have been smudges."

There was a long silence. Then Gazzo said, "Okay, Kelly, we'll take a look."

When we got to the hall in front of the late-Presidente's suite, I figured it was really the eighty-six, the endsville, for Slot-Machine. A fat cop was in a chair leaning comfortable against the wall right by the door to the suite. The cop had his jacket open and his shirt unbuttoned, he didn't look worried about anything. Gazzo took one look and started to chew out the cop.

Slot-Machine shut him up. "Hold it down, Gazzo!"

"Kelly, don't you tell—"

Slot-Machine didn't let him finish. He kicked that door in again with one kick. Slot's got legs like a kangaroo. The door went down, Slot was in the room, and the light was on. Gazzo and his boys crowded in after Slot-Machine. I sort of eased in ready to duck.

There were two of them. One was our little friend Perez. The other was a Police Captain. Only one look told me this guy never went through the Police Academy or the Civil Service. He looked like a Captain all right, but no Captain of Police ever looked that good. I mean, the guy was neat and rich looking.

The two of them were at the wall safe, and they had papers in their hands. Perez was the first of the two to make with the protest. The little guy bristled right up to his one-line mustache.

"What is this the meaning of! These they are the private papers! You will leave us, yes?"

"We will leave you, no," Slot-Machine said. "There's a man on his way up, Gazzo. Those papers are very private. So private only the late lamented Presidente and his Cabinet Secretary are supposed to know where they are. That was the call I made. I told the Cabinet Secretary to call Perez and tell him the papers had to be moved tomorrow and taken back to their country, so would Perez make arrangements for a private plane. It worked. Perez and his killer chum bit like hungry herring at mating time.

"I figured they'd use the Captain's uniform again to get past your cop at the door. I mean, it worked once. And they were in a hurry and would figure it would work again. If you just wait for the Cabinet Secretary, he'll tell you about those papers.

"You see, Gazzo, that's a reform plan for their country. Señor Perez, he is against reform, yes? I figure he planned to destroy the papers, hot foot it back to the country, and start a shooting-up of patriots that'd keep the country boiling a long time, and keep Señor Perez rich and powerful. Right, Señor?"

Perez snarled, "The stupid weakling was going to hold elections. No more graft for me! He wasn't going to get away with—"

"Hey," Slot-Machine said, "What happened to the it was so bad the English?"

"I speak ten languages perfectly, cripple!" Perez snarled, and that was as far as Perez got.

The guy in the phony Captain's uniform had another knife it seems. The shiv missed Slot-Machine by maybe an inch and went maybe three inches into the wall.

Slot had the guy before he made one foot out the window. The guy put up a fight. I guess Slot had to break his arm.

After the Cabinet Secretary had arrived and finished telling Perez and his bogus-Captain buddy what he thought of them in very choice Spanish, they took the pair away.

Gazzo said, "Okay, Kelly, you made it again. How?"

Slot-Machine grinned. "I remembered seeing something. When I got up here last night, that Captain of Police was walking past. I guess they had to do it that way to keep down the time he had to be on that fire-escape. Someone might have seen him and started hollering copper. So anyway, I saw him walk past your two guards. You know what? Those patrolmen of yours had their jackets open and their shirt's unbuttoned just like tonight. And that Captain walked right past without batting an eye.

"You ever see a New York Police Captain walk past two cops out of uniform on the job without chewing them out? I mean, it's a reflex, even for you, Gazzo. Besides, I saw his hands. The guy had a manicure. Now what New York Police Captain gets a manicure?"

Gazzo turned only a light purple this time. The Captain ain't really a bad guy, I guess, so he just sort of cursed Slot-Machine a little and waited for the rest of the story.

"Well," Slot-Machine said, "I knew Puerto was killed from outside the window. Only there was no one on the fire escape, and your boys in the alley would have stopped him if he went down that way. So tonight I took a look in the men's room.

"There's a ledge runs around from the men's room window to the fire escape. He came that way after passing your guards, and he went back that way. Who noticed one Police Captain in the ruckus after Puerto was killed?

"Those patriot kids gave me the motive. The Dictator was going to reform the country, they would lose their hold. Perez was the only one who could have called me, and Joe told me he lied about it. The topper was that when Puerto told me I wasn't any use as a hidden bodyguard he was right, I wasn't, so why call me again unless someone wanted a patsy? I got to admit they timed it sweet, and that phony-Captain is real handy with a shiv."

Gazzo looked like a truck had hit him. The Captain took out a long cigar and started to chew it. Gazzo didn't even light the stogie, he just chewed. "Kelly, you got luck."

"Cheer up, Gazzo, next time you'll get me," Slot-Machine said.

"I'll dream about it," Gazzo said.

After we got out of there Slot-Machine needed a drink. So did I. We was on our third when I said, "One thing I don't get. You had to know that call was crazy. I mean, you said Puerto was right in firing you. So you must have figured Perez was crazy to hire you back. Why'd you fall for it?"

Slot-Machine looked surprised over his whisky. "Hell, Joe, the guy owed me five hundred clams. I hadda go."

CARRIER PIGEON

A few weeks after I sent "If The Whisky Don't, The Women Will" to MSMM, *Leo Margulies, the owner of Renown Publications who published* MSMM, *called me. He said he thought, from reading my story, that I could write the monthly "novel" by Brett Halliday that featured Shayne himself, would I like to try one? Being a novice at the time, I asked if Mr. Halliday was away or sick, and learned to my surprise that Halliday wrote none of them, he'd simply traded his and Shayne's name to Leo for a share in the magazine. In fact, Brett Halliday did not exist, he was a pen name of Davis Dresser, who also wrote westerns under various pseudonyms among other literary endeavors.*

I didn't want to write under another man's name, real or pen, so I hemmed and hawed. For "Whisky" I'd been paid a penny-a-word, the going rate at Renown. For the "novels" Leo told me he paid a penny-and-a-half-a-word. New York hadn't become any less expensive. I said, "Thank you very much, I'd give it my best try."

I worked hard to catch the light, breezy style, the flamboyance of the "big redhead" Shayne, and the idiosyncracies of all the other stock characters that filled Shayne novels and whom readers loved. When I finished I had 30,000-words entitled "The Friendly Corpse" and a $350 payday. (Rent and groceries for a month.)

Leo howled like a butchered pig. It seems the "novels" never ran over 20,000 words, and he had never paid over $250. Three hundred and fifty was like draining his blood. But he liked the piece, bought it, and told me I could write as many as I wanted for him—but never more than 20,000 words, give or take five bucks.

A few months later, Dave Dresser himself paid me $500 for the right to turn the piece into a full novel for his series. He put it more into his voice, added perhaps 12,000 words (his full novels at the time rarely ran over 40–45,000 words), and changed the title to Too Friendly, Too Dead.

In the end I turned out 88 Shayne "novels" for MSMM *over about eight years, and scholars, collectors, and fanzines have been trying to identify which they were ever since. (You see, I have a record of when I was paid for most of them, but not of the month they appeared in, and Leo changed all the titles!)*

But doing the novellas, plus some one-shots and free-lance editing, cut into the production of the Kelly stories, so after "The Bodyguard" I had Slot-Machine stories in back-to-back issues of MSMM *only once more.*

This one came out three months after "The Bodyguard."

WHEN YOU GET a phone call from Slot-Machine Kelly at 9:30 A.M., you know it's got to be important. I mean, that's about the time Slot-Machine goes to bed most of the time. So I turned the bar over to Manny and made tracks to Slot's office. When I got there the office was empty. I had a sort of elevator feeling in my stomach. Then Slot-Machine's head came up from behind his desk. He was crawl-ing around on the floor.

"I'm not serving a summons," I said.

"Someone searched the place last night," Slot said. "I'm looking for clues like in the movies and television."

"You wouldn't know a clue if it had a label," I said, and I looked around the office. Neat as a pin. By me you couldn't tell the office had been searched.

Slot watched me. "Yeh, a real clean job. They was pros, I'll tell you. But they went over this place with a vacuum cleaner, believe me."

"Why?"

"You got the cigar, want to try for a kewpie doll?" Slot-Machine said. "Yeh, why? All I got on tap's that Jameson job with the diamonds. It's today. I don't even pick up the stones for maybe two hours."

"With Jameson it got to be crooked," I said. "That fink sold hot diapers when he was a day old."

Slot-Machine was still on his knees. He stood up now, and I saw he was wearing the special guard uniform. It was sort of grey-blue. The badge on the cap shined like a rhinestone in the belly button of a stripper, and the .45 looked as big as a cannon with its belt as full of bullets as the bandolier of a Mexican bandit.

"Viva Zapata," I said. "Slot-Machine Kelly the one-armed bandit. You goin' to a fancy dress ball?"

"Pretty, ain't it," Slot said. "So Jameson's got diamonds in the bag and maybe rubies in his shoes, how do I know? I'm clean. I guard the diamonds. His shoes ain't my business."

"On the edge you're hangin' again," I said. "Someone searched, and Jameson's a crook. Maybe the Treasury boys went over the joint."

"I'll watch Jameson. Stop screaming."

"I got principles."

"He's payin' half a grand on the line," Slot-Machine said.

"I lost my principles," I said. "Don't crease the uniform, he might fire you."

Slot looked real good in that uniform even with the empty sleeve where he didn't have his left arm. And we needed the $500. Bartending don't pay for a lot of groceries for two guys who eats like me and Slot. Only I didn't like it. Jameson would steal a beer off the bar and try to sell it back to the bartender.

Slot looked worried, too. I said it for him. "Who pays half a grand for a two-day guard job?"

"Okay, so there's got to be an angle. So what? I'm clean. I got clearance from the cops and Customs. I'll keep both eyes on Jameson. A small-timer like him, what can he do?"

"Someone searched this place," I said. "Real pros you said. Where did Jameson get the five hundred? Who's looking for what?"

Slot stood by the window looking out. You know, the way a guy does when he's thinking. Only all you could see out of the office window was a brick wall, and the dirt was so thick on the windows even the brick wall could have been in Yonkers.

Slot gave up and sat down. "You been around bad company too much. Okay, he says the diamonds are a consignment job, the half grand is from the big diamond man who hired him. The big man is real scared someone will lift the ice. Jameson's doin' me a favor."

"Jameson don't do favors for himself," I said.

"So Jameson got a full grand, he gets me and keeps the change. I don't knock another guy's racket."

"A grand? There must be an Army after those diamonds," I said. "Who searches for diamonds *before* they're delivered?"

"Life is dangerous," Slot said. "We don't need the five hundred?"

So that was that. I went back to work. I poured rye for Scotch, and bourbon for muscatel. The winos loved me that day. I sweated that job.

The ship docked at noon. Slot was to go out on the pilot boat with Jameson and get the stones. When they got to the dock Slot-Machine was to lead the way down the plank with his hand on the .45 and a mean look on his face. He was supposed to stand by, sort of grim and determined looking, while Customs checked it all out, then lead the way to a taxi to Jameson's office. After that it would be a job of 24-hour guard in the office, with Jameson of course, until the guy who owned the diamonds came for them.

Simple, sure. But it smelled bad. It *was* bad. Slot called me from the dock. His voice was sort of tired, like he knew it was going to happen but sort of wished it had gone smooth.

"Get over here, Joe," he said. "I need a character witness."

"Me? You been smoking the hard stuff," I said.

"I need some help, it looks bad."

"On my way," I said.

I turned the bar over to Manny, the second barkeep, and made it to the dock by cab. They had Slot-Machine and Jameson in an office. From the look of Jameson they'd held him up by the heels, and shaken him. Slot didn't look mussed, but he looked worried.

Slot said, "They run Jameson through a laundry wringer and out came some extra ice. Like, maybe two dozen extra. Sewed inside his tie. It took maybe two minutes flat."

"Jameson ain't that stupid," I said.

"That's why we're still here," Slot said. "They don't think Jameson's that stupid. I think they sent for a surgeon to cut him open."

"It might be interesting to see what he got inside."

"A buck gets you fifty it ain't diamonds," Slot said. "Joe, he's scared honest. He's so scared it's like he figures a smuggling rap is a favor. Like he was real happy to go away a couple of years in a nice cell."

"He ain't dumb enough to hide rocks in a tie," I said.

"The stones was planted," Slot said. "On the ship. Jameson was surprised as hell when they found the ice. Only he got over the surprise in ten seconds and started confessing. He said he should've known better than to try such a dumb trick. He talked like words was going out of style. He wants that cell real bad."

"Jameson's a fink," I said, "but he don't scare easy."

"Yeh," Slot said. "And you know what? He cleared me. He told them I was clean. He said I was legit, the owner of the diamonds really hired me for protection. He practically got down on his knees to clear me."

"That ain't like Jameson," I said.

"Maybe," Slot said. "Only someone was after the rocks."

"Fill me in."

"It was after we got out there and got the stones from the safe. We was on our way up on deck when the lights went out. The hard way. Whoever hit us must of used a crowbar, I still got a lump. When I came out of it Jameson was still out and a guy was working over us. I started pawing for the ice. It was all there. The guy who was working over us said he saw two men run away when he come down the corridor.

"Jameson came to and after he counted the diamonds, and checked them to see they was still the real stones. He figured the boys with the crowbar was scared off. I figured the same until the Customs boys found those other stones in Jameson's tie. Then it figured we got tapped so they could make the switch. Only why does Jameson start singing like he was so guilty he couldn't stand it?"

"You tell me," I said.

"I figure it got to be someone wants him out of the way, and he knows it, and he's scared enough to go along. Now maybe it's someone after the stones, and maybe it ain't, but I got you down here just in case. I figure you'll take the legit stones out of here. I'll go a different way. They don't know you."

I started to leave. "My grandfather's sick, see you around."

"Your grandfather's been dead twenty years."

"That'd make anyone sick," I said. "See you at the U.N."

"Stop shaking," Slot said. "We'll make the switch in here. I'll take the briefcase, and you can take the stones in a paper bag. On you it'll look like your lunch."

The Custom guys kept Jameson who, I got to admit, looked real happy about it and I was wishing I was him. They let me and Slot go with the stones. When we got outside the pier I saw them. Remember how when you was a kid and you was looking through your old man's dresser drawer and all of a sudden there your old man was right behind you?

You dropped anything you had and ran. That was what I wanted to do. There were two of them. Max Marsten and Little Fiore. Two of Big Mike Frascati's best executioners. They were leaning against a support of the West Side Highway. Slot stopped, shook my hand, and stalked off carrying that briefcase. I headed the other way. When I looked back I saw them following Slot. I said a small novena for Slot, and beat it for the nearest cab.

Only all the way to Jameson's office in the cab one thing was going around in my head like two prelim boys in a Garden six rounder. What were two of Big Mike's best boys doing trailing a load of diamonds? All the diamonds in South Africa wouldn't match Big Mike's yearly take from the rackets.

When I made Jameson's office, breathing hard, Slot wasn't there. Now that would've worried me, with those two unfriendly types on his tail, except I took one look in that office and went so numb I couldn't have gotten out of the way of a tank coming at me.

Slot wasn't there, but someone was. Joey Capallo. Once I had the honor of serving Capallo a beer. He'd paid for the beer with a fifty dollar bill and he took all the change, he was that type. The bulge under his arm wasn't his wallet. He didn't smile much. When he did smile you sort of wished he hadn't. I mean, his smile was meaner than most guys' best scowl.

Only—he wasn't smiling now. He was lying down on the floor with four holes in him. Like, he was dead. I sat down and started to really shake. Capallo had friends and I was alone with his corpse. Capallo's friends don't ask questions. It looked like Joey had enemies, too. I mean he was very dead, only with Capallo his friends worried me more.

After I'd shaken about five minutes steady, I locked all the windows and the door. I tossed the diamonds on the desk. Diamonds are swell, but the corpse of Big Mike Frascati's best boy had sort of a way of making them unimportant. In a room with Capallo's body you think of the really big things, like your life.

I called Gazzo at Homicide. I mean, diamonds are just pretty rocks when you got a syndicate corpse for company. I told Gazzo, and then I waited.

SLOT-MACHINE got there about ten minutes after Gazzo and his boys in blue. The body was long gone—even the Coroner had looked scared to touch Capallo— when Gazzo started around for the tenth time.

The Captain sure don't like to let a point drop. He had a big point. "Joey Capallo don't get killed for a bag of diamonds."

"He don't get killed for a house of diamonds," I said.

"Shut up, Harris," Gazzo said. Homicide cops got no sense of conversation. The Captain said, "Kelly, I buy you being stupid enough to go along with Jameson, especially for five hundred bucks. I buy Harris walking in on Capallo dead, because Harris would have been too scared to shoot Joey with a slingshot if Joey was tied down.

"What I don't buy is who kills Capallo for a bag of diamonds? What was Capallo doing going after a bag of diamonds? Who planted Jameson, and how come a fink like that cops a guilty plea? Jameson would take a parking ticket to the Supreme Court. And who got the guts to kill Joey Capallo?" And Captain Gazzo stopped.

For a homicide fuzz the Captain ain't dumb. "How come Harris beat you here by a half an hour? You know, you just might be dumb enough to kill Joey, peeper."

"I stopped for a beer," Slot said.

"You want to stop in a cell a while?" Gazzo said.

"Okay, I was followed, I took the long way around to lose them."

"Who?"

"Marsten and Osso," Slot said.

The Captain didn't even breathe for about fifty seconds.

"Little Fiore," Slot said.

Gazzo sighed. "Okay, Kelly, something smells real bad. I'd tell you not to leave town, only with those two around, and friendly Joey dead, I figure you won't leave the room."

And Gazzo went away. Maybe there was a time I was more unhappy to see someone leave, but I don't remember when that was. After Gazzo and his blue-boys had gone, I said, "Something smells, the Captain got a brain."

"Joe boy," Slot said, "something don't figure. Now Marsten and Little Fiore, they're bright boys. They both took off after me, you know? They didn't even look at you."

"Alaska?" I said.

"Siberia ain't safe. Jameson was scared enough to take a smuggling rap. Marsten and Little Fiore expected to see two guys come out, you could of been Jameson. So who framed him? They followed me all the way. They wasn't in a hurry. I lost them, they didn't even try to stay with me too hard. And don't look but they're out there in the street right now. I spotted Little Fiore."

I didn't look. I said, "I wish it was big brother Tony Osso, he just likes to break arms. Now Fiore, he's real mean."

"The only thing figures is they knew Capallo was up here waiting for me. That means they knew all about the whole deal."

"Maybe the South Pole?" I said.

"They got a Eskimo branch," Slot said.

"That's the North Pole, down South it's penguins," I said. "What do we do now?"

"We wait for the guy to come for his ice," Slot said. "Someone owes me half a grand."

We waited. Like I always said, Slot-Machine he likes his money. I mean, it was dark now, and that meant Slot had a broad waiting somewhere. A broad or a bottle, probably both. Only he sat in Jameson's office with the bag of ice waiting for the buyer. Whisky and dames is Slot's hobby, only the loot don't wait and the dames do. So Slot sat there fiddling with that .45 while I sweated. He was loading and unloading the cannon when we heard the noise.

Footsteps. Real soft footsteps out in the hall. They was coming slow down the hall toward Jameson's door. Slot moved. Slot moves faster than any guy I know. He had that .45 in his fist and he got behind the door and waited. Me, I sort of froze. The door was that frosted glass and the shadow on it was real small. I began to wish I hadn't locked all the windows.

The door opened fast and Little Fiore was in the room. Slot swung the cannon. Little Fiore had eyes on all sides. The little guy blocked Slot's swing, the .45 went flying, and Little Fiore had his own artillery out. Slot's next swing caught Fiore on the neck. The little guy went down.

Slot had Fiore's gun hand and Little Fiore let out a yell. The gun dropped and Fiore went out like a light. Slot felt Fiore's wrist to see if it was broken. It wasn't. Slot had the little hoodlum propped in a chair by the time he opened his eyes.

"Santa Claus was here," Slot said to Fiore.

Fiore took it all in. Me, Slot holding the .45 on him, the empty holster under his arm. The little punk shrugged. The shrug said we had him, but he wasn't scared. He knew who he was, and he knew we knew.

The little killer said, "Okay, shamus, I'll let you off easy this time."

Slot said, "Where's Marsten?"

"Watching the front door, peeper. How about taking a walk with us? I come to invite you."

"You're a pal," Slot said.

"We was just waitin' for the fuzz to blow," Fiore explained out of nowhere. "Five minutes and you go home."

"Walking or carried?" Slot said.

"We wouldn't touch you, Kelly. We like you."

Slot said, "How come you guys work for diamonds now?"

Fiore shrugged. "Diamonds are a skirt's best friend."

"On the desk," Slot said. "The paper bag. Joe carried them."

"Brains, peeper, you got real brains," Little Fiore said.

Only the half-pint killer didn't even look at the desk. Fiore never even turned his head to look at anything. He stared right at Slot-Machine. I started to feel I wasn't even in the office.

Fiore said, "Fuzz take Capallo?"

"Yeh," Slot said.

"How'd they know he was here?"

"I called them."

Fiore's pig eyes narrowed. "That ain't brains, shamus, that's real dumb. Joey plays square. We figured you'd fingered him. That was real dumb, Kelly. Now I tell you what you do, you just hand over—"

Slot said, "They took him in a basket, Fiore."

Little Fiore blinked. "What?"

"He's decoratin' a slab," I said.

Little Fiore still blinked like it was having a hard time getting through to his brain. "Basket? What the hell—"

And then it slid into the little killer's brain. Slid? It must have hit him like an atom bomb. Fiore's kind of a dark punk. He wasn't dark now. He was whiter than Snow White. He was so white he looked like he was going to fade away if he didn't fall off the chair first.

The little killer looked like he wished he could fade away, far away. "Joey? A slab? Who—"

"Not me, trigger-man, how about you or Marsten?" Slot said.

"Not you?" Little Fiore was having trouble with the brains he had. "Not you—"

For a while I though the little killer was paralyzed. His pin head went up and down, up and down, like even he knew Slot-Machine wouldn't tangle with Joey Capallo. Then Fiore looked up once and if I ever seen fear that was it. The little killer looked up once, and then he was gone.

He went so fast I didn't see him, and Slot hadn't time to move the .45 two inches. Fiore went so fast he didn't even ask for his artillery. Slot had started after Fiore when the telephone rang. Slot stopped. We looked at the phone.

Slot-Machine picked it up. "Yeh?"

I waited. For a second I thought I heard a car move slow out on the street. Slot was listening to someone on the phone. I walked to the window, but there was nothing out there. A deserted street. Too deserted.

Slot said, "Okay, half an hour. I got the address. Yeh." And Slot hung up.

"The diamond guy," Slot said. "He wants us to come to his place with the rocks. Says he thinks someone's watching him. He thinks it's Gazzo's men, but he ain't sure so we should come to him."

Slot gave me the address and we started out. Jameson's office was in a two-bit building. That figured, so there wasn't no elevator. I told Slot about the street being too empty. He nodded, and told me where to take the stones just in case we had to split up and I got the ice. We had the stones back in the briefcase.

We went out real careful. The street was still empty. There wasn't even a parked car in sight. We started for the corner to flag a cab. Maybe fifty feet down the block there was a street lamp. It didn't give a lot of light, but when we got close to it we saw what we was supposed to see.

High up something was hanging from it. We got closer. He wasn't pretty to look at. I figure he never made it out the door. Little Fiore had about six red stains on his shirt, and he was hanging from that lamppost like a side of meat.

The rope was tied to the post, and the other end was a longshoreman's cargo hook tied to the rope on one end and hooked right through Fiore's neck on the other end. The only look on the dead punk's face was fear. Cold fear.

"We got a war," I said. "Slot, let's run, let's run fast."

"Where do we run?" Slot said. "We don't even know what the hell they want?"

"Who?"

"Yeh," Slot said. "Who? Who kills Capallo and Fiore? Who scares Little Fiore so bad he runs out without his cannon?"

"Marsten?" I said.

Only it wasn't Marsten. We found him at the corner. They'd stuffed him down a sewer head first so all we saw was his legs sticking up in the air. And we didn't have any more time to wonder about who. The car came slow down the street. It's lights was out. The second car came from the other end of the block.

Slot took a quick look, grabbed my arm, and we were down an alley. We got over the fence at the end of the alley and there were three of them waiting for us. They read military books, the boys of the syndicate. They pinned us down with those cars, and then waited where we had to run. Real smart. Maybe too smart. Like an army they was overconfident.

Slot took the first one with the edge of his hand to the windpipe. The guy went down for good. I got the second with a knee in the groin. I figure that one's still screaming. The third got off one shot that missed me and Slot broke his arm. Some others were coming over the fence behind us by then. Slot tossed me the briefcase and I ran.

Slot stayed around long enough to drop the first one, to give me a head start, and then I saw him make like a racehorse. It took me three blocks to realize no one was running after me. About three blocks after I realized that I believed it and slowed down. For Slot all I could do was pray a little.

THE DIAMOND DEALER stared at me. It had taken me ten rings of his bell to wake him up. When he came to the door he was in his pajamas. "Yes?"

"Kelly sent me," I said.

"Go away, you're crazy." And the guy shut the door.

I rang the bell. I rang five times this time. The guy opened the door. "The police I call."

"Call away," I said. "You don't want your diamonds?"

"My diamonds?"

"They sure ain't mine?" I said.

"At this hour? You are a crazy man. You think I do business at such an hour?"

"I'm a crazy man, only we do business, okay?"

The man hesitated, then shrugged, and we went inside. He was a good business-man, the diamond man, he counted every stone before he said another word. When he did start talking I wished he hadn't. The first thing was the telephone call.

"Call? I made no call?"

"No call?" I said.

"You think I'm crazy, too. I should make a call at such a time of night? I'm a legitimate businessman. I do my work by day."

Okay, the call I should have figured. I mean with those hard boys waiting for us it didn't take an Einstein to figure out who made the call to get us out in the street. It was the next thing. The money.

"Five hundred dollars? For a few hours work? Everyone is crazy? I hire this Jameson to bring in my diamonds. I pay him one hundred dollars, no more. I know nothing of this Kelly, this guard. A man who pays five hundred to bring in a little shipment, he should be locked up."

"Yeh," Slot-Machine's voice said.

I turned fast. Slot was standing in the door to the room. Like I said, he moves like a cat. And he's got one of the best ring of keys in the city. He says he can open anything and I believe him.

"Don't panic, friends," he said, "only we should get ready for visitors."

"Who are you?" the diamond man wanted to know.

I was beginning to feel sorry for him. He was confused. So was I.

"Kelly," Slot said, "the guy you didn't contract to pay. I called Gazzo, he oughta get here in ten minutes. We got to hold out ten minutes. You know something, Joe, those three are the only ones killed today. Now ain't that funny?"

I was going to tell him it was hilarious, and then kick him, when a window broke in the next room. Slot knocked out the lights. I hit the floor. There was a hell of a noise of someone hitting someone. That's another thing about Slot, he sees in the dark. I don't.

But I got a leg in my face and I grabbed and twisted. A head hit the floor. I hit the head. Then the lights went on and there were three guys sleeping on the floor. Mine, and two Slot had put to sleep. Mine was Big Tony Osso. I decided I should faint. But I did not faint.

It was too interesting to watch Slot. He had hold of one of the guys, who was Maxie Pisano which should mean something to you but I hope it don't. Maxie was about on the same level with Big Mike Frascati as the late Joey Capallo. If you know Maxie you ain't nice people. Slot was handling Maxie like he never heard of Maxie. He was twisting Maxie's arm. Maxie was awake.

Slot had the arm and said, "Okay, Pisano, call the all clear. Go on, call!"

"You're a corpse, Kelly," Pisano said.

"Call, Pisano, or I break the arm first and then I kill you! Call!"

Slot gave the arm a twist, and Maxie sang out. "It's okay, come on in. It's okay, we got the fink!"

Slot knocked Pisano stone cold then, and jumped behind the door. Me, I was too frozen to move. I had Big Tony Osso's gun and I was holding it steady with both hands. I never did find out what ever happened to the diamond merchant. He was long gone somewhere. At the time I didn't care, you know? I mean, not after the outside door opened, and someone walked toward the room.

And then there he was standing in the doorway big as life—Big Mike Frascati himself. All two-hundred and forty pounds of Frascati blubber. I froze solid with Osso's cannon pointed straight at Big Mike.

Big Mike didn't freeze. That blubber mountain moved almost as fast as Slot-Machine. I don't figure I could of remembered to shoot. Big Mike had his gun out and half way to leveling on me when Slot's hand came down like a knife.

Even I heard the bone snap in Big Mike's gun wrist. Big Mike didn't even wince. A broken wrist must be about the worst pain you can get. Frascati didn't even blink. The gun fell out of the hand, and that was all. Except that Big Mike looked at Slot-Machine.

"Kelly, I even liked Capallo."

"Me you don't like," Slot said.

"You, no," Frascati said. "I don't think I like you. But I'll settle for the stuff. I might even let you live a few weeks."

"Gazzo's on his way," Slot said.

"That's too bad," Big Mike said. "Now I can't let you live five minutes. Okay, Tony."

I guess it was my fault. I had been staring so hard at Big Mike I forgot to watch Tony Osso. Osso was up and had Slot in his big arms in a split second. Osso grabbed for Slot's .45, got it, ripped that nice grey-blue uniform, and pushed Slot half across the room.

"Shoot!" Big Mike said.

Slot stood there. I sat holding a gun I just had time to start to turn toward Osso.

"Now!" Frascati said.

Osso shot. And Slot began to laugh. Osso pulled that trigger on the .45 four times. Nothing happened. Slot laughed and laughed, only he remembered to get to me and take the gun from my hand. Osso tried once more. The .45 didn't fire. Slot covered both of them.

"Heroin don't make good gunpowder," Slot said, and then I really thought he would bust laughing.

By the time Gazzo showed up we had them all lined up. I guess Big Mike hadn't bothered to tell Osso about the death of Little Fiore. When Tony Osso heard his brother was hanging from a lamppost he got so mad he spilled the whole story of the three killings. Or maybe he wasn't mad. Maybe Tony just figured that Big Mike wasn't going to trust a man whose brother he'd killed.

After Gazzo herded them off, the Captain sat down and just looked at Slot-Machine.

Slot said, "It had to be Big Mike himself. No one would put out a contract on Capallo, or even Fiore and Marsten, if Big Mike didn't know about it. And if someone had killed them without Big Mike ordering it, then I figured Big Mike would've had the killers in cement by now. You said there was no other killings on record."

"He kills three of his own best men and lets you live?" Gazzo said. "He just chases you?"

"He didn't know where the stuff was," Slot-Machine said. "Capallo was crossing him, he heard about it, but he didn't know the details. That was why he had my office searched. He figured I was in on it and had stashed the stuff. A man like Big Mike always looks on the bad side. I'll bet he never even thought that I wasn't in on it.

"What tipped me was the way they followed me. I mean, they wasn't even interested in the diamonds, not ever. Little Fiore didn't even look at the stones, Marsten didn't care, and there in the alley they chased me even after they saw me toss the ice to Joe. It was me they wanted.

"So I started thinking. I knew I wasn't carrying anything. But they knew I was carrying. So it had to be planted on me out there on the ship when I was laid out. The diamonds on Jameson had to be a blind. It didn't take me long to figure out the bullets and the gun belt. I mean, the one thing Jameson made me do was wear this uniform."

Gazzo said. "In all the bullets, and inside the belt, too. A lot of heroin, uncut. If I was Big Mike I'd of been mad."

"Capallo, Fiore, and Marsten got greedy," Slot said. "They heard about Jameson's deal and cooked up the guard gimmick. I don't figure Jameson was hard to convince. When he saw he was framed he knew it was Capallo and a jail cell looked good."

Gazzo sighed. "Kelly, someday you'll get too greedy."

"Ain't that the truth," Slot said.

After we'd given our statement down at Homicide, we went back to my bar. I still had some hours to put in. Manny, the second barkeep, he keeps a good record and I owed him some hours. I served up a big shot for Slot.

"It's discouraging, Joe boy," Slot said, "they always figure I'm a good pigeon."

"You are," I said.

"I ain't a carrier pigeon," Slot said, and started to laugh like hell again. "God, the look on Big Mike's face when that cannon didn't fire!"

"You should of seen the look on mine before Osso tried to fire it."

"You got no faith in me," Slot said.

"None whatsoever," I said.

"I'm hurt," Slot said.

"You're also broke again."

"I'll sue Capallo's estate for the half grand," Slot said.

That one made me pour a drink for myself. I guess I would have told Slot what I was thinking of him, except a red-headed dame came slithering in then and Slot wouldn't have heard me. He's like that, Slot-Machine is.

THE BLUE HAND

This was the first "novelette" length Kelly I wrote for MSMM. *(Remember, Leo paid by the word, and New York was still expensive, so when there was any opportunity to write long, I wrote long.) It was also the first time I made the switch from the first person "Dr. Watson" style of Joe Harris telling the story, to a more distant authorial third person style. By doing that, I focused the camera far more on Slot, and what he did without Joe having to be around to report it. This greatly reduced Joe's role and increased Slot's. I was finding a "Watson" cumbersome, not my style.*

The plot itself was essentially a combination of the old "doubles" trick used by kings and potentates since the dawn of time, and revived most recently by Saddam Hussein, and Conan Doyle's Sign of Four. *Always steal from the best.*

What I don't understand about this story is that half way through Slot suddenly starts to drink bourbon. Now Slot would drink whatever was free, but he never drank anything but Irish if Joe poured or he had to pay for it. I have no idea what I was thinking, or why I did it, unless it was pure carelessness, which is always possible since these pieces were written so fast.

IT WAS AN ordinary night. Slot-Machine Kelly was beating Joe Harris out of the price of his booze with the best trained dice this side of Hong Kong. Slot watched Joe's boss turn purple as Joe lost and poured the booze. A regular night. Until the three big guys walked in.

Slot-Machine was Joe's best friend, room mate, and private charity. It wasn't that Slot was such a free-loader, which he was, but he just didn't like work, and, anyway, a private eye doesn't get rich around the waterfront. "Stop howlin'," Slot always said to Joe, "you got a trade."

Joe once said he learned bartending to support his old lady, only now he supported Slot-Machine, so he might as well let Slot roll for the booze since that made Slot-Machine feel better.

"That way I earns my gargle," Slot explained.

"If you lose, no booze, right?" Joe said.

"Don't get carried away, Joe boy," Slot said.

Slot was five drinks ahead when the big guys showed up. Joe's boss was way past purple and turning black as he watched Joe giving his booze away, when the three guys walked in.

They were big men. All three of them could have walked out on a basketball court and fitted right in. Their shoulders were so wide they touched both sides of the doorway coming in. Their hair was grey but all there, and they had fat on them, but not so much Slot would have wanted to tangle with them in a fair fight. Not that Slot for a moment ever thought of fighting fair.

50

Joe got a grip on his billy club when Slot nodded his head toward them. They looked like triple trouble.

They didn't exactly come in together. One came in first and leaned on the end of the bar nearest the door. The second one came in about two minutes later. He leaned on the bar near the back. Five minutes after the second, the third one came in. This one stood next to Slot-Machine.

They all ordered bourbon. They were all dressed exactly alike. They looked like triplets.

The one next to Slot-Machine looked down at Joe and said, "You Harris?"

"That's what my income tax says," Joe said. "My mother wasn't so sure."

"I heard you was funny," the big man said. "I want to talk to Kelly."

"Kelly who?" Joe said.

"I want to buy him a free drink," the man said.

Slot-Machine grinned. "This is your lucky day, I'm Kelly, and I'll have a double Irish."

The big man looked at Slot. "One arm'n all, I guess you are Kelly. Okay, peeper, I got a job for you."

Now Slot-Machine liked whisky. He liked free whisky almost better than breathing. But he didn't like people to talk about his missing arm. He could talk about it, and Joe could call him Slot-Machine the one-armed bandit, but he liked strangers to call him Mr. Kelly, or "Hey you," or something like that.

So Slot looked up at the big guy, he never claimed to be a big man himself, and said, "I got only one to break, you got two, which one you want busted first?"

"Why you punk!"

The other two big guys moved so fast around Slot that it looked like Slot-Machine was standing on Wall Street with those tall buildings all around him. Slot's hand went inside his coat to where he carries his Luger. He even had a permit. Captain Gazzo had signed the permit one day when the Captain was drunk.

"It's dark down here," Slot-Machine said, "stand back a way, okay boys?"

The second big man held the first one back. The second big guy said, "Okay, Kelly, I said I got a job for you."

"What happened to the whisky?" Slot said. "And that first guy said he had a job. Is it two jobs, or are you all one guy?"

The third big guy waved to Harris. Joe took down the bottle of good whisky and poured for all of them. Bourbon for the big men, Irish for Slot. Slot drank his down as if he thought they were going to stop making it.

"You got a thirst," the third big guy said. "You got brains to go with it?"

"Who wants to use my brains?" Slot said.

"Frank O'Hara," the second big man said.

Slot-Machine was not easily impressed. Frank O'Hara impressed him. Frank O'Hara was a big man, in all ways. O'Hara was president of the biggest stevedoring company on the docks, and if the whispers were half true he ran the docks and maybe the city.

"Why does O'Hara need me?" Slot-Machine said.

The third big man said, "I want a twenty-four hour tail job, I'll pay good."

Slot-Machine looked at the third big man. "You're O'Hara?"

Because that was the strange thing about Frank O'Hara, everyone had heard of him, but very few had ever seen him. He was that important. He only worked in person with shipowners, the Mayor, labor bosses, and hoodlums. That was O'Hara's city.

"You want the job?" the second big man said.

Slot-Machine realized any one of them could be O'Hara, and they were not going to tell him which one. O'Hara was very scared of someone.

"Why me?" Slot said.

"You was recommended," the first big man said.

"My mother wouldn't recommend me," Slot said. "Try again."

They were all scared, Slot could see that as clear as a dime in the gutter. Big and tough as they were, at least one of them, the real O'Hara, was very scared. That was, Slot guessed, why they looked like king-sized Bobbsey Twins, or triplets. Old time kings used that trick, the dressing other guys to look just like the king himself so that in battle the enemy wasn't sure which one was the real king.

"Don't worry about it," the third big man said. "I got your name, you want the job or not?"

Slot shrugged. "Who can say no if the price is right?"

"The price is right," the first big man said.

Slot shrugged and picked up his drink. His arm hit the edge of the bar, as if by accident, and the whisky sprayed all over the three big men. They all swore and jumped back. Two of them started to mop the whisky off the third. The third big man just stood there swearing while the other two mopped at him with their handkerchiefs.

Slot-Machine grinned at the third big man. "Now we know, right, Mr. O'Hara?"

The third big man, the one who was being mopped, looked at Slot-Machine kind of thoughtful. He pushed the other two away from him.

"Maybe you do have some brains, Kelly," said the third big man, who was Frank O'Hara himself. "That was a cute trick."

"I figure flunkies just can't get out of the habit of wet-nursing the boss," Slot said. "Why do you need me, O'Hara? You've got enough strong-arm boys to handle an army?"

"I can handle hoodlums, finks, and the Government," O'Hara said, "but this is different. This is someone who won't give up, not ever. All this one wants is me dead, and that's hard to handle. This one can't be bought, fixed, scared, or conned, and by now he'll know all my regular boys on sight."

"You're scared, O'Hara," Slot said. "Why?"

"If I could tell you I wouldn't need you. I'll pay good, and I can tell you what to watch for."

"Tell me," Slot said.

"You look for four men, all sailors. One has a bad limp, left leg. One has only one eye, the left eye is missing, he wears a patch sometimes. You look for a giant, a real giant, maybe seven feet and strong as he looks. That was what they were like the last time I saw them."

"When was that?"

"Twenty-five years ago."

"Great," Slot said. "That was three guys, you said four."

"Yeh, four. But really only one, he's the brains, and he's the one wants me stiff. All I can tell you about him is he looked like me, sort of, last time I saw him. Same size and all. Twenty-five years ago he gave me this."

O'Hara opened his coat and shirt and showed a bullet scar on his right shoulder. The scar was directly under a tattoo of a four-inch blue hand. The bullet had not missed paydirt by much. "I even changed my name since those days, but he's found me."

"That's some tattoo," Slot said. "You and your friends was maybe shipmates?"

"That's all you get, Kelly," O'Hara said. "You hired?"

"Make me feel hired," Slot said.

O'Hara counted out five one-hundred dollar bills and laid them on the bar. "The same every week I stay alive."

"You got a long life ahead of you," Slot-Machine said.

O'Hara whistled up his doubles and they left one at a time about three minutes apart. Slot-Machine started to recount the money.

II

SLOT-MACHINE KELLY's feet ached. He leaned back in his chair and put his feet up on his desk to rest them. It had been nearly a week since Frank O'Hara had hired him. He had seen nothing the whole week, and tomorrow the second $500 was due. All-in-all a good week, with Joe spelling him on the tail, and Slot-Machine's feet began to hurt more when he realized he would have to relieve Joe pretty soon.

Still, it had been so long since he had seen $1000 in two weeks that the income tax people had almost offered *him* money the last time he'd filed a return. It would be good to buy drinks for Joe, not that he felt guilty about living off Joe. You lived how you could, and if you had to hold your hat in your hand to get a free drink, a hat in the hand was better than an empty glass.

Besides, supporting him was Joe's kick, Joe's way of getting through the days, and Slot-Machine never knocked another man's way of getting through. Everyone had his way out, his gimmick. And he rubbed the stump of his arm with his one hand, just about ready to sigh and get up to go to relieve Joe on the tail, when the door opened and the bald man walked in. The man walked straight up to the desk.

"You Kelly?"

"You buyin' or sellin'?"

"I want to hire Kelly," the bald man said.

"I'm Kelly," Slot-Machine said.

The man sat down. A tall, thin man as bald as an eight ball. But there was muscle on the thin body, and the man wore no hat despite the cold. Slot-Machine took in the man's expensive clothes and commanding manner.

"What are you doing for Frank O'Hara?" the bald man said.

"I like to know who the hell I'm talkin' to," Slot said.

"Hanley," the man said. "Mike Hanley, I'm exec vice president of O'Hara's stevedoring company. Now what did O'Hara hire you for?"

"Confidential," Slot-Machine said. "It ain't ethical to talk about a client."

"All right," Hanley said, and the bald man reached into his coat pocket.

Slot-Machine hunched his shoulder and reached for his Luger. But the bald man's hand came out of his pocket with a fistful of green bills. Hanley tossed the bills onto the desk.

"Three hundred," Hanley said, "cash. I want to hire you."

Slot-Machine looked at the bills. He could feel his greed watering. "To do what?"

"Tail O'Hara, and report to me everything he does," Hanley said.

Slot-Machine looked at the bills. "You know I can't do that. It's maybe not illegal, but it sure ain't gonna help me keep my license. If O'Hara found out I maybe don't even keep my health. It ain't ethical, I'm workin' for O'Hara."

"Three hundred every week to work for me," Hanley said.

Slot-Machine fought a short battle with his conscience, and reached for the money. Conscience didn't buy booze. Besides, O'Hara was safe as a church, and this $300 a week Joe wouldn't even know about, and what Joe didn't know wouldn't hurt him. He'd held out on Joe before, it was a hard world.

"Good thing I ain't ethical," Slot said to Hanley.

"I figured," Hanley said dryly. "Okay, now what are you doing for O'Hara?"

"Sort of bodyguard," Slot-Machine said to his new client. And then he explained about the four men and O'Hara's obvious fear. It had crossed his mind that Hanley could be the fourth man, but, then, O'Hara should have told him. And O'Hara had talked like the man out to kill him was sort of a stranger, not his exec vice president.

Hanley listened to the story, and then snorted. "That sounds like a bull story to me, Kelly."

"It is kinda thin," Slot-Machine admitted. "Tell me your story."

"Simple," Hanley said. "Money's been missing from the till, a lot of money, two hundred and fifty thousand dollars so far. O'Hara keeps track of the books, but I pay the accountant to tip me. I want to know where that money is and why."

"It's your money?"

"No, I'm only on salary. O'Hara owns the business all out."

"So he's stealin' his own money," Slot-Machine said.

"Not quite," Hanley said. "The D.A., and the Feds, have been trying to pin something on Frank for years, we've heard they got a case this time. If he goes, I run the company, you get it?"

"I got it," Slot said. "You figure Frank is taking what he can before they boot him out of his own company."

Hanley nodded. "Legally, it's the company's money. We got a Board of Directors and all, even if Frank really handles the company alone. He incorporated, and that makes it the company's money."

"So why not go to the cops?"

Hanley shook his head. "Right now Frank would just say it was working capital, for some deal, he has that right as president. Besides, maybe he didn't take it."

"And he's a mean man."

"Very mean, I been with him a long time," Hanley said. "I just want to keep track of that money for when the fireworks start."

"If he took it," Slot-Machine said.

"Why do you think he hired you? I figure he's got you watching for the Feds and the D.A.'s men so they don't get too close. They'd know his own boys."

"Could be," Slot said, "and that'd make him kinda not ethical, right?"

Hanley stood up. "I'll expect a report every day."

"I always do what a client wants," Slot-Machine said.

After Hanley had gone, Slot-Machine sat and rubbed his stump thoughtfully. He sighed. People were so crooked. Now here was O'Hara with a story, and Hanley with a story, and maybe both of them were lying.

Hanley could easily want Slot to watch O'Hara because he, Hanley, had taken the $250,000 and wanted to keep an eye on O'Hara. Then O'Hara's yarn about the strange characters who wanted to kill him sounded fishy, too.

Slot was still thinking about how phony O'Hara's story sounded now, when the telephone rang. He picked up the receiver. It was Joe Harris. "They showed up, at least the big guy did. Get over here!"

"I'm on my way," Slot said into the telephone.

On his way out Slot began to wonder about Hanley, it looked like O'Hara had told a true story, so maybe Hanley was the liar. Then, who cared? As long as they both paid.

III

THE MAN WAS so big he would have made Frank O'Hara look like an undersized midget. A giant. Slot-Machine eased back into the doorway beside Joe. He did not want a giant like that to get angry by seeing him. The giant was about fifty feet away on this side of the street. Frank O'Hara's penthouse was in the building across the street. The giant was staring at the doorway of O'Hara's building.

"How long he been here?" Slot whispered to Joe.

"Maybe a half hour," Joe said. "You was late, I'm chargin' you overtime."

"Picket me," Slot-Machine Kelly said.

And then, with the sort of sixth-sense a one-armed man develops to survive on the docks, Slot-Machine became aware that there were other men watching.

The street was full of watching men.

There was a shadow close against O'Hara's building across the street. A shadow that suddenly lighted a quick match. In the light of the match Slot saw a face with a black eye patch.

Near the corner on Slot's side of the street a man stood under a street lamp. The man paced up and down, and the man had a limp in his left leg.

And, like a twin to Slot and Joe, a figure lurked far back in another doorway on the far side of the street.

Six of them, all together, each immobile as if at a post of guard, while the traffic passed on the street, and the pedestrians hurried to wherever it was legitimate people went. A street full of people and cars in the night, but the people and cars did not count, only the six of them waiting for something. Because, that, Slot realized, was what they were all doing.

And it came. A shot. A single shot high and distant as if from the sky.

The shot came and the watchers moved. They all moved at once. Joe stepped out of the doorway. The giant started to run across the street toward O'Hara's building. The man with the eye patch ran toward the giant. The man with the limp was hobbling toward the building where O'Hara lived. The man in the far door-way stepped out into the light of a street lamp.

The giant, the eye patch, and the limp all met in front of the building. The man with the eye patch was shouting. For a long moment the three of them stood there. Slot waited in the doorway for the fourth man, the man from the far doorway, to join them. Then the giant, the limp, and the eye patch turned and ran to the nearest corner and vanished.

Slot was about to grab Joe and go after them when he realized that the other man was not with them. He looked for the fourth man. The man was under a street lamp looking up toward O'Hara's penthouse. Slot recognized him. His name was Ed Green, and he was a private detective.

Slot-Machine swore in the night as he realized his mistake. Green was not the mysterious other man O'Hara was afraid of. Slot pushed Joe toward the corner where the three men had vanished.

"Trail them! Quick!" Slot-Machine said.

He ran across the street and into the lobby of the apartment house. The lobby was empty. In the self-service elevator he swore at himself. He should have real-ized that the three men had been waiting for the fourth—and the fourth was inside the apartment building! And, faint, as if far above, he thought he heard a second shot.

Slot stepped out into the hall in front of the penthouse. The doors of the eleva-tor closed behind him. In the silence of the hall he heard the elevator move on upwards.

The door to the penthouse was closed. Slot tried the door. It was locked. He knocked loudly but there was no answer. He backed off and kicked the door down.

The apartment was empty. A smell of gunpowder hung in the air. Slot turned and looked at the broken lock on the door. The key was in the lock—on the inside. Slot went through the penthouse room by room. It was empty, all doors were locked on the inside. On the terrace there was no one. But as he looked over the edge he saw, far below, a crowd gathered about something on the sidewalk.

"Checking your handiwork, Kelly?"

The voice came from behind him. He whirled, his hand reaching for his Luger, but even as he turned he recognized the voice. Captain Gazzo stood there. The Homicide detective was not smiling. Neither was Sergeant Jonas behind the Captain.

"He's dead, if it worries you," Gazzo said.

"Who?" Slot-Machine said innocently.

"Don't you even ask their names, Kelly?" Sergeant Jonas said.

"The door was locked inside, I kicked it down."

"A kicked-in door can be faked," Jonas said.

Gazzo said, "What's the story, Kelly?"

Slot-Machine gave Gazzo the details, without, of course, mentioning Hanley and his second job. "So I was going after the three of them when it hit me—the shot was up here! So I made it up here fast. I figure you must of found Ed Green down there, he probably saw me, right?"

"He saw you," Gazzo said, "that's the only reason you're not in the paddy wagon already. He says you were there until after the shot."

"He could of heaved the guy off the terrace," Jonas said.

"Could have, but didn't," Slot said. "You know how I hate hard work. Now maybe you can tell me who the corpse is?"

Captain Gazzo looked surprised. "O'Hara, who else?"

"It could of been the other guy," Slot said, and then he groaned. "Kiss bye-bye to five hundred bucks. Some luck I got."

"O'Hara had worse luck," Gazzo said. "Some bodyguard. A man hires you doesn't need an enemy."

"Very funny," Slot said. "Only I'm out a fat fee. Who made the ident?"

"Two of his boys, they were in the lobby," Gazzo said.

"Not when I came through," Slot said. "That lobby was as empty as a Met ballpark when the Cubs come in."

"Let's talk to them," Gazzo said.

By the time they reached the street most of the crowd of good citizens had gone on their way in search of the next cheap thrill. The meat wagon was waiting for the body. The Coroner still worked over the corpse. Under the gimlet eye of Lieutenant Jacobs of Homicide, the two doubles for O'Hara were nervous and angry. Slot-Machine walked to the body.

The big man had landed partly on his face. Not that there was much face. Every bone in the body looked broken from the fall, but the fall had not killed him. He had been shot in the back of the head at close range, and half his face had been missing before he took the long trip down. The corpse's shirt had torn wide open, and Slot-Machine looked sourly at the tattooed blue hand on the shoulder with the bullet scar under it. Good-bye $500.

"What hit him?" Slot asked the Coroner.

The Coroner stood up, rubbed his hands together, and looked down at the corpse appreciatively. "I'd say nine mm, real close, a lovely job, never knew what hit him. Shot probably knocked him over the edge. Neat job, whoever did it."

"You carry a Luger, right Kelly?" Sergeant Jonas said. "A Luger's nine mm."

"Keep hoping, Jonas," Slot-Machine said. He turned his back to Jonas and walked to where Gazzo was standing with the two big doubles for O'Hara.

"Well?" Gazzo said.

Slot shrugged. "Looks like O'Hara."

"It's Frank, damn you, Kelly," one of the two hoods said.

"Kelly's just worrying about his fee," Gazzo said.

"I'm worryin' about how come these boys wasn't in the lobby when I came through," Slot-Machine said.

The two big men looked annoyed and angry. One of them said, "Just a lousy break. We'd been there maybe three hours watchin' people go in when Frank called down. He wanted some tobacco and some beer. He told us to make it fast, he said we should both go and hurry back."

"That was stupid," Gazzo said.

"Frank told us," the second hoodlum protested.

"Frank was careless," Slot-Machine said.

The first hood snarled, "Maybe he figured *you'd* protect him, peeper."

Slot-Machine looked thoughtful. "Maybe he did, that was kinda careless, too."

Both hoodlums opened their mouths as if to say something when there was a stir in the group and Lieutenant Jacobs pushed his way through. Jacobs was grinning and holding tight to Joe Harris.

"Look what I found," Jacobs said.

"Hello, Harris," Gazzo said. "Where'd you hide your three suspicious friends?"

"I lost them," Joe Harris said, and he said to Slot, "A car picked 'em up, big car. There was a big guy in the front seat, and—" Harris stopped as if puzzled.

"And what?" Gazzo snapped.

Harris said to Slot, "I don't know, but I swear there was a kid in the car, too. I mean before the three characters got in."

"A big guy?" Slot-Machine said. "O'Hara said the fourth man was big like him, right?"

"Yeh!" one of the hoods, exclaimed. "Find them, Kelly, all of 'em! You go and find them!"

Gazzo said, "You stay out of it, Kelly."

Slot-Machine shrugged. "I'm out of it, my client's dead, right? No client, no work."

"You stay on the job!" one of the hoods said.

"Who pays me?" Slot-Machine said. "No tickee, no shirtee, as the Chinaman said."

"Why you cheap—" the first hood began.

The second hood stopped him. "We'll pay you, Kelly."

"I'm back on the job," Slot-Machine said.

IV

ED GREEN WAS not pleased to see Slot-Machine. The small detective looked sour under his RAF-type mustache, and looked at Slot the way you look at a beetle. "I don't talk about clients, Kelly."

"My client's dead," Slot said, "maybe you noticed last night. How about your client. I figure he's dead, too."

"Okay," Green said. "O'Hara hired me, too."

"I figured. I wonder how many of us he bought?"

"He was mighty scared," Green said.

"A big, hard man like him," Slot said. "What yarn did he give you?"

It was the same story, detail for detail. While Green talked, Slot looked around the small detective's office. It was an old office, exposed pipes and all, but it was better than Slot's office. He began to wonder if he could get Green to work shares with him. But then he dismissed the idea. He might really have to work.

"So," Green finished, "I got the job, and tailed them."

"How about the other one? The leader?"

"Never saw him," Green said. "You know, O'Hara was damned careless. I mean, he sent those boys of his away at the wrong time, and he went out himself about ten minutes before he got it."

Slot snapped, "He went out? You saw him?"

"Not exactly," Green said. "I saw him go in twice."

"Twice? You're sure it was O'Hara, both times?"

"Of course I'm sure," Green said. "I know Frank, and I was pretty close in that doorway."

"Yeh," Slot said. "Well, got any ideas?"

He said the last hopefully. Maybe Green would come up with some ideas and save him a lot of work. Slot had no objection to making his money the easy way. But Green had no ideas. Green was off the case, and Slot left.

In the street he stopped to think. At the edge of the curb his eyes searched the gutter for any loose change. Once he had found a ten dollar bill. That had been a happy day. But there was nothing in the gutter this time, and it looked like he was going to have to work.

Only he needed a lead. He could search the town for his three suspicious characters, talk to some stoolies, but that could take weeks. He needed a short-cut, a solid lead, and he had a strong idea that the lead was somewhere in O'Hara's past twenty-five years ago. A killer had to have a good reason to hate for twenty-five years.

He hailed a taxi and rode to the waterfront offices of the O'Hara Stevedoring Company, Inc. The blonde receptionist looked with pity at his missing arm.

"I lent it to a friend," Slot said to the blonde. "He was left-handed, he needed it."

The blonde blushed. "I'm sorry, I didn't mean—"

"Tell Hanley Mr. Patrick Xavier Kelly is here," Slot said, "and what you got planned for tonight, sister?"

The blonde bristled. "Do you have an appointment?"

"You'd be surprised what I can do with one arm, honey!" Slot leered at the blonde.

"If you think you—"

"Okay, okay, you're loss, girlie," Slot said. "Now lower the gates, Hanley knows me."

Hanley was behind a desk about half as long as the Queen Mary. The bald man was all business. "What can I do for you, Kelly?"

"I'm reportin', remember?"

"Forget it," Hanley said. "No problems now."

"You found the money?" Slot asked.

Hanley shook his head. "No, but with Frank dead it really doesn't matter."

"You mean with O'Hara dead it looks like maybe he didn't take the money?" Slot said. "Maybe you got the company and the money."

Hanley stood up abruptly. "Beat it, Kelly!"

"Easy, easy," Slot grinned. "You need me, Hanley. Now the cops'd love to know about you hiring me, you know? I mean, maybe you stole the money and killed O'Hara when he found out. You hired me to tail him to keep an eye on him."

Hanley sat down. "What do you want? Blackmail?"

"Well, that's not a bad idea. Did you steal the money?"

"No."

"Okay, I'll believe you for now," Slot said. "Tell me all about O'Hara."

"He started the company twenty-three years ago. It went great guns right from the start. You know the rest."

"Before that," Slot said.

"Who knows? He showed up here one day and started the company. I think maybe he was a sailor before that."

"A sailor with enough loot to start a company and make a go of it right off?" Slot said.

"That's the way it was," Hanley said.

"Okay," Slot said. "He got the money to start with from somewhere. It figures. That kind of money might be worth rememberin' for twenty-five years. Where'd he come from?"

Hanley shook his head again. "Can't help you. Frank never did have a past. The only thing I remember is that he said something once at a party. He was drunk, and he got to talking about Africa, and he said, 'The Congo's a bloody river.'"

"The Congo?"

"Where they just had all the fireworks," Hanley said.

Slot rubbed the stump of his arm. The Congo. It could be something, or it could be nothing. There was one thing about the four men O'Hara had been afraid of, they all sounded like sailors, And they were all about O'Hara's age. Maybe Green would remember more if he asked about the Congo.

"Don't go anywheres, Hanley," Slot said. "I maybe'll have to throw you to Gazzo yet. You're sure you ain't got that quarter of a million? I mean, I'll take about one-third and I never heard of you."

"Get out of here, Kelly!"

Slot grinned at the bald man and left. He patted the blonde receptionist on the shoulder as he passed. Her look would have frozen the Equator. He caught another taxi and went back to Green's office.

As he walked into the small detective's inner office he had one quick glimpse of Green slumped over the desk before it all went dark.

It went dark after the pain. And the pain came from a very solid object contacting his skull.

V

SLOT-MACHINE KELLY came awake. He was lying on a floor. It took him a few minutes to decide what floor he was on. Then he remembered, and looked for Ed Green. The small detective was still lying on his desk.

Slot stumbled to his feet and staggered to Green. The small man was breathing. Green's left shoulder was a bloody mess. The result of a close-range nine mm bullet, from the look of it. There was another hole in Green's chest. Slot called Gazzo.

By the time the Captain from Homicide arrived with his crew, Slot had searched Green's office from one end to the other and found nothing. Green kept neat, accurate records, but in the file on Frank O'Hara there was nothing Slot did not know.

"He'll live," Gazzo said after they had taken Green away. "Let's hear it all, Kelly."

Slot told Gazzo the whole thing, what he knew about it, which was not much. As Slot explained, "I went to sleep pretty fast when I walked in, Gazzo."

"Too bad he didn't hit harder," Gazzo said. "What you think it's all about?"

"Shut him up," Slot said, "what else. Those shots was meant to kill."

"What did Green know?"

"Nothin'," Slot said. "At least not that he told me."

Gazzo lighted a cigarette and sat down in the chair behind the desk. "It stinks, Kelly. O'Hara had a lot of enemies—hoods, the syndicate, all of it. But they all check out clean. The D.A. was after him, almost had him I hear, just a matter of weeks before he closed in. I'd figure it was someone in his company, but the D.A.

says the company's clean, too. It was just Frank they had pinned down for crooked dealings.

"The kicker is we can't figure how he got killed. I mean, how the killer got into a locked apartment, and got out again. I figured the terrace, but the only way to get up to the roof garden is an awning fixture and a drain pipe. They wouldn't hold anyone over ninety pounds soaking wet, we tested them."

"You got a motive at least?" Slot asked.

"No motive even," Gazzo said. "I mean, it stinks."

"Green knew something," Slot said. "Or at least the killer thought he did."

"You're a big help, Kelly," Gazzo said.

"I aims to please," Slot said. "Can I go now?"

"Get out of here," Gazzo said in disgust.

Slot-Machine was thirsty. He'd worked almost half the day, not to mention the bump on his head, he felt he deserved a drink. And, anyway, he wanted to think. Green had known something, but whatever it was Green knew, Green didn't even know he knew.

All the way to the saloon where Joe Harris worked, Slot sat in the taxi wondering what Green knew, and why he, Slot, hadn't been shot. Whatever Green knew, he probably knew. The only explanation was that the guy who had hit him didn't know him. That meant he had not been spotted by the four men. If it was the four men. Hanley would know him, but, then, Hanley could hire a strong-arm type who maybe didn't know Slot.

When he walked in to Joe's saloon he ordered bourbon. Joe made him pay for it. It had been a bad day all around.

"What I don't figure is how that killer got in past you and Green," Slot said to Joe.

"Ain't nobody went in that lobby except O'Hara, his two doubles. O'Hara went in twice."

"Green said that, O'Hara went in twice. Maybe you saw him come out?"

"Nope, just go in," Joe said.

"You and Green both couldn't of been star-gazin'. How did he get out? Maybe it wasn't O'Hara the second time." Slot looked speculatively at his reflection in the bar mirror. "Frank said the other guy did look like him."

"Same clothes, same size, same walk, same face."

"Yeh," Slot said. "Size, I buy, same walk, okay, and at that distance a lot of faces look alike. What I don't get is the same clothes. I mean, if anyone got that close to Frank you or me would of seen him, right?"

"Right," Joe said, "and you still got a locked penthouse and a drainpipe couldn't hold a man as big as O'Hara."

"Maybe he had a midget friend," Slot said.

"There was that kid I thought I saw in the car," Joe said.

"Yeh," Slot said, "that kid. Maybe our killer brought his kid to help."

"What an imagination," Joe said.

Slot sighed, the work was tiring his brain. Joe had to pour for paying customers, and Slot sat looking at his own face and drinking until it was dark outside and the night crowd of drunks and shysters and grifters had started to drift into the saloon.

He was trying to decide whether to stay drinking, or go scare up a crap game for the night, when the telephone rang in the back. Joe went to answer. The whisky had made Slot feel better. Joe came up and made him feel worse again.

"That was Gazzo," Joe said. "They found one of our three boys. The big guy. He was floatin' in the river. Gazzo says he don't look so big no more, he wants you should take a look."

Slot took a cab to the morgue. Gazzo was waiting for him. The Captain was getting madder by the minute. Gazzo said, "All I got is corpses and no killer. I don't even know how this one got killed. Coroner says full autopsy. I say nuts!"

"Looks like our killer don't like witnesses," Slot said. "What you find on him?"

"About five dollars cold cash, a clasp knife, a plug of chew, a hotel room key, and sort of carved doll."

"Doll? Ain't he kinda big for playin' with dolls?"

"Looks like a good luck charm," Gazzo said. "See?"

Gazzo held it out to him. A small, black doll about the size of a rabbit's foot. Hand carved and good. A grinning little idol. Slot held the doll and began to think about the Congo.

"Let's see the body," Slot said.

Gazzo nodded to the attendant who lifted the sheet. The big man was not pretty. His face was contorted into a rigid grimace. There did not seem to be a mark on him. But it was not the face, or the marks, that made Slot-Machine stare at the corpse. On the right shoulder he saw a four inch tattoo. The tattoo of a blue hand.

"Yeh," Gazzo said, "the same tattoo. So?"

"I don't know," Slot said, "but I got an idea."

"Everybody got an idea," Gazzo said. "So tell me."

Slot shook his head. "I ain't sure. Only Frank forgot to tell me there was any more tattoos like his. Come to think of it, he forget to tell Green. You think maybe there's more?"

"So what if there is?"

"I ain't sure, Captain," Slot said. "I'll let you know when I figure it out."

"You do that."

A blue hand. Two identical tattoos. And maybe Frank O'Hara had just forgotten to tell him, or maybe Frank O'Hara had a reason for not telling. A blue hand, a carved doll, and the Congo. Maybe it was nothing. Only O'Hara, and four other guys, had to have come from somewhere. Some place where the four guys had found a reason bad enough to wait twenty-five years to kill.

Slot walked out of the morgue. He sighed in the night. Tomorrow looked like a day of work.

VI

IT TOOK THREE days of work. At the end of the three days Slot had what he wanted, but he was very tired. It had taken a day in the main library poring over old newspaper microfilms, a day talking to the Belgian people, half a day with the new Congo people, and another half day in the library. But he had it. Only he didn't know yet what he had.

Slot said to Joe Harris, "I got it, the motive, only it don't change much, you know?"

"You figure they all got that blue hand tattoo?" Joe said.

"All of 'em, those Congo prison records said so. They was all off the same ship. They must of planned it. There was six of them. They had this race riot in Stanleyville, and while everyone was shooting, these six guys hauled off with about a half-million dollars in diamonds.

"It was a big haul, made all the papers back then. Four of them got caught and sent up for life 'cause they killed some native guards on the haul. They would of got away, all of them, only someone ratted to the cops. Two got away. They found one of the two dead a few days later, but they never found the diamonds. The new Government down there let the four guys out six months ago."

"The one got away was Frank O'Hara?" Joe said.

Slot nodded. "I figure that. He had a different name then, Frank Sullivan. The Belgian cops traced him as far as Singapore in those days, then they lost him. Besides, the guys in jail never talked, and they couldn't of proved it was Frank who got away.

"Only the description fits, and they all had that blue hand tattoo. The four guys waited twenty-five years to get Frank. Looks like they made it. What I don't figure, is why the big guy got killed? I mean, Gazzo says nothin' was missin' from Frank's place. They didn't get away with nothin', so they couldn't of had a fight over the loot."

"Twenty-five years is a long time," Joe said. "I mean, five hundred thousand dollars is a lot of dough, and ratting on friends ain't nice, but twenty-five years in jail oughta cool folks down some."

Slot stared at his face in the mirror. "I guess I forgot to tell you their names. The big guy was Max Perkins. The one-eyed guy is Blinky O'Donnell, and the one with the limp is Pat Adamson."

Slot turned his eyes toward Joe Harris. "The other guy in jail is Mike Sullivan, and the one who got away but got killed two days later was Tim Sullivan."

Slot sat there and drank for a long time in silence. Joe poured. Joe poured a double shot for himself. After a time, Joe poured himself another double, and said, "So six guys made a big haul, Frank O'Hara, or Sullivan, ratted on them all, left three friends and a brother to rot in a Congo jail, killed a second brother, and ran with the loot."

Slot nodded slowly. "A real nice guy, Big Frank."

"Maybe he deserved killing," Joe said. "I guess I'd remember twenty-five years."

"Yeh," Slot said. "Let Gazzo find them guys. I guess it'll be easy enough. Gazzo sent for pictures and prints on the three left, he's got all the seamen's hirin' halls covered, they got to show sooner or later."

"So that's it," Joe said. "I guess it was that Mike Sullivan, or O'Hara, or whatever he calls himself, I saw go in the apartment house the second time."

"Must have been," Slot said. "Come on, Joe boy, they stopped makin' the booze? I'm dry. Buy one on the house."

"Boss is watchin'," Joe said, "slip me some loose pennies anyhow. I guess Gazzo thanked you for getting him his motive and the names."

"Gazzo wouldn't thank Santa Claus," Slot said. "Pour."

"Okay, okay," Joe said. Joe poured. He had one eye on the boss who was watching suspiciously. "I still don't figure how he got out of the place, Mike Sullivan, I mean. He's as big as Frank was, you said."

Slot shrugged. "Maybe he had help, that kid, or midget, or whatever you saw in the car. Come to think of it, I sort of remember a second shot, and that elevator was going up when I got out, the killer was on the roof, and—" Slot stopped.

He stared at his face in the mirror. "You know, how would Mike Sullivan know about that elevator goin' on up to the roof? And how would he know he could get up there at all?"

"He cased the joint," Joe said.

"No!" Slot shook his head. "I'd of seen him. Frank's address wasn't listed nowhere, Frank was too careful for that." And Slot stood up. "I'll be back."

Hanley would have known about the roof and the elevator. Slot decided he would ask Hanley a few more questions. There was still something very smelly about the whole set-up. For a scared man Frank O'Hara, or Sullivan if that was his real name, had been very careless about it all, unless O'Hara had had no reason to suspect the man who killed him.

As he walked across town toward the river, Slot decided that Big Frank had been very, very careless. Unless maybe someone else, not Mike Sullivan, had taken advantage of the whole Congo bit to kill O'Hara and blame it on Mike and the other Congo men. He was thinking like that, mulling it all over, when he noticed the shadow.

The sun was to his left toward the river. The shadow was directly in front of him at the mouth of a narrow alley. A regular shadow as he walked toward it, but—too small! Like the shadow of a kid. And something seemed to be sticking out of the head of the shadow. Like a kid with a beanshooter in his mouth.

Slot watched the strange little shadow, and then it moved, the shadow. A kid with a beanshooter moving out of the alley toward the street just where Slot would pass. And then Slot saw it, the face. A small, black face with wild, red-streaked eyes. The beanshooter in its mouth was aimed right at Slot. And then Slot saw it all!

He dived to the pavement. His shoulder smashed hard on the concrete. Pain shot through his stump. And he heard a sound like a sharp puff of breath, and a faint click on the sidewalk behind him. Then he was up and running. In the alley and running after the figure of the tiny black man who was nearly to the far end of the alley.

The black man, Pygmy, because that was what the man was, went over a fence like a cat. Slot scrambled after the man. As he raised his head above the fence he had another glimpse of the wild face looking straight at him, the blow-gun pointed, Slot ducked. This time the dart stuck in the fence just below where his head had been.

The Pygmy turned and ran again. Slot went over the fence after the Pygmy. As he ran he thought about this strangest Pygmy he'd ever seen. The little man couldn't be more than four feet tall, the wizened face of all Pygmies, and yet the man wore normal Western clothes.

Slot went down the back yards of the houses, over fences, warily, until the Pygmy went up a small tree and over a high fence. Slot stopped then. The tree would not hold his weight.

But under the tree Slot found a key. A hotel room key. Hotel Marsden. Slot walked back to the street and turned toward where he knew the Hotel Marsden was. The Marsden was a cheap flop for sailors and carnival workers who worked the 42nd Street and Coney Island clip joints.

As usual at the Marsden the desk clerk was missing. Slot slid through the lobby and up the stairs to the third floor where the room of the key was, Room 339. Slot fitted the key and pushed the door open quickly. The room was empty. The Pygmy was a smart man. He had probably missed the key, and he was not coming back to the room.

There was not much to come back to in the room. Slot found a small suitcase with a few extra clothes. The clothes were expensive, and they had a tailor's label from Stanleyville. He found, in a drawer, a leather bag of wicked little blow-gun darts. Extras, he thought grimly, the Pygmy probably carried a good supply.

There were some Coney Island trinkets, a large bag of cheap beads, and a slip of paper with the address of Frank O'Hara's penthouse on it. It was the other three addresses on the slip of paper that made Slot turn and run for the door. One of the three addresses was the same hotel where the dead giant had lived.

Slot headed for the other two addresses on the run.

VII

IT WAS DARK outside Homicide Headquarters. Captain Grazzo sat behind his desk in the dim light of the single lamp. The Captain looked like a man who had seen a ghost and didn't believe in ghosts.

"A Pygmy?" Gazzo said. The tone of his voice was not exactly one of disbelief, it was more of amazement.

"We should of figured it," Slot said. "The only way out of that apartment was up that awning and drain pipe."

Gazzo nodded. "That big guy, Perkins, it all checks out now. The Coroner reported he was poisoned, some nerve poison. The Doc said it looked like a hypodermic in the neck, only I couldn't figure how anyone got close enough to a guy that big to jab him with a hypo. Now we know. A blow-gun dart."

"He must have come from the Congo with them," Slot said. "Too bad I was too late for the other two when I went to their places."

Because Kelly could still see them. The man with the eye-patch, O'Donnell, bolt upright in the chair when Slot had broken in. Dead with the dart sticking out of his neck. And the man with the limp, Adamson, rigid as a board on the floor of the second address on the Pygmy's list.

"That's all of them," Slot said, "all three, except Mike Sullivan."

"I can count," Gazzo said. "He won't get far. You can't hide a Pygmy, and we got a full description on Mike Sullivan."

Slot rubbed at the stump of his arm. "I still don't get it. Why? You know? Unless—"

"You got an idea?"

"Maybe Mike intends to go back for some loot. Maybe he knows where it is."

"We got a twenty-four hour tail on all of O'Hara's boys, and a stake-out on the apartment." And Gazzo looked suddenly puzzled. He said, "Funny thing, I forgot to tell you, we found a slug in the wall of the apartment. A forty-five slug, kind of high up. You hear a second shot from up there?"

Slot nodded. "Yeh, I heard what I thought was a second shot. It was muffled, like, as if it was silenced."

"That explains it," Gazzo said.

"Yeh," Slot said. "Maybe. So who fired it?"

"Who cares? It missed," Gazzo said.

"Yeh," Slot said. "You know, Gazzo, I'd still like to know how Mike Sullivan and that Pygmy found O'Hara and knew about the roof elevator. Frank wasn't that easy to get to."

"Somebody tipped them," Gazzo said.

"That's the way I figure it. I think I'll take a walk. When you get that report on the Pygmy from Stanleyville, call me."

"Okay, Kelly, I guess you got it coming," Gazzo said.

Once outside Slot-Machine went straight to a telephone in the nearest saloon. He called Hanley. The bald man was not in his office this late. Slot called Hanley's home. The vice president answered himself. Hanley was annoyed.

"I told you to stop bothering me!"

"Or you'll go to the cops?" Slot said into the receiver. "Knock it off, Hanley. I got a riddle for you. What does Hanley and Stanley have in common?"

The bald man's voice was angry. "Get off my back, Kelly."

"Tell me, is there a Hanleyville anywhere?"

This time there was only silence at the other end of the line. Then Hanley said, "Okay, Kelly, come on over here."

All the way to Hanley's Park Avenue apartment Slot-Machine thought it all over.

It would fit. Hanley had taken the money from the company, Hanley wanted his boss out of the way. It would fit.

The bald vice president was waiting in his living room. Slot-Machine wasted no time.

"So you knew about the Congo all along?"

The bald man admitted it. "Okay, I put two-and-two together just like you did. Frank was scared to death of his brother and those other men. I was worried about the company, so I hired you to watch Frank. I was afraid he'd take a run out, or maybe bleed the company to pay off his brother."

"I believe you," Slot-Machine said. "I always believe my clients, but maybe Gazzo won't. Somebody tipped off the brother and the Pygmy about how to get Frank."

"Not me," Hanley said. "Listen, when Frank took that trip to the Congo about a year ago I followed him. That trip cost a lot of money and there was no company reason for it. So I went over, too. That's how I found out about Frank's brother."

"You went to Stanleyville?"

"I did. Frank saw his brother there. That was when he found out Mike was getting out. I guess he couldn't make a deal."

"Maybe you did?"

Hanley was frightened now. "I didn't kill Frank!"

"You just helped Mike and the Pygmy do it," Slot said.

"No! Listen, Kelly, it was just all that missing money! I mean, when it started going out I wanted to know why, that was all! You got to believe me!"

The bald man was scared, really scared. Slot-Machine could not decide if Hanley was scared because he was innocent, or because he was guilty. If it was Hanley, it would make sense to get rid of all the men from the Congo. If it was Hanley, the next body could be that of Mike Sullivan. But maybe it wasn't Hanley.

Slot said, "When did that money start vanishing from the company?"

"About six months ago." Hanley said. "Why?"

"Maybe Frank wanted it to make a deal with his brother."

Hanley was eager. "I think you've got it, Kelly! Sure, that would fit just right. The brother got out of prison about six months ago."

Slot said, "Then why did the brother kill Frank?"

Hanley hesitated, then blurted out, "Frank tried to double-cross him, that would be like Frank!"

"It could be," Slot admitted. "Okay, Hanley, just don't go anywhere."

Slot left the bald man still shaking. But Slot walked carefully down the street. If it was Hanley, Slot didn't want to be the next corpse on the Pygmy's list. But nothing happened, and Slot made it to a taxi and went home to get some sleep. All the way across town to his room he was bothered by something that buzzed in his mind and wouldn't settle down.

VIII

SLOT-MACHINE AWOKE with a start. The sun was high outside his window. Joe Harris was snoring in the next bed. And the buzzing in his mind had settled down. It was a question: Why had Frank O'Hara been killed with a 9 mm bullet? Why any bullet? All the others had died from a blow gun dart.

Slot jumped out of bed and went fast to the telephone. Gazzo didn't wait for him to speak. The Captain was boiling like superheated steam.

"We found him and lost him! That damned Pygmy! Some police force I got to run. Spotted him early this morning up by City Island, had him dead to rights, and he skinned through a hole in a boathouse. My fat cops couldn't make it! By the time they got around the front, no Pygmy!"

"City Island?" Slot said.

"Yeh, maybe he's figurin' on swimmin' back to the Congo. I got the report. No trouble at all. Do they know maybe a Pygmy who'd be over here? I think they almost laughed. Gave me name, rank, and serial number in nothing flat. Name's Mbola, calls himself Peter Mbola, and he's got a record as long as the Congo River. Seems it's so damned rare for a Pygmy to even leave the jungle, much less go Western. Mbola is the only Pygmy they know ain't killing lions."

"What else," Slot said. "I mean, how come Peter Mbola is over here?"

Gazzo seemed to be strangling on the other end of the phone. "They don't know. Mbola showed up with a lot of money about a year, ten months ago. Was a good boy for maybe six months, then vanished. They been lookin' for him. Ain't that a help?"

"Maybe it is," Slot said. "Listen, Gazzo, did you run an autopsy on Frank O'Hara?"

Gazzo was silent. Then the Captain's voice said cautiously, "Should we?"

Slot said, "I just got a hunch. I mean, if you got a blow-gun, and you use it, why change to a messy gun? I mean, it was that shot brought me runnin', you know? A blow-gun I'd still be standin' down in that street watchin'. I sure wouldn't have heard it."

Gazzo's voice was ominous. "You better get down here, Kelly, I mean it."

Slot heard the warning. "Why?"

"Because I had that autopsy run last night," Gazzo said. "Seems we had the same idea, if yours is a guess not personal information. You better come and talk."

"What really killed him, Gazzo."

"You guessed it, the same poison. Coroner found the mark on his neck, too."

"Where on the neck?"

"What?"

"I said, where on the neck," Slot said.

"The back. Right under the hair line in the back."

"I'll call you later," Slot said, and he hung up.

He stood there in the sunny room with Joe snoring behind him and thought for a long minute. Then he picked up the telephone again. The voice that answered this time said, "Doctor's Hospital."

"Let me talk to Ed Green," Slot said.

Green's voice was very weak. Slot said hello and then said, "One question, Green. Did O'Hara let you see that tattoo real plain?"

"The blue hand? He sure did. He showed me what the guy who was after him had done to him."

"Thank's, Green, kiss a nurse for me."

Slot-Machine hung up and turned to Joe. He shook his best friend. Joe woke up with a start, saw Slot, and began to swear. "I was on the night shift, Slot, let me sleep!"

"I got a question."

"Awright, go ahead."

"You remember seein' that kid, the Pygmy, go into O'Hara's apartment?"

Joe groaned. "I told you already I didn't see no one except Frank, or maybe the brother dressed up just like Frank. Now go away." And Joe turned over onto his face and began to snore at once.

Slot sat on the edge of the bed. He reached toward the telephone again. He had it now, and he should tell Gazzo. But his hand came away from the phone. Maybe he was wrong, and if he was wrong Gazzo would hang him. He stood up and dressed. Then he left the room, walked down the stairs into the street, and hailed a cab.

"City Island," he told the driver.

The driver started to swear. Slot grinned at the back of the irate drive's head. The driver mumbled to himself all the way up the East River Drive, across the bridge, and through the Bronx.

By the time they reached City Island the driver was still talking to himself. Slot got out, paid, and gave the driver a dime.

"A dime!" the driver screamed. "You lousy bum."

Slot just walked away.

He walked slowly and carefully, but straight down to a large dock on the north side of the island. The boat was there. It was where Frank O'Hara had always kept his boat. The police had searched it the day after the murder. That made it a very good hideout for a killer.

Slot worked his way carefully to the edge of the water out of sight from the boat. He stepped into a rowboat, untied it, and slowly paddled to the seaward side of O'Hara's boat. He left the rowboat and climbed aboard. There were voices in the cabin. About now Slot was cursing himself for not calling Gazzo.

He lay there listening to the voices. They were speaking French. Slot wrestled with his well-developed sense of self-preservation. He lost. He started to crawl back to the edge of the boat. If he had to swim, and if he gave them time to get away, he was going to call Gazzo.

He was too late. A small, black head emerged from below. The Pygmy came out onto the deck. In another second the Pygmy would see Slot. Slot sighed to himself and lunged to his feet.

The edge of his hand caught the Pygmy on the back of the neck. The little man went down without a gurgle.

Slot dived down the stairs, kicked open the cabin door, and fell inside with his Luger ready. The big man stared at him. Slot got to his feet, the Luger pointed at the big man's chest.

"Hello, friend," Slot said.

The big man just stood there. He was as big as Frank O'Hara, about the same age, the same height, the same grey hair. Only this man was wearing a grey beard and a thick grey mustache.

"Who the hell are you?" the big man wanted to know.

"Phony beard and all," Slot said. "Now you didn't have a beard the day of the murder, did you? Joe Harris and Ed Green would of seen it."

"Murder?" the big man said. "What murder."

Slot grinned. "Funny you should ask that. Open your shirt."

"Now you listen you stupid—" The big man was very angry. He even made a motion toward his coat. Slot waved his Luger, and the man stopped moving.

"That's better, now open that shirt," Slot said.

The big man opened his shirt. The tattoo of the blue hand seemed to shine in the sunlight through the portholes. Slot looked carefully at the tattoo.

Slot said, "No scar, that's what I figured. A nice, clean blue hand."

The big man sagged. "Okay, you win, mister. It was Frank had the scar. But I didn't kill him. It was Mbola. He killed all of them, you hear? I just wanted to scare Frank, make a deal, get some of the money. I guess you know about the money. I mean, Frank was a big man, I didn't want Mbola to kill him. That little savage just got to kill, I tried—"

Slot shook his head slowly in the cabin. "Maybe you're right, but you brought Mbola here, mister. Now maybe the police will—"

And Slot suddenly reached out, caught the beard, and pulled hard. Then he grinned again. He said, "Well hello, Frank, long time no see."

The big man, Frank O'Hara himself, just stood there. Slot-Machine said, "See, I do got brains after all, right? I didn't get it right away, O'Hara, but after a while I got to thinking that it was Mike, your poor dear brother, who was shot back there in the Congo. So it figured he had the real scar, the one you showed me and Green must of been a phony just for us."

The big man said, "Okay, Kelly, you got me. Look, I got a lot of money, I'll pay you, anything you say. It really was Mbola who killed Mike and the others. I'll give Mbola to you, you can let me go, right? I'll make you rich, Kelly. You like a buck. Take Mbola, they won't believe a lousy little—Get him, Mbola!"

Slot heard the sound a split second before O'Hara shouted. A faint sound. Slot went over sideways, his Luger coming around toward the door. But he would have been a lot too late. The Pygmy had his blow-gun leveled and Slot would have been a dead man. If the Pygmy had been aiming at him. Mbola wasn't aiming at him. Mbola was aiming at Frank O'Hara.

Mbola spat. "*Lache! Cochon!*"

Frank O'Hara did not even have time to be scared. The dart caught him full in the throat. O'Hara shivered where he stood. Slot-Machine turned his Luger toward Mbola. But the Pygmy was gone, vanished with the speed of a snake. By the time Slot turned back to Frank O'Hara, the big man was lying on the floor a rigid grin on his dead face.

IX

LATER, AFTER GAZZO had come and gone, after they had cornered the Pygmy in a sail loft on City Island and the police had gone in and pulled Mbola out writhing like a snake, Slot-Machine sat at the bar and sighed with pleasure as he drank off his fourth bourbon.

Joe Harris looked disgusted. "For one free whisky you get shot at with blowguns. It'll get you yet, that thirst."

"Women or whisky," Slot said. "Us guys with brains always go that way."

"Awright," Joe said, "dazzle me, tell me how you done it?"

"Like I told Gazzo, I smelled it from the start, the body havin' no face an' all."

"Don't kid me. You smelled nothin' from the start but five bills."

Slot grinned. "Okay, so I got lucky. I mean, I did kinda wonder about Big Frank bein' so careless like, and I wondered some about Frank bein' so scared he hired both me and Green when he had his own boys. Then it was funny he never said all of them had that same tattoo, you know?

"But what really started me thinkin' was why anyone would kill all of them. I mean, if Mike had killed Big Frank, why kill his own buddies? If it was Frank had killed Mike, then it'd make sense, right? Then there was the real stink, how did Mike and Mbola know all about Frank's penthouse? See?"

"Slot," Joe said, "you are one lucky guesser!"

"Yeh, ain't I? Only it just had to be Frank. When you come down to it, he was the only logical one. The D.A. was after him, his brother was after him, and he figured out a scheme to stop his brother and get away from the D.A. He was goin' to vanish and take that quarter of a million bucks with him. He set it up when he went to the Congo. He hired Mbola to get in with Mike, and he talked Mike into comin' to New York for a payoff. After twenty-five years, Mike and his friends figured some money to get started again was better than revenge. Poor Mike."

"You figured all that out by yourself?" Joe said.

Slot shrugged. "Mbola told us after we caught him."

"We?" Joe said. "Gazzo said you was hiding under a boat."

"I'm the thinkin' type."

"Tell me more," Joe said.

"You pour, I tell more," Slot said. He watched Joe pour another bourbon. He tasted it. "We all figured Mike was dressed up like Frank, only it was Frank who was dressed like Mike, see? Mbola tipped off Frank about what to wear so the body would look like Mike. You said Mbola didn't go into the apartment, so he had to be already there, right? That meant he was working for Frank, not Mike.

"Mbola spilled it. Frank arranged for Mike to come for a payoff. Mbola and Frank was ready. Only Mike saw what was happening and pulled his gun. The shot went wild because Mbola got him with the blow gun in the back of the neck. Then they blew Mike's face off with a Luger, and dumped him over the ledge for good measure. That was the silenced shot I heard.

"Only they heard me and had to move fast. Frank went out the side way, Mbola locked the doors and skinned up to the roof. Frank looked enough like Mike to meet the other guys in a dark car with Mbola with him. Then he got them one at a time. He figured on beating it when the heat was off, and he had his dough."

"Slot," Joe Harris said, "you just figured most of that out right here with the booze."

"Ain't that the truth," Slot said. And he said, "You think maybe we could sue Frank's estate for a couple more weeks fee?"

Joe did not even answer that one. He poured another bourbon without a word. Slot drank it off and sighed happily.

THE PRICE OF A DOLLAR

This was another "novelette." Sheila, my wife, was pregnant, I was still struggling with the mainstream novel, I had taken on more free-lance writing and editing for a chemical magazine, and more money from more words looked good. Alas, the pressure of juggling all these disparate demands on my time, the haste it engendered, and the stretching of a basically small idea, resulted in the sloppiest writing of all the Kelly stories.

The plot again uses my experiences during World War Two, a fairly standard Mafia turn, and Slot-Machine's sleaziness and constant need of money. I remember chortling when I thought of the basic plot element of stealing the cash from the bar as the initiating moment, but I'm afraid the effect is diminished by the length and the generally hasty writing. I probably sold this to MSMM without rereading it closely, if at all.

Making your living as a writer has its drawbacks, especially if you try to have a relatively normal life with wife, family, etc.

IT WAS A bad time for Slot-Machine Kelly. Until yesterday Joe Harris had been out of work for over a month and, besides, Slot had been separated from a job himself for all of six weeks. So when he saw the money lying loose and abandoned on the bar, he moved his hand fast enough to catch a fly, swept up the money unseen by the bartender or the six men at the bar. He sauntered slowly out of the *La Bomba Club*.

After he reached the darkness of Eighth Avenue, he made a wide circle in the night to an alley he knew, shoved the loot behind a loose brick without even looking at it, and then went for a swim at the McBurney YMCA.

They liked him at the YMCA. He was an example to others what you could do even with one arm. He had learned to swim pretty well with his one arm, and tonight he swam around for about an hour, played a little fast handball for another half hour, dressed slowly, and went to pick up the money.

He carried it to his office, sure no one had seen him or was after him. He switched on the light with the door switch, crossed the two-bit office above Twenty-Eighth Street, and sat down at his battered desk to count the take. There were two fives and three singles.

Disgusted, he shoved the bills back into his pocket. The *La Bomba* was a call-girl hangout, and the big blonde dame who'd left the money lying loose while she plied her trade out among the tables had looked like at least a hundred-a-night. Still, thirteen bucks was thirteen more than Slot had right now, and at least he would not have to drink any of Joe Harris' rotgut booze. He was already tasting the fine clean bite of good Irish whisky when the man slid into the office.

He did not actually see the man. He saw a hand reach for his light switch, and he had a brief glimpse of a face, and then the office was dark. He moved

74

two quick steps away from his chair and froze. That brief glimpse had turned him to ice.

The face was Oriental, he was sure of that, and it looked like Packy Chen. The Chinese giant was the only Chinese hood on the East Coast, and as far as anyone knew he was an expert in broken arms. That alone made him one of Mike Booher's best boys.

"Throw your money on the desk, mister! All of it."

The voice was muffled, as if talking through a cloth. If it was Packy Chen he didn't want Slot to know it. That was strange, because the big Chinese knew Slot and knew Slot would give him just about anything he wanted. And what was Packy Chen doing on a holdup job?

"Don't try to think, one-arm," the muffled voice warned.

Slot moved very softly to his left until he was against the wall, with the window directly across the room. He made it just in time. A giant shadow crossed the lighter square of the window, and he felt the edge of a hand across his nose, hard.

He felt his nose break. He wasn't worried about his looks. His nose had been broken a few times in the past, and before the dark figure could hit again, Slot caught the hand and threw the man across the room. There was a crash of chairs and bookcases.

He did not wait to see where the attacker had landed. He felt no call to battle. Without hesitating for a split second he ran out the door. He was two flights down and picking up speed by the time he heard feet pounding above him down the stairs. In the friendly dark of the street, Slot faded into a doorway hidden behind a thick wire gate that only he knew was there. He saw the attacker run out and stop.

The man was in shadow, but it still looked like Packy Chen. He was a giant all right, and the face was definitely Oriental. Slot watched him shrug his shoulders and turn back into the office building. He would probably do a wrecking job, but Slot had nothing in his office the Salvation Army would even take, so it didn't bother him. His nose did. It was bleeding and it hurt now. In a few hours he would have two lovely black eyes. He headed for Doc Moriarty.

After Moriarty had patched him up, he went to the tavern where Joe Harris had just started working. Joe took one look at him and glanced toward his new boss.

"I don't know you," Joe said.

"Make it Irish," Slot said, "I'm a wounded man." And he told Joe about Packy Chen—if it had been Packy. He did not tell about the thirteen dollars. You could carry friendship too far.

"Packy Chen is mean," Joe said. "Mike Booher is worse."

"I didn't do anything," Slot protested.

"Chen don't work for nothin'," Joe said. "Tell Gazzo."

"I don't run to the cops," Slot said, "especially not to Captain Gazzo. He ain't friendly, you know?"

"Packy Chen ain't a buddy exactly," Joe said. "Come on. What you been up to?"

Slot sighed, leaned his one arm on the bar, and told Joe about the thirteen dollars.

"Thirteen bucks? Slot-Machine Kelly, the one-armed bandit. The one-armed penny ante boy," Joe said. "You tryin' to tell me Packy Chen would go after a guy for thirteen bucks?"

"It don't figure, does it," Slot said. "Only I'm sure it was Chen."

II

AND THEN THE cops found Slot. It was not Captain Gazzo. Gazzo was Homicide, and the cop that walked into the tavern and straight up to Slot was Lieutenant Mathews of the waterfront precinct. Mathews even liked Slot-Machine a little. The Lieutenant looked at Slot's nose.

"That's a pretty nose, Kelly," Mathews said. "Packy Chen hits hard."

"He don't run so fast," Slot said. "How'd you know it was Packy? In fact, how'd you know I got hit?"

"Doc Moriarty talks sometimes, if you ask nice," Mathews said.

"And you asked?"

"I asked," the Lieutenant said.

"How come?" Slot said. "Anyway, Doc didn't know it was Chen."

"I knew it was Chen, Kelly," Mathews explained. "Doc just told me it was you. Seems I had an epidemic tonight. Six muggings in the streets, three of them claiming it was a big Chinese guy that laid it on them. So I called all the neighborhood Docs, routine check, and found you. You want to tell me about it?"

"He walked in, he wanted money," Slot said. "I didn't stay around to ask why. And I ain't sure it was Packy. I didn't get a clear look at him."

Mathews was not convinced. "You don't know why?"

"Not a whisper," Slot said.

"He'll be back after you," Mathews said.

"I'll keep off dark streets."

"You do that," Mathews said. "You don't know why, eh? Now that's really funny, because that's part of my epidemic. None of the victims knows why. They all got the arm. Some went out, some didn't, but nothing was taken from any of them."

"Nothing?" Slot said.

"They were frisked, their dough taken, and put back," Mathews said. "They all said the same thing. And one more thing, Kelly. Were you in the *La Bomba Club* tonight? Left maybe about nine o'clock?"

Slot raised his drink and drank slowly so that he would not show his surprise. It had been just ten minutes after nine when he left the *La Bomba* with the thirteen dollars. He put down his glass.

"Me in that clip joint?" he said. "Never, Lieutenant."

"Well, you're the only one then," Mathews said. "All six of my sleeping beauties had been at the *La Bomba* bar. They all left about nine, and they all got mugged about fifteen minutes to an hour or so later. I figure Chen didn't do it all. There must have been other boys. It could be coincidence, but I don't think so."

"Life is strange," Slot-Machine said.

"Yeh, well, if you remember anything, call me. And try to do it before Packy Chen finds you. I want you able to talk."

"It was all a mistake, Lieutenant," Joe said.

Mathews shrugged. "Let's hope it was Packy who made the mistake."

Slot hoped it was Packy Chen who had made the mistake. He watched the Lieutenant leave with a certain regret. The big Chinese strong boy did not make mistakes, and that had to mean that for some reason Mike Booher thought that he, Slot, had something Mike wanted. Booher was the number one big man in just about everything dirty and illegal in New York—dope, white slaving, protection, the docks, you name it. If he put the finger on you it was curtains.

The only people who gave Mike Booher orders were somewhere overseas, probably in Naples. The only man who gave Packy Chen orders was Mike Booher. So Mike wanted something. The question was: What did Mike want that Slot had, and how badly did Booher want it?

"Packy Chen ain't after thirteen bucks," Joe said, "even if he did lose his shirt in Max Waller's poker game last week."

"No," Slot said. He tried to think. Nothing else had happened in the *La Bomba*. Two drinks, the eye for a couple of dames, casing the six men at the bar for a possible touch or easy mark, but—Six men!

"How many guys got worked over did Mathews say?" Slot said.

"Six."

"There was exactly six other guys in *La Bomba* around nine," Slot-Machine said.

"So Mike Booher thinks one of seven guys has something," Joe said. "It's probably one of the other guys."

"Maybe," Slot said, "but from the sound of it I was about the last on the list. If he'd found what they was after before he got to me, he wouldn't have come."

Slot-Machine became thoughtful. He reached into his pocket, took out the thirteen dollars, and spread the two fives and the three ones out on the bar. He studied them for a long time, and then he shrugged.

"I don't see nothin'," Slot said. "How about you, Joe?"

Joe looked at each bill. The bartender began to shake his head, and then he stared at one bill. Joe picked up that bill. It was one of the singles. A plain dollar bill. Joe stared at it.

"I'll be damned," Joe said, "this is a funny one, Slot."

"What's funny?"

"The seal," Joe said. "It's gold. I didn't notice it at first. Who looks at the seal on a bill? Only this one's gold. I ain't seen a bill like that for fifteen, seventeen years. I figured there wasn't any around."

"So what's so big about a gold seal?" Slot said.

Joe explained. "It was the war. I mean, regular dollars got blue seals, fives and tens and higher denominations blue or red or green seals. I learned to keep my eyes peeled for things like that to keep from getting stuck with counterfeits."

"Get to the point."

Joe Harris laughed. "If you'd really lost that wing in the war, like you tell everyone, you'd know. Gold seals was on the bills they printed for using overseas in the war. They was special."

"They never used them back here?"

"I think it was illegal," Joe said. "They got pulled in."

"This one didn't," Slot said, picking up the bill.

"That one didn't," Joe said.

Slot said, "Okay, Joe, I'll see you, I hope."

"Where you going?"

"To give thirteen dollars to Mike Booher, if that's what he wants. He can have it all."

"My hero," Joe said.

"Better chicken than cold turkey," Slot said.

III

SLOT CAUGHT A taxi to ride uptown to Mike Booher's place above an elegant restaurant on Ninth Avenue. Booher liked a good front, which tied in with the way he liked to eat. As Slot got into the cab he was sure he saw a large figure run from a doorway and get into a waiting car. It looked a lot like Packy Chen. Slot sweated all the way to Mike Booher's place.

When he reached the restaurant there was no one behind him. He told Lou Gotz on the private door he wanted to see Mike Booher. Gotz checked by phone, and thumbed Slot to follow him. When he reached Booher's private office, Mike did not wait for a formal greeting.

"Listen, cripple, Mathews was here ahead of you. Now you tell me about Packy Chen. Talk fast, Kelly!"

Slot told all he knew, but he did not mention the thirteen dollars to Booher either. There was something peculiar about Mike's anger. Slot had feared that almost anything in the threat line might be used to get the money out of him, but he had not expected outraged anger.

"So you don't even know if it was Packy?" Booher said.

"I ain't sure," Slot admitted. "Mathews thinks it was him."

Booher exploded. "Every time a Chink does a strong arm in this town you all blame Packy! And everyone knows that Packy Chen only does what Mike Booher orders. How do you think that makes me look? I got enough trouble, Kelly, without you lying about me."

"You didn't order Packy to work me over?" Slot said.

"You? What the hell is a small-time cripple like you to me? If I ordered Chen to get you, Kelly, you'd be dead or a bloody mess by now. You know that, don't you?"

Slot nodded, "You got a point, Booher."

It was true. If Packy Chen had been on a job for Booher, he, Slot, would have been handled neat and clean. And when did Mike Booher ever send just one man to do a job?

"Listen, Kelly, I got enough problems. Okay? Now I'm gonna tell you something I told Mathews, just to shut you up. Chen's been in Chicago for a week. I sent him. He ain't even in town. You got that?"

"Packy's in Chicago?"

"I said he was in Chicago," Booher said. "He's due back any minute. I had Lou there call him. Right Lou?"

"Right," Lou Gotz said. "I called Packy. He's flyin' back. Ought to be here by now."

"Okay, we'll wait. Right, Kelly?" Booher said.

"You are right," Slot said. You did not disagree with Mike Booher.

While he sat waiting, and sweating, Slot-Machine tried to puzzle it out. The attacker had looked enough like Packy Chen to have been Chen's twin brother. So who was impersonating Packy? Slot did not have a guess. But it explained the turned-out light, the muffled voice, and the fact that he was still walking around. Packy Chen did not make mistakes. So it had to be someone else. And that someone was after him.

Chen arrived about a half hour later. The big Chinese hood stared at Slot when Mike Booher explained the charge against him. Chen did not smile. Packy Chen never smiled. The Oriental muscleman only stared at Slot.

"You look too good for a guy *I* worked over, one-arm," Chen said. "Tell me, why would I bother with a bum like you?"

"You know, that's what I'm wondering, Packy," Slot said. Because once again he was not sure. The big Chinese looked too much like his attacker, and the voice was very much the same.

"You're funny, ain't you, Kelly? I do what Mike says, no more. You got that?" Chen was very annoyed. Maybe too annoyed.

"I got it, Packy."

"Mr. Chen to you, cripple," Chen said.

"Of course, Mr. Chen," Slot said. Only he noticed that Chen seemed to be favoring his right arm as if someone had thrown him across a room by that arm.

"Get out of here, Kelly," Mike Booher said.

Slot left. He went home to sleep. Joe was already snoring, it was that late. But Slot lay awake quite a while trying to figure it out. He had a hunch about that dollar.

After breakfast next day, Slot grabbed a taxi to the *La Bomba Club*. Again he was sure someone was following him. And again it looked just like Chen.

When he walked into the *La Bomba Club* he was not alone. Captain Gazzo turned to look at him as he came in. Slot stopped in his tracks. The Captain had four of his best men with him. Sergeant Jonas saw Slot-Machine and began to grin.

"Well, well, my old pal the one-armed bandit," Jonas said. "Can we help you with something special, Kelly?"

"My mistake," Slot said, "I thought this was the library. See you around."

Slot spun on his heel and started for the door. He did not hear the five cops move. Then he heard Gazzo's voice. The Captain sounded tired.

"All right, Kelly, how come you come walkin' in here at ten in the morning? The dancin' don't start for a long time, Kelly."

"I was lookin' for a friend," Slot said.

"You ain't got a friend," Sergeant Jonas said.

"That's why I'm lookin' for one. Maybe you'll be my friend, Jonas?"

Captain Gazzo said, "This friend, would he be alive or dead, Kelly?"

"You know somethin' I don't, Cap'n?" Slot said.

"I got a very stiff friend of someone's," Gazzo said.

"I just remembered I got to visit my dentist," Slot said. "He's in Miami. See you boys again soon, heah?"

Jonas said, "The owner there says you was in here last night, Kelly."

"Not me, Sergeant," Slot lied.

"Kelly, don't you never learn?" Captain Gazzo said.

Slot turned back, shrugged, and walked to Captain Gazzo. From the scared look on the face of the owner of the *La Bomba*, and the grim faces of the cops, Slot knew this was not petty larceny. Gazzo and his boys were Homicide.

"Okay, Gazzo, how come Homicide's in on this?" Slot said.

"In on what, Kelly?" Gazzo asked.

Slot explained what he knew, and what Lieutenant Mathews had told him. But he did not mention the thirteen dollars to Gazzo any more than he had mentioned that to Mathews.

"Maybe you should ask Packy Chen," he said, "he's right outside."

Gazzo snapped to Jonas, "Take a look."

When Jonas had gone, Slot-Machine said, "Who's the stiff?"

"Name was Myrna Velton," Gazzo said. "She was a hooker. A hundred bucks gets you a happy night. At least, it did. Myrna ain't having no more happy nights. You know her, Kelly?"

"Big blonde, a real looker, shakes it nice and looks like maybe a hundred bucks a night is a bargain?" Slot said.

"That's her," Gazzo said.

"I didn't know her," Slot said.

"That was a good description."

"I seen her around," Slot said, "she hung out in here."

"That's why we're here," Gazzo said. "The owner there says he doesn't know why she was killed."

"One of her customers maybe?" Slot said. "They came from all walks of life."

Gazzo nodded. "Could be. She was beaten to death, a drunk trick kills that way. How about you? You look like you'd pay for Myrna."

"When did I have a hundred bucks?" Slot said.

"You got a point," Gazzo said. "But it doesn't clear you."

Sergeant Jonas came back alone. Jonas looked at Slot-Machine and shook his head in mock sadness and worry.

"He was there," Jonas said, "but he spotted me and was long gone. Too bad, Kelly, with Chen after me I'd pay up my life insurance. After he gets you, we'll get him. How's that?"

"Thanks," Slot-Machine said. "You're being real generous—with my life."

"Okay, Kelly, beat it," Gazzo said. "Only sort of stay in town."

"You gonna check all her customers out?"

"We are," Gazzo said.

IV

SLOT LEFT. If he knew Myrna Velton, Gazzo would be busy for weeks checking out her paying lovers. One thing was sure, the thirteen dollars was beginning to look more and more like a very hot thirteen dollars. Myrna Velton was the woman he'd stolen the money from. And Myrna was dead.

Slot went to a telephone and called Joe Harris. He got Myrna Velton's address. There wasn't a call-girl in New York Joe didn't know; it was part of the bartending business. Joe had supported both of them many times on the tips he got from steering customers to call girls.

Slot found the brownstone where Myrna had lived and climbed the stairs carefully. The door opened the first time he knocked. A small, pale-faced man stared at him. The man's eyes were red from crying.

"What the hell you want?" the man said.

"Myrna," Slot said.

"She's dead," the small man said dully.

"Yeh," Slot said. "I ain't a customer. I figure maybe I'm next on the list."

The man stared at him. Then the small man shrugged and waved him inside. The apartment was elegant and expensive. Call-girls do all right. But there was something about the room that was puzzling. It was a warm room, lived in, and there were pipes and other men's things around. The small man saw Slot looking at the place.

"We got four rooms," the man said. "We lived in these two. We was happy. I'm her husband. Sam Paxton, that's me. Myrna was Mrs. Sam Paxton. I loved her, you know?"

"You lived good," Slot said.

"I work," the man said. "I make money, but she liked expensive things. I mean, she liked a lot of money."

"Yeh," Slot said.

"It was her work. I didn't want to lose her, so I tried not to let it torment me too much. I kept telling myself it didn't count, it was just her work."

"What happened?" Slot said. "The night she got it?"

The small man, Sam Paxton, sat down. "It was last night. He came in through the back entrance. I didn't see him, you know? I mean, I thought it was a customer, so I waited in here. But I heard—"

"Tell me," Slot said.

The small man shrugged. "He wanted something. I figured he was a customer at first, but then I heard them start arguing, and I recognized his voice. He'd been up before. I'd never seen him, you know, just the voice. So they started arguing. I heard the door lock click shut and then she started screaming.

"I could hear him hitting her. I tried to bust the door down, but it's a metal door. I half killed myself hurling my shoulders against it without realizing how hopeless it was. She just kept on screaming, and this guy kept yelling, 'Where is it! Don't lie to me! *Where is it!*' And I heard her say, 'It got stolen. How do I know!'

"By the time I made it around to the other door, and busted it down, she was dead and the guy was gone out the window and down the fire escape. She wasn't really dead yet. She died right after I found her. Her jaw was broken and she couldn't talk."

"You didn't see the man?" Slot said.

"No."

"Thanks," Slot said, and as he was leaving he turned and said, "Sorry, Paxton."

"Yeh," Paxton said.

And it had to be the thirteen dollars. Slot thought of poor Myrna Velton trying to convince someone she had lost the money. Paxton had said he knew the voice. So the killer had been with Myrna before. Probably a regular. And maybe the thirteen dollars was part of the money he had paid Myrna for her favors one night.

There could be no doubt at all that the killer wanted the thirteen dollars very badly. Chen could easily kill with his hands. Whoever Myrna's visitor had been he probably hadn't intended to kill her, and Packy Chen was strong enough to kill a woman by accident. Or a man. Slot knew one more thing. If it was Chen he had better find out why the big Chinese wanted that money before he met him again.

If Chen, or anyone else, got to him before he knew why, he wouldn't be able to talk his way out of it. Myrna's slayer would kill him first, and take the money, and ask no questions. There was something about that money which left no doubt in Slot's mind that he had to get it back to the killer without the killer thinking he knew why it was so important. Protesting that he didn't know wouldn't save him. He'd never be believed.

After he left Paxton he took a cab down to the tavern where Joe worked. Joe was just going on duty. Slot sat down at the bar and didn't even ask for a whisky. He spread out the money and stared at it again. There was nothing unusual about any of it, except that gold seal on the one dollar bill.

"Hold it up to the light," Joe said.

"Maybe I should look for secret ink?"

"Why not?"

Slot sat up straight. "A message! Maybe that's it, but how?"

He studied all the bills. There was nothing about them that rang a bell. He studied the bills one by one, and found nothing. Until he took the gold-seal bill and stared at it a long time. Then he saw it! The serial number. *X 82622217 A.*

Slot snapped; "Joe, what's the date?"

"August the second, why?"

"August the second, nineteen sixty-two. Right?"

"Last time I looked," Joe said.

"Okay, now listen," Slot said. "Call Mathews and Gazzo and tell them to stay around their offices if they want something maybe big. Got that?"

"Where you goin'?"

"To try to give a dollar back to a killer," Slot said.

He had two stops to make first. If his hunch was right, it explained why Packy Chen had been working alone, and why Mike Booher had stated flatly that Packy wasn't doing anything. The one thing that had puzzled Slot all along was the secret way Chen had gone about committing mayhem and murder.

He headed straight for Mike Booher's restaurant. Lou Gotz was on the door as usual. Lou gave Slot a fish eye.

"Fly away, peeper, Mike ain't friends today," Gotz said.

"Listen, Gotz. I got a question that may be real important to Mike."

"So ask Mike."

"I ain't sure about it," Slot-Machine said. "When you called Packy out in Chicago, did you talk to Packy?"

Gotz laughed. "You got rocks in your head, shamus? You know better. Nobody talks to Packy when Packy's workin'. I got a message to him."

"How?"

"We got lots of ways to send messages, peeper," Gotz said.

"Yeh, I know," Slot-Machine said. He did not wait for more polite conversation. He knew it might not stay polite.

Slot-Machine's second stop was just as brief. He called on Eddie Purvis, the loan shark. Eddie shook his head when Slot asked for $1,000. Slot-Machine wasn't surprised by that and settled for $500. Eddie made it clear that payments must not be allowed to lapse and that interest was important. It was very high interest, about 100 percent if payments were made on time. But Slot needed the money too badly to worry about that.

Packy Chen had one weakness—poker. Chen knew every poker game in the city. Max Weller's game was Chen's favorite. A poker game was the only way Slot could think of to get the hot dollar back to Packy without turning Chen's suspicion that he knew too much into a dead certainty. Even that might not work, but it was worth a try.

V

THERE WERE FIVE players in the game when Slot arrived. None of them were Mike Booher's men, but he was sure that sooner or later Chen would appear. As Slot walked in and took an empty chair, a man stepped out of the shadows, stared at him for a moment, and walked quickly out the door. Slot had an idea Chen would appear very soon.

"Dollar ante," Max Weller said. Max was his own dealer. It was a five card stud game, and they played for business here. "Big king, a ten, nine is fine, five for the ride, with a Jack, and the eight can wait. Sing, king," Max Weller chanted.

Slot had the Jack up and a nine down and he folded. The play went on. Slot folded every hand. Until the tenth deal after he got there.

"Ante the buck," Max called. "Deuce, big ace, with a trey, and spades the ten, the king is red, a queen. You got the handle, ace."

The ace bet five dollars. Slot looked under his red king, and stared at a second red king. He raised twenty. The ace saw, the three called, and the queen behind him. He decided the ace was sucking, the three had to be paired, and the queen could be.

Max called, "Seven for the ace, treys a pair, eight for the big king, ace to the queen. Treys says."

The pair of threes showing bet fifty dollars. That had to be three threes already. Slot called with his kings. The queen-ace raised fifty. The ace-seven went out. The threes re-raised. Slot called and so did the queen-ace. Now Slot figured the queen-ace was not a pair of queens but an ace in the hole, a pair of aces. And there were no kings or eights showing.

"Ace for the treys," Max Weller called. "The kings are paired, the queens are paired. Take off, kings."

When Slot saw the black king drop on his showing red king he forgot why he was there. He bet fifty, the threes raised fifty, the pair of queens with an ace just called. Slot re-raised fifty. He knew he was betting against three three's and two pair, aces and queens, and with all the aces out he had a good chance. The threes and queens saw him.

"Queen for the threes," Max called. "An eight for the kings and two pair showin,' a third queen on the board. Three ladies make the play."

Slot tried to look calm.

The three queens checked to him. He bet a hundred dollars, the three's went out swearing. The three queens showing raised him a hundred. He was just about out of money, so he only called. The queens showed a pair of aces for a full house. Slot showed his three kings with the two eights, the queens cursed, and Slot reached for the pot. And he heard a sound behind him.

The door had opened and closed. Slot sensed the looming presence of a large man behind him. He raked in his money casually. Then, as if at random, he picked the gold-seal dollar from his pile and threw it in for the next ante. He heard a sharp intake of breath behind him, then a step, and a hesitation.

Max Weller dealt the cards. The man behind him seemed to be making a decision. Slot forced himself to sit casually, and he forced himself to look carefully at his hole card. He had a ten up and a three in the hole, but he raised twenty dollars on the first bet. He seemed to be intent only on his cards.

The light breathing behind him did not go away. There was a sudden stir of movement, and the man walked to the table, leaned over to say something to one of the players, and expertly palmed the gold-seal bill, dropping another bill in its place. It was done so quickly Slot would not have seen if he had not been watching. The man walked back behind Slot.

Slot's next card was a seven. He raised fifty and casually lighted a cigarette with his one arm. For a long second the person behind him did not move. Then there was a sense of someone going away, and the door opened and closed. Slot went weak inside and folded his cards and stood up and walked out of the game without a word.

The street was empty. Slot did not even stop to count his winnings. He walked quickly to the nearest tavern and called Gazzo and Mathews. He told them to meet him at 221 Seventh Avenue right away.

He was waiting in the shadows by the time Gazzo and Mathews and their men arrived.

"What's up, Kelly?" Gazzo said. "It better be good."

"Packy Chen just walked inside there. I don't know which apartment."

He had been in the shadows when he had seen the big Chinese drive up, park a block away, and walk slowly back and into the building. Chen had been playing it very cautious.

"Why is he in there?" Mathews asked.

"I ain't sure yet," Slot-Machine said. "All I know is he's got an appointment there tonight. I've a hunch, though."

"Tell it," Gazzo said.

"Well," Slot explained, "it has to be big. Chen was real anxious to get back a certain dollar bill." He explained about the dollar bill, and Myrna Velton, and the poker game. "Mike Booher says Chen was out of town when the muggings and the killing took place. Lou Gotz says the same thing. I think they're telling it true. They really think Chen was out of town.

"Like Booher says, if he ordered Chen to get me I'd be out of circulation now. But I know it was Chen who jumped me and those other guys, so he has to be workin' for himself. That's why I'm still around. Chen's being real careful. If Mike Booher was out to mug seven men and a dame, he's got plenty of boys. He'd make sure the job was done quick and efficient. He wouldn't send just Chen, no matter how reliable Chen is.

"Lou Gotz admits he didn't actually talk to Chen out in Chicago. And the guy that fingered me at the game wasn't one of Mike Booher's boys. The way I figure it—Chen is on a private deal. He ducked back into town, and didn't want anyone to know about it. So he had a cover out in Chicago in case Mike called him."

"What private job, Kelly?" Gazzo said.

"Well, I ain't sure, but ten'll get you a hundred if Mike Booher don't show in the next ten minutes," Slot said.

"So what? So Mike and Chen are meetin' here, and—"

Mathews whispered, "Look!"

VI

A TAXI PULLED up near the building at 221 Seventh Avenue. A man got out. The man stood there in the light from the lobby and carefully looked up and down the street. It was Mike Booher.

"He got ten cars to use," Slot hissed, "why a taxi?"

"And alone," Mathews said. "He don't want anyone to know he's here."

"Stop him!" Slot cried. "Get him, quick!"

But by the time Gazzo had led them all to the building, Mike Booher had vanished inside. Gazzo rang a bell, the buzzer answered, and the cops went in. Slot heard Gazzo send men to ring every doorbell in the building. Slot stayed outside. It was a mistake.

The shots were so muffled they had to be silenced. There was a woman's scream. Slot looked up to the window on the fourth floor where the scream had come from. A big shadow was already more than half way down the fire escape.

Packy Chen came down the alley from the fire escape like a runaway express train. Chen had a very large gun in his hand. Later, Slot swore to Joe that he must have been temporarily insane. He never did find out what happened to the gun. He came out of the dark and caught Chen full in the throat with the edge of his one hand.

Anyone but Chen would never have gotten up again. Chen got up. The Chinese caught Slot under the chin with the heel of his hand. That blow would have killed Slot-Machine then and there, except that Chen was still gasping from Slot's blow. He was off balance, and the stroke did not catch Slot full.

As he reeled backwards, Slot kicked Chen in the solar plexus. Chen gasped. Slot recovered and kicked Chen in the groin. The Chinese doubled over. Slot-Machine chopped Chen down with a karate blow to the back of the neck. Chen did not get up.

By that time the cops were all around Slot-Machine and he left them to take care of Chen. He went upstairs to the fourth floor. A beautiful, dark-haired woman was crying in a chair. On the floor the body of Mike Booher lay very dead.

"All right," Gazzo said, "tell me about it, Kelly."

Slot-Machine shrugged. "I told you most already. The whole deal smelled of Chen working for himself. I didn't think Mike Booher was lying, so Chen had to be lying. Why, you know? I mean lying to Mike Booher was dangerous business. Working alone when you are one of Mike Booher's boys was real bad. *Unless Mike was on his way out!*

"I mean, it would have to be real big for Chen to work on something Mike didn't know about. I couldn't figure it unless the stake was real big. And that dollar bill was important enough for seven muggings and a murder. The only thing I could think of that was big enough would be Mike on his way out, and Packy Chen on his way in! I was just guessin', of course. I still am, but maybe the dame can tell us."

The beautiful woman looked at Slot-Machine. Her voice was low and dull. "I warned him. Poor Mike. He loved me, you know? He was going to get out, go somewhere with me. His wife wouldn't divorce him. He just wanted to get out of it all and be with me."

"And no one gets out," Gazzo said. "The big men overseas wouldn't like that."

Slot-Machine nodded. "That's about what I figured. Who knows, maybe Mike had made some mistakes already. A dame can mix up a guy. I guess we'll never know. Packy Chen won't talk. But just trying to run out with this dame would be enough to get the finger put on Mike.

"It was Lou Gotz who said it, those people have a lot of ways of sending messages. I figure Mike was real careful about visiting this dame. He thought he was safe, but they found out overseas somehow. They got word to Chen. Packy would kill his mother for the top spot.

"When the big boys overseas were ready for the hit on Mike, they had to tell Chen. They would usually send a messenger, but Mike Booher might have known a messenger. A messenger to Chen instead of to him would have warned him. The same goes for a letter. Mike could have spotted it.

"I've seen them use the numbers on a laundry list, the prices on a menu, cigarette packages, all sorts of ways. Anything that looks innocent and no one who isn't looking for the message would figure it out.

"It was the serial number on the dollar bill. *X 82622217 A*. It ain't easy to get a bill with just the right number, that's why they had to use one of those gold seal bills. It was all they could find that fitted. Most people wouldn't notice the seal.

"I figure the X was the tip-off it was the contract on Mike. The number was the message: *X 82622217 A*. August the second, nineteen sixty-two, at Two Hundred Twenty-One Seventh Avenue. No one except someone *looking* for the message would get it. Later, people would laugh if you cops said the serial number was a message. They picked the dame's apartment because they knew Mike always came alone. He was being real careful. It cost him."

"I warned him," the sobbing woman said. "I always told him not to come here alone."

"Dame's are always trouble," Slot-Machine said.

Gazzo shook his head sadly, "So Packy was double-crossing Mike. He won't talk, like you say, Kelly, but we got him cold anyhow. I guess Chen had to do the job himself. To prove he was tough enough, and he couldn't trust anyone else. You guessed he lost the bill in Max Weller's poker game?"

Slot nodded. "Yeh. Chen never could think of anything else when he played poker. He probably tossed it into a pot without even thinking, probably was sure he had the winnin' hand. When he lost and saw what he'd done, he couldn't risk anyone guessin' what that bill meant.

"He faked that Chicago trip and traced the bill. I figure the guy who won it gave it to Myrna Velton, probably to buy coffee or cigarettes or some petty-cash deal like that. Chen found her but I'd already lifted the bill from the bar at *La Bomba*. Chen didn't believe her and beat her up. He just killed her by accident, he was too strong.

"Then he went after anyone who maybe *had* taken the bill from the bar. He wasn't sure which one of us had it. Only he had to play it careful, at least careful for him, or Mike might have gotten suspicious. Chen was supposed to be in Chicago."

Gazzo took Chen away. After Slot-Machine had made his statement he headed straight for the tavern where Joe Harris was working. He told Joe the story. Joe agreed that Slot had been insane to tackle Chen.

"I'm still shakin'," Slot said. "I need medicine, make it a double Irish."

"Better have a triple," Joe said, "that one was close."

"Too close. I think I'll go straight."

"And the ocean'll dry up," Joe said. "How come Chen didn't blast you at that poker game?"

"Too many witnesses even for Packy," Slot said. "I counted on that. Besides, Mike Booher might have got wind and started thinking. I mean, Mike Booher didn't buy my story about Chen jumping me, he thought I was a dumb cripple. Too bad, it cost him big."

"It could of cost you big," Joe said.

Slot-Machine shivered. "Pour the booze. My skill at poker has made us rich."

Joe went for the good bottle. When he came back Slot-Machine was still shivering, but he was busily counting his poker winnings.

EVEN BARTENDERS DIE

I returned to the shorter story, with a notable improvement in the writing, and even maybe in the logic. I have always preferred to write short and incisive, and that applies to novels too. (For the last eight years I have been trying to write a "Big" thriller. In its long form it wasn't bad, but it wasn't good enough either. Not to the marketplace, and not to me. Especially not to me. I'll give it one more shot as the kind of shorter, sharper book I think I do best.)

This story itself is the first example of a theme I used in many variations in subsequent stories. It is essentially the theme of the effect of "chance," of how often our lives turn on a combination of events over which we have little or no control. I combined it with a particular trait that appears only too often in the personalities of the rich and the powerful. It is a certain pettiness blended with a strong sense of entitlement. I got the idea first from a habit of Napoleon's that was later repeated by Richard Nixon, and almost certainly by hundreds of such movers and shakers.

Napoleon's favorite wine was a great Burgundian Pinot Noir from the Cote Nuit, Le Chambertin. He described it as a "great purple robe," and it went with him everywhere including Egypt and Russia. When he gave a state dinner, he drank his Chambertin, but had everyone else served a considerably lesser wine! Almost two centuries later, Nixon did exactly the same thing with his favorite expensive wine. The "good" stuff was only for them.

The characterization and imagination improve considerably in this piece, especially witness the "lover" who appears near the end.

SLOT-MACHINE KELLY was thirsty. There was nothing unusual about that, but this was more of a problem. He had been sitting for an hour in the saloon where Joe Harris was working this week. Joe had not shown up.

"He's an hour late," the relief bartender said. "He owes me an hour."

Slot-Machine was worried. If Joe didn't show soon, he might have to buy a drink. The relief man wouldn't give a blind man a push in the right direction. Not that Slot was broke. He had ten dollars in his pocket left from the last job he'd done. That had been the Hasting's divorce set-up, three weeks ago, but he still had the ten spot. It wasn't the money, it was the principle. Slot-Machine didn't want to set an ugly precedent by buying a drink in Joe Harris's bar.

He was also worried about Joe. Not that he would have admitted that openly. On the docks no one worries about anyone else, not even his best friend. It was enough of a problem to get in and out of one's own trouble. It was hard, but it was honest, except Slot had to admit, at least to himself, that he *was* worried about Joe.

He did not have long to worry. Or, better, he did not have long to wait to have a real worry. Manny Hornberg came in for his evening six cans of beer. It was just five o'clock. Manny was as good as a fifty-jewel watch to tell time by.

"Hey," Manny said. "I seen them pick up your buddy, Kelly."

"What buddy, and who picked him up?" Slot said.

"If you got two friends you should throw a party," Manny said. "It wasn't Elizabeth Taylor picked him up."

"Funny, funny," Slot-Machine said. "Give before I bend your beer can opener and you die of thirst."

"Okay, okay," Manny said.

Slot-Machine was only five foot eight and not too heavy, but he could use his one arm better than most men could use two arms. People weren't afraid of Slot, but no one called him "Slot-Machine" to his face. Only Joe Harris could call him Slot-Machine, the One-Armed Bandit.

"It was Gazzo, who else?" Manny Hornberg said. "It was about an hour ago, maybe two hours. I was working my truck and I forgot the time. I was deliverin' by the Munich Delicatessen. They take six cases of my best soda, when I sees Gazzo and Jonas come out of McGuire's place with Harris in tow."

"Gazzo and Jonas?" Slot said.

"In person," Manny said, "and they didn't look like they was takin' Harris to no policeman's social."

Slot-Machine caught a taxi out front on Tenth Avenue and made the Precinct House in four minutes. When he arrived the Desk Sergeant grinned at him. The Sergeant seemed very pleased. It did not pay to be Slot-Machine Kelly's friend.

"Well, well," the Sergeant said from behind his high desk, "You gonna charge Harris half price because he's a friend?"

"Where is he, Perwolak?"

"Coolin', Kelly, coolin'," the Desk Sergeant said. "We got him on ice. Too bad it ain't you. Hey, who's gonna buy you your booze now?"

"What's the charge?"

"Associatin' with a fink like you is charge enough," Perwolak said.

"That's about your speed, Perwolak," Slot said. "Where's Gazzo?"

"Sweatin' your boy, I hope," Perwolak said.

Slot-Machine found Captain Gazzo in his office. Sergeant Jonas was there. The two homicide cops did not like Slot, but they were good cops. They did not look happy. Slot raised his black eyebrows in question.

"Murder one," Gazzo said. The Captain looked really puzzled. "I can't figure Harris, you know, Kelly?"

Slot-Machine sat down hard in a chair. Murder one. He did not feel like joking right then.

"If it was you, I'd say okay," Sergeant Jonas said. "But Harris ain't a bad guy for a friend of yours."

"Tell it straight," Slot-Machine said.

He sat there in the chair in the perpetually dim and airless office of Captain

Gazzo. One sickly bulb burned in a green shade that dangled from the ceiling. Captain Gazzo did not live in the lap of luxury. The Captain told it straight.

Joe and Sam McGurie had been drinking in McGurie's apartment above the Munich Delicatessen. After about a half hour Mrs. McGurie came home and found Sam slumped over the table with Joe bending over him. She had called the cops. Gazzo had taken one look at Sam and guessed poison. They had brought Joe in on suspicion.

"The whisky McGurie was drinking tested out for arsenic—enough to kill a horse. McGurie ain't dead yet, but he ain't got a chance, the Doc says," Gazzo told him. "Harris didn't happen to drink any of that whisky. He says he brought his own."

"He would," Slot said. "He likes his own brand."

"Maybe," Gazzo said. "Only maybe he brought both bottles. Mrs. McGurie don't remember the bottle Sam had. It wasn't his regular stuff. She hadn't ever seen it, and it wasn't full when he started. The cap wasn't there. Someone had just put a wine cork in it to carry it. Even Joe admits that much."

"McGurie was a lousy bartender, but Joe doesn't kill the competition," Slot said. "What's the motive?"

"Joe and McGurie had a fight last week," Jonas said. "That'll do for a start."

"His prints were on the bottle," Gazzo said. "Just his and Sam McGurie's prints, Kelly. He was there. The bottle wasn't one Mrs. McGurie ever seen. It'll hold for a while."

Slot-Machine remembered the fight. It looked bad for Joe. It would look worse when Gazzo and Jonas found out that the fight had been over Joe's girlfriend, Moira Jones.

Sam was a ladies man, wife or no wife, and Joe was jealous over Moira. Joe was always jealous over his girls when they were less than a year old with him. Moira was six months old. It looked very bad for Joe. Gazza was no fool. It wouldn't take him long to find out about Moira Jones.

"What about McGurie's wife? Sam was a skirt-chaser," Slot said.

"She's got an alibi a mile deep." Jonas said.

"She could have doctored the bottle, wiped it clean, and left it," Slot-Machine pointed out.

"She could have," Gazzo admitted, "we're checking out. She swears the bottle wasn't there, and even Joe admits she came in after Sam was down and out. She says she got two witnesses to prove there wasn't any whisky in the house when she left this morning."

"What does Sam say?"

Gazzo shook his head. "Sam ain't talkin'. He's in a coma."

"Can I see Joe?" Slot said.

"Sure, come on," Jonas said.

Jonas led Slot-Machine down the dim corridors of the precinct house. In the cells in the rear four drunks were sleeping it off with bad dreams. From time to time one or more of them screamed in his sleep. The cells smelled of stale whisky and a broken toilet.

Joe Harris was alone in a corner cell. Jonas left Slot to talk to Joe.

"You kept me waiting," Slot-Machine said.

"Sue me," Joe Harris said.

"I'll admit it looks bad," Slot said.

"From in here it looks worse."

"Did you kill him?"

"What do you think?"

"He had it coming," Slot-Machine said. "He was a louse."

"He was a louse," Joe said, "but I didn't kill him."

"Tell it," Slot-Machine said.

Joe was sitting on the edge of the bunk set in the concrete wall of the dingy cell. The bartender shrugged. Joe looked scared, really scared.

"What's to tell?" Joe said. "McGurie calls me and says come on over for a drink. He's got something to tell me about Moira. I figure, okay I'll listen. I'm a jerk, I guess. So I goes over there. I take my own booze, you know?

"I get there and all the bum wants is to apologize! Who's gonna believe that? He's got this maybe three-quarters full fifth of real good Scotch. He said it was the best Scotch. I was almost tempted to drink it when he offers it to me, only I like my bourbon.

"We talks for a while. There was yellin', I admit it. He wants to apologize but he starts talking dirt about Moira, you know that kind of fink. So I yell and we get loud. After a while I figures he was gettin' drunk mighty quick. He starts to weave, he looks sick, he gets pale, he vomits—only nothin' comes up.

"Then he collapses. He must of drunk almost all that whisky. He's sprawled there on the table and I'm wonderin' if I should call the Doc and all. I mean, maybe he won't like it if he's just blasted with booze. I'm still thinking when his old woman walks in. You know the rest."

Joe sat there on the edge of the bunk looking as if he could hardly believe his own story himself. It was a thin story. It told nothing. Slot-Machine was worried. There was one strange thing.

"He offered you some of the whisky?"

"Yeh, I should have drunk it," Joe said.

"It would have made you look better," Slot-Machine admitted. "How come he offered? He was a stingy crum?"

"He was sure proud of that bottle," Joe said. "It puzzled me."

"Proud?" Slot said.

Joe nodded. "Yeh, and you know, he brought it home with him. I'm sure of it. It was still in a paper bag."

Slot-Machine was about to ask if Joe was sure of that when Sergeant Jonas came down the dank hall between the cells. Jonas was grim. The Sergeant stopped and looked in at Joe Harris.

"McGurie's dead," Jonas said. "He didn't talk."

Slot-Machine felt a little sick. Joe Harris held his head in his hands there inside the dark cell.

NO ONE BELIEVED Joe Harris except Slot-Machine. Everyone agreed it was a stupid murder. Poison wasn't Joe Harris' weapon, and Joe wasn't a murderer. But as Captain Gazzo said, "Who else we got? He was there, his prints are on the bottle, he had a motive."

The Captain had questioned and found out about Moira Jones. Moira herself was long gone. A good, loyal woman, Moira.

The cops were looking for Moira Jones. Slot-Machine was looking for a suspect. Any suspect would do. Gazzo was ready to believe any reasonable doubt. Slot-Machine went to work. He had only one passing moment of regret that this case would be a free ride.

Slot started with Sam McGurie's widow. Velma McGurie was no bargain even for a fink like Sam McGurie. The woman was small, skinny, grey, loud, and a shrew. She was in her late forties. She hadn't looked much like a female since she was twenty. Velma and Sam had lived for twenty years on the bliss of mutual hatred. Only now Velma was full of grief.

"I didn't ever think Joe Harris was like that. My poor Sam," Velma said in the dingy apartment above the Munich Delicatessen.

She brushed a fake tear from her eye and pushed back a stringy strand of dirty grey hair. She held a shabby housecoat tight around her dessicated body. Booze and Sam McGurie had made her look more like a dry fence post than a woman.

"Joe ain't like that," Slot-Machine said. "You know it."

"I should give him a medal maybe?" Velma sneered.

"They got a hotter prize in mind. You sure you didn't fill that booze with the one-way ticket?"

"Get the hell out of here, Kelly!"

"Was it Sam's money, or maybe you got a lover on the side?"

The sleazy woman turned purple. She knew an insult when she heard one. She looked like she was going to grab for something to demolish Slot-Machine with. Then she suddenly began to cackle like a lizard. She was laughing.

"Lissen, peeper, I got two witnesses say there wasn't no booze in this dump when I left. Sam's own brother, he should rot with Sam, swears there was no booze. And he's a lush. He come here and searched. Sam's brother hates my guts. He's the best proof I could get.

"My sister was with me all mornin' and she swears there was no booze. The cops asked all around for who buys arsenic? Not me. Go watch your friend fry, Kelly."

"You're a sweetheart," Slot-Machine said. "If Sam killed himself, I could understand it."

"Go to hell!"

Slot-Machine grew thoughtful. "That money ain't such a bad idea at that. Sam have insurance?"

"Go find out, shamus. Now beat it!"

Slot-Machine left. In the Munich Delicatessen he called Gazzo. The Captain was not helpful. Yes, Gazzo had checked out the insurance. There was a measly $5,000 policy, borrowed to the hilt. The brother hated Velma, but admitted that he had searched for booze and found none. The brother agreed that the woman wasn't born who could hide booze from his thirst. It was possible there was a hidden policy somewhere. Everything was possible, but it didn't look good.

Slot-Machine hung up and walked out into the thin sun of the New York slum. A fine haze was blowing over the river from Bayonne and the Jersey Flats. He lighted a cigarette and thought about his next move. He didn't have a next move. His suspects started and ended with Velma McGurie.

He went into the *Mona Lisa Tavern*. He had a drink. He had two drinks. He had three drinks. He still had no more suspects. In his mind he ran down the list of names who did not like Sam McGurie, and he came up blank. Everyone had an alibi. No one had been seen anywhere near McGurie's apartment. Otto in the Munich Delicatessen had a clear view of anyone who went in and out of McGurie's building.

"Sam 'n Joe, no one else, Kelly," Otto had said. "Sorry! I see no one. It is bad, yes?"

It was bad. Slot had a fourth drink. He added up the case. Velma McGurie had a hundred and one reasons for killing Sam, and she was clear. Joe had no reason to kill Sam, and he was hooked. Joe hadn't killed Sam McGurie. Fact one. Fact two: no one else had. Answer: suicide. With arsenic?

Slot began to think about arsenic. Arsenic was a slow poison. If caught in time it could be pumped out and antidoted easy. If someone wanted to kill a man fast then arsenic was a bad weapon. Arsenic killers plan a long time. Arsenic … Slot sighed. It was no use. No one had killed Sam McGurie.

There it was: the killer was no one. The killer was one bottle of real fine Scotch. Sam McGurie had had a bottle of Scotch he was proud of and it had killed him. All by itself. A wine cork, and …

Slot-Machine sat up as if he'd been shot. He blinked. He jumped up and ran out of the *Mona Lisa Tavern*. He hailed a taxi. When he arrived at the precinct house Gazzo stared at him. The Captain was looking sadder as each day passed and Joe sat in the cell. In a few days Gazzo would have to turn Joe over to the D.A. for indictment.

"You got something, Kelly?" Gazzo said.

"Maybe," Slot said. "Maybe I have. You got that whisky bottle?"

"Sure," Gazzo said. The Captain reached into a locked drawer and brought out the bottle. "I been over it with a ouija board, and there's nothin' on it but Sam's prints, Joe's prints, and two ounces of whisky with arsenic flavoring. Not even a dog hair."

Slot-Machine did not touch the bottle. He just sat in a chair and looked at it. It was a tall, green bottle with a simple label printed in red on ivory. There was a wine cork in the neck. Originally the bottle had had a screw cap.

"It's just plain Scotch, regular stuff," Gazzo said. "I checked the brand. It's a house brand carried by about ten stores around here. They bring it over in kegs, bottle it out in Brooklyn at Bush Terminal, save money that way. They can sell it cheaper. But it's the real stuff."

Slot-Machine stared at the whisky bottle. He read the label. DRURY'S SCOTCH WHISKY, *A Blend, 86 Proof, 4/5 of a quart.* Slot's eyes began to narrow and he hunched in his chair. Gazzo looked at Slot, then at the bottle.

"You got an idea, Kelly?"

Slot-Machine nodded slowly. "Maybe. I know Joe didn't kill McGurie, and you know it. What we don't have is anyone else who could have done it, right?"

"Right. We got no real reason except Velma and she's in the clear."

"Maybe there wasn't any reason," Slot-Machine said. He stood up. "I'll be back."

Slot-Machine left Gazzo sitting there with his mouth open. What Slot had in mind was too hazy to tell anyone yet. He was looking for a killer without a reason.

IN HIS TWO-BY-FOUR office, Slot-Machine Kelly took another sip of whisky and dialed his telephone again. On his desk was a list of names. There were five names on the list. Each time Slot dialed he shook his desk and dust flew up into the dim air.

"Hello? Mrs. Morgan? My name is Kelly. That's right. No, you don't know me, but I know you. I'm calling about a bottle of Scotch whisky. Yes, Scotch. I want half a grand to let you have it. Yes, I've got it. Five hundred, cheap at the price."

Slot listened to the woman's voice. He heard outrage, talk of police, shouting to someone else in the distant room. He hung up. There were two more names on his list. He dialed. Again it was a woman who answered.

"Mrs. Euclid? My name is Kelly. No, you wouldn't know any Kelly. I'm calling to ask if you'd like to buy some Scotch whisky. That's right, Scotch. I've got a fine brand. I'd say it was worth maybe five hundred dollars a bottle. Yes, I've got one bottle, just one. That's it, half a grand in small bills right here in my office. Fourteen-ten West Twenty-eighth Street, third … Mrs. Euclid?"

The woman had hung up. But she had not hollered copper. She was the first one on his list who had not screamed for the fuzz. Slot-Machine began to grin. Still, he could be wrong. He called the last name on his list. It was a man. The man hung up at the first mention of $500. It sounded like the Euclid woman.

Slot-Machine looked at his watch. He had maybe a half an hour; the address of the Euclid woman was high in the East Seventies. Slot stood up and walked across the hall to the office of Doc Madison. The Doc was an old quack who was known to have a door that opened onto the fire escape and lights that burned late at night in a windowless room. The Doc was a plastic artist. Gazzo couldn't prove it.

"Hello, Kelly," the Doc said from his desk. The desk was almost as dirty as Slot-Machine's desk. "You got a nice, hot client?"

"I got a hot friend," Slot said.

"Yeh," the Doc said sympathetically. "I heard."

"Do me a favor, Doc."

The old Doc was cautious. He had been in business a long time and hadn't copped one arrest.

"Like what?" the Doc said.

"Make a phone call. I want a Doc to do it just in case the party asks questions. You know the symptoms of slow arsenic poisoning?"

"Maybe," the Doc said.

"Is it hard to spot?"

"If the Doc don't know it's there, yes. It's a classic way of no return."

"Okay, call this number. Tell the woman you're a Doc and you heard her husband's been sick. The symptoms sound interesting. That's all unless she asks questions. Then give her the arsenic symptoms."

"For how much?"

"Ten bucks and a friend."

"Twenty-five," the Doc said. "I got a friend."

"Make the call."

"Convince me," the Doc said.

Slot-Machine put twenty-five dollars on the desk. The Doc picked up the money and the telephone. The Doc dialed the number of the Euclid woman. The Doc said what Slot-Machine had told him to say. There was a pause. Then the Doc hung up slowly. He looked at Slot-Machine.

"She just breathed, Kelly. Pay dirt?"

"I think so," Slot said.

Out in the hall Slot-Machine paused. He looked around. There was the broom closet. He opened the door of the tiny closet and squeezed in beside the mop bucket. He left the door open a crack and waited.

While Slot waited he went over it again in his mind. The bottle had given him the idea. Sam McGurie was a hungry little fink. Sam worked days in the tavern on Tenth Avenue. At night, Slot had remembered, Sam often took jobs bartending for private parties and banquets. Maybe Sam just wanted to stay away from Velma.

Anyway, Slot had checked with Velma, Otto in the Munich Delicatessen where Sam took business calls, and a bartender's agency. There had been the five names of people who had hired Sam in the past week. Mrs. Euclid had been only two days ago. Slot was still thinking when he heard the noise.

He peeked out his crack. It was a man. A tall, elegant looking man who wore a beautiful cashmere overcoat. The man had his hand in the pocket of the fine coat. The man tried Slot-Machine's office door. Slot stepped out of his closet, his Luger in his hand.

"Bring the hand out of the pocket slow, friend," Slot-Machine said. He should have expected a man.

The man froze. There was a moment of hesitation in his rigid back.

"Don't try it, sonny," Slot-Machine said. "This'll hurt more than a cell. I figure you ain't killed no one yet."

The man brought his hand out of his pocket empty. The man started to turn.

"Don't turn, friend. Just open the door and walk straight ahead and put your hands flat on the desk. Go on."

The man did as he was told. Slot-Machine went up behind him and took the gun from the man's pocket. It was a small .25 calibre Beretta. It had a pearl handle. A woman's gun. Slot-Machine reached into the other pocket of the man's coat and came out with $500 tied in a rubber band.

"Well, well," Slot said, "I see you came prepared for any possibility. Very smart."

Too late Slot-Machine heard the soft step. He felt the other person behind him.

"Smarter than you, Mr. Kelly," a woman's voice said. "Now you put the gun down."

Slot-Machine obeyed. It was a rule of his. If they got a gun on you smile and don't even breathe mean. The tall man picked up his own gun. Slot turned around. The woman was small and very pretty. She was holding a twin of the .25 Beretta Slot had taken from the tall man.

"The whisky, Kelly," the woman said.

"Whisky?" Slot said innocently.

"Yes, the whisky! Thomas, search!"

The man began to search. Slot noticed with reluctant approval that the woman was in her stocking feet. Most women would forget how loud their heels could sound in a hallway. Slot-Machine watched the man searching and waited. At last the man reached the left hand bottom drawer. Slot tensed.

The man opened the bottom drawer. The shot rang out like a cannon explosion. It was a booby trap blank cartridge Slot always left in that drawer. The man almost fell backwards. The woman turned her pistol toward the man and the sound of the shot.

Slot-Machine leaped. He caught the woman on the neck just as she swung back toward him and fired. The bullet seared his side. The woman went down and out as if pole-axed. Her small pistol skidded across the floor toward the tall man.

Slot-Machine turned, crouched, and faced the tall man. For a long minute the tall man stood with his pistol pointed at Slot. Slot-Machine prepared to lunge sideways and forward and pray. Then the tall man shrugged and put down his pistol. The tall man looked down at the woman.

"It's her problem," the tall man said. "I'm clean. I don't know anything."

Slot-Machine looked at the tall man in disgust. The tall man lighted a cigarette.

"I think she must have been crazy," the tall man said. "I just came here as a favor. Poor girl."

The tall man carefully wiped his Beretta and dropped it. Slot-Machine picked up his Luger and called Gazzo. The tall man was still smoking when Gazzo arrived. The woman was sitting in a chair holding her neck and swearing at Slot-Machine.

Slot-Machine explained to Gazzo. "What tipped me was the bottle. I mean, Joe was innocent, that much I knew. So someone else did it, check? But even Joe said Sam brought the bottle home himself. Joe said it was real fine Scotch and Sam was proud of it.

"Only the bottle you have, Gazzo, ain't real fine Scotch. It's plain old eight-year-old house Scotch. Sam McGurie was a hungry and cheap fink. I checked and found he'd worked five jobs that week. I figured at one of those jobs someone was using arsenic poisoning.

"You see, it's an old bartender's trick to take home unused whisky. In this case I figured if someone was using whisky to slow poison, and maybe this dose was to be the killer, then the whisky would have to be real special. Private whisky, you know? You'll probably find that Mr. Euclid, if he's still alive, has a real fine special Scotch *no one else in his house dares touch.*

"But Mrs. Euclid there made the mistake of hiring Sam McGurie to bartend her party. I bet it was a cheer-up party for her poor sick husband, something to make him feel better, and to make her look the loving wife. Right Mrs. Euclid?"

The small woman was not so pretty now. There was a deep bruise growing on her neck. She said nothing. She only glared. The man just sat and smiled and acted very innocent. Slot-Machine almost felt sorry for the woman. Some lover to kill for.

"Anyway," Slot went on, "she hired Sam McGurie. Fink that he was, he spotted the real fine Scotch no one was drinking right then, and *he switched whiskies!* He probably figured that the good stuff would be missed, but not the bar stuff Mrs. Euclid had bought for the other guests, see? So he poured the real fine Scotch into a cheap bottle and took it home."

Slot sighed, "Poor Sam. He killed himself with his cheap stealing. I expect you'll find Mr. Euclid mighty sick and it'll be arsenic in him. I don't know if you can get the woman for Sam's death, that's your job. Anyway, it shouldn't be hard to find witnesses who saw Sam there.

"Maybe you can get Mrs. Euclid to confess. You got her on attempted murder anyhow, and Sam's death wasn't premeditated. If you get the whisky you got left analyzed it'll be a lot better than the Drury that's supposed to be in that bottle, Gazzo."

The Captain looked grim. "We'll work it out, Kelly. I knew Joe wasn't a killer. Okay, folks, let's go now."

After the woman and her lover had been booked for attempted murder (the husband was sick of arsenic poisoning), Slot-Machine and Joe Harris walked out of the station house. Joe was very thirsty. They went to Joe's bar and sat on stools. Joe tossed down three in a row. All bourbon.

"I never want to see no Scotch again," Joe said. "When I think of all the pay we lost—"

Slot-Machine laughed. "Don't give it a thought, Joe boy. I got paid pretty good. You know, you think Gazzo'll ever believe that dame gave me half a grand for a bottle of whisky she never got? That boyfriend won't breathe a word, it might involve him."

Slot-Machine tossed the $500 onto the bar and laughed like hell. He began to count the money. It was all in small bills. He was still laughing when he finished counting and Joe Harris was on his fourth bourbon and smiling without pain.

DEATH FOR DINNER

My wife had a book describing the fine wines of the world, with particular emphasis on those of France's two great regions: Bordeaux and Burgundy. I read it, my interest was raised, and I did what I have done all my life—started learning all I could about these wines, and, inevitably, buying them. The first one I tried I found in a bin in Nussbaum's Liquor Store down near Wall Street for $3.98 a bottle: Lafitte Rothschild 1958. Simply put, it was an experience. After that first glass, I realized I had never known what real wine tasted like. I was hooked. We stretched a tight budget to buy two cases, and had 24 wonderful experiences at dinner, which, at the time, we needed.

After that I discovered the Astor Place Liquor Store, and bought almost every classified Bordeaux of the 1958 vintage. They were dirt cheap even at Sixties prices, because the year had been rated poorly, but turned out to be not a bad vintage, only a soft one that would mature rapidly and would not last long enough to lay down. After that I began on the more expensive, and far more complicated, matter of the Burgundian wines. Over the years I've tried almost all of them, but to this day I have never had a La Romanee Conti!

In this story, I think, the characterization, the imagination, the structure, notably improves. I was beginning to use my experience in the literary mainstream world in the detective story. (It also shows the arrogance of the "amateur expert" full of his new found knowledge. The mellowing of more experience has taught me that the key turning point I use is far less rigid and definite than I make it here. Sigh.)

SLOT-MACHINE KELLY groaned in his bed and reached for his morning cigarette. He snapped a match alight with his one hand. Only after he had taken four deep, sighing drags on the cigarette did the one-armed detective open his eyes to look at the dismal grey light that struggled through the one window of his shabby bedroom.

A quick glance told him that Joe Harris was long gone to work in his saloon. The thought of Joe and work brought Slot's mind around to the problem of money. This was so painful that he closed his eyes again. He groaned again. He decided to think about something else. He thought of Gloria, his latest find in the female line. He groaned again. Gloria made him think of money.

A mouse, foraging in a far corner for anything edible, scurried away at the last groan. Slot-Machine fixed a beady eye on the small animal. A new mouse, the old ones were accustomed to the groans from the rumpled bed.

"We got more turnover in mice than any flop-joint in New York City," Joe Harris had said yesterday. "The old ones know better than to look for food in here."

And that made Slot-Machine think of money. Slot stopped fighting it. Okay, money. His cigarette finished, the one-armed detective got up, crossed the room, and felt in his pants pocket. He came out with twenty-seven cents and a German pfennig good for a subway token until they fixed the turnstiles. Now he carried the pfennig for luck.

Slot-Machine knew better than to check his wallet. Joe would bring home tips, but Joe frowned on Slot's taste for expensive Irish when the room-mates were this low, which was most of the time. There was no hope for it, he would have to do some work.

Without dressing, Slot wrapped a sleazy bathrobe around his small but solid frame, and went out into the hall to make the telephone call. He had run out of subpoenas to serve, he was into old Maxwell for $300 advance in Maxwell's perennial need to have his wife tailed, and the only job left was the snooping for J. Ellsworth Farley.

At the telephone Slot-Machine hesitated. J. Ellsworth Farley was a gold-plated louse. No, J. Ellsworth was a solid gold louse. Slot had turned down Farley four times this week. No other private cop would even bother to turn down the rotten job.

J. Ellsworth Farley was a self-made dictator of smut. The oily man had made a fortune out of the dirt in everyone's hidden corners. He tyrannized everyone who worked for him and his cheap but highly lucrative magazine. He was hated by half the population of the show business world of five states, and he was detested by his relatives who were painfully waiting for him to die. It was one of the relatives, a nephew, J. Ellsworth Farley wanted ruined this time.

Slot had half turned from the phone when he saw the small grey mouse come shuffling out of his apartment, look at him once in sheer disgust, and head down the hall for greener pastures. Slot-Machine sighed. Even a mouse had to eat. He reached for the telephone.

J. E. FARLEY was a fat, bald, grotesque man who affected striped silk westkits that bulged over his paunch. Usually there was a food stain somewhere on his expensive suits. Farley was a gourmet. The fat man was also a gluttonous slob. The stain this morning was eggs benedict.

"You know what I pay, and I want the expenses itemized down to the cost of a toothpick," J. Ellsworth said nastily.

"I get my toothpicks wholesale, no charge, just for you," Slot-Machine said.

"You'll laugh your way into the poorhouse," Farley said.

The smut-czar's office was in the rear of his Park Avenue apartment—ten stories up, no fire escape, a double police lock on the door, and he could deduct two-thirds of his rent as business expenses. The desk that separated Farley from Slot-Machine was big, and heavy, and second-hand.

"I want Murray followed, every move. I want his wife followed. Hire a man, I'll pay half what I pay you."

"You'll pay full, double," Slot-Machine said.

"That's all, Kelly. I'll get another man."

"You couldn't get a dog-catcher," Slot-Machine said. "No one except me is low enough."

The fat man began to swear. Slot-Machine toyed with the small, Japanese Samurai dagger Farley used for a paper knife. Farley wriggled in his chair like a stuck pig while he swore.

"All right, peeper," Farley said. "Double. Now here's what I want. I don't care how you do it, but I want my nephew's marriage broken up. That wife is putting ideas into his head of getting some of his money."

"His money?"

"His mother, my late and stupid sister, left it to him in my trust. He gets it when he's thirty, or when he has his first child. I want him unmarried. You fix it. You find the facts, or frame him, I don't care which, and I'll tell the story in print. That should do it."

"You're a sweet fellow," Slot-Machine said.

"Why not? The punk gets it all, mine as well as his money, when I die. The stupid bum is my only relative."

"Leave it to charity and cheat him," Slot said.

"Even Murray's better than charity," Farley said.

"You'll find a way to take it with you."

"Get out of here, Kelly. You're on my time," Farley said.

Slot-Machine was about to stand up when there was shouting in the outer apartment and the door burst open. A tall, angry man stalked into the room. The tall man wasted no time on polite chit-chat. He reached over the desk and punched Farley squarely on the nose. Blood spurted and the fat man went over backwards in a tangle of legs, arms, chair legs, and striped westkit.

"That's for an introduction," the tall man said. "Next time I'll use a gun."

"You … you …" Farley sputtered. "I'm bleeding! Kelly, do something! Call the police!"

"I charges double for bodyguarding," Slot-Machine said placidly. "Pay me first, and I'll protect you." ·

"You …" Farley sputtered as he disentangled himself from the chair, blood staining his fine striped westkit.

"In case you don't know," the tall man said, "my name is Walters, Philip Walters, and if you print one word of your lies I will happily kill you."

The tall man turned and stalked out, nodding, as he went, to Phyllis Thaxon, Farley's secretary. Miss Thaxon paled as she saw the scene. The woman was literally shaking as Walters passed her and vanished, his tall back as still and straight as a ramrod.

"He just pushed past me and—" Miss Thaxon began to stammer.

J. Ellsworth Farley was on his feet. The fat man walked to his secretary and slapped her hard across the face.

"You stupid witch!"

Miss Thaxon fell back against the door. The woman was in tears, her hand up to her face.

"You let him in! You were in it with him. I'll have the police on both of you!"

As Farley raised his hand to strike again, the woman cringed. Slot-Machine caught Farley's arm and held it. The fat man struggled. But, big as he was, Farley was soft and no match for Slot even with two arms. Slot-Machine hurled the fat man across the room.

"Don't, Mr. Kelly," Miss Thaxon said. "You can't help."

"Why do you let him push you around?"

"That's my business," Miss Thaxon said.

Across the room J. Ellsworth Farley began to laugh. It was a sneering, nasty laugh. The fat man laughed until he noticed his ruined westkit. Then Farley began to swear.

"This will come out of your salary, Miss Thaxon. You should have stopped him."

"With what?" Slot said. "Indian wrestling?"

"She has a gun for such eventualities," Farley said.

"You get a lot of visitors with fists?" Slot asked.

"People should keep their noses clean if they don't want to get hurt," Farley said. "Now get to work, Kelly. Remember, I want that boy ruined good and proper."

The fat man's face was twisted in a grotesque leer. Farley enjoyed the thought of ruining his nephew's marriage. That pleasant thought had already erased the rage he'd experienced when the tall man had punched him squarely on the nose. The nasty leer mixed on the fat man's face with the dried blood and swollen nose into a demonic mask. Slot-Machine felt almost sick.

"I've changed my mind," Slot-Machine said. "Go look in a deeper sewer for your man."

"I'll get your license, Kelly! I hired you; you better do your job if you know what's good for you!"

Slot-Machine stepped up to Farley and slapped him hard. The pain must have been intense, for Slot had slapped Farley squarely on the nose. The fat man roared, and the blood started flowing again.

"You're good at threats, fat man," Slot-Machine said. "Maybe I'll take care of you myself."

"You're through, Kelly. You hear?!"

Slot-Machine laughed. He turned to go while what was left of his sense of decency, after twenty years in the private snooping business, was still stronger than his memory of how empty his pockets were. At the door he stopped.

"Come to think of it, you owe me for two hours," Slot said. He grinned at Farley. "That's ten bucks, plus taxi both ways, making it twelve and a quarter. I'll just help myself."

He leaned across the desk, opened the top right-hand drawer where he knew Farley kept his petty cash, and lifted out fifteen dollars.

"I'll keep the change. Thanks, Farley, see you around."

Behind him J. Ellsworth Farley was still screaming for his secretary to call the police as Slot-Machine walked out of the apartment.

THE CALL CAME for Slot-Machine while he was nursing a cheap rye in the Halstead Tavern on 11th Avenue where Joe Harris worked. Slot had already begun to regret his noble gesture for the poor and downtrodden. From where he sat there weren't many poorer, and how far down could you get trod?

"It's for you, Slot," Joe Harris said. "Start runnin', it's Gazzo."

"I'm in Pago Pago," Slot-Machine said.

"That ain't far enough," Joe said. "They got extradition."

"I'll turn Communist and be safe," Slot said.

"They wouldn't take you, you're a capitalist. Let me tell Gazzo you just croaked, yeh?"

Slot stood up and walked to the telephone. Captain Gazzo was Homicide, and Homicide was an unfriendly word to Slot-Machine. Gazzo did not paint a delicate picture.

"You had a run-in with a J. Ellsworth Farley today, peeper?" Gazzo's voice said.

"Never heard of him."

"Your name's all over his appointment book, and his secretary says you threatened to kill him."

"That was the other Kelly, second cousin three times removed," Slot-Machine said into the phone.

"You could be removed, Kelly," Gazzo's grim voice said. "He got himself killed. Get down here—now!"

Gazzo hung up. For a long minute Slot-Machine stared at the wall of the telephone booth. Then his battered face split into a wide and happy grin. He laughed aloud. J. Ellsworth Farley was finally dead. Someone had done it at last!

Then he stopped grinning. Who? There would be a conservative list of a few thousand candidates, and the police did not like odds like that. And he, Slot, would be on their list.

He filled Joe in on the caper, and left the tavern. All the way up town to Park Avenue in the cab he went over it in his mind. Almost anyone could have killed J. Ellsworth Farley, and he was not even sure he had a passable alibi himself. It all depended on when and how Farley had reaped his well-deserved reward.

After he had left Farley he had tried to contact the nephew, Walter Murray, but Murray had been out. Mrs. Murray had been there the first time, but the last time he had called, at exactly seven o'clock, she too had not been at home.

He, himself, had been wandering the streets alone all day. He was all right for the time from leaving Farley until six that night, because he had been seen by many people who knew him. And he was all right from about 9:20, when he had entered the bar where Joe worked, until now, which was 10:30.

In between he had been alone down by the river watching the ships. A hell of an alibi.

Gazzo thought is was a hell of an alibi. Sergeant Jonas thought it was hilarious.

"Watchin' the ships? Kelly, you're a real comic. That's a swell alibi, right Captain?"

Jonas, Gazzo, and three uniformed cops had escorted Slot into the apartment when he had arrived. One look told Slot-Machine that Gazzo had wasted no time. Phyllis Thaxon, Farley's put upon secretary was there, as were Phillip Walters, the irate puncher of that morning, and Mr. and Mrs. Walter Murray, the bereaved next-of-kin. Mrs. Murray could hardly keep down her smiles. Murray himself seemed almost really grieved.

"Fill me in, Gazzo," Slot-Machine said.

"*Captain* Gazzo, peeper," Sergeant Jonas said.

"*Captain* Gazzo," Slot-Machine said. "I goofed."

"Maybe you really goofed, Kelly," Captain Gazzo said. "Here it is. We found him about nine-thirty. He was down behind the desk right where he is now. That Samurai knife isn't in his chest for decoration.

"Medical Examiner puts the time at about eight-thirty. You can see he was eating his dinner. Miss Thaxon said he always ate at exactly eight o'clock, and usually alone. He had good food, good wines, and I gather he didn't like to share them."

"That sounds like our late friend," Slot-Machine said.

"Miss Thaxon found the body. Farley had called her at home at about eight o'clock, told her he was just eating, but wanted her in the office by nine-thirty for work. She showed up and he was dead.

"We checked the service. They brought up his dinner at ten to eight. He was alive and kicking about the price. No one has a real alibi for the time from about seven-thirty to nine-thirty, except Miss Thaxon, and she could have made it here ten minutes before nine-thirty. The coroner admits he could be off by as much as a half hour."

Gazzo paused, and Miss Thaxon, the secretary who seemed almost distraught by the death of her tyrannical employer, burst out suddenly.

"But I didn't. He was dead when I arrived! He called me and told me he was eating, and that I should come at nine-thirty. My sister knows I was home. I was in my bed with a headache until almost nine o'clock. My sister almost wouldn't let Mr. Farley speak to me."

"Where do you live, Miss Thaxon?" Slot asked.

"On Third Avenue, a few blocks from here," the secretary said. "Mr. Farley insisted I be close."

Phillip Walters, the tall man who had punched Farley, leaned forward where he sat in a leather armchair.

"If you want a motive, I have a good one. I'm glad he is dead, I wish I had done it, and I was alone in my apartment during the crucial hours."

Gazzo looked at the tall man sourly.

"Thanks. I'll keep you in mind. You're one of about two hundred Farley had on his hook for smut stories, so relax."

Gazzo turned his sharp eyes toward the Murrays. The young couple seemed nervous now.

"I'm with Mr. Walters. I wish I'd done it," Mrs. Murray said.

"You two have the best motive," Gazzo said. "Miss Thaxon tells me you stand to inherit about a half a million dollars all-in-all. Now that's a motive I like."

Gazzo paused. "Let's see, you, Mrs. Murray, were home until six o'clock, then you went for a long drive to think about what to do about Farley, right? And Mr. Murray, you were right across the street trying to get up nerve to call on your uncle and hit him for a loan."

"Yes," Walter Murray said. "No one saw me. I was just walking around all day trying to get the nerve to ask."

Slot-Machine looked at the nephew. "Farley wouldn't lend a glass of water to a choking man. It sounds phony to me."

"Well, it isn't!" Murray exclaimed.

Gazzo turned to Slot-Machine.

"While you're solving the crime for me, tell me how it happens that only *your* fingerprints are on the knife!"

In the sudden silence Slot-Machine remembered the knife, and the way he had toyed with it that morning. Gloves, of course, and yet why were the prints still clear? It was almost as if the killer had *seen* him handle the knife and held it with special care. Only Miss Thaxon and Phillip Walters could have seen that, unless someone else had been hiding in the office.

They were all looking at him. Jonas and Gazzo warily. The Murrays with surprise. Walters with what could only be a jealous admiration. And Miss Thaxon with what looked like a mixture of fear and understanding.

"Well, peeper?" Gazzo said.

Slot-Machine looked around the large room. The body lay behind the desk. Nothing else was disturbed. The dead smut-merchant's files were all closed and undisturbed. Nothing had been broken into.

Slot walked to the desk and checked the petty cash while they all watched him. It was all there. Then he looked at the meal still laid out on the desk. Chicken bones, and the remains of asparagus and *Noodles Romanoff*, were all that were on the plate. Beside the plate stood an almost empty bottle of Romanee-Conti, 1949, a fine vintage year.

"I don't figure your motive, Kelly. But Miss Thaxon told us about the threat, and we'll work something out," Gazzo said.

"He called you back and put on the screws, and you lost your temper," Jonas said. "Maybe you can cop-out with manslaughter, second."

Slot-Machine did not seem to hear them. He was staring again at the remains of Farley's elegant dinner. Suddenly he swung about.

"Miss Thaxon, you say Farley called you at eight o'clock and told you he was eating and that you should come to the office at nine-thirty?"

"Yes, Mr. Kelly, and I found ..."

"He gave you an hour and a half? That doesn't sound like Farley," Slot said. "I mean, he wanted you close. It figures he was the type who called and said jump—drop everything and come right away."

"I said he was eating," Miss Thaxon said.

"Yeh, you did, didn't you," Slot said. "What did he want you for?"

The secretary looked evenly into Slot's eyes. She did not flinch or move her eyes away.

"If you must know, it was to draft a letter charging you with malpractice, Mr. Kelly. He was going to have the police take your license away. He was going to say you stole money, and I was to be the witness."

"Nice work, Kelly, you just give us the motive. You came back here and found out what Farley was going to do. You fought and killed him. Take manslaughter second, peeper. We got you this time."

Slot-Machine smiled. He turned back to the desk. He picked up the bottle of wine. The deep ruby liquid still in the bottle gave off a rich, fruity odor. Slot read the label aloud.

"Romanee-Conti," Slot read, "you like Italian wine, Miss Thaxon?"

"I don't drink, Mr. Kelly," the secretary said.

"Not even good Italian wine. It's the best, believe me."

"Especially not Italian wine," Miss Thaxon said. "And it should be the best. Mr. Farley always drank the best."

"You're not interested in wine, I guess," Slot said, "Now take this Italian …"

Phillip Walters had been staring at Slot-Machine for some time. Now the tall man suddenly said, "It's not Italian wine, for God's sake, Kelly. It's just about the best red Burgundy there is."

Phillip Walters stopped. He stared at Slot-Machine and then his eyes turned toward Miss Thaxon.

"That's right, Mr. Walters, and thanks," Slot said. "I never thought it was you who killed the louse, because the files haven't been touched. If you'd done the job you'd at least have taken what he had in the files about you. I expect we'll find the dope still there, right?

"Now, Mr. and Mrs. Murray there, they have servants, and they move in the best circles. I imagine they can prove they know enough about wine to know that a gourmet like Farley would kill himself before he drank Romanee-Conti *with chicken.*"

Miss Thaxon had turned white. The secretary leaned against the wall. But there was fire in her eyes.

"Red wine can be used with chicken, Mr. Kelly. I've often heard Mr. Farley say people who thought red wine could not go with chicken were stupid."

Slot-Machine nodded.

"Sure, light red wines, fine. But never Romanee-Conti. It's a great wine, Miss Thaxon. Farley probably never even showed the bottle to you. It's for the best steaks and roasts, and not even a second-rate gourmet would drink it with chicken. Besides, you really ought to have read the label when you remembered Farley always had wine with his dinner and grabbed any bottle. I mean, it's a French wine, not Italian, like Walters says.

"The way I figure it, you got the call at about eight o'clock. You were telling the truth about that. Only, like I said, Farley told you to get over here on the run. I guess maybe you knew something was wrong, maybe because of this morning and all. But you decided to sneak out, so your sister would think you was still in your room.

"You got here and you had a fight about something, and you grabbed the knife and killed him. I figure just about the time you reached for the knife you remembered seeing me put my prints on it, and decided I'd do for a patsy.

"After you killed him you saw the dinner. He hadn't even started on it, so you forced yourself to eat it, and you grabbed a bottle of his wine and poured most of it down the toilet.

"Then you went home and snuck back in, so your sister could see you come out and head over here for a nine-thirty appointment. What did he have on you, Miss Thaxon? He had some hold. Maybe if you can prove he was blackmailing you, you could plead second degree manslaughter, like Jonas says."

The secretary seemed frozen rigid against the wall. Her eyes were wide and staring. Her mouth moved convulsively. Her hands twitched. Then she collapsed in a heap on the floor as they all stared.

IN THE TAVERN, Joe Harris served the third special deluxe Irish to Slot-Machine. Slot sipped it slowly and smacked his lips.

"Damn good thing I'm a connoisseur," Slot said.

"You can't even spell the word," Joe said.

"Just 'cause I'm a one-armed bum, people thinks I don't know nothing," Slot complained. "I'm a bum 'cause I like it that way, right? I been a wine drinker since my sailor-boy days. I finished that Romanee while Gazzo was pickin' up the dame."

"So the dame said Farley told her he was going to fire her," Joe Harris said, "and she was afraid if he fired her he'd print all that stuff he had about her being a prostitute once, with the names of her boyfriends and family and all."

"That was about it," Slot said. "He treated her like dirt, because he could ruin her family anytime and she knew it. He was a diamond-studded louse. Too bad. I wish she'd gotten away with it, but she shouldn't have tried to frame me."

"You're going to testify for her, you said?"

"Sure I am, maybe get her off light. Walter Murray's puttin' up the cash. He wants her to get off, too, because he's a nice guy. He said he just *had* to pay me my full rate for a week. Come on, pour that good Irish. We're rich."

"The gourmet," Joe said as he poured.

Joe Harris looked around, and then poured a double for himself. Slot and Joe touched glass and grinned at each other and at the pile of green money on the bar between them.

THE HECKLER

This story is shorter, tighter, smoother, with less wasted words than any previous Kelly. Slot-Machine was moving away from the tongue-in-cheek near-caricature of the private eye. There are fewer references to his tawdriness, he takes charge more. Gazzo's scorn is easing, he is treating Slot with more respect, taking him more seriously. It's subtle, but it's there. This is a different Slot, and the story is far better as a story than, say, "The Price of a Dollar."

Perhaps I'd had a small epiphany. My first daughter was born on the 25th of November, and that changed much in what had been the relatively wild and free-wheeling life of an aspiring artist back from a war and in New York. The story was written before Katie's birth, of course, but probably no more than a month before, and the imminent event had to have been on my mind. The lark inherent in the writing of the first Kelly stories is much toned down. The undercurrent of mockery is fading. I am coming to like the form of the detective story, seeing how I can perhaps use it for my more serious purposes, and how I can make a living as a writer.

All in all, I think I see the start of Dan Fortune and my other detectives: Paul Shaw; Kane Jackson; and the various sleuths of Buena Costa County. The start of a career.

THE MAN WAS tall and emaciated, as thin as a walking cadaver. His sunken eyes were like two black holes above his long hawk nose as he shouted into the night.

"The blood and flesh of beasts! Surely that is the Devil's food! Unclean, unclean! Is it not written in the Scriptures that those who live by blood shall perish from the earth?"

High above the crowd, the man stood on the park bench in the dark night and howled his message. The crowd murmured its agreement or protest. The man's voice was loud and deep: it carried all across Union Square, and inexorably attracted a larger and larger crowd.

The large crowd shuffled and muttered under the spell of the booming voice. The cadaverous man's hawk nose and deep eyes seemed to slash and bore into the night. Suddenly a small man at the rear of the crowd began to laugh.

"He's off his rocker!" the man said as he laughed. "Screwballs like him oughta be locked up. Pipe down and eat a steak, mister. You look like you could use one."

There was more laughter in the crowd. The hawk-nosed man turned in fury toward his heckler.

"The Devil speaks through the lips of fools!" the tall man shouted. "But those who listen are greater fools in the Lord's sight."

"I say we shut the screwball up!" the short man said.

"Turn ye and rend the Devil!" the cadaverous speaker shouted into the night.

"I'll shut the bum up!" the small heckler said, suddenly angry.

In the crowd other voices took up the fight. There were voices that shouted with the heckler, and there were others who defended the speaker.

"Let him say his piece. Maybe he isn't so crazy."

"Knock him down out of there."

"It's a free country."

"Send for the paddy wagon!"

"He's a nut."

"He's got a right to speak his mind. Give him a chance."

"You ought to be locked up, too!"

"Listen you …"

Suddenly the crowd surged. Someone shouted an oath and a punch was thrown. And then the crowd became a seething mass of shouting, pushing, swearing men.

At the edge of the roaring crowd, Slot-Machine Kelly stood and grinned until he was propelled abruptly backward by a lurching drunk. Then the one-armed detective ducked into the shelter of a statue.

"It's all yours, boys," Slot-Machine muttered aloud, and sighed as he watched the crowd turn into a cursing melee.

Slot-Machine, tired after an all-day pursuit of a small-time businessman who owed forty dollars and was being hailed into small-claims court, had stopped some minutes before to watch the hawk-nosed man deliver his speech. There was a bruise on his left cheek where the claim-ducker's wife had hit him with a plate when he had finally served the summons on her husband.

With five dollars for the summons job in his pocket Slot had been on his way across town to the tavern where Joe Harris was bartending tonight, and had stopped briefly to watch the haranguing fanatic. He was still shaking his head in quiet disapproval when he suddenly noticed that the cadaverous speaker had vanished.

Then he saw the tall man down among the crowd flailing about like a skinny windmill. Slot looked for the heckler who had started the fracas. He spotted him after a moment working his way through the crowd, as if he were in haste to get to the cadaverous speaker, and start more trouble.

Slot was curious about what would happen when the heckler and the speaker met for the second time. But police whistles had started to blow, so he gave up watching and vanished out of the Square into the friendly dark, and emptiness of 16th Street.

As he walked west a slight smile hovered on his lips. Union Square was usually an interesting spot. Fanatics and madmen, all speaking their pieces. In a way, there was something good about it. Even the battle had been "democratic."

Slot-Machine was less than a block from the Square when he stopped and listened. Something was decidedly wrong, and suddenly he realized what it was. Behind him, in the Square where the rioters should have been furiously battling the police, there was a dead silence.

The only sound was the wailing of endless police sirens.

Riots did not end that quickly.

Slot turned and walked back to the Square. As he reached the edge of the wide open space, the first thing he saw that made him walk faster was the figure of Captain Gazzo. The Captain was Homicide.

Police were milling all across the Square, and the crowd had melted away like butter on a hot day. The police had collared about twenty of the rioters, but the rest of the Square was occupied solely by the police.

In the center of the open space near the statue where the fanatic had been shouting his piece, a group of five policemen stood over a man who lay sprawled out on the ground. Captain Gazzo was bending over him, flashing a light in his face.

As Slot-Machine walked up the Captain straightened and regarded him steadily for a moment.

"Well, well, Kelly the vulture," Gazzo said. "Looking for a client, Kelly? Or maybe you know this one? He looks like most of your clients. I mean, he's stone cold dead."

"How come Homicide interests itself in a riot?" Slot-Machine said. "Maybe they took you off Homicide—I hope?"

"Take a look, peeper," Gazzo said. "I said he was dead. And that interests Homicide."

Slot looked. The man on the ground was flat on his back, and there was a very fatal-looking knife protruding from the center of his chest.

The man was also small, and short, and had once been a very loud heckler.

"The heckler!" Slot said.

"Okay, suppose you tell us about it," Gazzo said. "Maybe you *do* know him?"

Slot explained about his nocturnal tarrying of a few minutes earlier, when he had watched the cadaverous speaker and the heckler almost coming to blows.

Gazzo sighed. "So someone was enraged by the heckling," he said. "Enraged enough to kill. They oughtta stop these speakers—too much trouble. A guy opens his mouth, and someone shivs him for fun to settle the argument."

"Maybe," Slot-Machine said thoughtfully. "Only it's funny. That guy really started the whole battle. He was out to cause trouble."

"Meaning?" Gazzo said.

"Meaning maybe he wanted to start the riot. Where's the speechmaker now?"

"We got him over there," Gazzo said. "He was flat on his back forty feet away when we arrived—out cold. He's in the clear."

"I've seen a lot of these speechmakers," Slot said. "They usually ignore hecklers. If you start debating with a heckler it nearly always ruins your speech."

"So?" Gazzo said.

"Our walking-corpse talked right back to the dead guy. You might even say they started the riot together." Slot frowned. "Who was the dead guy? You asked me, but you could be the one who knows!"

Gazzo shrugged. "I don't! No identification on him. No papers, no wallet, no nothing."

"Nothing?" Slot said.

"Probably a bum," Gazzo said. "Or maybe his wallet was lifted."

"Why lifted?" Slot asked.

"Four guys had their wallets lifted," Gazzo said. "You know how the dips work crowds like this for wallets."

"Did you find the wallets?"

"Are you kidding?" Gazzo said. "You beat it fast, right? Well—so would a dip. Anyway, we've had no time to check on the four complaints."

"So you think our heckler was the victim of a riot killing?" Slot asked.

"Looks that way. Maybe you'd like to come down the station and give us your story?" Gazzo said.

"Do I have a choice?"

"Why not? You can ride with me, or in the wagon with the rest of the crowd we've got our hands on," Gazzo said.

"You got a better car," Slot said.

At the station house Slot gave his story. Across the room the cadaverous speaker had started declaiming again, now that the bump on his head had been treated.

"The wrath of the Lord descended upon him!" the tall fanatic cried out. "The scoffer was struck down even as he defied the Lord's messenger."

"Get him out of here," Gazzo said to the desk sergeant.

"You dare to scoff, Captain!" the tall fanatic said. "You too shall perish!"

"Okay, okay," the desk sergeant said. "Take your junk and beat it! One bible, one hymn book, one free pass to the Paramount, forty-six cents, a wallet, one mustard-stained handkerchief, two keys, a subway token, and one pawn ticket. All here. Now blow, mister!"

The tall fanatic picked up his belongings and turned toward the door. As he turned he stopped, drew himself up, and intoned to the room. "Ye shall die by the blood ye live by!"

And the cadaverous fanatic stalked out of the station without a backward glance, his shoulders held straight.

Slot-Machine stood staring after the departing man with a puzzled frown on his face. Something had flashed across his mind, but he could not place it. He was almost sure that the gaunt apparition had smiled just before he'd walked out.

"You know," Slot said to Gazzo. "I swear he smiled. Like he'd gotten away with something, and was secretly congratulating himself."

"He's a nut," Gazzo said. "Forget it. We've got our motive."

"What motive?"

"We checked the dead guy's prints. His name was Joe Peddlar, and he has a police record of four arrests for bunco and picking pockets. Looks like he was caught with his hand in some other guy's pocket."

"You're sure about his record?" Slot said.

"Yeh, we got his wife on the way down to make the ident positive," Gazzo said. "You can beat it now, Kelly."

"You know, Captain, I think I'll stick around. How'd you like me to hand you a murderer?"

"You're as crazy as that religious crank," Gazzo said.

Slot grinned. "Make it worth my while. Say, fifty bucks if I hand you a killer?"

"Five to one," Gazzo said. "Ten bucks for me if you don't."

"You got yourself a wager, Captain," Slot-Machine said.

Slot sat down on a bench and lighted a cigarette. He began to rub the stump of his left arm. That was a habit of the one-armed detective when he was thinking hard.

THE WOMAN, Anna Peddlar, got out of her taxi at the corner of Amsterdam Avenue and Seventy-fourth Street. She was a small, pretty woman who looked about fifteen years younger than her recently-departed husband. She walked up Seventy-fourth toward Columbus Avenue.

Slot-Machine Kelly paid off his taxi driver, and hurried after her. He followed her as she walked all the way to Columbus Avenue. Slot began to grin. The woman had turned left on Columbus Avenue, and then left again on Seventy-fifth. She was obviously trying to cover her tracks.

When the woman reached Amsterdam Avenue for the second time she walked into the *Manhattan Tavern* in the middle of the block. Slot ambled into the tavern and took an unobtrusive seat in a corner away from the television set.

The woman ordered a beer and stared at the lighted screen. She seemed to be waiting for someone. Every few minutes she glanced at the door to check on the newly-arriving patrons. The sixth man to come in caught her eye almost instantly and crossed directly to her table. She nodded in recognition and they sat talking together for a few minutes.

Slot-Machine felt better and better. The man who had walked straight up to the slain man's wife was familiar to him. It was one of the bystanders who had debated with the dead heckler in Union Square. Slot distinctly remembered him, because he had been one of the eight or ten men who had strenuously insisted that the fanatic had a right to speak.

Slot was feeling so good, that he almost failed to see the man and woman leave. He raced out and looked up Seventy-fifth Street. They were just going into the Hotel Lincoln Square.

Slot stood in the entrance until they had picked up a key from the desk and gone up in the elevator. Then he crossed to the desk and flashed his badge. He asked for the room number of the couple who had just come in.

"Room Two-D," he clerk said, reluctantly.

"What name?" Slot snapped.

"Peddlar," the clerk said. "The dame an' her husband. The other guy I don't know."

"Which other guy?" Slot said.

"I don't know neither of them," the clerk said.

"Thanks," Slot said, "that's what I wanted to know. Where's your phone?"

The clerk pointed. Slot-Machine went to the telephone, and called Captain Gazzo. Then he sat in the lobby with his eyes fixed on the two elevator doors, and the stairway door on the opposite side of the lobby. There were no other ways out. Slot knew this hotel.

Fifteen minutes later Gazzo arrived with Jonas and two other men. Gazzo was looking sour, but the sergeant had a broad grin on his face.

"This better be good," Jonas said.

"It will be," Slot-Machine promised. "Got your fifty, Captain?"

Sergeant Jonas laughed. "I can't lose. Gazzo clips you and hands you thirty days for conning the police, or you clip him for fifty. I ain't seen you part with fifty bucks in ten years, Captain."

"Shut up," Gazzo snapped. "Okay, Kelly, make it good."

"Room Two-D," Slot-Machine said. "Better be ready with the artillery. This guy has killed once. It could happen again."

The police and Slot-Machine took the elevator to the second floor.

"They're on the second floor, so they can jump if they have to," Slot pointed out. "You better watch the window."

"Don't worry, we will," Gazzo said. Slot led the way to the door of room 2-D. At the door he stepped back into the protection of a broom and dustpan alcove, and motioned to Gazzo.

"You get paid for walking in. I don't, so be my guest."

"Ain't you tired of being gutless, Kelly?" Jonas said.

"I ain't tired of being alive," Slot said.

"Where's your spirit of adventure?"

"I drank it," Slot said. "Besides, I'm the thinking type."

Gazzo swore softly, and nodded to Jonas. The big Sergeant braced himself and kicked in the door. It took three good kicks, the door was solid. There were shouts inside the room.

The door swung open and Jonas plunged through. Two shots rang our explosively. Then there was silence.

Slot walked into the room behind Gazzo. Three people stood in different parts of the room with their hands up.

The woman stood beside the bed. The man who had joined her at the *Manhattan Tavern* was at the window trying to get it up. The tall, cadaverous fanatic stood beside the woman.

"What the hell is this!" the fanatic wanted to know.

Slot-Machine pointed to the bed. On the bed there were eleven wallets lying in a neat pile. Beside the wallets, there was a neat stack of money.

"There it is," Slot-Machine said. "I figured they were in it together. It's a neat operation. Our boyfriend makes his spiel, the other two guys start the fight by heckling, and in the melee they pick pockets.

"The woman probably waits in a car for the boys to hand her the wallets. Only this time she didn't. She cleaned out her husband after he was dead. Who knows why? Maybe our speech-maker there was sweet on her and decided to get rid of the husband."

The tall fanatic shrugged. His fire-and-brimstone manner of speech had suddenly vanished. He lighted a cigarette, and shrugged again.

"Okay, so you got us. The shamus has it figured out. We worked the crowds like he says. Only we don't know nothing about poor Joe getting killed. We were as surprised as you. Why would we kill poor Joe?"

"Nuts," Slot-Machine said, turning to Gazzo. "If someone else had killed Peddlar, they wouldn't have taken the wallets. It was all planned. I figure the tall guy knifed Peddlar, the woman grabbed the wallets and slugged the tall guy to make it look good. I mean, it might have looked like the tall guy killed the heckler out of spite. The tall guy wanted to be there when you cops arrived, so the woman grabbed the wallets from Peddlar."

"Prove it, peeper," the speechmaker said. "Prove Joe even had those wallets. I say we picked them ourselves. We didn't go near Joe. We didn't even know he was dead. I was out cold, and Anna wasn't even there."

"What about it, Kelly?" Gazzo said.

"Easy," Slot said. "I figure you'll find *Peddlar's own wallet* right in that pile! The woman probably grabbed it by mistake. They knew you'd identify Peddlar, so they didn't need to take his wallet. You'll find her prints on Peddlar's wallet."

"Why you stupid, dumb broad, I ought to—" the tall man began to shout.

"You ought to what!" the woman cried. "You and your stupid ideas! We were meant for each other, you and me! Kill Joe, you said, and we can make sweet music! Well, I didn't kill him! You did! You can burn alone! It was his idea, copper. He knifed Joe!"

The tall man gave a strangled cry and lunged at the woman. Sergeant Jonas dropped him with a single, neat punch to the jaw. Then the police herded the three crooks out to the street to wait for the wagon.

In the street, Slot-Machine held out his hand. Captain Gazzo swore the whole time he was counting out the fifty dollars, bill by bill.

"Thanks, Captain," Slot said. "It's a pleasure to work with you."

"Okay, they're singing, but how'd you figure it would be the tall guy? How'd you figure he was in on it?"

"Trade secret, Gazzo," Slot said. "Us detectives got to keep our secrets."

Slot-Machine laughed all the way down to the tavern where Joe Harris worked. In the tavern, he counted out the fifty dollars on the bar.

"Sweet, very sweet," Slot said to Joe. "It's like Gazzo's blood."

"It is Gazzo's blood," Joe said. "And tell me how you figured the tall guy was a phony?"

"A mustard-stained handkerchief," Slot said. "It was on the list of stuff the cops found on him and gave back. Now why would a guy who hated meat-eating have mustard? A phony all the way, Joe. You know, I bet he wouldn't even have married that woman after all. She must have been crazy to trust him."

"A mustard stain?" Joe said.

"Sure, it was obvious, you know? I mean, once I found out Peddlar was a pickpocket."

"Maybe he liked mustard on carrots." Joe said. "You pulled another lucky one."

"It's all in the brains, Joe," Slot-Machine said. "Now let's have some good booze. It was a good night."

And Slot closed his eyes in appreciation as he let the good whisky run slowly down his dry throat.

NO WAY OUT

Here it is, the sea change that had been slowly developing. This story is truly a story, not simply a narrative. The first one that definitely brings to the Kelly series, and to my detective stories in general, all I had learned in writing my mainstream short stories and novels. It is written, not simply told. It is dramatized, shaped to have the most impact, to get it right, to make the reader look at what I want him or her to look at. It is economical, it focuses the reader, and can therefore be written shorter. It compresses narrative time, and leaves more space and emphasis for the events that really count.

It was, and is, a giant step forward from "The Heckler," although, as I said earlier, that story was already more controlled than the previous Slot pieces, and contained strong hints of where I was going. The big difference, I'm convinced, is the total application of mainstream experience to the crime writing field. In short, I had finally realized I liked writing detective stories, was pretty good at it, and the quickest and surest way to make a living as a writer was to write detective novels. It was time to give the field the same dedication and attention as my mainstream work.

Apparently I wasn't the only one to see all this in "No Way Out," because it was selected by Anthony Boucher for inclusion in his Best Detective Stories of the Year 1965. *The same year, one of my mainstream stories was selected for* The Best American Short Stories 1965. *And, of course, Katie had just been born.*

It was a good year.

And three years later there was a corollary to Tony Boucher's praise of the story. When Act of Fear *was published in 1967, with Dan Fortune as the detective, he excoriated me because I had created two one-armed detectives, and had used a pseudonym for the novel, Michael Collins. I've always thought it was because he had praised Slot-Machine Kelly, and I had dropped Kelly in favor of Fortune, and he felt betrayed. But maybe I'm wrong.*

NEXT TO WINE, women, and whisky, Slot-Machine Kelly's favorite kick was reading those real puzzle-type mysteries. You know, the kind where the victim gets his on top of a flagpole and they can't find the weapon because it was an icicle and melted away.

"There was this one I liked special," Slot-Machine told Joe Harris. "Guy was knocked off in an attic room. The guy was alone; there was a cop right outside the door; and another cop was down in the street watching the one window. The guy got shot twice—once from far, once from real close. Oh, yes—and there were powder burns on him. The cops got into the room in one second flat, and there was no one there except the stiff. How about that baby?"

"I'm crazy with suspense," Joe said as he mopped the bar with his specially dirty rag.

116

"Simple," Slot explained. "The killer shot from another attic across the street; that was the first shot. Then he tossed the gun across, through the window, and it hit the floor. It had a hair trigger, and it just happened to hit the victim again!"

"You're kidding," Joe said. "You mean someone wants you to believe odds like that?"

"It's possible," Slot said.

"So's snow in July," Joe said. "The guy who wrote that one drinks cheaper booze than you do."

"Don't just promise, pour," Slot-Machine said.

Slot-Machine liked these wild stories because things like that never happened in his world. When he got a murder it was ninety-nine per cent sure to be something about as exotic as a drunk belting his broad with a beer bottle in front of forty-two talkative witnesses at high noon.

"Did you know that ninety per cent of all murders are committed by guys with criminal records?" Slot went on informatively. "The victim usually has a record, too, and they usually know each other. A lot of them take place in bars. It's near midnight, and both guys are swinging on the gargle."

"And the bartender gets hauled in for serving whisky to drunks," Joe said.

"Life is dull," Slot sighed.

Which was why this time Slot-Machine Kelly was not even aware that he had a puzzler until it happened. Things like this just didn't happen in Slot-Machine's world. When they did there had to be a logical explanation and a reason. In the real world a man has to figure the odds and forget about guns with improbable hair triggers. Only no matter how you sliced it, there was no reason for the guard to be dead, no way the rubies could have been stolen, and no way out of that tenth-story room. It was a hundred percent impossible. But it had happened.

It all started with the usual routine. Mr. Jason Moomer, of Moomer, Moomer & McNamara, Jewel Merchants, came to Slot's dusty office one bright morning with a job offer. The morning was bright, but Slot-Machine wasn't. He was nursing a fine hangover from a bottle of Lafite-Rothschild '53 he had found in Nussbaum's Liquor Store. The price had been right, and Slot had killed the bottle happily over a plebeian steak.

"It was the brandy afterward," Slot explained to Moomer. "Speak soft; my skull's wide open."

"For this job you stay sober," Moomer said.

"Don't ask for miracles," Slot said.

"You did a good job for us before," Moomer said. "My partners think you're not reliable, but I vouched for you."

"You're a brave man," Slot said.

"You know the setup," Moomer said. "We're displaying the rubies in a suite at the North American Hotel. They're on display all day for three days, and they're locked in the safe at night. Twenty-four-hour watch on all doors, at the safe, with the jewels when they're out. We're hiring three shifts of Burns guards, five men to a shift to cover the three doors, the safe, and the elevators, just in case. We're hiring a private detective to work with each shift, to keep his eyes and ears open."

"You got more protection than a South American dictator," Slot-Machine said.

"There are five rubies, a matched set. They're worth perhaps a quarter of a million dollars."

"Maybe you need the Army," Slot-Machine said.

"You'll change shifts each day," Moomer went on. "I'm hiring Ed Green and Manny Lewis for the other shifts. You'll all wear uniforms, so you'll look like ordinary guards."

"A tight setup," Slot said.

Slot-Machine disliked regular work, and he particularly disliked uniformed-guard work. But, as usual, his bank account looked like a tip for a hashhouse waitress, and Joe's current employer was already beginning to count the shots in the Irish-whisky bottle every time Slot appeared in Joe's bar.

"You got a deal," Slot said. "I have a little free time. You're lucky."

"Well," Moomer said, "if you're so busy, you won't need any money in advance."

"You're dreaming again," Slot said.

Moomer grinned, paid $50 in advance, and left. Slot counted the money four times. He sighed unhappily. It always came out to $50. He hated clients who could count. At least, he decided, it would be easy work except for the wear and tear on his feet.

He was wrong. Before it was over, he had a dead man, five missing rubies, a very unfriendly Jason Moomer, a suspicious Captain Gazzo, and a room from which there was no way out except for a bird.

FOR TWO DAYS all the trouble Slot-Machine had was tired feet. The suite in the North American was crowded with ruby-lovers, and jewelry dealers who loved only money, for the whole two days. The uniformed guards, and the three private detectives, earned their pay.

During the day the guard at the elevator checked credentials. Slot-Machine knew that this was necessary, but it was not a very valuable precaution. Moomer, Moomer & McNamara wanted to see their rubies sold, and almost anyone could get an invitation.

There were three doors to the suite. Two were locked on both sides, but a uniformed guard was stationed at each door anyway, as an additional security measure. The third door was the only entrance and exit to the suite. The Burns man there kept his pistol in plain sight. There was no need for guards on the windows. The suite was ten floors up without a fire escape.

The fifth Burns guard stood like an eagle-eyed statue right behind the display case. It would have taken an invisible man with wings to steal the rubies during the day. Which did not stop the Messrs. Moomer and McNamara from prowling like frightened hyenas.

"If you see anything suspicious, get to the alarm fast," Jason Moomer explained to the guard at the display case. "The alarm is wired to the case itself, but there's the extra switch just in case."

"You're in charge of your shift, Kelly," Maximilian Moomer said. "Just stay sober!"

Old Maximilian did not like Slot-Machine. That came from the fee Slot had charged for finding a stolen diamond tiara a few years ago. Maximilian was a skinflint, and he had always suspected Slot of stealing the tiara and returning it for the handsome fee. Slot hadn't, but he had thought it a good idea.

"Bringing in detectives is ridiculous anyway," Maximilian Moomer said. "The uniformed guards are enough."

"I think we should have had the showing in our own strong room," Angus McNamara said. The tall Scotsman seemed the most nervous of the three owners.

But nothing happened for the first two days, and at night everything was quiet. The Burns men remained on guard at all the doors; the elevator remained under watch; and the man inside the suite camped in front of the safe.

Day or night, Slot-Machine Kelly, Ed Green, and Manny Lewis kept a roving eye on everything as they wandered through the rooms and halls in their uniforms. The detectives could not be told from the other Burns guards. For two days Slot-Machine cat-footed through the four rooms, eying the rubies and the guests and sneaking some of the free liquor when no one was looking. The only incident occurred on the second day when Slot was off duty.

Ed Green was on duty at the time. It happened just as the dayshift was going off. The swingshift guards had taken their stations, and Ed Green was talking to Manny Lewis outside the room, when the alarm went off like a scared air-raid siren.

People started to mill and shout. Manny Lewis ran to check the other doors. Ed Green and the uniformed guards poured into the main room and surrounded the display case. The guard at the case already had his gun out.

"What is it!" Green had snapped.

A very nervous and embarrassed young woman stood near the alarm switch. "I turned it," she said. "I'm sorry. I thought it was for the waiter."

Green swore angrily, and the Moomer brothers insisted that the attractive of-fender be taken to the police. The young woman did not seem to mind too much. She checked out nice and clean; she was the legitimate secretary of a small mer-chant named Julius Honder.

"The dame was just curious," Green said to Slot-Machine. "At least we got sort of a drill."

The guard system had worked fine. No one on the doors had left his post, and the Moomers and McNamara seemed happier. The final precaution, the electronic scanner that was set up to cover the elevators during the day and the single exit from the lobby of the hotel at night, was working perfectly.

"It's a vacation with pay," Slot told Joe before he went on duty on the third day. "A cockroach couldn't get into that room, and a germ couldn't get out."

IT HAPPENED ON the third day.

Slot-Machine had the lobster shift—midnight to eight o'clock in the weary morning. He had stopped for a couple of quick whiskies at Joe's tavern, and when he arrived he had to hurry into his uniform. The five Burns men of his shift were ready and waiting.

Ed Green greeted Slot-Machine. After the shift had been changed and Slot's men were in their places at the locked doors and in front of the safe, Green and Slot had a cigarette just outside the main door to the suite. The Burns men of Green's shift relaxed in the hallway.

The two shots exploded the silence a second or two before the alarm went off.

The shots were inside the suite. The alarm clanged like a wounded elephant.

"Come on!" Green shouted.

The Burns guards poured into the suite.

"Stay alert!" Slot snapped to his Burns man who was on the front door.

He watched his man pull his gun and stand alert, and then he hurried inside the suite and into the room where the safe was. The first thing he saw was the open safe. The second thing he saw was the body of the guard lying in front of the safe with Ed Green bending over it.

"Twice, right through the heart!" Green said.

"Search the place!" Slot snapped. "Tear it apart."

Slot-Machine and Green checked the safe. It was clean as a whistle. It had been neatly and expertly burned open. The torch was still on the floor. The safe was a small one, and it had not taken much burning.

Ed Green called the police. Slot-Machine called the Burns men on the single night exit from the hotel downstairs, and told them to start the scanner and let no one out of the hotel without checking them. By this time all the Burns guards had torn the apartment apart and had found nothing at all.

By the time Captain Gazzo of Homicide arrived, in company with Sergeant Jonas and Lieutenant Mingo of Safe and Loft, the Moomers and McNamara were also there. Maximilian Moomer was almost hysterical.

"Search them all! Search Kelly! No one could have gotten in or out of this room!" Maximilian wailed.

"He's got a point," Captain Gazzo said to Slot-Machine.

"Green and I were together," Slot said.

"I wouldn't trust Green too far, either," Sergeant Jonas said.

Lieutenant Mingo had finished his examination of the suite. Now he broke in on the hysterical owners of the rubies.

"Here it is, Captain. Safe was torched—an easy job. All windows are locked inside. A caterpillar couldn't have come up or down those walls outside anyway. The torch is still here. We searched all the guards, nothing on them. The Burns men on the doors never left their posts."

Gazzo turned to the Burns man who had remained at the front door of the suite the whole time.

"No one came out?"

"No, sir," the Burns man said. "I never budged. The guy at the elevators never moved, and no one came out except Green, Kelly, and the other guards."

"In other words," Gazzo said. "No one went in, no one came out. Only— we've got a dead man and we don't have five rubies worth a quarter of a million in real cold money."

In the room everyone looked at everyone else. The Moomers and McNamara were ready to cry like babies.

It was an hour later, and Gazzo and Mingo had been over and over the situation fifty times with Slot-Machine Kelly and Ed Green. The morgue wagon had come, and the white-suited attendants were packing the body in its final basket.

"The Burns boys from my shift want to go home," Green said. "We've searched every part of them except their appendix."

"OK," Gazzo said. "But you'd better check them through that scanner downstairs, just in case."

"That's some machine," Lieutenant Mingo said admiringly. "You just dab the rubies with a little radioactive material, and the scanner spots them forty feet away."

"It also spots radium watch dials and false teeth," Gazzo pointed out. "Let's get back to our little puzzle, OK? First, how did anyone get into the room?"

Everyone looked blank. Slot-Machine rubbed the stump of his missing arm. It was an old habit he had when he was thinking.

"It's impossible," Slot-Machine said, "so there has to be an answer. Look at the odds. It's a million to one against the guy being invisible. It's two million to one against him having wings. It's a couple of hundred to one against that guard having shot himself."

"Very funny, Kelly," Gazzo said.

"Wait," Slot-Machine said. "I'm serious. We got to rule out science fiction, weird tales, and magic. So how did he get *into* the room past all of Green's guards? Be simple. There's only one way—he was already in the room."

"Kelly's shootin' the vein again," Jonas said.

Even the morgue attendants turned to look at Slot-Machine. They had the body by head and feet, and they paused with it in mid-air, their mouths open. Gazzo looked disgusted. But Ed Green and Lieutenant Mingo did not.

"He's right," Ed Green said. "We never searched, never thought of it."

"It's not an uncommon MO," Lieutenant Mingo agreed. "Now that I think of it, the suite is full of closets piled with junk. It wouldn't have been hard as long as the guy knew the guards didn't search."

Captain Gazzo morosely watched the morgue attendants close their basket and carry it out. The captain did not seem very pleased about the whole matter.

"Which means the joint was cased," Gazzo said. "OK, it figures. Our ghost has to be a pro. He got in by hiding here for about five hours. Now, how did he get out?"

"Yeah," Sergeant Jonas said. "You guys didn't search the place because a snake couldn't have sneaked out of this suite."

"You had twelve guards around and in the suite, damn it," Gazzo said. "Twelve! A worm couldn't have crawled out!"

Slot-Machine seemed to be watching something very interesting in the center of the far wall. His one good hand was busily rubbing away at the stump of his left arm. Now he began to talk without taking his eyes away from the blank wall.

"Let's talk it out," Slot said. "He didn't fly out, he didn't crawl out, he didn't dig out, he …"

"Trap door?" Sergeant Jonas said.

Lieutenant Mingo shook his head.

"First thing I checked. The floors are solid. Checked the rooms below, too," Mingo added.

"Secret doors in the walls?" Gazzo suggested.

"Hell, Captain," Ed Green said, "we know a little about our work. We went over the walls with a microscope."

Slot rubbed his stump and nodded. "Keep it up; we're ruling out. Look, the guy was a pro; he was in the room; he had to have his plan to get out. It had to be workable. It had to be simple."

"Maybe he's still inside the room," Green said.

"Negative," Mingo replied. "I combed the place."

"What do we have?" Slot-Machine said. "He's in here, and there are eleven guards outside and one inside with him. He shoots the guard, torches the safe, and … Hold on! That's not right. He burned that safe fast, but not fast enough to do it between the time of the shots and all of us busting in.

"So he must have torched the safe *first*—then shot the guard and set off the alarm! He couldn't have torched the safe with the guard still awake, so it follows that he must have knocked the guard out. But why did he kill the guard later? He knew the shots would bring us running. He must have *wanted* the shots to bring us in just when it happened. Why did he pull the job at the exact moment when there were twelve guards instead of six? He timed it for the shift change."

There was a long silence in the room. Sergeant Jonas looked blank. Ed Green was obviously trying to think. Mingo shook his head. Only Gazzo seemed to see what Slot-Machine was seeing on the blank wall.

"No one came out," Gazzo said softly. "There was no way out. Only a killer got out with five rubies. So, like Kelly says, we rule out magic, and somehow a guy walked out."

Gazzo turned to the Burns guard who had been on the main door.

"Do you know *all* the guards who work with you?" Gazzo asked.

"Sure, Captain," the Burns man said. "Well, I mean, I know most of them to look at. I know the boys in my shift, and—"

"Yeah," Gazzo cut him short. "There it is. So damned simple. He just walked out in the confusion. Right, Kelly? He was probably behind the front door waiting. He probably even helped search the suite with all of you. He was just …"

"Wearing a Burns uniform," Slot-Machine said. "He simply mingled in with us.

That's why he timed it for two shifts to be here. He mingled with us, and walked out through the front door."

The swearing in the room would have done credit to a Foreign Legion barrack. Everyone began to move at once. Mingo called in to alert the Safe and Loft Squad to start watching all fences in the city. Ed Green went to check with the guard on the elevator. Jonas called downstairs to the single exit door. Gazzo just swore. Ed Green came back.

"Burns man on the elevator says he did see a Burns man go for the stairs," Green said. "God, he was lucky! How could he know we wouldn't search him? I mean, we searched all the guards mighty quick. He couldn't be sure he could get away so fast. He took a hell of a risk."

Sergeant Jonas hung up the telephone in anger.

"Green's shift of Burns men passed out twenty minutes ago," Jonas said, "and they were all clean. That scanner didn't find anything on them."

"How many men?" Gazzo said.

"Six," Jonas said.

Gazzo cursed. "He's out!"

"But the rubies aren't," Green said. "He must have stashed them somewhere inside. That means he plans to come back for them."

Slot-Machine shook his head. "I don't know. He planned this mighty careful. We could have searched him right here in the room like Green says."

"All right, genius," Gazzo said. "You've figured how he got into the suite and how he got out. Now tell us how he plans to get the stones out if he didn't stash them. No one's gone out of this hotel since it happened except through that front door where the scanner is."

"He just had to know about the scanner," Slot-Machine said. "This was a fool-proof plan. So he must have figured a way around that scanner."

"Great," Gazzo said. "Only, no one got out of here without being checked."

Slot-Machine stood up suddenly.

"One person did! Gazzo, come on!"

Slot-Machine led them all from the suite in a fast dash for the first elevator.

THE NIGHT WAS dark on the city. The streets were bare and cold in the night. Traffic moved in small tight groups down Sixth Avenue as the lights changed. The late night revelers staggered their weary way home. In the all-night delicatessens the clerks yawned behind their counters.

In Gazzo's unmarked car the five sat alert and waiting. Gazzo swore softly, and Ed Green smoked hard on his cigarette. Slot-Machine leaned forward tensely and watched the car-exit below the towering glass and steel of the North American Hotel. Suddenly Slot leaned over and touched Jonas, who was behind the wheel.

The morgue wagon came out from under the hotel and turned left down Sixth Avenue. Jonas eased the car away from the curb and followed the morgue wagon.

They drove down Sixth Avenue, turned across town toward the west, and the morgue wagon moved steadily on its way a half a block ahead. The silent procession turned again on Ninth Avenue and continued on downtown toward the morgue.

Suddenly, as the morgue wagon slowed at a traffic light, the back door of the wagon opened. A man jumped out. The man hit the pavement, stumbled, and then began to run fast toward the west.

The man wore the uniform of a Burns guard.

The morgue wagon continued on its grim journey. Jonas swung the police car in a squealing turn and gunned the motor down the side street. The running man was forty feet ahead. Jonas roared after him. The man heard the motor, looked back, and then dashed toward a fence. In a flash he was over the fence, and gone.

Slot-Machine and Gazzo were out of the police car before Jonas had brought it to a halt. Mingo and Green were close behind them. Slot-Machine was the first of the three over the fence with a powerful pull of his single arm.

The man in the Burns uniform was scrambling over a second fence just ahead.

The chase went on down the rows of back yards and fences in the silent darkness of the night. At each fence Slot-Machine gained on the uniformed runner. As he went over the last fence before a looming dark building ended the row of back yards, the uniformed man turned and shot.

Slot-Machine ducked but didn't stop. He went over the last fence in a mad leap and dive. Another shot hit just below him, and wood splinters cut his cheek. In the next second, Slot-Machine was on the uniformed man who was trying frantically to get off one more shot.

The man in uniform never made it. Slot-Machine drove him back against the brick wall of the building with the force of his rush. His pivoting body slammed into the wall, his gun went flying, and he came off the wall like a rebounding cue ball on a lively pool table.

Slot's one good hand caught the uniformed man across the throat. He collapsed with a single choking squawk like the dying gurgle of a beheaded chicken.

By the time Gazzo, Green, and Mingo had caught up with Slot and his victim, Slot was holding the rubies in his hand. In the beam of light from Mingo's flashlight, the deep red stones shone like wet blood.

Slot-Machine handed the pistol to Gazzo.

"This'll be the murder weapon," he said. "It's a regulation Burns pistol; he was a meticulous type."

Mingo was bending over the supine man, who had not even begun to wake up. The lieutenant looked up at Gazzo and shook his head.

"No one I recognize," Mingo said. "Chances are, he's not a known jewel thief."

"That figures," Slot said. "I think you'll find his name is Julius Honder, a legitimate jewel merchant."

"Why Honder?" Ed Green said.

"He had to have cased the job," Slot said. "He knew we'd all go running into the suite. Remember that woman? The one who thought the alarm was a waiter's button? She was Honder's secretary. I expect we'll find her waiting at Honder's office for the boss to bring home the loot."

From the dark, Sergeant Jonas came up. The Homicide sergeant looked down at the sleeping killer and thief.

"So he made another change," Jonas said, "and played one of the morgue boys?"

Slot-Machine shook his head.

"Too risky," Slot-Machine said. "Gazzo said no one had gotten out of the building through the front door. You don't take a stiff out the front way, right? He knew that. The stiff went out through the basement. What tipped me was what I said myself—why did he kill the guard *after* he'd opened the safe and got the stones? To get us into the room, I said.

"Only the *alarm* alone would have done that. There had to be another reason. All at once it came to me. He killed the guard just to have a way of hiding the stones on the body and getting them out!"

They all looked down at the uniformed man who was just beginning to groan as he came awake. There was a certain admiration in the eyes of the police.

"He knew we wouldn't search the dead man until you got him to the morgue," Slot-Machine said. "So he had to get the stones from the body before it reached the slab. It was quite simple. He just hid in the wagon. Who would think to look for him there?"

Later, in the tavern where Joe Harris was working, Ed Green leaned on the bar beside Slot-Machine Kelly and bought Slot a fourth expensive Irish whisky. Green was still admiring Slot.

"You just got to think logical," Slot-Machine explained. "Figure the odds. Miracles are out, so there has to be a simple explanation. The more complicated it looks in real life, the simpler it has to be when you figure it out."

"You make it sound easy," Green said. "Have another shot."

"Twist his arm," Joe said as he poured. "The thinker. So it turned out it was Julius Honder, right?"

"Yeah," Slot said as he tasted his Irish whisky happily. "He needed cash. Too bad he needed a corpse. He'll fry crisp as bacon."

WINNER PAY OFF

The new direction of the Kelly stories continues in this one. There is a greater attention to detail, characterization, and a certain newly acquired gravitas in Slot's manner, speech and actions. He's still given to quick cracks and smart-mouth repartee, but there is a sober edge to them, to everything. The plot is complicated, and could have been stretched much farther, perhaps to novel length, with more development of each major character, and a subplot or two drawn from what was already there. (Velma's husband and child for example.) There are even a few touches of the social commentary that will be a main part of the Dan Fortune books and stories. This Slot is not the Slot of the earlier stories. He is not quite Dan Fortune yet, but the lineaments are already there.

Perhaps because of the changes coming over Slot-Machine, some "ticks" struck me. I noticed how often in these stories another character says in response to a succinct rebuttal from Slot of a suggestion they've made: "You got a point." It runs through all the stories. This kind of thing is something all writers have. It can be maddening or endearing. Sort of a familiar trademark readers come to like and expect.

Then there is Velma. This is the third time I am aware of, and there may be more, I used the name for a tough, smart, hard, sexy woman who is no better than she should be. On the shady side of the law. It's an obvious pickup from Chandler I was clearly unaware of using. The price of need and haste.

THE WORD WAS out on Morgan Palmer. The word said that the small-time crook and big-time drunk was broke, and no bookie in New York would take his bet. So Morgan Palmer was scared.

He had been broke before, of course. But no one had refused to take his bets before. This time Palmer tried all night to place his bet. He *had* to place the bet. He ran like a hounded rabbit through the dark streets of the city. By midnight he was desperate. So desperate, in fact, that he went to Slot-Machine Kelly for help.

Joe Harris brought Palmer to Slot-Machine. Before Joe called, Slot-Machine had been alone in his one-room office with its fine view of the air-shaft through its one grimy window. The one-armed detective was having a midnight meal to help take the ache from the arm that wasn't there.

His meal consisted of two hamburgers, rare, and a bottle of *Chateau Haut Brion*, 1953. The hamburgers had cost $1.20, and the wine had cost $10.00, but that was Slot-Machine. When he had some money, which was not often, Slot bought good wines and laid them away in a dry corner of the cellar of his shabby building where he shared an apartment with Joe Harris. It was his hobby, and, besides, as he said, it tasted good.

"You can take the taste of a bottle with you," Slot-Machine liked to explain. "Furniture, cars, and a bank account you got to leave behind."

Slot was half way through the bottle when Joe Harris called. Morgan Palmer had just dropped in at the saloon where Joe had been working a one-week shift, and spilled his troubles to the bar-keep.

Joe did not waste words. "Palmer's got trouble," Joe told Slot. "He's in deep."

"Who ain't?" Slot said sympathetically.

"He's broke, and no one'll take a lay-off bet," Joe explained.

"Palmer's always broke," Slot said.

"He needs help," Joe said.

"How does he pay me?" Slot said.

"Maybe later."

"I'll count on it for my old age," Slot-Machine said.

"What'll I do?" Joe said.

Slot-Machine sighed. "Bring him around."

The one-armed detective finished his bottle of Haut Brion and sighed again. An empty bottle made him sad. He was about to wrap up the remains of his hamburger, and throw them into his wastebasket, when he glanced toward the darker corner of his shabby office.

A very neat hole decorated the baseboard in the corner. Slot stood up and carried the remains of the meal to the corner. He laid them out on a piece of wax paper. Even a mouse had to eat, and Slot's uncomplaining mice had slim enough pickings.

Back at his desk, Slot-Machine took out his file on Morgan Palmer. There was little in it he didn't know. Palmer was an ex-Marine who had come home from Korea with a chip on his shoulder against the world, and a big thirst. Palmer hated the world, and loved the booze. The combination had led the ex-Marine to the dark corners of the waterfront where he could pick up a loose buck or two without working, and where the booze was as cheap as it came.

Neither the file nor the man had changed much. When Joe led Morgan Palmer into the office, Slot saw that Palmer was still big, and flabby, and bleary-eyed. Only one thing was different. Palmer was usually tough and bitter. Now the ex-Marine was only scared.

"What's so important about a bet?" Slot asked.

"I got to make a lay-off," Palmer explained. "I'm flat broke."

"A lay-off on what?"

"I bet one thousand clams on Fuentes to take the ten-rounder Friday," Palmer said. "Okay, it was stupid. This broad got me drunk, and Fuentes is a three to one favorite. The guy made the bet even money."

Slot-Machine raised an eyebrow. He looked at Joe Harris. Joe shrugged eloquently. They both knew Palmer would try almost anything for a fast buck. And this bet sounded like a really good bet.

"You found a sucker," Slot-Machine said. "It's a good bet. Why won't anyone lay it off?"

"That's what I can't figure," Palmer said.

"Who'd you make the bet with?" Slot asked.

"I bet with Ace Mulloy."

Joe Harris had to brace himself to keep from falling off his chair. Slot-Machine blinked as if someone had just hit him with a two-by-four. Someone had. Ace Mulloy was not small-time. Ace Mulloy was very big time indeed. And Ace Mulloy had a very nasty streak in him. He killed people.

II

"ACE MULLOY MADE a bet like that?" Slot-Machine said. "You sure this isn't all a gin-dream, Palmer?"

"I wish it was," Palmer said. "I'm scared. I can't pay."

"I'd be scared," Slot-Machine said. "And I can pay. Why the hell would Mulloy make a sucker bet like that? He could have laid the bet at three to one on the other pug anywhere."

"When I sobered up, that's what worried me," Palmer said.

"Cheer up," Joe Harris said. "Maybe you'll win."

Palmer began to shake. "This afternoon I got the word it's a tank job. Fuentes is going to dive."

"That figures," Slot-Machine said.

"Mulloy, or someone, is on my tail," Palmer said. "I seen him behind me all night."

In the silence of the room Palmer shook so hard the chair he was in began to rattle. Joe Harris was watching the office mouse dining on the remains of Slot's midnight meal. Slot-Machine rubbed the stump of his left arm. He was beginning to feel a very bad pain in the missing arm.

At last Slot-Machine leaned forward over his desk. "What has Mulloy got against you?" he asked.

"I don't know," Palmer said.

"You're sure? It looks like he's setting you up for some pressure," Slot said. "Have you got anything?"

"I been clean for months," Palmer protested. "I just told you—I'm broke. I ain't been near a heist or anything. I ain't been working for no one."

"What do you want me to do?" Slot asked.

"Make them take my lay-off bet," Palmer said. The big man's flabby face was sweating, and it was cold in Slot-Machine's office.

"I can try," Slot said.

"You got to make them take the lay-off!" Palmer cried.

"I said I'd try."

"He'll kill me if I can't pay!"

"Yeh," Slot-Machine said, "he probably will."

"God, I must have been crazy drunk," Morgan Palmer said.

The big ex-Marine held his face in his hands. In the chair, the flabby punk leaned forward like a man in terrible pain.

"All right," Slot-Machine said, "tell me how it happened—all of it."

Palmer still sat with his hands covering his face. The drunk was shivering like a whipped cur. His whole big, flabby body shook like a dead, sapless tree in a high wind. Palmer did not look up or take his hands away from his face all the time he talked.

"I met this blonde, nice and all dolled up, you know?" Palmer said. "I told her I was broke, but she acted like she didn't care. She acted like she wanted me bad. I figured I had a real good thing going. She was willing to pay for the booze, so we made the rounds.

"Maybe the ninth or tenth joint we was in, Ace Mulloy is there. He starts needling me, you know? Me, I don't know Mulloy so good, but he acts like he knows me. He gave me the business good. How I was a two-bit punk, and a no-good Marine, and all that. I ain't proud, so I just lets the broad buy me drinks.

"After a while, Mulloy's still needling, and the broad gets mad. She starts telling me to stand up to Mulloy. I'm drunk by then, so I ain't thinking so straight. After a while Mulloy says I'm so yellow I wouldn't bet on a sure thing in a soap-box race.

"I was real drunk, so I says I'll bet on anything that looks good. Mulloy says, okay, he'll bet a grand on the fight. He says he'll bet a grand against Fuentes and make it even money just to show how chicken I am. Now me, I was boiled. Only I ain't never so boiled I can't see a miracle. Fuentes is three to one, and Mulloy wants to give me Fuentes even money. So ..."

"So you took the bet," Slot-Machine said. "The dame got you drunk enough to forget who you were betting with, and how much money you didn't have. A real sucker set-up, if I ever saw one. Who was the dame?"

"Never saw her before," Palmer said sullenly. "Name was Velma."

"Yeh, that fits," Slot-Machine said. "Okay, Palmer, I'll try to save your skin. Only I ain't sure it's worth it."

"You'll make them take my lay-off?"

"I'll give it a try."

"Maybe you could talk to Mulloy?" Palmer said. "Maybe you could talk him out of the bet?"

"Get the hell out of here, Palmer," Slot-Machine said.

III

SLOT-MACHINE KELLY knew every bookie in the city. He talked to half of them that night. He got nowhere.

No bookie would take Morgan Palmer's lay-off bet, and no bookie would say why. They all insisted that Morgan Palmer was known to be flat broke, and it made sense for them not to take the bet.

"Since when did that stop you taking a man's bet?" Slot-Machine asked Moe Mantell. "You stop taking markers and you're out of business. You guys live on guys without funds."

Moe Mantell was a friend of Slot's. Mantell was as much a friend as the bookie could be a friend to anyone. Bookmaking is not a profession that breeds deep friendships.

"We don't take bad markers," Mantell said.

"Who says it's bad?" Slot-Machine said. "Besides, Palmer wants to bet on the loser."

"Is that what he says?" Mantell asked.

"So you've heard Fuentes is in the tank, too?" Slot said.

"Is he?" Mantell said.

"So the little bird seems to be whispering," Slot-Machine said drily. "Who's the little bird, Moe?"

"I wouldn't know."

"Okay. But even if Palmer is sure to lose, he's been on your cuff before this," Slot-Machine said. "The town's papered with Palmer's markers, and he always finds the bread somewhere."

"Palmer don't welsh, most of the time," Mantell agreed.

"So someone passed the word," Slot-Machine said. "Who?"

"What word?" Mantell said. "I told you, we all decided Palmer's a bad risk."

"Don't con me," Slot-Machine said. "I'll find out who's pulling the string."

"Don't," Mantell said. "Lay off this one. It could hurt. And, Slot, tell Palmer to put on his track shoes. Ace Mulloy don't play *mah jong*."

"That's your advice?"

"Far and fast," Mantell said, and the bookie turned back to his poker game.

Slot-Machine left Mantell holding three kings in four cards at five-card stud. The bookie had an angelic expression on his greedy face. Slot saw five hundred dollars move quietly into the pot in front of Mantell's hand. Someone else pushed a matching five hundred into the pot. Mantell looked benignly at his unknown benefactor.

Slot-Machine got no more from the other bookies. He began to look for the unknown woman who had been so eager to have Morgan Palmer defend his honor with a sure-thing bet. The woman figured to be a B-girl, and that should make it easy. It did not make it easy. No one recalled a blonde named Velma.

Whoever the woman had been, she seemed to have vanished from this green earth. Five bartenders in a row remembered the woman and Palmer the night before, but none of them recalled having ever seen her before. The fifth bartender did recall something else.

"Sure, I remembers them," the bartender said. "Palmer's been combed out of here loaded so many times I see him in my sleep. He was lapping the sauce like, you should excuse the expression, Prohibition was coming back. The dame was buying. It's funny, but she was cold sober, you know?"

"Not drinking?" Slot said, in surprise.

"Maybe one with water. And that's funny, 'cause any dame Palmer ever come in with was as big a lush as him. Ace Mulloy was drinking real slow, too."

"Ace Mulloy?" Slot snapped.

"In person," the bartender said. "Him and Mel Throne come in after Palmer. I know 'cause I was surprised to see Ace. He's supposed to be kind of warm."

"Ace is hot?"

"Just rumor, you know? Robbery Squad man tipped me Ace is supposed to have been in on a couple of big hauls recent like."

"When isn't Ace hot?" Slot-Machine said.

"You got a point," the bartender admitted.

"You're sure he was here?"

"Sure I'm sure. Him and Throne, one of Freddie Tucci's hard boys," the bartender said.

Slot paid for his whisky and left. Ace Mulloy had been in this bar when Palmer was there. And this was *not* the bar where Palmer and Mulloy had made their bet. In the next four saloons along the dim and dismal waterfront, Slot added Ace Mulloy to his list of persons-to-be-asked-after. Ace had been in each one when Palmer was.

The woman was still a shadow to all the bistros. Until Slot reached the saloon where Ace Mulloy had made his sucker bet. The bartender had nothing to offer, but Bax Cantenac, the owner of the saloon, did.

"Yeh, I seen her once before," Cantenac said.

Then Slot-Machine found out why he had been unable to get a lead on the woman.

"B-girl?" Cantenac said, "hell no. Not her. She come in here maybe six months ago with Mel Throne. I think she's from out of town—a real cool dame. Name's Velma O'Hara."

A real cool dame from out of town who had been seen once before in the unsavory company of Mel Throne, one of Freddie Tucci's gunmen. Slot-Machine was sure now that there was more to this than a bet, and that someone was setting Palmer up for something. Only what?

If Palmer lost his bet, who gained by having Palmer owe Ace Mulloy money? A cool woman conned Palmer into making what looked like a good bet, word got out that the bet was a loser because Fuentes was going to do a dive, and then when Palmer tried to lay it off, word got out to shut Palmer off. Why?

The only answer Slot-Machine could find that made sense was that Ace Mulloy wanted a hold on Palmer. He decided that, despite shivers up and down his careful spine, he would have to try to find Ace Mulloy.

He tried. He did not find Ace Mulloy. Like the woman, Ace Mulloy had vanished. Wearily, Slot-Machine retraced his path through the saloons. No one had heard of Ace Mulloy since last night. Swearing at himself for breaking his back on a job that would probably never pay a counterfeit dime, Slot kept on asking for Mulloy.

He visited every poker table, and every floating crap game on the waterfront. At Big Dike Collona's crap game Slot finally struck pay-dirt. Only it wasn't what he had expected to find.

Big Dike was paying off a winner at the door. "Go, friend, and tell 'em where you got it," Collona was saying. "Tell 'em it was easy."

The stickman was droning his chatter as he raked the money.

"Little Joe, the hard way, four's the point, get your bets down, bets down, man's coming out, a seven a loser, the night's young, next man's hot, roll the pot, a six don't mix, bets down, six the point ..."

Slot-Machine felt his palm itch for the dice, but he had business on his mind. Besides, he had no money. He was about to ask Collona if he had seen Ace Mulloy when his eyes lighted on the woman. She was blonde, beautiful, dolled up, and she looked smart.

She was looking at Slot-Machine. When she saw that he saw her, she vanished through the side door. Slot was close behind her.

IV

SLOT-MACHINE FOUND himself in a dim corridor. He had a fleeting glimpse of the dame disappearing around a corner. He went after her at a quick walk. As he rounded the bend he saw a door close just ahead. He darted to the door and went through it fast.

He was in an alley. A flick of a very trim leg went through another door down the alley. Slot was just behind. In the new building, he got a good view of the woman as she ascended a flight of stairs to the second floor. Slot-Machine followed two steps at a time. Her legs were just going through the door of a room on the second floor.

Slot-Machine stopped dead for an instant. Then cautiously he advanced along the hall, rubbing the stump of his arm. At the far end of the hall a red light glowed over a fire exit. Slot-Machine headed for the fire door. He opened it and stepped out onto the fire escape. He looked down, but the alley below was as empty as a deserted theater.

He stepped softly along the fire escape to the window of the room in which the woman had disappeared. Crouched low, he crept up to the window sill and peered into the room. The woman was there. She was very much there, and she looked as if she was expecting company.

She was expecting Slot-Machine.

He could tell by the ugly little .32 automatic she held in one well-manicured hand. She was just out of the line of sight from him. Slot was crouching. But she was watching the door expectantly. The gun was trained on the door, and she appeared to be concentrating. Slot-Machine could see every round muscle in her body under her thin silk blouse. She was tense and ready.

Slot-Machine eased himself silently through the window. The woman was so intent on the door, so sure that Slot would come barging into the room, that she did not hear him enter until he was all the way in and two steps toward her.

Suddenly she heard, or sensed that he was there. She moved like oiled steel. The snub little automatic swung toward Slot. His own .38 Police Special was in his hand.

"Easy does it, honey," Slot-Machine said pleasantly.

The woman stopped moving her hand. The little automatic was pointed at the wall half way between the woman and Slot.

"Lay it down gently, honey," Slot said. "On the floor, that's it. Now push it slow with your foot—nice and slow."

The woman laid down her automatic, and pushed it slowly away from her with her foot. Slot grinned as he picked up the weapon.

"Now that was a good girl," Slot-Machine said.

"You're smarter than you look," the woman said.

She reached into her handbag and extracted a cigarette. She lighted the cigarette with a handsome silver lighter. She crossed her very trim legs and blew smoke.

"A lot smarter than you look," the woman said.

"I'm smarter than that," Slot-Machine said. "Sometimes I surprise myself. Only I didn't have to be very smart to smell out I was being led a chase, honey."

"A chase?" the woman said. "What are you talking about? I just thought you were a sex-maniac on my trail."

Slot grinned. He looked around the bare and dirty room. The room looked like someone's storeroom.

"Sure you did," Slot said. "You were just coming up here for a beauty sleep. Okay, honey, you know me, and I know you. The only problem is why you were waiting to lead me the chase from the crap game? Who told you I was looking for you?"

"Were you?" the woman said.

"Look, honey, I know you're Velma O'Hara, and I know you heard I was asking for you. Now let's make it easy."

"I'm Velma O'Hara," the woman admitted coolly. "But who are you? And why were you looking for me?"

"What are you, honey, Ace Mulloy's girl?" Slot said. "Or are you just a hired shill?"

"Who's Ace Mulloy?"

"A very nasty gent you met last night. Only you were with his friends six months ago, and didn't need an introduction."

"Mulloy?" Velma O'Hara said. "Oh, you mean the big guy in the bar last night. I thought I remembered him from somewhere. So I knew him, did I? I got to do something about my memory."

"So you admit you saw Mulloy last night," Slot-Machine said. "That's the first step anyway. We're making progress. Now why did you con Palmer into that bet, and where is Mulloy?"

"Mulloy? How should I know?" she said calmly.

She was still smoking, and her long, smooth leg was showing more and more at the rate of an inch a minute. Her tight skirt was hiking up as she swung her crossed leg. Slot fought a silent battle with himself. He would much rather have been working *for* this woman than against her. He sighed. The woman smiled and continued to swing her leg.

"Okay, we'll pass that for a minute. What about Palmer?"

"You mean the big, flabby type?" Velma O'Hara said. "He did things to me. One look and I swooned. Only he got so drunk he was as much use as a wet towel."

"You crawled half the saloons on the West Side," Slot said.

"Like I said, I went for him, a girl's got to live," Velma said. She arched a perfect eyebrow at Slot. "You look interesting. That one arm now; that looks interesting."

"Let's try again," Slot-Machine said, ignoring the invitation with heroic self-denial. "Why did you set up Palmer for Mulloy?"

The woman stubbed out her cigarette. She bent and ground it out on the floor, and her skirt hiked up another two inches. Three more inches and Slot-Machine would get a clear view of the label on her underwear—if she was wearing any, which was doubtful considering the smooth line of the tight skirt.

"Look," Velma O'Hara said. "Let's stop playing, okay? I don't know who you are, or why you want me. I picked up this Palmer because he rang a bell in me. Maybe I got bad taste, but I'm new in town, I was lonesome, and the flabby big man sent me. If we talked to this Mulloy, it was just barroom conversation. If I had met this Mulloy, I didn't remember."

"Then why con Palmer into betting with Mulloy?" Slot said.

"Betting?" Velma O'Hara said. "What bet?"

"Palmer and Mulloy put up one grand even-money, Palmer took Fuentes."

"When did they do this?" Velma O'Hara said.

Slot-Machine stared at the woman. She was beginning to annoy him. He stepped toward her, his revolver steady.

"Honey, I'd hate to bring harm to that pretty face, but ..."

The woman reached into her handbag for another cigarette. She brought out the silver lighter, and then she brought out a twin of the .32 automatic. Slot-Machine blinked. The split second in which he had assumed she would come out with her pack of cigarettes was all she needed. She brought the automatic out firing.

Slot-Machine did three things: he dived for the floor, he fired his .38 in her direction, and he cursed himself for an idiot. She had set him up good with the first cigarette she had taken from her handbag. It had been then he had watched for a trick. A smart dame.

Lucky for Slot-Machine, she had fired so fast she had missed him by about half the width of a hair. Slot-Machine felt the slug gently nudge his scalp as he went down. Colored lights flashed in his head. His own shot went as wild as her shot. But it made her decide not to wait around for a steadier aim at him. She was out the door before Slot-Machine could clear his head, untangle himself, and fire again.

On his feet he went after her. The door had swung half-closed behind her. As Slot reached it, a second shot from her little automatic lipped splinters from the door frame. The shot hit high and wide. She had probably fired in full flight without taking aim. But Slot-Machine was in no hurry to make sure of that.

He stopped inside the door and let her go. Her high heels clicked rapidly on the stairs going down. He heard the front door slam. Slot lighted a cigarette and gave the woman a long count of a hundred and fifty. Then he peered cautiously out into the hallway. There was no one in sight. He went slowly down the stairs and out into the street.

In the grey light of dawn the street appeared deserted. Slot studied every dark doorway. He looked at the windows of the buildings. It looked clear, and he stepped out and headed for home.

It was now Friday. Fuentes was fighting tonight. Palmer said there was a bet. The woman said there wasn't a bet. Ace Mulloy wasn't around to say anything. The whole case was getting smellier and smellier.

Still puzzling over Velma O'Hara's denial of the bet, Slot broke a rule. He passed an alley without looking in. There were three of them in the alley, and they moved fast. Slot dropped one of them with a karate chop to the neck. He sent one into the street with a sharp kick to the groin. The third one dropped Slot-Machine with a less sophisticated, but equally effective, blackjack.

After the blackjack, all three of them worked him over neatly with the pointed toes of their shoes. They had big, hard feet. Before he finally went to sleep on the cold ground, Slot recognized one of them. Mel Throne.

V

"MEL THRONE?" Joe Harris said. "Freddie Tucci's strong man?"

"Himself," Slot-Machine said as he touched the lump on his head and winced. All his ribs were on fire, he had a black eye, there was a faint trace of blood where Velma O'Hara's bullet had grazed, and he was one raw bruise. In brief, he was a mess.

Joe had been sleeping when Slot-Machine had staggered in after waking up in the alley. While Slot-Machine braced himself with some booze, and tended to his wounds, Joe offered advice.

"It's more than a bet," Joe said. "Tucci's in it, so tell Palmer to fly low, and retire from this one."

"I don't like getting kicked," Slot-Machine said.

"Forget this one," Joe said. "Mulloy's forgotten it."

"Why would he set Palmer to lose a thousand bucks he knows the guy don't have? It has got to be a set-up, Mulloy could have stood to win a thousand for less than four hundred dollars with any bookie. He wouldn't risk a thousand when he didn't have to," Slot-Machine said. "And why won't the bookies take a lay-off on the underdog which they figure to win?"

"Maybe they've got the word Mulloy won't pay," Joe Harris said.

"Could be," Slot-Machine mused. "Only Mulloy's no welsher. If the bookies would *take* the layoff, I'd figure it better. That way Palmer would owe if Fuentes *won*, and if Mulloy didn't pay he'd be in trouble."

"Not if they knew it was a tank job," Joe said. "Maybe they got word Fuentes would lose."

"From who?" Slot said.

"Maybe they just heard the rumor like Palmer," Joe said. "Or maybe from Freddie Tucci. Tucci's big enough to get them to shut-off Palmer. He owns a piece of Fuentes according to the wise boys, and ..."

"And word has it Mulloy and Tucci get close sometimes," Slot broke in. "Okay, but why? If Fuentes loses, and Palmer made no lay-off, Mulloy's out a thousand bucks. If he wanted to kill Palmer, he wouldn't need an excuse."

"Maybe Mulloy just made a bad bet, didn't know Palmer was broke, and the bookies won't take the lay-off just because they know Fuentes is going to dive. Maybe the bet and the shut-off ain't even connected," Joe Harris said. "It could have been that way."

"Maybe," Slot said, "but I doubt it. No, Mulloy wants a hold on Palmer. I figure Mulloy's got something in mind. For some reason, Tucci don't want me to find Mulloy. The only guy in all this really big enough to have Palmer shut-off all over town, is Tucci."

"Everybody runs fast?" said Joe hopefully.

"Nobody runs yet," Slot said. "I got to talk to Tucci."

"You like lumps on your head?" Joe said.

"This time I'll see them coming."

"That'll help a lot," Joe said.

Slot-Machine finished his ministrations to the lump and left the apartment. Freddie Tucci had his office in the back of a candy store on Eleventh Avenue and Seventeenth Street. Tucci was big time. Getting into the back of the candy store was like getting to see J. Edgar Hoover with a machine-gun in your hand.

Four very un-juvenile delinquents were playing the pin ball machines when Slot-Machine walked into the candy store. Mel Throne was not one of them, but they were friends of Throne's. One of them had a bruised neck. This one did not look pleased to see Slot-Machine. The one-armed detective grinned.

"Anyone know where I can get a two-cent licorice stick?" Slot said.

"Well, well, our old pal Kelly," one of the boys said.

"You like lying in alleys, one-arm?" the boy with the bruised neck said.

"I got the word from Throne," Slot-Machine said. "I figure I'd hear better if Tucci told me himself."

"Get lost, peeper," another boy said.

The four of them began to walk toward Slot-Machine. Slot backed against a fairly solid wall. He was just about to reach for the revolver snuggled under his stump, when Freddie Tucci appeared. The short gangster was smiling.

"Hello, Kelly," Tucci said. "Come on in."

The four hard ones stepped back reluctantly to let Slot pass. In the back office Mel Throne was cleaning his fingernails. Tucci sat down and waved Slot-Machine to a chair.

Slot sat.

"What's up, Kelly?" Tucci asked.

"You tell me," Slot said. "Ace Mulloy is setting up a hold on Morgan Palmer. Why?"

"A hold? How's that?" Tucci said.

"You passed the word," Slot-Machine said.

Tucci looked at him in apparent bewilderment.

"Word?"

"To shut-off Palmer."

Tucci laughed. "Not me Kelly. I heard the bookies was shutting him off, he's a fink and he's broke."

"Where's Ace Mulloy?" Slot asked.

"How should I know?" Tucci said. "I ain't seen Ace in months."

"Throne has," Slot-Machine said.

Tucci looked surprised. The small gang leader looked over at his hired hand.

"You been seeing Ace, Mel?" Tucci asked.

"I had some beers with him," Throne admitted.

Slot-Machine laughed. "Cut it out, Tucci. Throne and two friends played ping-pong on my skull this morning. You got to have ordered it."

"They did it for me, peeper," Mel Throne said. "Me and Ace we got a deal. I don't like peepers looking for Ace."

"Deal?" Slot said. "You wouldn't need Palmer in the deal, would you? Maybe you both set up the sucker bet."

Mel Throne continued to clean his fingernails. The muscleman seemed very interested in his nails. He did not even look up when he spoke again.

"What bet?" Mel Throne said.

"A bet?" Freddie Tucci said. "Who made a bet?"

"Ace Mulloy and Palmer laid a thousand even money on tonight's fight and you know it," Slot-Machine said. "Ace bet against Fuentes."

Freddie Tucci's mouth dropped open like a fish gasping for air. Mel Throne began to guffaw. Both gangsters laughed as if they had never heard anything so funny.

"You telling me Ace Mulloy laid even money against a favorite when he could get three to one?" Tucci said.

"You must have lost half your brain, too," Mel Throne said.

Slot-Machine blinked. He looked at Throne. "You were there, Throne."

"I was with Ace all last night," Mel Throne said. "I didn't see no bet."

When Slot-Machine left the candy store he could make no sense out of it. Had there been a bet? Palmer was one hell of an actor if there hadn't been. Slot headed for the saloon where Palmer said he made the bet. The night barkeep was off-duty. Slot got his address. He woke the bartender from a deep sleep.

"Bet?" the bartender said. "What bet?"

Slot-Machine refreshed the bartender's sleepy memory with the details of the Palmer-Mulloy wager. The bartender seemed as amused as Tucci had been.

"Ace wouldn't make a bet like that," the bartender said.

"You had to see it happen," Slot-Machine said. "You saw the dame, you saw Palmer, and you saw Ace."

"Only I seen no bet," the bartender said.

"Who told you to lie?"

"That's all you get, Kelly," the bartender said.

"You know there was a bet, damn it," Slot said.

"Maybe," the bartender said. "Only I forgot. I got a real bad memory."

Slot-Machine could get no more out of the man. As he headed for his office, a nagging thought kept running through his mind. *No one seemed to know, or admit, that there had ever been a bet between Ace Mulloy and Morgan Palmer.* No one except Ace Mulloy, who was nowhere in sight, and Morgan Palmer, who could be lying.

VI

MORGAN PALMER SAID, "I told you I made that bet. Ain't I scared enough?"

Palmer was definitely scared enough. The big man was sweating in the cold of Slot-Machine's office. It was late afternoon. Palmer and Joe Harris had had no more luck than Slot in getting down the lay-off bet for Palmer. And the fight was no more than eight hours away. Palmer had a packed suitcase with him.

"Who's holding the stakes?" Slot said.

Palmer reddened. "The dame."

"You let a strange dame hold two thousand dollars on a bet?"

Palmer shrugged. "Mine was only a marker."

"But Ace put up cash?" Slot-Machine said.

"Yeh."

Joe Harris whistled low. "Ace let a strange dame hold one thousand dollars of real money when you put up only a market? This gets worse and worse."

Slot-Machine rubbed the stump of his arm. He reached into his pocket for a cigarette, deftly flipped the cigarette high in the pack, and clamped his lips on it. He put the pack away and producing a wooden match he snapped it alight on his thumb-nail. He smoked.

"Okay," Slot-Machine said, "let's look at it. Ace Mulloy, a smart and tough boy, makes a sucker bet. He lets a dame he's not supposed to know hold the stakes. The dame herself conned you into the bet. Now Ace is missing, the dame clams up on Ace, no one even knows there was a bet."

"I know," Palmer said.

"Yeh," Slot-Machine said, "you know. And you know you can't pay. Everyone else knows you can't pay. All the proof we've got that there ever was a bet is your word. As far as the town knows, Palmer, you couldn't afford that bet, and everyone knows Ace Mulloy wouldn't make a bet like that."

"I made the bet!" Palmer said.

"You know it," Slot said.

"And Ace knows it," Joe Harris said.

Slot-Machine nodded slowly, and blew a stream of smoke into the cold air of the office.

"Yeh, Ace Mulloy knows it," Slot-Machine said, "and the dame knows it, because she's holding Palmer's marker and Mulloy's grand. What I just don't figure is what does Mulloy get out of winning a bet he knows can't be paid off?"

"Maybe he's a masochist," Joe Harris said. "He likes to win money he never gets paid."

"And why is he hiding?" Slot-Machine said.

"Who knows?" Joe said. "But it's a good idea. Palmer better start hiding fast. Maybe if he runs far enough Ace will forget about the money in a hundred years or so."

"I guess that's all there is," Slot agreed. "Run far and fast."

"That's what everyone says," Joe said.

Palmer shook harder. "You got to lend me fifty bucks," he said.

"Some clients I get," Slot said as he counted out twenty-two dollars.

Joe added the rest. They were almost down to counting it out in dimes before they made it.

"Get a job and send it back," Slot-Machine said. "And fifty bucks extra for my fee. Maybe I'll go to work for Mulloy. He's got cash."

Palmer did not appreciate the joke. Neither Slot nor Joe had the money to cover a thousand dollar loss. Slot-Machine was not sure Palmer's hide was worth a thousand anyway. No one else in the whole wide city would lend Morgan Palmer taxi fare. Palmer was a drunk, a crook, and a cheat. But Palmer was in some kind of trouble that was other people's doing, and Slot-Machine didn't like that to be done even to Palmer.

Slot and Joe lent Palmer the fifty bucks. The ex-Marine went out of the office carrying his bag and a heavy load of pure fright. Slot and Joe went down to the street with Palmer. Slot-Machine was rubbing the stump of his arm and scowling. He had the definite feeling that somehow he had gotten hold of the wrong end of the whole affair.

It bothered Slot that the best he could do was to help Palmer run away the way everyone else agreed Palmer had to run. It was the only way out now, but ... Slot-Machine stopped rubbing his stump. He narrowed his eyes in his ugly face. They were at the door of his building. He stopped Joe.

"We'll watch from here, Palmer," Slot-Machine said. "You grab a taxi. When you get where you're going, send me a wire, right away, okay?"

"Sure," Palmer said. "Only I'll call at your home number. If you don't answer, I hang up."

"Good," Slot-Machine said, nodding.

From the shadow of his doorway, Slot-Machine and Joe watched Palmer hail a taxi, get in, and drive slowly off into the traffic. Slot-Machine scanned the whole block carefully. A large, black car seemed to materialize from an alley.

"Damn!" Slot swore.

Joe looked at the car. There were four people in the car. The driver was Mel Throne. The other two men were two more of Freddie Tucci's lads. The fourth person was a woman, a blonde woman.

"Velma O'Hara," Slot-Machine said to Joe.

"You think they're going to get Palmer now?" Joe said.

"No," Slot said, "I think they're tailing him."

"For Ace Mulloy?"

"What else?" Slot-Machine said. "I heard Ace was hot. He's probably hiding out, but that wouldn't make him forget a sure-thing bet of one grand. Except, damn it, what does Tucci get?"

"Inner satisfaction from helping a pal," Joe said.

"Why the hell would Mel Throne lie about the bet?"

"Maybe Mel *is* in this on his own," Joe said. "Maybe Mel and Ace are just in it for the thousand dollars."

"Do you believe that?"

"No," Joe said.

"What I don't get is why they all lie about the bet," Slot said.

"What does it matter?" Joe said. "As long as Mulloy says there was a bet, and Palmer knows there was a bet, who else matters?"

"I don't know yet, Joe," Slot-Machine said, "but I don't like the whole deal. Why is Mulloy in hiding? If he's sure to win that bet, he should be parading the town laughing at Palmer."

"Maybe he don't think it's funny," Joe said.

EIGHT AND A half hours later, at precisely forty-two minutes after ten o'clock that Friday night, Slot-Machine remembered Joe's words. Slot-Machine and Joe were outside Madison Square Garden They had just come from the Garden. They had not waited for the last fight. They had come out the moment the main bout ended, and now they stood alone on the sidewalk in front of the Garden. Joe was looking dazed.

"As long as Mulloy says there was a bet," Slot-Machine said. "You said it Joe. Ace didn't think it was so funny."

Joe shook his head as if still in a daze. Joe's voice was incredulous. "Fuentes won!" he said. "Palmer's got a thousand bucks coming."

"Yeh," Slot-Machine said as he stared up into the dark Manhattan sky. "Fuentes won. If I ever saw a fighter take a dive, it was the other guy who took the dive."

"The other guy was in the tank," Joe said. "The boys had it all wrong. You get paid, you know? That is, if Palmer can ever find the dame with the cash. He's a winner, and he's run away."

Slot-Machine still stared up at the dark city sky. Fuentes had won the fight. A sucker bet by Ace Mulloy was going to cost the gangster $1000 when it should have cost him no more than $400. If Velma O'Hara paid off. And Velma would pay off. Suddenly, Slot knew Velma would pay off. The other fighter had been in the tank, so it was no accident.

"Palmer won't have any trouble getting paid," Slot said. "It'll be real easy. Damn it, Joe, we got to move fast! It may be too late already."

"Too late for …"

"You go get Captain Gazzo," Slot-Machine snapped. "Get him, and bring him to Palmer's flop-house. Bring him fast, and tell him to come with a lot of help."

Joe Harris remained alone on the sidewalk as Slot-Machine ran for a taxi. All around Joe the audience was now coming out of the Garden. The lovers of the Manly Art were screaming blue murder about the dive Fuentes' opponent had taken.

VII

SLOT-MACHINE KELLY eased his revolver from its holster under the stump of his left arm as he approached the sleazy rooming-house type hotel where Morgan Palmer lived. He approached the flea-bag cautiously. He saw a shadowy figure lurking across the street from the one-dollar-a-night hotel. The figure had a clear view of the entrance and the alley behind the fleabag.

Slot-Machine went into the building next to Palmer's hotel. He climbed up the stairs to the roof. He went over the roof to the roof of the hotel, and went down the fire escape that hung over the alley. Palmer's room was on the fourth floor and opened onto the fire escape.

Slot-Machine climbed in the window, after using his jimmy to open it. He searched the one grimy room, and found nothing but three empty whisky bottles. In a trap like this, the maid service was not of the finest. And Morgan Palmer would not have told anyone he was leaving, not, at least, the way he had left—in a hurry with Ace Mulloy hanging over him.

Satisfied, Slot-Machine went into the single closet, which was empty now, and crouched down with the closet door barely open so that he could see. He did not have long to wait.

First, there was the sound of the ancient elevator somewhere out in the corridor. Then there were voices. Someone was explaining something. That, Slot guessed, would be the man who had been watching the room explaining to a new arrival that no one had gone into the room.

Slot-Machine waited. His legs were beginning to ache from his crouching position. The elevator went down.

There was the sound of a heavy door opening. That would be the door to the back stairs. Heavy footsteps came down the hall toward the door to Palmer's room. Slot-Machine licked his dry lips and waited.

Light suddenly flooded the room. The door to the hall had been opened. For an instant there was heavy breathing, the scuffling of feet, and then darkness as the door closed.

The lights in the room went on.

Through the crack between the closet door and the closet, Slot-Machine saw two men carrying a large, heavy sack. These two vanished, and another man appeared in Slot-Machine's line of sight. It was Mel Throne.

There was a fourth man in the room. Slot-Machine could not see this man. He did not have to. He pushed open the closet door, stepped out with his revolver leveled, and grinned.

"Surprise, Tucci," Slot-Machine said.

The two men carrying the sack were so startled they didn't even drop the sack. They just stood there with their mouths open staring at Slot-Machine. Mel Throne was just loose enough to turn around to face Slot.

Freddie Tucci himself started a fluid motion toward his shoulder holster.

"Easy, Tucci!" Slot-Machine warned.

Tucci went on reaching for his gun.

Slot-Machine fired.

The bullet fanned waves in Freddie Tucci's hair. The gang boss froze like a pillar of salt. Slot-Machine grinned again.

"That's a real smart boy," Slot-Machine said. "Now why don't we all just sit down and relax. Who knows, Tucci, maybe you can blame it all on Mel there."

"Kelly, you stupid ..." Mel Throne began.

"Shut up, Mel!" Tucci snapped. The suave little gang lord smiled at Slot-Machine. "Okay, Kelly, so you're smart. I like smart men. It's good. Now be real smart. How much?"

"You're trying to bribe me," Slot-Machine said.

"Ten grand," Tucci said. "There's a lot in this. Ten grand for you because I like you."

"That much? It must have been some haul," Slot-Machine said.

"It was," Tucci said.

Mel Throne snarled. "Don't play with this one-armed fink! Listen, cripple, I'll blow ..."

"I said shut up, Mel!!" Tucci said again. "Look, Kelly, there's four of us. One of us'll get you. Be smart, take the money."

"I figure I can get two of you first," Slot-Machine said. "I let you out of here, a hundred grand wouldn't take me far enough away from your boys knowing what I know."

"What do you know, Kelly?" Tucci said.

"I know who's in that sack," Slot-Machine said.

"Real smart, real smart!" Tucci said. "You ain't getting out of here alive, Kelly!"

Too late Slot-Machine realized that Tucci had been talking very loud. The man in the hall! He heard the door click open. He fired at the door without looking. There was a loud grunt. Slot-Machine had no time to look toward the door to be sure his man was down for good.

Mel Throne had his gun out. Tucci had his half way out. The two men with the sack had dropped the sack and were clawing for hardware. Slot fired once. Mel Throne went down.

Tucci had his gun leveled now. Slot-Machine could not get his revolver around in time. He stared at the muzzle of Tucci's gun.

Then the gun was gone from Tucci's hand.

Slot-Machine heard the shot a split second after Tucci's gun vanished. The other two men had their hands up. Tucci was cursing and holding his right hand with his left. In the doorway Captain Gazzo, Homicide, surveyed the scene with five of his men behind him. Joe Harris pushed through to stand beside Gazzo.

"Nice timing, Gazzo," Slot-Machine said.

Then Slot sat down hard on the edge of the shabby bed. His knees were shaking. Captain Gazzo led his men into the room.

"Okay, Kelly, you want to start telling me all about it?" Gazzo said.

"Open the sack," Slot-Machine said.

Gazzo motioned to Sergeant Jonas. The Sergeant opened the sack, and with the help of a patrolman, dumped the contents on the floor. The contents were the body of a man. A very dead man.

"Meet Ace Mulloy," Slot-Machine said.

"We've met," Gazzo said. "Why did Tucci kill Mulloy, Kelly? Do you know?"

"You tell me, Captain," Slot-Machine said. "I heard Ace was hot, a couple of big hauls. Take a look in Mulloy's pockets. I figure you'll find some bills, some big bills, and you ought to be able to identify them."

Jonas searched the body. The Sergeant brought out fifty hundred-dollar bills. Jonas handed them to Gazzo. The Captain looked at the money. Gazzo nodded.

"I'm not sure without my sheet," Gazzo said, "but from the numbers I'd say they were part of the Wells Fargo Armored Car haul about six weeks ago."

"Did you suspect Mulloy?" Slot said.

"Yeh, we suspected," Gazzo said. "But we had nothing on him."

"How many men on that job?"

"Two, Kelly," Gazzo said. "Just two, but real well planned. Three guards were killed."

Slot-Machine nodded. "That's what I figured. Mulloy always was trigger-happy. I figure Mel Throne was the other man, but Tucci planned it. Only with three dead guards, Tucci wanted out. He wanted to keep the money, too. So he got a real bright idea.

"He talked Ace Mulloy into making a bet with Morgan Palmer. Ace was to pay off with part of the loot. Ace wasn't too smart. Tucci sold him on the idea that if the police caught Palmer it would take the heat off. Palmer would say there had been a bet, but who would believe him? Everyone denied the bet, you would know that a bet like that wasn't something Ace Mulloy would do."

"It won't play, Kelly," Gazzo said. "That wouldn't have saved Mulloy. There were two men on the job."

"Sure, but Ace forgot about that," Slot-Machine said. "Tucci had a lot better plan. After Ace made the bet, Tucci snatched him, and hid him out. Then he put out the rumor that Fuentes was in the tank, which scared Palmer, then stopped Palmer from laying off the bet. That fixed it so Palmer would run. Everyone said he should run. Even me.

"Palmer ran. Tucci killed Mulloy right then. When the Coroner gets here you'll find that Mulloy has been dead maybe nine hours, a little more maybe. Tucci dumps Mulloy's body here, you find it. Palmer has run out, and you find some of the loot on Mulloy. You look for Palmer. When you locate him you find some more of the robbery loot on him.

"That's it. Two men on the robbery. One is dead, and he's found in the room of the other man. *He was killed just about the time Palmer got a train*, and when you catch Palmer, he's got some of the money on him. Q.E.D. Case closed. Sure, you look for the money, and Palmer tells his story. But who would believe Palmer with Ace Mulloy's body right here in his room and Palmer on the run?"

"How do you know Palmer's got the money?" Gazzo said.

"Because by now Velma O'Hara's paid off the bet," Slot said. "She tailed Palmer wherever he went. As soon as Fuentes lost, she paid, and called Tucci. He's had Mulloy's body ready since about an hour before Palmer got on the train. Throne and the other boys were following Palmer everywhere. When Palmer left my office with his suitcase, Throne called Tucci and Mulloy was shot right then.

"In a flea-bag hotel like this all they had to do was watch to be sure no one went into Palmer's room. They had the door locked, it was easy. They didn't even think they had to worry about me. I just saw Palmer get in a taxi. He could have come back here, killed Mulloy, and still made the train. With Mulloy dead, you'd never have believed Palmer's story about the bet."

Gazzo whistled. "Some plan."

"It was good," Slot-Machine said. "I just couldn't figure *why* Mulloy would make such a sucker bet."

"They had to worry about you after all," Gazzo said.

"Yeh," Slot-Machine said. "They made a mistake when Throne only tapped me around to warn me."

When the Coroner arrived he confirmed the time of death as that afternoon about a half hour to two hours before Palmer had left town. Morgan Palmer called from Syracuse, New York. Palmer was happy as a sand boy. He had been paid off precisely at eleven o'clock, and had wondered how the woman had found him. Gazzo had an all-points out on Velma O'Hara. Slot-Machine had both elbows on the bar at the tavern where Joe Harris was working that week.

"Everyone said Palmer had better run," Slot said to Joe as Slot drained his third Irish, "and you said the rest. You said the bet was good as long as Ace Mulloy said it was. Right then I began to figure I had the wrong end of the stick. When Fuentes *won*, I got the picture—someone *wanted* Palmer to run. Someone *wanted* to pay off Palmer. With Ace Mulloy missing, the rest was easy."

"You guess good," Joe said, pouring another shot. "Palmer was cooked if it had worked, because no one would have believed that bet, not even you and me. Once they found Mulloy's body in his room and dead that long, Palmer wouldn't have convinced his mother he was innocent. Palmer should be one happy boy."

"He ain't," Slot-Machine said. "He figures he's out one grand drinking money. The cops took the loot. Palmer's screaming for his grand."

"You do good work," Joe said, "for nothing."

"I got paid," Slot-Machine said.

Slot held up a crisp one-hundred-dollar bill. He smoothed it lovingly on the bar.

"Gazzo won't miss just one," Slot-Machine said. "I palmed it off Mulloy's roll."

"Gazzo'll have your skin," Joe said.

"After I spend it," Slot said. "Besides, Palmer owes us fifty."

"You're out of your mind," Joe said.

"Just pour," Slot said. "I got to spend this hundred fast."

Slot-Machine glanced over his shoulder. There were no police in sight. Slot-Machine began to laugh as he smoothed out his one-hundred-dollar bill. Joe Harris poured another drink.

THE HERO

The first eleven Slot-Machine stories were written and published in MSMM *between August 1962 and May 1964, at fairly regular intervals. But after "Winner Pay Off," this twelfth story did not appear until May 1965, a full year later.*

There were many reasons for this: I was writing mainstream stuff; I was doing more free-lance writing and editing of chemical business magazines because we had Katie now and needed money; I was writing more non-series crime stories between Kellys; I was doing all the monthly 20,000-word Mike Shayne novelettes for MSMM; *and I had changed.*

So for a year I wrote other things, and thought about what kind of crime stories I wanted to write. What kind of book? What kind of hero? The result was the private detective in "The Hero." He is not the Slot-Machine Kelly of the first nine stories. Not even the Kelly of "No Way Out" or "Winner Pay Off." They had changed from the earlier stories, yes, but they were not yet the Slot of "The Hero," and the Slot of "The Hero" is not yet Dan Fortune. But he is very close.

Dan is already there in a new point of view—first person. What had begun as a series with a Dr. Watson narrator, and changed to an authorial third, is now in the voice of the detective. It is almost Dan's voice. So much so that many years later I reshaped the piece into a real Fortune story.

THE NAME IS Patrick Kelly, and I'm writing this one myself. I knew Paul Asher and Constantine Zaretzki, and you had to know Zaretzki to tell this one right. Besides, I'm tired of having a ghost write about me. I've got enough ghosts in my life. Just ask any cop in half the cities of this damned world, not to mention a lot of sea captains and most of the bartenders.

"Very impressive," Joe said when I showed him my first paragraph.

"I think I've got the hang of this writing now," I said.

"You forgot to mention that most of the ghosts are bottles," Joe said.

Joe Harris is my best friend and roommate. He tends bar and pays the bills when I'm not working, which is most of the time. You've got to have a reason to work, besides money, and it's been a long time since I found any reason except money. Joe understands me.

"Slot-Machine Kelly," Joe said, "the one-armed bandit. You just don't want to split the pay."

"Why split when I can get it all?" I said. "I got the hang of this writing. Besides, you got to understand Asher and Zaretzki to write about them."

Let them call me Slot-Machine, the one-armed bandit. All it means is that I've got the hang of that too, the hang of living in a world that made Asher and Zaretzki. Everybody's got something missing somewhere, one way or another, and everyone's some kind of a bandit. You've got to be a bandit to face a world that made Asher and Zaretzki and still go right on drinking your beer and propositioning waitresses.

"That was a close one," Joe said, dirtying up the bar with a rag dirtier than the bartop. "I don't want to understand Asher. I get nightmares."

Do you know that we've killed fifty million people in fifty years? Give or take a couple of million here and there. From 1914 to 1964. And I mean _killed_, not just died in hurricanes, or famines, or earthquakes, or other accidents like those we ought to be fighting instead of each other. Fifty million! Now maybe you think this is a hell of a way to start a murder story, but it isn't. In a way it's the whole story.

I want you to think about those fifty million corpses. They all figured they died for a reason, or most of them did. Now when one man dies for a cause, that seems okay, even good. It takes a good man to go out and die for a cause. I've seen them.

But what cause is worth fifty million deaths? How many causes have fifty million people to spare? You got to begin to wonder if maybe the cause doesn't go down in that ocean of blood. You got to begin to think about what fifty million corpses can do to people.

I'm not playing games. I'm not talking about _your_ cause, or _my_ cause, or _his_ cause, or _their_ cause. I'm talking about everyone, everywhere. I'm talking about people who can swallow fifty million dead bodies without even a trickle of vomit.

I'm talking about people who see those fifty million corpses, and face maybe seven hundred or eight hundred million more potential dead bodies every day, every minute, and still go right on swilling beer and making passes at the ladies.

I'm talking about Paul Asher and Constantine Zaretzki and what they had missing somewhere inside that was a lot worse than a left arm.

It was a rainy Monday afternoon when Paul Asher came to find me in _Hogan's Tavern_ on Twenty-Second Street near the docks. When I say _Hogan's_ Place is near the docks, I mean near. Another fifty feet west and _Hogan's_ patrons would have been seagulls. You can smell the river like it was flowing deep behind the seedy bar.

I like the smell of salt mud and a big river like the Hudson; the smell of oil and floating wood and debris; the sound of ships. There's something simple and honest about a river, all the rivers that flow into all the dark oceans. I was listening to the river when Asher found me.

It was a slow Monday, so I'd left a note on my office door to tell any prospective clients that they could find me at _Hogan's_ if they wanted me that bad. I was on my third beer. Cash was low and Joe was new at _Hogan's_, so beer was all he could put on the cuff right then. Actually we were playing poker for the beers, but I was cold-decking Joe like always, and he knew it, so it was really getting the beer on the cuff.

I don't mind cheating Hogan. He's the kind of guy who worries so much about being cheated and made to look like a sucker that he wouldn't a throw rope to a drowning kid for fear it was some kind of a trick to sucker him. That kind of guy deserves to get cheated.

Besides, Hogan thinks a one-armed man is just another cripple and can't do anything like normal people. He has no idea what you can do to a deck of cards with one good hand. It's a pleasure to cheat him.

Paul Asher was something else. You couldn't cheat Asher.

"You're Kelly?" Asher said.

He seemed to sort of come up out of the floor right beside me. He was a small man, dark, and he moved like a cat. I never saw him come into *Hogan's*, or walk toward me. He was just there all of a sudden. He had dark hair, grown long, and he smelled like he took a bath maybe on his birthday if it happened to be warm that day. His clothes were dark and maybe bought from some fire sale in Bulgaria. He was dark all over, colorless. Nothing reached out to tell you about him. In the twilight he would have been invisible. Only his eyes said something, told you he was, after all, alive. They were dark, and hard, and cold.

"Are you buying or selling?" I said.

"I want to hire you," Asher said.

"Then I'm Kelly," I said, "if I don't have to work too hard for my hire."

"You must deliver a package," Paul Asher said. He said it plain and flat. Humor was not part of Paul Asher.

Asher had an accent, that much I could hear. But it was an accent from no-where. And not exactly an accent at that. It was more a kind of flat, toneless, very precise way of speaking the English language that showed that English was not his home-town language. There was no way of telling just what language he had spoken when he was a kid, if he had ever been a kid. I couldn't place the accent, and I couldn't place Asher. He could have come from anywhere or nowhere.

"I'm a detective, kind of," I said, "not a messenger."

"I will pay five hundred dollars," Asher said.

"I'm a messenger," I said. "What's in the package, a shrunken head?"

Joe looked worried. Joe always looks worried. I've talked to Joe about that, about how when you've got nothing to lose in this world you shouldn't look worried all the time. It doesn't help. Joe likes to worry. He should have been a scoutmaster or a politician.

"That's a lot of bread for a messenger," Joe said, his eyebrows at high noon to warn me that this looked fishy. Warning me is Joe's favorite occupation. It gives him a reason to stay alive and worrying.

"The five hundred is so that you will not ask what is in the package," Asher said simply, "and because Zaretski is a dangerous person."

"Zaretzki?" I said.

"Constantine Zaretzki," Asher said. "He would kill me. I must deliver to him this package, but I would not live."

"You're afraid of him?" I said.

"And he is afraid of me," Asher said.

"I don't carry a package unless I know what's in it," I said.

"I have valuable papers to sell to Zaretzki," Asher said.

Joe's eyebrows went up another notch. "Blackmail! Slot, you better—"

"No," Asher said, "not blackmail. Simply a sale. The papers are not a danger to Zaretzki. They are merely valuable to him. I will sell them to him. If I went myself he would kill me. You will take the package?"

"Let's see it," I said.

Asher produced a small, flat package about as big as a paperback book but twice as thick. I took it. They make bombs smaller every day, but this package was too light. It had the weight and feel of papers, no more. I thought of everything lethal that could be that light, and came up with a blank. It hefted like a package of papers and nothing else. Even a deadly gas needs a container, and plastic would have had a different feel.

"Why me?" I said. "I'm not in Dun and Bradstreet."

"I have friends," Asher said. "You are a man who asks few questions, and you need money."

"You've been talking to the right people," I said. "Okay, I just take this package to Constantine Zaretzki. Does he pay me anything?"

"No," Asher said. "The package is a sample. You give it to him, no more."

"Pay now?" I asked.

Asher counted out five hundred in dirty old twenties and laid them on the bar. I took the money and the package. Asher turned to leave.

"The address?" I said.

"It is on the package," Asher said.

"How do I contact you?"

"You do not. There is no need. If I need you, I will find you," Asher said.

Asher continued on out the door and was gone. I went back to my beer—five hundred dollars richer. I left one of the fine old twenties on the bar when I shoved the rest into my pocket. They made a nice bulge. I grinned at Joe.

"Whisky for the whole house," I said grandly.

Joe looked up and down the bar. With Asher gone, there was no one in the room except Joe and me and old Hogan sitting alone at a rear table smoking a cigar and watching the cockroaches to make sure they didn't steal his whisky. Hogan doesn't drink, at least not his own watered booze.

"You're a sport," Joe said. "You going through with this?"

"I got paid," I said. "Besides, I've got a hunch Asher'll be watching me."

"You're crazy," Joe said.

Maybe Joe was right. When I got close to the address on the package, I began to wonder about just how crazy I was. After my whisky at *Hogan's*, I grabbed a taxi to the uptown East Side address where I was supposed to deliver the package to Constantine Zaretzki. It was way over by the East River, and the street was dark. Dark but not deserted. There was no one on the street, but I could feel eyes.

I knew that Asher would be somewhere around watching me to make sure I delivered. But I felt other eyes. When you grow up near the docks, and you start stealing early because you have to eat even when your mother is a lush and your father took a bunk to parts unknown long before, you learn to feel eyes.

When you sail ships through a war zone, you learn to feel eyes on you from under water. When you get paid to spy and snoop around the back streets of most of the cities of the world, you can feel eyes watching from a thousand yards.

I felt eyes watching.

I walked slowly down that dark street. I can spot shadows of shadows, and I knew I was not alone. I had the feeling that no one walked down that street alone. It was in the air, a sort of alert, watching silence all around me. Then I began to see them.

At the far end of the dark street two men leaned against a building in the shadows. Behind me at the corner I had come from, two more men lurked. At a window directly across from the address of Constantine Zaretzki, there was a head, watching.

I went up the flight of steps to the door of the brownstone. I had my finger on the bell when I heard a footstep behind me. I turned. A short, powerful man stood four steps below me. He had a very nasty looking automatic in his left hand. He just stood there, another man behind him at the foot of the steps. I turned again to face the door. Too late. Hands reached out, and an arm went around my throat. The arm clamped tight, and I was dragged into the darkness of the entrance hall.

YOU CAN'T TIE a one-armed man's hands behind his back. It creates a problem. They had solved it neatly. I was tied expertly to the chair around the chest. It wasn't comfortable, but that did not seem to bother them. I counted six different men who came and went in the small room, but they barely looked at me. They were busy.

The short, powerful man seemed to be the leader. He barked out orders like a drill sergeant, sending the other men in and out of the room. They were speaking a language I didn't understand, but I didn't have to understand them to know what they were doing.

They were searching the street, the house, the backyards, the roofs, everywhere close by for anyone who might have come with me. They were quick, sure, and silent. Only the stocky leader barked his orders, the others hurrying in and out in silence, answering only in nods and short grunts. They were all armed, and they knew their business.

It was another half an hour before they got around to me. The stocky leader slapped my mouth, hard.

"Who are you, and what do you want here?" he demanded.

The others stood covering all of the doors and windows. The windows were heavily curtained, and I had the feeling that they were boarded up behind the curtains.

"I wondered when you'd get around to that," I said. "I could have saved you all the motions. I came alone."

"Why?"

"To deliver that package over there," I said.

The package was on a small side table, unopened. The stocky man looked at it.

"Deliver it to who, Mr. Kelly?" he asked, "if that is your name."

"Someone named Zaretzki," I said. "Constantine Zaretzki. Is that you?"

The stocky man ignored my question. "From who did the package come?" he said.

"Paul Asher," I said. "He said it was something Zaretzki would buy."

"Asher?" the stocky man said. "I know no Asher. You are lying, Mr. Kelly. Your papers say you are a private detective. They hired you. Do not try to lie! You came here armed, to kill Zaretzki!"

"I don't even know Zaretzki," I said. "I mean, I don't know who he is, or why anyone would want to kill him. If you have reason to believe someone's trying to kill, why not go to the police?"

While I talked I had been watching their faces. These men did not look like gangsters. They were all grim and unsmiling. Then, as I watched, their expressions changed and I was aware that someone else had entered the room.

Whoever it was had come into the small room through a door behind me. I could feel him standing there. His voice was low but hard, and he spoke perfect English.

"The police could not save me, Mr. Kelly," the new voice said. "The police would be of no help."

There was an air of command in the voice, of absolute confidence. The stocky man had come so rigidly to attention that I had little doubt that the newcomer was Constantine Zaretzki.

"I guess not," I said, "not if you were out to kill Asher. Maybe you're telling it backwards. Maybe it's Asher who should be afraid of you and your private army here."

"You miserable—" the stocky man began to say.

"Be silent, Emil!" the voice behind me said. I agreed with him. Emil was a lot more pleasant silent.

But Emil wasn't buying the silence bit. The stocky man was as suspicious as a Chinese Communist looking at a present from the Russians.

"He is another one! I can smell them," Emil cried. "I say kill him—now!"

"Perhaps," the voice of Zaretzki said behind me. "But let us find out if he *is* another one."

Emil swore in the unknown language. "What does it matter? We cannot take the chance. You must be safe at any cost."

I waited for Zaretzki's answer to that one, but the man behind me said nothing. I had a few answers myself, and was about to offer them free of charge, when a chair scraped against the floor and I could feel a hot breath close to my neck.

Zaretzki had sat down close behind me. That was okay. I liked the breath on my neck. As long as I could feel the breath, I was ahead of the game.

Zaretzki's voice, when he began to speak again, was cold and efficient.

"A man hired you to deliver a package to me at this address," he said. "Is that correct?"

"Correct," I said.

"What was his reason for using you?"

"He was afraid of you," I said.

"He gave you to believe I would kill him?"

"In spades," I said.

It was kind of weird, unreal, to be talking straight ahead into empty air. I had more than an urge to try to turn around and talk to Zaretzki straight, but I resisted the urge. I had a hunch that would be a bad play. The boys in the room looked jumpy enough already. A false move would have pretty certainly started a shooting gallery. It was in the air.

"And his name was Paul Asher?" Zaretzki said behind me.

"Check," I said.

"I do not know anyone named Asher, but that does not surprise me. Can you describe this Asher?"

I described Paul Asher down to the stain on the small man's tie. I had been played for some kind of sucker, as usual. The trouble was I didn't know yet just *what* kind.

"I do not recognize the description," Zaretzki said behind me, "but that does not surprise me either, Mr. Kelly. However, I think you have saved your life."

Emil almost hopped up and down, he was so mad. The stocky man with the big gun in his fist obviously did not like my being reprieved by his boss. If Emil had his way I would have been feeling nothing but dirt in my face in some empty lot.

"We cannot take the risk!" Emil cried.

"No, Emil," Zaretzki said calmly behind me. "If Mr. Kelly were anything more than he says he is he would not have described this Asher. He could be lying, but I think not. He has acted exactly as he should have acted. You found no one else with him. He clearly does not know what was in the package or he would have told a better story."

The last point seemed to make Emil think. It made me wonder. What had been in the package that would have made me tell a better story if I had known? At the moment I didn't waste much more time thinking about it. I was too busy wondering about Paul Asher and his angle, whatever it was. Zaretzki seemed to be reading my mind.

"One thing puzzles me, and I cannot afford to be puzzled," Zaretzki said. "There was some reason for sending you to me, but I cannot understand what it is. I must know why you were sent. Tell me your story once more, Mr. Kelly."

I told him. I gave him chapter and verse. When I have nothing to tell, I always tell the truth. I knew I had nothing to tell Zaretzki. I had no idea why Paul Asher had hired me. It was possible that it was Zaretzki and not Asher who was working the con job on me. Zaretzki had dismissed the package as of no importance, but I noticed that it was gone from the side table.

Maybe the package was just what Asher said it was—valuable papers. Maybe

Zaretzki was conning me into leading him back to Asher and the rest of the papers. It wouldn't help him. I couldn't have led him to Asher if my life depended on it. Asher wasn't dumb.

"I cannot understand it," Zaretzki said when I had finished the second show of my yarn. "But at least you have done me one service, Mr. Kelly. If you are not lying, I now know what this Asher looks like. I will be ready for whatever he plans. If you are lying, it does not matter, I will be ready now."

"Ready?" I said. I didn't need a blueprint to figure out what Zaretzki had in mind if he ever ran into Paul Asher on a dark night. But I wanted to hear it.

"I will kill him, Mr. Kelly," Zaretzki said simply. "It would be necessary."

"You boys play rough," I said.

"We are not boys, and we do not play," Emil said.

"That's too bad," I said.

There was movement again behind me. The chair scraped and the hot breath on my neck went away. All the hard-looking boys stood at attention again.

"Take your five hundred, Mr. Kelly, and forget you ever heard of me or Paul Asher," Zaretzki said.

Then I could tell that Zaretzki had gone away. A door closed behind me.

Emil untied me. The stocky man's heart wasn't in it, but his boss had spoken. While I got the circulation back in my arm, I took a chance to have a quick look around. The door behind me was closed.

I saw the package I had carried. It was lying on a table behind where I had been sitting, the brown paper torn open, and exposing a thick stack of what looked like folded papers. The package looked innocent enough. Just papers, like Asher had said, and he could have been telling the truth.

They didn't give me a chance to see more. There was something damned odd about that package, but I was too busy wondering if I was going to make it out alive to give it much thought.

The boys hustled me from the room and out into a long hall. We went down another hall and came to the door I recognized. The next thing I knew I was back out on the steps and walking down to the dark street. It was still deserted, and I could still feel the eyes watching me.

I didn't look back. I was out, I planned to stay out. I had no interest in Zaretzki and Asher and their private feud, whatever it was. I walked down that street as fast as I could without running. To run would have made me look like a coward.

I didn't run until I got around the corner. I made the next block faster. In fact I was on Third Avenue before I decided to be brave and stop running. I took the subway on Lexington.

By the time I got home to my apartment on Twenty-Seventh Street, I had forgotten all about Zaretzki and Asher. I worked on forgetting. There was too much I didn't know about those two boys. When I don't know something, I find out or forget it fast. It's safer that way.

Joe wasn't home yet, so I had a fast whisky and felt better. I was five hundred dollars richer and still alive. I figured I was home free. I should have known better. My arm, the one I don't have, had begun to ache. That's always a sign. When the missing wing starts to hurt where there isn't any arm to feel pain, I've got trouble coming.

I LOST THAT arm when I fell into the hold of a Dutchman ship on a small stealing expedition when I was just a kid. I got the loot out a porthole, so all they got me for was trespassing, but I lost the arm. I usually tell people I lost it in the war. It makes them feel better to think I'm a wounded hero. It makes me feel better too, the war stories I tell.

After all, I did lose the wing in a war—a war to stay alive and eating in those days, a war against playing it the way someone had dealt me the cards. I'm still fighting that way. I won't play the game they say I've got to play. I won't buy their stupid game of success, money, and power. But that's another story.

This is the story of Asher and Zaretzki, and I should have known it wasn't over when the missing arm started to ache. Not the stump, the arm itself. You got to be a cripple to know what I mean. It's always the missing piece of you that aches most, that hurts when the days are bad. But maybe you do know. We're all cripples one way or another.

It was still dark, but getting light in the east, when they began pounding a tom-tom on my door. Joe was asleep in the next bed. Joe can sleep through almost anything. I took a look at the grey dawn outside the window of the bedroom, and I lay there listening to them pound on the door. It was a cop type of pounding, and it was barely dawn. I had trouble.

Captain Gazzo himself led the boys in blue into my living room when I opened the door.

"Paul Asher," Gazzo said.

"A nice name," I said. "You got more?"

"We don't need more," Sergeant Jonas said. "One name like that don't need no more."

Sergeant Jonas doesn't like me. Captain Gazzo isn't exactly a buddy, either. It was Gazzo who gave me the name, Slot-Machine Kelly the one-armed bandit, but the Captain doesn't hate me. Jonas hates me. With Jonas his job is important. He's protecting The Game, the way it's played, the right and good and proper, and I don't play so he's got to crush me if he can. So he hates me, and right now in the grey light Jonas was happy.

"Shut up, Jonas," Captain Gazzo snapped. "Was Asher a client of yours, Slot?"

"You know I can't tell—" I began with righteous and legal indignation. I stopped. "Was? You said 'was?'."

"Stiff as all your clients, Kelly," Jonas said.

"Asher's dead?" I said.

Gazzo nodded. "We found him about an hour ago dumped under the George Washington Bridge. Shot up like swiss cheese. Don't ask what weapon, the killers used them all on him. You got any ideas?"

I had one idea. The George Washington Bridge is a long way from Zaretzki's stronghold and on the other side of the city. That was it. If I'd knocked off Asher on the East Side, I'd have dumped him on the upper West Side, too. I'd have dumped him in Jersey, but I'm very careful.

"Constantine Zaretzki," I said, "and a playful boy named Emil, and a half a dozen other retainers."

"Give us the story," Gazzo said.

I gave. I knew it as well as a good dealer knows his favorite poker deck by now. Chapter and verse again. Gazzo listened. Jonas listened as if he couldn't believe anyone could have been dumb enough to swallow Asher's yarn in the first place, not even me. Maybe he was right. Gazzo didn't care about me.

"Asher said Zaretzki was out to kill him," the Captain said, "Zaretzki said he would kill Asher, and you think Zaretzki was afraid of Asher. Okay, let's pick him up."

But I had a question. It puzzled me. On the way up in Gazzo's unmarked Homicide car, with a platoon of squad cars behind us, I asked my question.

"How'd you know I was working for Asher?" I asked.

"Your cards," Gazzo said without looking at me. The Captain was barking orders into his radio-phone. Gazzo's a good cop; he still gets excited about a murder.

"Cards?" I said.

"What do you do, Kelly?" Jonas said. "Give them out by the dozen? Asher must have had ten in his pockets."

"He also had a little notebook with your name and office address in it, and a notation of five hundred dollars paid," Gazzo said.

"He should get his money back," Jonas said.

I was thinking. I hadn't given Asher my card, not even one. Business cards cost money. As far as I knew Asher had never been in my office. He had met me in *Hogan's*, and, besides, I keep the cards locked up. I do give the cards out to uptown contacts in case anyone wants a kidnapped poodle found. Asher must have gotten the cards from whoever sent him to me. Before he ever met me or hired me.

By this time we had reached my favorite dark street on the East Side. It wasn't dark now, just grey in the dawn, but it was as deserted as ever. And I knew the eyes were still watching. The squad cars came from both ends of the street like a stampede of buffalo to a water hole. Only in this case the water hole was the brownstone house where I had delivered the package last night.

The squad cars nosed in toward the silent house like thirsty horses. The police aren't exactly quiet about their work. As Gazzo and Jonas got out of the Homicide car to lead their troops, windows began to pop open all up and down the block. Nothing popped open in the brownstone where Constantine Zaretzki lived with his private little army.

The brownstone was as dark and silent as a medieval fortress. It turned out to be almost as hard to crack into.

As they say in the communiques, Gazzo's men encountered determined resistance.

Knocks, shouts, and threats did not open the door. The windows remained closed. Gazzo ordered his men to break down the door. It was a strong door, but they finally did the job. The door went down. Gazzo stepped into the hallway inside.

Instantly, windows opened in the house and guns protruded aimed down into the street at the police. In the hallway Gazzo stood frozen and facing the stocky man named Emil. Emil had his gun in his hand. Behind Emil a voice spoke. The speaker, Constantine Zaretzki, was hidden somewhere in the gloom of the hall. I could not see him from where I stood in the shelter of the stairs, but I knew that voice by now.

"You are the police?"

"Call your men off, Zaretzki. We only want to talk to you," Gazzo said.

"How do I know you are the police?" the voice said.

Gazzo looked around at the blue uniforms that filled the hallway and the sidewalk in front of the building.

"You mean you think we're *all* fake police?" Gazzo said. I could hear a roar of anger growing in the Captain's throat. Gazzo does not like to be kidded by anyone. This did not bother Zaretzki.

"I have seen them try bigger tricks," the voice of Zaretzki said. "Tell me your name, number, and I will call to check."

"Now you tell you're damned men to—" Gazzo roared.

"I do not want trouble, I will check on you."

Gazzo clamped his mouth shut. He was so surprised that I heard him give his name and shield number. That was not like Gazzo, but, then, this was not like any homicide case I had ever been on. It did not take Zaretzki long.

I could imagine the scene at Police Headquarters when they received the call asking about a Captain Gazzo and would they please describe Gazzo! They must have given a good description. This time Constantine Zaretzki stepped out and I saw him for the first time.

"All right, Captain, won't you step in?" Zaretzki said.

The guns vanished from the windows. Emil followed his chief into the same small room where they had held me. I was watching Zaretzki. The man was small and thick, as wide as he was tall. He had powerful shoulders and a bullet head. The head shined in the light of the boarded-up room like a billiard ball. Zaretzki's head was shaved and was set like a thick egg on a bull neck.

In the small room, with his men around him, Zaretzki waved Gazzo to a seat. The Captain remained standing. I stayed out in the hall where I could watch and listen, but where Zaretzki could not get a glimpse of me.

"Just who are you, Mr. Zaretzki? Why do you have armed men guarding you?" Gazzo said to the bullet-headed Zaretzki. Gazzo spoke quietly enough, but I could hear the edge of menace in the Captain's voice. Gazzo does not like private armies in his city.

"A poor exile, Captain Gazzo," Zaretzki said softly. "And these are merely some loyal friends. They have permits for their weapons."

"An exile from where?" Gazzo said.

"Albania, Captain. We are simple Albanians," Zaretzki said.

Then I understood. Albania. That was the language I did not recognize, Albanian.

"Was Paul Asher an Albanian, too," Gazzo snapped. "Is that why you were afraid of him? Is that why you killed him!"

Zaretzki stared at Gazzo. The bullet-headed Albanian seemed puzzled. Then his thick face broke into a smile.

"He is dead? Good! I am glad! He is one we will not have to kill. You bring me good news, Captain, but how——?" Zaretzki stopped. The bullet head nodded suddenly. "Of course, you have talked with that Mr. Kelly! I should have guessed. Are you here again, Mr. Kelly?"

I stepped into the room. I flashed my bravest smile toward the glowering Emil and the bullet-headed Zaretzki. And I missed it. I almost missed the whole, murderous, impossible thing.

SOMETIMES I WONDER if there is anyone left who has not killed. I know there are many, but sometimes it doesn't seem like there can be anyone who hasn't. I've killed, not in the army the way I like to tell it for free beers in the bars, but I've worked for the Government, and I've worked for myself, and in my work you kill sooner or later. Maybe that was why I missed the clue in what Zaretzki had said.

I remember a time when we used to say that a really inhuman, animal type of man killed for the fun of it. Today they kill without even having any fun out of it. They just kill. It is their job, their duty, their work, their assigned role. They kill the way another man reports the dog show. It is those fifty million rotted corpses swallowed without need even of an aspirin.

In that small room I grinned at Zaretzki.

"Maybe you shouldn't have let me go," I said.

Emil growled like a frustrated lion. Zaretzki started to answer. Gazzo waved us all to silence.

"You're saying you didn't kill this Paul Asher?" Gazzo said.

"We did not," Zaretzki said.

"But you would have?" Gazzo said.

"Yes, Captain."

"Because he was out to kill you?" Gazzo asked.

"Yes," Zaretzki said.

"Why didn't you come to us for protection?"

Zaretzki smiled. "The police? No, Captain. You see, I am not precisely a friend of your Government. Let me tell you what I am. I am a Communist, an Albanian Communist. I have no love for your weak and stupid capitalist regime. They have no love for me. In my country I had, shall we say, an argument with the present leaders. They wish me dead. They must have me dead. Someday I will go back and they will run if I am not dead.

"Six times in six countries they have tried to kill me. In four of those countries, before I knew it would not help, I had police protection. It did not help, it did not stop them. I was many times almost killed, I have killed five of them. But they do not give up. They will never give up. If I were them, I would not give up. Someday I will kill all of them!"

It was right then that I first began to think about the fifty million corpses in fifty years. Zaretzki said the word *kill* the way most men say *work*—a fact of life, a necessity, sometimes good and sometimes bad, a tool of living. And I don't mean that it had anything to do with being a Communist. It is not only the Communists who have swallowed those fifty million dead men like so many faceless jelly beans.

"In the meantime you protect yourself," Gazzo said. "Like not even trusting the police."

"I trust no one, Captain. It is why I am alive. But I do not kill for nothing, even my enemies know that. No one can reach me without great danger, Captain, but I do not kill unless I know my enemy."

"You knew Asher," Gazzo said. "Kelly described him."

"Yes, but he never came here," Zaretzki said.

Gazzo stood up. "Okay, I think you all better come to Headquarters. Maybe you didn't kill Asher, but I need a lot more proof."

"Very well, Captain. And my friends?"

"Them, too," Gazzo said. And Gazzo instructed his men. "Take their guns, search this house from top to bottom."

I watched as Gazzo's men herded Zaretzki and the others out of the small room. Other police had already begun to search. In the small room I felt sick when I thought about Constantine Zaretzki. The bullet-headed Albanian would kill every enemy, or friend, who even bothered him. In cold blood, without hate or remorse. He drew the line at killing without *some* reason, and he was very proud of that. He considered that it made him a moral man. I didn't knock it; that was what had kept me alive, but it was not exactly high morality.

I looked down the hall from the doorway. I could still see the bullet-head of Zaretzki surrounded by police. Emil seemed to be giving the cops some trouble. He was probably reluctant to give up his gun. Cold-blooded killers, all of them, and yet I was sure they had *not* killed Asher.

They were not the type to wait around if they had. They must have known that I would tell the police about them and Asher. If they had killed him they would have been long gone before the police could connect me to Asher, and I could connect Zaretzki to Asher.

It was then that I got it.

Right then. I was there in the doorway to the small room, ready to walk down the hall and out, and I got it. *I was the only one who could connect Asher and Zaretzki.* The bullet-headed Albanian had said that himself, he had known it had to be me who brought the cops. Asher, dead, had sent Gazzo to me with my cards in his pockets, and I had brought Gazzo to Zaretzki. I got it, but I didn't want it. I felt colder than I had ever been in my life.

I walked back into the small room. Ran, not walked. The package was still there where I had seen it lying open. I looked at it. What I had remembered was right. I knew what was wrong with the package. The folded sheets of paper were all blank. A two-inch thick sheaf of blank paper, that was what had been in the package I had carried.

Now I knew why Zaretzki had told Emil that if I had known what was in the package I would have told a better story. I would not have said that I had been sent with valuable documents! When you knew what actually was in the package, it was a stupid story. And Asher had known that. Asher had known that Zaretzki would work me over.

Asher had sent me to Zaretzki with a phony package of blank paper. Nothing more.

All this had taken only seconds. Before I had finished that last thought, I was out of the room and half way down the hall toward the front door—running. I went out that front door like Peter Snell finishing the 800 meters. Gazzo and Zaretzki had just reached the foot of the stairs down to the street. The Homicide car waited with Jonas holding the door open.

I had my revolver out and cocked.

I saw him standing not two feet from Jonas, just where Gazzo and Zaretzki would have to pass.

He was a tall, thin man. I had never seen him before in my life. But I knew him. The police uniform was a good fit, but it was not his uniform. The revolver already in his hand was long and deadly and not a police pistol. He stepped one step out toward Zaretzki just as I got half way down the steps.

I had no time to aim. There wasn't even time to think. Gazzo and Zaretzki had seen the man. Emil had seen the phony cop. Jonas had seen the leveled pistol. None of them could have made a move in time.

I fired three shots.

I never did find out where the first shot went. Into a wall across that street, I guess.

The second shot caught Jonas in the leg. The sergeant still thinks I aimed at him.

The third shot got the phony cop in the arm. It wasn't much; it barely needed a bandage later. But it was enough. It made that assassin jerk to his right, and his first shot missed Zaretzki by an inch.

That phony cop never got off a second shot. Gazzo, Emil, and five husky real cops swarmed him under like an avalanche there on the East Side street.

LIKE I SAID at the start, everyone's got something missing somewhere. You've got to be at least a bandit to stand up and face a world that could have made Paul Asher.

The cops never got anything important out of that phony cop who had been waiting there on the street to kill Constantine Zaretzki. I had saved Zaretzki, but that didn't make me feel good. They were a pair, Asher and Zaretzki, but even Zaretzki had not imagined just how much Asher had missing inside.

I don't know Asher's real name, or who he was, or where he came from. No one knows, and no one ever will. A corpse in a Potters Field grave on Harts Island;

under a marker with a false name on it. No one will ever visit that grave. Paul Asher died faceless, nameless, and unknown even to his partner the phony cop.

The phony cop who had shot at Zaretzki never gave his real name, no one came forward to visit him. But he did not mind telling his story now that it was over. The plan had been Paul Asher's. The job had been to kill Constantine Zaretzki. They had almost succeeded. Zaretzki himself had not guessed why I had been hired to deliver that package. It was too cold even for Zaretzki.

"Himself?" Joe said, his hand hanging paralyzed above the bar. "Asher killed himself just to send the cops to pick up Zaretzki?"

"To smoke him out into the open where his partner could get a clear shot," I said.

It was late evening now, it wasn't raining, but here in *Hogan's Tavern* I watched the door anyway. I sort of expected that the river would flow right up over its banks and drown us all right now. Old Hogan was still sitting in the back watching to make sure I didn't get his cheap whisky free. I almost felt I liked Hogan. Greed is a human thing, at least—often a little apart from killing.

"They couldn't get to Zaretzki, a lot of others had tried," I said. I drained my whisky and pushed the glass toward Joe. "It was Asher's own plan. The phony cop told us all about it, he was *proud* of Asher and himself. Asher hired me just to have a private cop know that Zaretzki wanted Asher dead. Then he put my business cards in his pocket so the cops would come to me and ask questions. Then he killed himself. His partner, the phony cop, shot up the body afterwards to make it look like he'd been killed by a gang."

"And you took the cops to Zaretzki," Joe said. "The other killer, the phony cop, was waiting. It almost worked."

"Yeh," I said, "it almost worked. You know, Joe, every assassin expects to die if he succeeds in his job, maybe even if he fails in the attempt, but Asher died without any chance of knowing if the plan would work or not. He had no way of knowing I would tell the cops about Zaretzki, or that they would listen to me. A million things could have gone wrong. He killed himself just on the chance the plan would work and Zaretzki would be killed."

"The guy wasn't human," Joe said.

"No," I said. "Asher was human. That's the real horror."

And it is the real horror. I had five hundred dollars, and the rest of that night I drank whisky as fast as Joe could pour, but half a grand didn't buy enough whisky. Paul Asher, or whatever his real name was, was a human being. He had a cause and a job to do. But even a rat fights to survive, kills to stay alive. Paul Asher died just to kill. He killed himself the way you and I would step on a cockroach. Just a tool in a plan, his own plan.

And somewhere there are probably people who think Asher was a hero. Fifty million corpses in fifty years, maybe eight hundred million corpses tomorrow or the next day, and we go right on drinking our beer and whisky.

VIKING BLOOD

The year 1965 was tumultuous. My first two novels, Combat Soldier *and* Uptown Downtown *(neither were my titles, those being:* Far Off is Our Land *and* Man With Guitar*) had been published in 1963 and 1964 but had earned little money and less notice. Katie was nearly a year and a half old, my wife was pregnant again, New York was not getting any less expensive, and I was still scrambling to make a living. There were going to be four of us, which meant moving to a bigger and far more expensive apartment than ours where Katie had the small bedroom and we slept on the pull-out couch, or leaving the city. Neither Connecticut nor New Jersey appealed.*

Back in 1959, I'd helped my mother move to Santa Barbara, and had, as I wrote earlier, spent three months there in 1960 working on my fourth mainstream novel. I had liked the small city (a lot smaller then than now), was tired of the constantly gray Eastern winter, and had mistakenly expected Santa Barbara to be far cheaper. (It was cheaper, but less than I had thought. I had not realized it was a playground of the rich.) So in May we moved across the country, and our second daughter, Deirdre, was born in Santa Barbara in September.

The result was that another year passed after "The Hero" before I wrote the thirteenth and last Slot-Machine story, "Viking Blood." It was far longer than any other Kelly story, and I wanted to make more than a penny a word, so sent it to Manhunt. *It came out in one of that legendary magazine's last issues.*

There were few changes from "The Hero," which had been the big leap toward Dan Fortune. Slot is still close to Dan, but still not there. The style is still wrong, and so is the voice. I had to know my own mind better, what I wanted to do with my writing, before the voice, the style, and world view would be right.

By 1965 I knew I was going to try to make my living at crime writing, and to do that I had to write a novel. "Viking Blood" already had a big enough plot, with some developing and thickening, and a basic theme strong enough to carry a novel, and that I wanted to explore. All it needed was a broader, surer, more thoughtful voice.

I thought about it all for another six months, and began to rewrite the story into my first Dan Fortune novel, Act of Fear. *Slot-Machine would finally become Dan, still with one arm, but a different person, in a different set of novels and stories, with a different voice, and a different mission.*

IT BEGAN WITH the mugging of the cop.

Person or persons unknown jumped the patrolman, dragged him into one of our dark alleys near the river, and cleaned him out. We all knew him: Patrolman Stettin on one of the river-front beats. A young cop, Stettin, not too long on the beat, and eager. The mugger took it all: billy club, gun, cuffs, summons book, watch, tie-clip and loose change.

161

The story went around the back rooms like the news of free drinks at some grand opening. Because it didn't figure. Who robs a cop?

"What's a harness bull got worth stealing?" Joe Harris said.

"The pistol," I said.

Joe thought about that while he poured me a second free shot of Paddy's good Irish. Packy Wilson, the owner of this saloon, was too busy talking to his other morning customer about Stettin's mugging to notice the free drinks. Some good comes out of everything.

"There're a lot easier ways to get a gun," Joe said.

Joe was right. Getting a gun isn't exactly like picking fruit off a tree, even here in Chelsea, but there are easier ways than mugging The Man. Kids born between the river and Broadway know that much before they're weaned.

"Cops make less than you do," Joe said. "When you get around to working."

Joe and I live together, we have for a lot of years, and his name is on my life insurance. That doesn't tempt him, and it says a lot about his character these days when you read about kids who kill their parents to get the insurance money to go to college. Joe thinks I should bring in more money, but I point out to him that he really likes tending bar and I need a reason to work.

"Try hunger," Joe said. "That's my reason."

"It's not enough," I said.

And it's not. You don't need much money to eat and sleep and get enough to drink to quiet the voices in your head or the pain in an arm that isn't there. The missing arm holds me back a little, but we make enough to eat. Real work is for something else. There has to be a reason for real work—a reason that's part of the work itself. That was a fact Jo-Jo Olsen had to face before it was all over.

That morning I hadn't even heard of Jo-Jo Olsen, and no one had mentioned the other robbery or the murder. Nothing is that neat in real life, and the cops don't tell all they know to the neighborhood grapevine. On the West Side we get maybe 40 burglaries a day alone, and another robbery isn't news. The mugging of a cop is news.

"A cop gets killed, that I figure," Packy Wilson said. The other morning customer had left and Packy had to talk to me. "It's the robbing and not killing I don't get."

Packy's Pub is kind of a fancy name for a Tenth Avenue saloon, but Packy has ideas of drawing the young executive crowd and their Vassar-girl secretaries. He might even do it. The bright kids are always running out of places to "discover" these days. It's a nervous time we have, everyone on the go-go. It doesn't matter where they go, just somewhere else.

"I guess it was the gun," Joe said, decided.

"Even an out-of-town hood oughta have better connections," Packy Wilson said. "Jumping a cop is the hard way."

"A junkie, maybe," Joe said. "A junkie could sell the gun, and the other stuff, for a couple of good fixes."

"Even you don't believe that," I said. "A junkie shakes when he sees a cop in the movies."

"Maybe just a cop-hater," Packy Wilson said. "And he took what he could while he was at it."

It was good for a lot of talk for a while, but after a week or so even I had almost forgotten it. People are strange. I mean, cops are killed somewhere every day, but cops don't get mugged and robbed very often. Yet a cop-killing rates headlines, and a mugging, which is real news, gets forgotten. People are more interested in death.

That's the way it is, and the talk about Stettin faded fast. I guess I would have forgotten it completely in a month. But I didn't get the month. I got Jo-Jo Olsen and a couple of killings, and I caused a lot of trouble myself.

The kid walked into my office about three weeks later. It was a Monday and Joe's day off. The Mets were away, it was too hot for fishing, and I was broke anyway. So I was in my office. The kid was looking for his friend Jo-Jo Olsen.

THE EXPERTS TELL you that a man can't think up an alias that won't give him away if you know enough about him. I believe that. A man can't have something inside his head that didn't have a start somewhere. Sometimes you have to know a lot, and sometimes not very much, but if you know enough about the man you'll spot the alias. That was one of the things I knew and Jo-Jo Olsen didn't know, and it almost cost him.

Another thing they tell you is that a good man is a man who faces up to his obligations, accepts his duty. Maybe that's true, too. Only I've seen too many who face up to every obligation except the hard one. The hard one is a man's obligation, duty, to himself. It's hard because it always has to hurt someone else, the way it had to for Jo-Jo Olsen in the end.

"You writing a gossip column," Joe said, "or you telling about Jo-Jo Olsen?"

Joe likes to read over my shoulder when I decide to write about all of it instead of working. He's my friend, and he's got the right, and most of the time he was there when it happened so he can help me tell it the way it was.

"They pay by the word," I said.

Joe thinks I go off on angles, don't tell it straight. He's right, and he's wrong. He wants me to tell the story of Jo-Jo Olsen. But what I've been telling is the story, the real story of Jo-Jo Olsen.

Most of the time it's not the facts, the events, that tell the story, it's the background, the scenery. It's all the things floating around a man in the air he breathes, the air he was born to and lives in. Things waiting for a spark to set them off. That's the real story of Jo-Jo Olsen, not the spark that blew it all up, or the dead faces he never knew.

Joe would say it started on the day Petey Vitanza happened to find me in my office that Monday morning. Or maybe on the day Patrolman Stettin was mugged, and the woman killed. But it really began the day Jo-Jo Olsen was born, or maybe a hell of a long time before that when the Vikings still roamed the seas. Petey

Vitanza, sitting in my dingy office with the brick wall for a view out the one window, was just one of the sparks.

"Almost three weeks, Mr. Kelly," Petey Vitanza said.

"A rabbit act?" I said. "Try the police."

"Jo-Jo wouldn't never stay away three weeks on his own," the Vitanza boy said. "He just bought a new bike. We was fixing it for racing."

The kid was scared. That was one of the things I mean. He was scared, and should have minded his own business, but Jo-Jo Olsen was his friend, so he came to me. He picked me because I'd known his father, Tony, before Tony Vitanza died building the Lincoln Tunnel so people could get to Atlantic City faster.

Missing persons are jobs for the police. Even when I was working steadier at private snooping, I didn't like them. Most of the rabbit cases I got were fathers after stray daughters, or wives after stray husbands who had all of a sudden wondered why they were working to their graves for women who weren't any fun. There could be a message. I mean, what happens between the time the daughter runs and the wife is run on? Makes a man think.

This time was different. Jo-Jo Olsen was a nineteen year old boy. He hadn't been lured into bad company, he'd been born into bad company. He wasn't married or even going steady.

"Sure," Petey Vitanza said, "we got girls, you know? Only no steady. Jo-Jo and me got motors, you know? I mean, Jo-Jo is studyin' hard by Automotive Institute. He's good. We're gonna go over 'n work for Ferrari someday. Maybe England, the Limeys sure knows cars."

And it wasn't Jo-Jo's parents who were looking for him.

"They said he went on a trip," Petey said. "His old man told me to stop botherin' him, and his old lady got mad. She said I should mind my own business and go dig dirt with the other hogs."

I didn't know the Olsens, and I was glad. From the crack about hogs, they sounded like people who think hard work is for suckers. We have a lot like that in Chelsea. They live around the rackets and the fast buck, and honest sandhogs get their contempt. The story sounded like that. It also sounded like a cover up.

"Is Jo-Jo in trouble, Petey?" I asked.

"Hell no!" Petey said, but he looked scared.

"It's got the sound," I said.

Petey was scared. "That cop, the one got beat up bad? The fuzz got it the day before Jo-Jo took off. The bull got beat right down the block from Schmidt's Garage."

"And you and Jo-Jo were working on the bike in Schmidt's?"

Petey nodded. "Jo-Jo works by Schmidt's. Only we been there near every day for months, the both of us! We was working on his new bike, fixin' the motor for racin'. It's a sweetheart, a Yamaha. I mean, we was together all the time!"

"A Yamaha costs real bread," I said.

"Jo-Jo he stashed his loot. He's a good mechanic, Mr. Kelly, and Schmidt pays him good."

I had a funny feeling in my arm, the left arm that isn't there. I get that when things don't sound right. This didn't sound right.

"He had a good job," I said, "he was studying hard at school, and he had a new cycle you were readying for racing. But a cop's been beaten right on the block where he works, and he's run."

Petey nodded. Nobody is with somebody else *all* the time. Like I said, my advice on rabbits is go to the cops. They have the tools. Most rabbits are repeaters. Once a man runs, unless the pressures change which they usually don't, he will run again. It's the rabbit's answer to run. Some men drink, some mainline, some watch TV, some beat their wives, some let everyone beat them to see how much they can take, and rabbits run.

But this sounded different. Jo-Jo Olsen had no reason to run, and a cop had been attacked on his block. Jo-Jo sounded like a straight kid, but in Chelsea if a man wants quick money his mind turns only one way, and it isn't to a bank loan. Besides, if Petey went to the police they would check with the parents and go home.

"Okay, Petey," I said. "You go home, I'll check it out."

I meant it, but you know how it is. It was summer and so hot the chewing gum on the streets turned liquid, and I was having my troubles with Marty again, and it all made me thirsty and tired.

Marty is my woman. Martine Adair, that's her name on the off-Broadway theater programs and the signs outside the tourist nightclubs on Third Street. Her real name doesn't matter. She changed her name, and I don't tell how I really lost my arm. She's fifteen years younger than me, and she gives me trouble. That's my own private business. I wouldn't mention Marty except that she was the reason I was almost too late, and she knew about Pappas.

Anyway, I did get around to checking with precinct on Jo-Jo. They had no record on the Olsen boy, but Lieutenant Marx was interested. Maybe it should have interested me, the fact that Jo-Jo had reached the age of nineteen in our neighborhood without picking up any record at all, and yet his name seemed to ring some kind of bell with Lieutenant Marx. But it didn't register at the time, and Marx didn't offer any comment. Most cops don't.

I put out a few other feelers asking for any information on Jo-Jo, and went back to my own problems. It could have stopped right there, too, but the spark had been set off. Marty got friendly again, and I got mauled a little, and they picked Petey Vitanza out of a gutter beaten blind, and Captain Gazzo down at Homicide told me about the other robbery—and about the killing.

THE GUY WHO mauled me was big but slow. I'm not big, and I'm not slow. When you've got only the average number and size of muscles, and you picked up a handicap like one arm along the way, you need good legs and fast thinking. It's called compensation, or adaptation, or just learning to use what you have in a world you can't do much about.

It was a night about a week after I'd talked with Petey Vitanza. Hotter than the engine room on some old coal-burners I've sailed on, and I was heading for *Packy's Pub*. I passed one of our convenient dark alleys, and he came down on me like a whole hod of bricks.

He hit me once on the right shoulder. He'd lunged off-balance, and he only got the shoulder. He was no trained fighter, but he had muscles, and his fist felt like a small bowling ball. I bounced off a wall. His second blow was slow, and I had time to roll with it. That was lucky because it was aimed at my chin and was more accurate. I think his trouble was that he had something on his mind, and his brain was too slow to think of two things at once.

"Lay off Jo-Jo!"

He grunted that message just as he swung the second punch at my jaw, and so he was slow, and I rolled with it. I threw one punch just to make him slow down, kicked his shin hard, and rolled two garbage cans into his path. He ducked the punch, howled when I got his shin, and sprawled over the cans as he lunged again. By the time he had picked himself up I was nothing but heels going away fast. I think I was leaning on Packy Wilson's bar, and half way through my first drink, before he was sure I had gone.

"A big guy," I described to Joe. "Blond, I think, or going grey. Kind of a square face, flabby. Dressed good in a suit from the little I got to see."

Joe shook his head. "He don't drink much, I don't know him."

"He drinks," Packy Wilson said, "only not in bars you work, Joe. He drinks in the good joints, the Clubs over in the Village and down Little Italy."

"The racket-owned places?" I said.

"If he's who I think, and it sounds like him," Packy said.

"Who?" I said. "Or are we guessing?"

"Olsen," Packy said. "Lars Olsen. They call him Swede only he's Norwegian, I think."

"Jo-Jo's old man?" I said. There is a big difference between not looking for a missing son, and trying to stop someone else from looking. Good or bad, Jo-Jo had some kind of trouble.

"Yeah," Packy said. "It was Jo-Jo told me they was really Norwegian. The kid come in here for a beer sometimes. He was real hipped on the Vikings and all, that's how he come to tell me they was Norwegians not Swedes."

"Vikings?" I said. "Jo-Jo knew history?"

"The kid knew the Vikings," Packy said. "Read all them old Sagas he said. He used to say they was tough, and brave, and always won because they was daring and could outsail anyone. He said they never took no handouts from no one."

I listened to Packy, but I was thinking of something else. In my mind Jo-Jo Olsen was moving down two streets. It didn't make sense. Everything that had happened, the events, put Jo-Jo more-and-more into trouble, some kind of trouble. But everything I heard about Jo-Jo made it more-and-more clear that he did not sound like a kid who would get into trouble.

"Those old kings sure had names," Packy said, remembering. "Harald the Stern, Sweyn Blue-Tooth, Halfdan The Black, Gorm The Old. The kid used to rattle them off like they tasted good just to say. He said that today was nothing, his old man even let guys call him Swede and didn't give a damn."

"History and motors and racing," I said. I was talking to myself. I rubbed the stump of my arm where sweat from the heat had made it sore. No record, history, motors, a bank account, and maybe joining Ferrari in Italy just didn't sound like either a cop-beater or a rabbit.

"They never come in here much," Packy said. "The old man is too good for the place, and the kid is saving his dough."

I needed a key, a link that would connect motors and racing and dreams of Ferrari in Italy, with a mugging-robbery of a cop that might make a man do a rabbit.

"Maybe saving his money wasn't fast enough," I said.

And Packy gave it to me. The possible zinger, the "maybe tie-in between a vanished kid, an angry father, and a mugged cop."

"You think maybe it was Jo-Jo pulled that job on the dame?" Packy said. "You know, I was thinking about that myself."

"What job?" I said.

"The couple-of-grand jewel heist down on Water Street," Packy said. "Maybe you didn't hear. The Man got it under the cool for some reason. Not much, just a few grand take, but the dame got killed. In one of them new buildings."

New York is a peculiar city. Most big cities have slums and rich areas, but the rivers make New York special. Manhattan is an island, so there isn't much space to move in, and the whole city moves in slow circles from good to bad to good and back to bad. You end up with tenements, businesses, factories, and luxury buildings all on the same block.

Water Street is a slum street near the river that is getting good again. There are three new apartment houses on the street, a lot of old-law tenements—and Schmidt's Garage. It is also on the beat of Patrolman Stettin. It is the street where Stettin got hit. Now it had another robbery, and a killing.

I waited until next morning to pay a call on Captain Gazzo down at Homicide.

"The killing and robbery happened the same day our man was mugged, Kelly," Gazzo said. "We made the connection too."

Gazzo is an old cop. He says he's crazy because the world he lives in is crazy and you have to be crazy to handle it. He says he wouldn't know what to do with a sane person, he never gets to meet any. He includes me with the crazy. Maybe he knows.

"Jo-Jo Olsen," I said. "He's done a rabbit it looks like."

"Olsen?" Gazzo said as if listening to the sound. "Any part of Swede Olsen?"

"Son," I said. "I think Swede doesn't like me."

I told him about the inefficient mangler of last night. He seemed interested, but with Gazzo you can't tell. I've known him over twenty years, and I don't know if he likes me or hates me. With Gazzo it doesn't make any difference, he does his job.

"The kid worked at Schmidt's Garage?" Gazzo said.

"He did," I said.

"Interesting," Gazzo said.

"Tell me about the murder, robbery and cop-jumping?" I said.

"I thought you gave up on the world?" Gazzo said.

"I try," I said, "but it just hangs around. What have you got, Captain."

Gazzo had a file, but it was thin. A woman named Myra Jones was robbed and killed. Fake name, Caucasian, 22 years old, blonde, five-foot-eight, profession: model and chorus girl. Two diamond rings and a diamond necklace stolen, value about $2800, nothing else missing and plenty left behind. She lived alone in a four room luxury apartment in a non-doorman building on Water Street with a self-service elevator. Death was quick from a massive brain hemorrhage. No suspects on record.

"It looks like a grab and run unintentional killing," Gazzo explained. "The stolen stuff must have been lying open, a lot more was left behind inside an unopened jewelry box. The girl hit her head on the corner of an andiron in front of one of those fake fireplaces. She hit hard. There was a big bruise on her chin."

"She surprised him in her pad, he panicked and hit too hard," I said.

"That's the way it reads right now," Gazzo said. "No one saw him leave who's talking to us. He went out the back way and into an alley from the look of it. Tell me about the Olsen kid."

"What could he see?" I said. "Two rings and a necklace don't show. Schmidt's Garage is at the other end of the block."

"Maybe he recognized the guy," Gazzo said.

"What, just walking on the street?" I said. "You just said the guy ducked out the alley. If he just killed a woman, he'd have been pretty careful not to be seen by anyone who knew him."

"Accidents happen, Kelly," Gazzo said drily.

For myself I was thinking about Swede Olsen. There aren't many men you would see on the street, just walking, and wonder what they were doing. But your father you might. For some reason this did not seem to have occurred to Gazzo, and I wasn't about to bring it up.

"What about the cop?" I said. "Maybe he saw the burglar and was slugged for that?"

Gazzo rubbed his chin. He needed a shave. He usually did need a shave unless City Hall wanted to see him. Gazzo took some acid in the face twelve years ago, and his skin is tender. The Captain was shaking his head.

"No one ever accused our men of being *slow* on the trigger, Kelly," Gazzo said. "If Stettin had seen anything there would have been a rumpus. And why would our killer just knock him out and rob him? Anyway, he's okay now, and he can't tell us anything."

"He was just jumped?" I said. "Persons unknown?"

"Unknown, unseen, and unexplained," Gazzo said sourly. "Poor Stettin is embarrassed. He's an eager rookie. It hurts him to have been slugged and not even guess why."

"Clues?" I asked. "That you can talk about?"

Gazzo grinned. "Clues? Sure, we got a clue. A losing stub on a slow nag at Monmouth Park the day before the job. It was the only thing we found didn't belong to the lady or her lover."

"Thanks," I said. Monmouth Park is a popular track. I'd hate to be chased down a dark street by half the losers there in a single day. "What about the times?"

Gazzo checked his file. "Woman died between five and six in the afternoon. Stettin was hit about six-thirty." And Gazzo looked up at me. "The kid play the horses?"

"Cars and motorcycles are his line," I said. I got up to leave. I had a breakfast date with Marty, and I hate to keep her waiting when she feels friendly. "I don't really see Olsen in this, Gazzo. I don't even know he's run. His family say he's just on a trip."

"Swede Olsen was only trying to give his boy some privacy, eh?" Gazzo said.

"Maybe he just doesn't like people talking to the cops about his family," I said.

"I believe that much," Gazzo said.

I left Gazzo putting in a call on Jo-Jo Olsen.

Out in the street I headed for the subway. The more I looked at it, the less I could see Jo-Jo in the robberies or the killing. I didn't think Gazzo could either. Police work on patterns, records, the facts. Jo-Jo had no record, and the pattern stank. In Chelsea kids are born knowing better than to pull a job on their own block—and then point the finger at themselves by running.

But it looked like Jo-Jo *was* running. Swede Olsen was worried. I thought again about the older Olsen, but it played rotten. If Swede was the killer, he should have run not Jo-Jo. Why would a boy run just because he knew too much about his father? Afraid? I doubted that. Ashamed? That was possible, but I didn't like it. If Swede was a thief, and Jo-Jo knew it, one accidental killing wouldn't be likely to bring sudden shame.

Since it wasn't noon yet, I had plenty of time for my breakfast date with Marty, so I took the local north. The local is more comfortable, there's more room to stand. While the local rattled, I went over it all again. The way it appeared now, I couldn't fit it to Jo-Jo, so maybe there was another way to look at it all.

I didn't like the way Myra Jones had died. You'd be surprised how few burglars panic—unless they are amateurs or junkies. Jo-Jo was an amateur, but he wasn't a junkie. I never heard of a junkie with money in the bank, or who needs wheels to roll.

I didn't much like the robbery. The thief had gotten in and out totally unseen and undetected, not a trace left behind. And yet the haul had been peanuts.

I didn't like two violent crimes on the same block so close together—but unconnected. Somewhere there should be a connection between the robbery and the attack on Officer Stettin.

By the time I climbed out of the subway into the 90° cool of Sixth Avenue, I was working on the other side. Burglars did panic. Junkies made clever but sloppy robberies, and grabbed and ran. And unconnected crimes happened on the same block every day in New York.

To wash it all away I stopped in a tavern a block from Marty's place. There was still a half an hour until noon and a decent breakfast hour for Marty. I planned to relax and think about her and get into the mood. Burglaries were a dime a dozen, the cop had probably written a ticket and got someone mad, and Jo-Jo Olsen had probably had a fight with his old lady. Marty was much better food for the inner man.

But they knew me in this saloon. Before I had a chance to blow the foam off my beer, I had heard all about Petey Vitanza. Marty isn't the kind of woman you forget about for any reason, so I called her and told her I'd be late. She didn't like it, and neither did I.

I like bars. Everything is cool and dim and simple in a man's relation to a glass of beer. And I don't like hospitals. But I left that bar and took a taxi down to St. Vincent's because I liked Petey Vitanza.

THEY TOLD ME that Petey would see again. He wasn't blind, it only looked that way. His face wasn't a face, it was a bandage. They had broken both arms. But the real serious damage was the splintered ribs and the internal injuries.

"Very complete job," the doctor said. "I had a case on the Bowery, but this is more complete."

The cops were there, since it was pretty clear that Petey had not fallen down some stairs. One old cop agreed that it was a good beating, but not professional.

"Amateurs," the old cop said. "They used their hands. Too much blood and damage without enough pain. Just amateurs."

Petey could not talk, but he could hear. They give me two minutes. They said that he would probably live and I could ask him more questions later. I asked him if he had known the ones who beat him. He shook his head, negative. I asked him if it had been anything to do with Jo-Jo Olsen, and he nodded that it had. I asked him if it had any connection to the robbery-killing, or the cop-mugging, and he seemed agitated. He passed out then.

When I came out of the hospital it was still summer and hot. It seemed that it should have been dark and cold.

At that point I didn't really care about Jo-Jo Olsen, or about law and order. But I cared about Petey Vitanza and men who would, or could, beat a boy that badly. It's like politics for me—I don't care much about Anti-Poverty Crusades by politicians, but I care a lot about the poor.

I had let enough normal lack-of-interest in another man's troubles slow me down. Now it was time to go to work. It was time to find Jo-Jo Olsen, and I had one new fact to go on. Petey knew Swede Olsen, and he had not known who beat him. Which meant that someone else had a strong interest in Jo-Jo Olsen beside his doting father.

It was past time to meet Swede Olsen and family formally. Not that I expected the Swedish Norwegian to want to tell me much. The big older Olsen had tried to dissuade my interest in Jo-Jo forcefully. The question was: was it only me he wanted to keep away from Jo-Jo, or was *all* outside interest a worry to him?

When I walked up to the building on Nineteenth Street, I was not surprised to find that the Olsens lived in the best big apartment in a not-too-good building near the river. And I was not surprised to find Swede at home at mid-day. Both Gazzo and Lieutenant Marx seemed to know Olsen, and from what Petey Vitanza had told me I had already guessed that the Olsens were not a hard working family.

Swede Olsen *was* surprised. The big man took one look at me and clenched his large fist. I dangled my not-so-large Police Special in my hand. I didn't point the gun, you understand, I just showed it. He had the muscles. I had the equalizer. He scowled, but he stepped back and let me walk inside.

"What you want, Kelly?" Olsen growled.

I looked around. The apartment was big and ugly. Not lack-of-money ugly, but just plain rotten-taste ugly. It fitted. I mean, everything about Olsen and his apartment talked of enough money but not much experience in spending the money wisely. The place had cost a lot to furnish, but it still looked like a slum room. The rent in such a building would be high for our section, but low for anywhere else.

Swede himself looked like a slob, and yet Packy Wilson said the big man went to the expensive bars for his beers. The whole picture was of making money too late. And the woman who came into the living room now fitted right in. She looked like one of those Okie women in *Grapes of Wrath*, except that her clothes had cost a bundle and her hands were clean. Too late. The woman had money for clothes and clean hands now, but the hands had been ruined long ago, and the years had left her nothing to hang the clothes on but a bag of old bones.

"Stay out of this, Magda," Olsen snapped at the woman.

"It's my business," the woman said. She looked at me as if I was a cockroach she knew too well. "You the one askin' about my boy?"

"I'm one of them," I said. "I'm the one who doesn't play so rough. The others are the mean type."

"Get lost," the woman said.

I turned to Olsen. "You don't want your boy found?"

"Who said he's missing?" the woman said.

"I say he's missing," I said. "The question I can't answer is the one about if he's missing from you, Mrs. Olsen."

"He ain't, Kelly," Olsen said.

"Then where is he? If the other guys find him they might play rougher."

There was a long silence. I watched them. Olsen looked unhappy, and he was sweating. The woman looked like the rock of Gibraltar. Olsen looked worried. The woman, Mrs. Olsen, looked determined. I got a funny feeling—they were worried about themselves, not about Jo-Jo.

"What did he run for?" I asked.

"He ain't run," Mrs. Olsen said. "Beat it."

"Did he jump that cop?" I snapped.

"No," Olsen said, cried, and realized he had shot his mouth off. He looked green. His wife, Magda Olsen, glared at him.

"He did nothing. He took a trip," Magda Olsen said.

I was ready to go on with the dance when the two boys came into the room. They were both big and both young. They looked enough like Swede to tell me I was looking at Jo-Jo's brothers. A pretty girl behind them told me Jo-Jo had at least one sister. The girl was pretty, but the boys weren't.

"Take off," Olsen said.

I went. But all the way down the stairs and out into the mid-afternoon sun, I knew I had learned a lot. They were worried. Not worried about Jo-Jo, but about themselves. All of them, as if they were all in some kind of collective trouble, but not police-type trouble. They were *angry* worried, not *scared* worried.

And they were not surprised that others were looking for Jo-Jo. Olsen knew Jo-Jo had not beaten and robbed Officer Stettin, and I had a pretty strong hunch that he knew who had. Olsen didn't like what he knew. The old lady, Magda Olsen, didn't like it all either, but she was standing pat. They were all like people on eggshells. They didn't want to breathe if that would rock the boat.

Only what was the boat? I'd have staked my reputation on them being clean about the killing and mugging. So it had to be that they *knew* something they wished they didn't know, and that maybe Jo-Jo knew it, too. Then why had only Jo-Jo run? And what was there about a simple robbery-murder, and even a cop-mugging, that knowing it would worry Olsen and his family so much? It didn't figure a small-time heist man would worry them.

It was a good question, and I thought about it all the way across town in the sun. A good question, and I got a good answer a lot faster than I expected.

I told you that Marty was my girl. I had kept her waiting all day. Or maybe it'd be truer to say I'd kept myself waiting. I liked Petey Vitanza, but a man has to think of himself. It was too late for breakfast at Marty's pad, so I met her at *O. Henry's*. Outside, at one of the sidewalk cafe tables.

I needed a drink by then, two drinks, and Marty matched me all the way. She's not so pretty, Marty, not really, but under the lights, and to me, she's beautiful.

"That's what counts," I said. "To your audience and your man you're beautiful."

I got a nice smile. She's small, and this month she was a redhead, and she's built. But the real thing is she's exciting, you know? She's alive, she never stops moving even sitting there doing nothing. When I'm with her she keeps me busy. That was why I missed Pappas until he was sitting down at the table.

I'VE KNOWN ANDY Pappas all my life. We're the same age, we grew up together on the river, we stole together, we learned to like girls together and we graduated high school together. Andy, me, and Joe Harris. That was where it ended. Joe is poor and hardworking. I'm poor and not so hardworking. Andy is rich and no one knows what he works at.

I mean, Andy is a boss. For the record, Andy Pappas is boss of a big stevedoring company on the docks. Off the record, Andy is the boss of something else. Everyone knows this something else is a racket and illegal. Only no one really knows just what Andy's racket is. He's got a piece of a lot of dirty pies, is my guess, but the main one is keeping the riverfront peaceful. He gets the ships unloaded—for a price and by force.

"Hello, Patrick," Pappas said. He's got a nice voice, low and even. He took lessons everyone says, but I remember he always had a good voice.

"Hello, Andy," I said. I nodded to Marty that she should leave. Andy grinned.

"Let the lady stay, I've seen her work," Andy Pappas said. "Besides, we're friends, right, Patrick?"

"You don't have a friend, Andy," I said. "You're the enemy of everyone."

Pappas nodded. He did not stop smiling. It was an old story with us.

"You don't soften up, do you, Pat?" Pappas said.

"And you never change," I said. "This isn't a social visit."

I nodded toward the lamppost a few feet away. It was one of those old gaslight lampposts *O. Henry's* had put up for atmosphere. Just leaning against it, pretending he was watching the little girl tourists pass, was Jake Roth. Roth wasn't watching girls, he was watching me. They say that Andy Pappas never carries a gun. But Jake Roth went to bed with a shoulder holster under his pajama top. Roth is Pappas's first lieutenant and top killer.

Across the street I could see Max Bangio. Bangio is Pappas's next best gun after Roth, and the little gunman was trying to read a newspaper in front of the stationery store by spelling out the words in the headline. Actually, Bangio was watching me in the store-front window.

Just up the block toward Sheridan Square, Pappas's long, black car was parked in front of a Japanese knick-knack shop. The driver sat behind the wheel with his cap down and his arms folded. I didn't need a ouija board to know that there was a pistol ready beneath those folded arms.

Pappas shrugged. "You said it, Patrick, everyone's my enemy."

"That isn't exactly what I said, but let it pass. What's on your mind, Andy?"

"Let's have a drink first, Patrick. You're my friend if I'm not yours," Pappas said.

"I don't drink with you, Andy. Those days went a long time ago," I said.

I know I go too far with Pappas. There was that glint in his cold eyes. I've seen it before, and I push too hard. It's not brave to refuse to back off from a mad dog, it's stupid. But with Andy I can't help it. I know him, and that makes it worse. It's one thing to hear about Andy Pappas and hate him, and another to really know him and hate him. I feel guilty around him, because in some way I failed and he's my fault. I have to share the blame.

I can't back off from Pappas, tread softly, because he is what is wrong with it all. A man like Andy Pappas is where we went off the track. All the men like Andy who believe that all that counts is some advantage, some victory, some success, here and now, no matter how or who gets hurt. The men who will destroy us all just to try to win something even if only King of The Graveyard.

"All right, Pat," Pappas said at last, "I'll make it short. Lay off Olsen and his family."

And there was the answer. Somehow, Andy Pappas was mixed up with this. If I were the Olsens I would be worried, too. I'm not the Olsens, and I knew nothing, and I was still worried as I watched Pappas.

"Why?" I said.

"Olsen works for me," Pappas said.

"Olsen?" I said, and the question was clear.

"Odd jobs, driving, stuff like that," Pappas said. "But he gets my protection."

"Does he need it now, Andy?" I said.

Pappas laughed. "Look, Patrick. I don't know everything. I don't want to know everything. All I know is that Olsen doesn't want you bothering him or his boys, okay?"

"Did he tell you why I'm bothering him?" I said.

"I didn't talk to him," Andy Pappas said. "I got the request through channels. If it was anyone except you, I'd have sent a punk to tell you."

"His boy's done a rabbit," I said.

"So it's a family matter," Pappas said. "Since when you work for the cops on a rabbit?"

"I'm not working for the cops," I said. "I'm working for a nice kid who wants to find his friend. A nice kid who got beaten ninety-percent to death today. You wouldn't know about that, would you, Andy?"

"I don't beat ninety percent, Pat," Pappas said. Pappas stood up. He was smiling, but his eyes were not smiling. "He's got my protection, Patrick, remember that."

When Pappas stands up it is a signal. I heard the motor start in the big car up the block. Max Bagnio crossed the street toward us. Jake Roth stepped up to the table. Roth never took his eyes off me. I watched Pappas.

"Olsen must be in real trouble, Andy," I said.

Jake Roth answered me. The tall, skinny killer leaned half down like a long-necked vulture. He stank of sweat.

"Listen, peeper, Mr. Pappas said lay off, forget it, you got that? Mr. Pappas said cool it, he means cool it. Forget you ever heard about Olsen."

Roth's black, luminous eyes seemed to float in water. His breath was thick, his breathing fast as he bent close to me. Andy Pappas touched Roth lightly. The skinny gunman jerked upright like a puppet on a string.

"I told him, Jake, that's enough," Andy Pappas said. "You can tell Olsen that Kelly got the word."

Roth nodded. Max Bagnio said nothing. The black car slid up to the curb. Andy Pappas touched his hat to Marty, and climbed into the back of his car. Roth climbed in beside him, and Max Bagnio went around to get in beside the driver. The car eased away into the traffic and turned uptown on Sixth Avenue. I didn't breathe until it was gone. Then I ordered a double for both of us. Marty was still staring after Pappas.

"I know you know him," Marty said, "but I'm surprised every time. Just seeing him makes me shiver."

"Join the club," I said.

The drinks came and we were busy gulping for a long minute. Then I sighed, let out my breath, and smiled as I sat back. Marty still looked toward where the black car had vanished.

"How can you talk to him like that, Patrick," Marty said.

"I can't talk to him any other way," I said. "What I never really understood is why he lets me. I guess even Andy needs to think he has some human feeling. I'm his charity."

Marty shuddered. "But now," she said. "I could hardly look at him. I heard he was almost insane he was so mad."

"Mad?" I said. "Now? Why now, Marty?"

"His girlfriend was killed, Patrick," Marty said.

"Killed? But Andy's married," I said slowly.

Marty gave me a withering look. "I never heard that marriage had much to do with a girlfriend, except to make it harder on the girl."

"How was she killed, Marty?" I said. "How do you know about it?"

I had forgotten my thirst. I was not holding my breath because I had no breath to hold. I was seeing Andy Pappas's smiling face as he told me to lay off the Olsens. I was remembering the thick air of worry in the Olsens' apartment.

"I know because she worked sometimes at the Club. Not much, she had no talent. Just a pretty girl," Marty said. "She had to tell someone about Pappas. She was a dumb girl."

"Did Pappas kill her?" I said.

"I don't know, Patrick. They say not. They told me it was just an accident, during a robbery," Marty said.

"Myra Jones," I said.

"You knew her?" Marty said.

"No," I said.

So there it was. I could imagine a sneak thief learning that he had killed the mistress of Andy Pappas. I could imagine the problems of *anyone* involved. Jo-Jo Olsen? I did not want to think about it. But I had to think, and I still did not see Jo-Jo Olsen as a thief. But I saw him as a witness. Everyone in Chelsea knew Andy Pappas. Men had killed their mistresses for thousands of years.

I wanted to talk to Gazzo.

CAPTAIN GAZZO LEANED back and shrugged when I walked in and told him what I knew. Gazzo looked tired, too tired to amuse himself with me.

"Why didn't you tell me she was Pappas's girl?" I said.

"You didn't ask, and it was none of your business," Gazzo said. "As a matter of fact, it still isn't your business."

"It might have saved a boy from almost being killed", I said.

"I doubt it," Gazzo said. "Pappas is pretty busted up."

"I'll bet," I said. "It's a classic, Gazzo. Andy always was jealous."

"If anyone got the Vitanza kid beat up it was you," Gazzo said. "You went around looking for Jo-Jo Olsen."

"I mean Pappas," I said. "It's a thousand to one he killed her! Who would kill Andy Pappas's girl friend?"

"No," Gazzo said.

I blinked. "No, what?"

"No, Pappas didn't kill her," Gazzo said.

I laughed. "Alibi? Of course Andy would have an alibi!"

Gazzo swore. "Knock it off, Kelly. Don't you think I've been around long enough to know a real air-tight alibi when I see one?"

"I'll listen," I said.

Gazzo smiled. "Andy Pappas was in Washington in front of a Congressional Committee at the exact time. He'd been there all day, and he was there half the night."

"All right, he had it done," I said. "That would be perfect. Pappas would pick just such a time. Were all his boys with him?"

"No," Gazzo said. "But they all have alibis."

"Sure. Each other, probably."

"No, Roth was at the Jersey shore swimming. Bagnio was in Philadelphia. All the others were in Washington or somewhere else they can prove."

"Air-tight alibis?" I said.

"Not like Pappas," Gazzo said. "No one saw any of them who could not be bought, I admit it. Roth has the best. Jake says he was on the beach all day. We checked that his car never left the shore. Bagnio was seen, off and on, in Philly, but only by other hoods. The rest can account for a lot of their time, but not all."

"It's got to be Pappas himself!" I said. I suppose I wanted it to be Andy. It's nice to think that evil always trips itself up; that a human monster like Andy Pappas would finally be betrayed by his one weakness—that he was, after all, human, and not a pure monster.

"I was there when we told him," Gazzo said. "I saw him. Pappas almost fainted when we broke it. I know real shock when I see it. He cried, Kelly. I mean, Pappas really cried."

"Touching," I said, but I wasn't as hard as I sounded. It was just that I wanted Andy to make the mistake that way. I wanted Andy to get it from something as stupid and simple as a jealous rage; some lousy little mistake anyone could make. I wanted it real bad.

"Give us some credit, Kelly," Gazzo said wearily. "I've been a cop a long time. The Man isn't all stupid, no matter what you hear around the city. We checked it all ways and upside down. Everything says that Pappas was really hooked on the girl, treated her almost like a daughter."

"Daughters cheat," I said, because I was still hoping.

"We dug deep, Kelly," Gazzo said. "There isn't a whisper that Pappas might have done it. A year ago he caught her holding hands with a young punk. He didn't do anything except tell the kid to get lost, and tell the Jones girl to choose. She's dumb, but not that dumb. She chose Pappas."

I had nothing to say.

"Think of the odds, Kelly," Gazzo said.

"What odds?" I said.

"The odds that a guy who meant to kill her would have been able to do it with one punch that happened to make her hit her head on an andiron. The Medical Examiner says it just about couldn't have been done any other way. The odds against it being deliberate, the way it happened, are so big you'd laugh."

"He knocked her out," I said, "and then belted her with the andiron. Then he arranged it to look good."

Gazzo shook his head. "The M.E. says it's possible, but only barely. I say it's impossible because the andiron had not been touched. It had clear, unsmudged prints of the girl and her maid, and no one else. It had not been wiped. It still had dust on it."

I gave up. Even Andy Pappas could not arrange for a girl to be killed by a real accident. I still had enough problems without Andy.

"Damn it, Gazzo, *someone* is looking for Jo-Jo Olsen," I said. "And I don't think it's some sneak thief or junkie. The kid has run, Pappas and the Olsen family are involved with each other, and Pappas's girl is dead. It's too much coincidence. Jo-Jo Olsen knows *something*."

"We'll know it too when we find him," Gazzo said.

"If we find him," I said.

I was thinking of the others looking for Jo-Jo. At least they were still looking. Which meant that Jo-Jo was not in some shallow grave yet—or he had not been about noon today.

I thought about them, the ones who had beaten Petey Vitanza, all the way down and out into the evening streets of the city. The old cop at the hospital had called them amateurs. He was probably right, and Andy Pappas did not use amateurs.

It was now evening, the city cooled down to a nice 89° in the shade, and I was getting a theory. I took a taxi uptown to get a wind in my face and think better. By the time the cab got to Fourth Street and Sixth Avenue I had the theory down solid. I looked in at *O.Henry's*, but Marty was gone. I went on down the block and into the dingy plebian silence of *Fugazy's Tavern*.

I had an Irish with my theory.

What had been wrong all along was the small-time nature of the bit. In Chelsea even the best of kids would not fink to the cops over a small-time robbery and accidental killing. Mind your own dirt is the motto here. Kids drink it from the bottle. No one would have been really afraid that Jo-Jo Olsen would run to the cops over such a crime—and the Olsens had the protection of Andy Pappas. If all it was was a simple robbery-killing, then silencing Jo-Jo would have been more dangerous than the original crime.

But Myra Jones had been Andy Pappas's girl. That changed it. Now the killer of the Jones girl had a reason to be scared. Now he had a reason to silence any witness. Now the Olsens had a reason to worry: two reasons. First, that the original killer might be after Jo-Jo. Second, that Pappas might be after Jo-Jo! It wasn't the cops the unknown killer was afraid of, it was Andy Pappas!

That was my new theory, and it made a lot of sense, but I didn't like it. There was still too much that rattled. A big loose piece was the killer himself—a small-timer who killed a woman in a robbery, and found out she was Pappas's girl, should have run far and fast. It was double-jeopardy: a felony murder that carried the chair; and a capital offense against Pappas that carried maybe worse than the chair. A small-time jewel thief would have run, not hung around trying to cover. Penny-ante crooks don't hire men to work for them, and I couldn't see even amateurs letting themselves be hired to get mixed up in the killing of Andy Pappas's woman!

The second big rattler was that the Olsens were tight with Pappas. If Jo-Jo knew something about who had killed Pappas's girl, why not tell Pappas? Even if Jo-Jo himself were not part of the Pappas-Olsen scene, he would have no reason to protect a killer from Pappas. From the cops, yes, that was the code, but tipping Pappas would only get him a medal, especially from his old man Swede Olsen.

Unless the killer was Swede Olsen! I could see Jo-Jo saving his father. But I could not buy Swede as the killer—he was not *that* worried.

Pappas himself was out as the killer, which was too bad because that would have explained it all. If I knew Pappas was a killer, I'd fly not run.

If Jo-Jo was the killer that would explain it all, too. But in this world you have to go on more than facts, and I did not see the Olsen kid as the man.

Which left me still nowhere, and with my one last big question: Officer Stettin. Somehow the mugged cop figured in this. He had to. You have to go on probability in this world. The pivot, the center, of this mess was Water Street. That street was all that Myra Jones, Pappas, Jo-Jo Olsen, Petey Vitanza and the unknown killer had in common. And Patrolman Stettin had Water Street, too.

I finished my Irish and headed across toward the river. The block I wanted on Water Street was right on top of the river. It was still twilight when I got there. I stood at the head of the block and looked down it toward the docks.

The apartment house stood up like a giant among shabby pygmies half way down the block. The other two good buildings were across the street and nearer to me. The alley beside the good building where Myra Jones had been killed opened on both Water Street and Sand Street behind it. Which meant that the killer had not come out on Water Street unless he was crazy.

Schmidt's Garage was all the way down at the far end and across the street. Cars were parked on both sides of the block, bumper to bumper at this hour, except in front of driveways and two loading docks. There was a light in Schmidt's office. And I thought of Schmidt. Maybe he had seen, or knew, something.

I was the second one to get that idea.

THEY HAD WORKED the old man over before they killed him. I don't think they meant to kill him. Amateurs again. His grey hair lay in a pool of blood that had poured from his nose and mouth. Blood that was still wet. I didn't look to see what they had done in detail to get him to talk. I called Gazzo.

Then I walked out into Water Street again. The old man had not told them, I was sure of that. He had not been killed on purpose after talking. He had died while they were still asking. Either he was, or had been, tough, or he had not known what they wanted. I figured it was the last. Schmidt had not known what they had killed him to find out.

I took deep breaths in the twilight of Water Street. I lighted a cigarette. At times like this the dangers of cigarettes don't seem so big. You have to live a while for the coffin-nails to kill you, and I'm not sure many of us are going to make it. The guys who control the bombs wear better clothes and speak better in more languages than the killers who worked Schmidt over, but they are the same kind of men.

Then I saw the cop. A patrolman walking lazily along the block. Officer Stettin's replacement until Stettin got back to work. This cop had his billy in his hand and was idly batting tires with it as he passed the parked cars. He stopped in front of the loading docks, and at the fire hydrants, and looked real close at the cars parked on either side of the open spaces. He seemed annoyed that no one had parked illegally.

That was when I heard the click in my head. Like a piece suddenly slipping into place in a busted motor. All of a sudden, the motor hummed as smooth as silk in my brain. The piece had fitted like a glove. The old missing link. I dropped my smoking butt into the gutter, and headed back toward the brighter lights of the avenues. I looked for a taxi, but there weren't any except six Off-Duty whizzers, and I walked all the way to St. Vincent's.

It took me ten minutes, but they finally let me see Petey Vitanza. He was propped in bed like a side of meat wrapped in cheesecloth. He could talk now. He could not see yet, and his words were like the speech of an idiot with a rag stuffed in his mouth, but he could talk.

"That day, Pete," I said. "The day before Jo-Jo ran, what were you doing?"

The boy shrugged.

"Anything and everything," I said. "They killed Schmidt."

Behind the bandages Petey did not move. Then his eyeless head nodded. His thick voice was shaky. They could easily come back.

"Two ... of ... them," he said, or he said something like that and I was able to translate. "Big guy ... fat ... with muscles. Twenty-five, dark hair, scar ... on his eye. Other guy ... maybe twenty ... real good build ... lifts weights type ... blond. Punks ... tryin' for the big ... time ... yeh."

I could fill in the picture. Two young hangers-on, eager to get in the "organization," and ready to do anything to please. Amateurs who wanted to be pros and live the good life. And that meant the one who had hired them was a man who could do them favors, get them "inside." It fitted with what I had had in mind.

"That day," I said.

Petey shrugged again. "Work ... on the bike. Same as always. Just work on the ... bike."

"At Schmidt's?" I said.

"Yeh ... the steering ... I remember," Petey said, nodded as eagerly as he could with a plaster neck. "Jo-Jo was doing ... turns ... you know, like figure ... eights and ... all."

"And you needed space?" I said. "You needed room to run the bike."

"Yeh, sure ... so ...?"

The angle of his head showed a question. I answered it.

"So you moved a car, maybe a couple of cars. You ..." I began.

I could not see his eyes, but I know that Petey blinked. It was just one of those little things that happen every day that you never remember you did. Like which car you got onto when you took the subway uptown. Like walking to the corner to drop your empty cigarette pack into a basket. Like nicking yourself shaving, and then wondering how blood got on your collar.

"One car," Petey said. "We shoved it down by the loading dock. We ... needed room ... to make ... the turns. A small ... black convertible ... guy left the brake ... off. Jo-Jo he saw ... the cop ..."

"And he took the ticket off," I said, because that was the click I had heard when I had watched that cop on Water Street. "The cop, Stettin, ticketed the car because you had shoved it into a No Parking zone. Jo-Jo got worried. He took the ticket off so the owner wouldn't get mad."

Petey nodded. "I forgot all ..."

"Yeh, of course. It was funny at the time," I said. "You shoved a car and it got a ticket. Only you had been on the street all day, and Jo-Jo figured the owner of the car would guess who had shoved his car, moved it. So he grabbed the ticket off, and you both beat it. Did you know whose car it was?"

Petey shook his head. No, the two kids would not have known at the time. But I guessed that Jo-Jo had found out later. He had grabbed the ticket, figuring that by the time the police got in touch with the car-owner, no one would remember the day. But he must have done a bad job.

"He must have left the string on the wipers, or wherever it was," I said. "The owner came back and saw the string. He knew he had been ticketed. That placed him on the spot, on that block, at that time. That was why he mugged Officer Stettin—to steal the summons book. The rest was window dressing."

It all fitted like a polished mechanism. And, of course, the killer was no burglar. I had not really believed he was a burglar all along. The grabbed jewels were a cover, grabbed after Myra had died. As smooth and simple as one of those Japanese *haiku* poems.

A man called on Myra Jones. A man who had an argument with her and hit her and she died by accident. A man who went out through the alley, circled the block, and came back to Water Street to his car. Only his car had been moved and ticketed! A man who knew there was a record of the ticket in Stettin's summons book. He jumped Stettin and stole the book. Then he went looking for the original ticket and the person who had taken it.

This left me with three questions: who, why he was so worried about the presence of his car being known, and how Jo-Jo Olsen had learned that the ticket was a danger. I had a pretty good idea of all three answers.

I did not know exactly *who*, but I had a picture. A man big enough to be able to hire men to go against Andy Pappas. A man who would beat and even kill to get what he wanted. A man the Olsens knew. Someone big enough to risk two-timing Andy Pappas with Myra, but not big enough to want Pappas to know.

Because that was the second answer. The mere presence of his car would not be enough for the police to nail him. The police would have to place him, somehow, in the apartment. No, the answer to why he was so worried about the ticket, had to be that it would tell *Pappas* he had been with Myra. Which meant that he was a man with an alibi, an alibi not intended to cover the killing, which had not been premeditated, but to cover that he was seeing Myra!

This left me with a sub-question. How would a summons have told Pappas? A summons would come back to the owner of the car. I thought I knew that, too, but I would find out for sure when I checked out my last question. How had Jo-Jo learned the danger of that ticket?

I had reached Swede Olsen's apartment before I had finished all those interesting thoughts. I had made a straight, fast passage from St. Vincent's to the Olsen pad. The big Swede and his sons were no happier to see me this time. The mother, Magda, was less happy than anyone. I faced her vicious face, and the clenched fists behind her.

Before they could swing into action I hit them with the crusher.

"What was it, Olsen? Was Jake Roth driving one of Pappas's own cars the day he killed Myra?"

Because I had remembered what Gazzo had said: Jake Roth's car never left the Jersey Shore that day. Roth had an alibi, he had been on the beach and his car had not moved. And Roth would have known Myra, could hire men afraid enough of *him* to risk bucking Pappas, and would kill to keep Andy Pappas from knowing what had really happened to Myra Jones.

IT TOOK SWEDE Olsen an hour to tell me what I already had guessed. When they heard what I knew, the man and boys had lost all fight. Only the old woman still would not budge. The girl sat silent in the gaudy, cheap room.

"He's my cousin," Swede Olsen said. "What could I do? His name ain't Roth, its Lindroth. Jake Lindroth, he's Norwegian. The stupid kid showed me the ticket. I knew the license number. I drive a lot for Jake and Mr. Pappas. I recognized the number, and I knew Mr. Pappas was in Washington."

"Roth was playing footsie with Myra Jones?" I asked for the record.

Olsen nodded. "Not really, he just wanted to, you know, Kelly? I mean, he made the pass, went to see her a couple of times. I don't know what happened, but there was a fight, I guess. Jake had used the car because he was supposed to be in Jersey."

"And when he saw that ticket, he was in trouble. The summons would come to Pappas sooner or later," I said. "And Jo-Jo had the original. If Pappas ever got wind of that ticket, he'd know who had been with Myra. I guess Roth was at Monmouth Park the day before?"

"Yeh, he was," Olsen said. "He even told Bagnio what horse he had lost on!"

Like I said, it wasn't the police who scared Roth so much, it was Pappas. That would have scared me, too. It would have been almost a death-warrant to be caught two-timing Pappas, much less killing his girl even by accident.

"How did Roth find out Jo-Jo had the ticket?" I said.

There was a long silence. The men all looked at each other. The old woman stared straight at me. Only the girl looked away. Magda Olsen, the mother, did not flinch.

"Jake Roth is our cousin. Lars works for Mr. Roth," the old woman said. "All this," and she waved her bony old hand around to indicate the whole, grotesque apartment, "is from Jake Roth. We got a duty to help Mr. Roth."

The silence got thicker. I watched the old woman. She gave me her Gibraltar face, a rock of granite.

After a while I said it. "You mean you told Roth? You told him it was Jo-Jo who had the ticket."

Swede Olsen was sweating. "I got to tell Jake. I made Jo-Jo beat it fast, and I told Jake it was okay. I mean, only us and Jo-Jo knew, and we wouldn't tell no one, see? I told Jake I got Jo-Jo safe out of town, he don't got to worry. Jake he was grateful like, he said I was okay."

"Then you come!" Magda Olsen hissed. "You! You got to ask questions, talk to cops! You got to tell them look for Jo-Jo!"

"You got Jake worried!" Olsen snarled.

"You're not worried?" I said.

This time the silence was like thick, sour cream. A room of black, heavy yogurt. If I stood up high enough I could have walked on that silence. All eyes were on the floor except those of the girl and me. I understood, but I didn't want to.

"You mean you really thought Jake Roth would leave Jo-Jo alone?" I said. "You really thought that? Even without the ticket Jo-Jo saw the car!"

"Jake Roth is family," Magda Olsen said.

"A fifty-fifty chance at best," I said. "You give him the ticket, and it's still fifty-fifty he kills Jo-Jo!"

For the first time the young girl, the daughter, spoke. She was pretty, Jo-Jo's sister, and her voice was small, light.

"They don't give him the ticket. Jo-Jo got the ticket," the young girl said.

I guess my mouth hung open.

"Jo-Jo went away. By himself," the girl said. "He wouldn't give the old man the ticket, and he went away."

"Shut up!" Magda Olsen said to her daughter. And she looked at me. "Mr. Roth he says okay. Even without the ticket! He trusts us. Then you! That stupid dirtpig Vitanza! You start asking questions."

"Sandhog," I said, but I got her message. Maybe she was right. Maybe Jake Roth would have trusted the Olsens, even Jo-Jo as long as Jo-Jo never came back. Maybe I did put the boy's neck in the noose, it happens that way when you start stirring up the muddy water in the detective business. But I *had* asked the questions, and the water *had* been stirred.

"Then?" I said. "After I started? You could have told the police, even Pappas. They would have stopped Roth. He's only a cousin and a killer."

Magda Olsen sat as stiff as steel. He voice was old and clear and steady.

"Lars is an old man. We live good. We got five kids. We got a lot to do for five kids. All our life Lars works like a pig on the docks. I work, sweat. We live like animals, now we live good. Lars asks Mr. Roth be a good cousin, get him good work with Mr. Pappas. Roth gets Lars good work.

"Mr. Pappas he is good to us because Roth tells him to be good. In one day for Mr. Pappas Lars he makes more money than two months on the docks! He is too old to go back to the docks! We got five kids, and we only got one Jake Roth!"

What do you say? You feel sick, yes, but what do you say? Do you tell them that no human being risks a child to help Jake Roth? Sure, that's true. Do you say that Lars Olsen and his worn-out old woman should work to death if they must to save their boy? I'm not so sure how true that is. How far is a father responsible for saving his son? How much must a father and mother endure for the mistakes of a child?

It is easy to feel sick when you are not asked to give up all that you want, no matter how rotten it may be. And what about the other four kids? Eh? Do you sacrifice one boy to give four better lives? Lars Olsen, back on the docks at his age, could do nothing for his children. Are you so sure? I'm not. But I made it easy on myself. My duty was to my client.

"You can go to the police now," I said.

"With what, a story? Jo-Jo has the ticket," Magda Olsen said. The old woman had made her decision.

I nodded. It was too late anyway. Roth would have his hired hands searching all over by now. Roth had had a man killed, the police would not take him quickly. But the old women did not rely on me.

"No," Magda Olsen said. "No!"

"Jo-Jo, he'll be okay," Swede Olsen said, but he did not believe it now.

"You don't know where he is?" I said.

"No," the old woman said.

"I do," the young girl said.

She was sitting up straight now, and all eyes turned toward her. A small, pretty young girl. I guessed that she was very close to her brother Jo-Jo.

"He wrote me a card," the girl said.

She handed me the postcard. It was from Daytona Beach, and that fitted. They have a big raceway, speedway for racing cars, at Daytona Beach. The card was unsigned. It said nothing that would show it was from Jo-Jo. Just a few cheery words about the fine weather, the fine racing cars, and a fine job he had selling programs. It could have been from anyone, but the girl knew who it was from.

"I got it yesterday," the girl said. "They didn't tell me about Mr. Roth. I knew Jo-Jo had some trouble, but they didn't tell me."

"We don't want to worry the kids," Swede Olsen explained.

But I was watching the girl. She was telling me something. I felt hollow all the way to my toes because I guessed what it was. I felt like a man on a roller coaster heading far down.

"Roth was here?" I said. "He saw the card?"

"Uncle Jake, we call him Uncle Jake, was here this morning," the girl said. "I didn't tell him, I know Jo-Jo is hiding. But he ..."

"But he saw the card? He read it?" I said.

"I think so. He was in my room. It was on the table," the girl said.

The boys, who had never spoken at all, sat and looked at the floor. The Olsen family had discipline. It did not come from Swede. The big old man blustered.

"Jo-Jo'll be okay. Jake he won't hurt my Jo-Jo," Olsen said. "Jake is okay. Jake is a good man."

He was trying to convince himself still. He was trying to convince his other sons. He was saying he was, after all, a good father and a big man.

The old woman did not bother. She knew. She knew the truth, and she faced it.

I left them sitting there. The old woman got up and went to prepare dinner. She had decided about her life and where her duty lay. I left and began to move in high. I had to if I was to help decide about Jo-Jo's life. I took a taxi to Idlewild.

DAYTONA BEACH WAS hot, and loud, and crowded in the night. There was action at the raceway, and I went straight there from my jet. The only lead I had was that he was selling programs, and I figured that Roth and his men had about two hours on me.

I gave myself that much break because of Schmidt and the jet schedules. Even though Roth had seen the postcard this morning, he apparently hadn't tumbled right away. Otherwise he would not have worked over Schmidt. I guessed that Roth had not known about Jo-Jo's interest in racing, or had forgotten it, and had not thought of it until his boys questioned Schmidt.

Jake Roth was not noted for his brains, that was pretty clear from his play with Myra Jones. I hoped I was right. If I was, the best flight out of New York after the death of Schmidt was only two hours before my jet. Even if I was right, two hours was a long time. It only takes seconds to kill a man.

At the raceway I found that it was closed for the night. That was strike one. I searched around until I found the office. There was light in the office. I went into the office, the door was not locked. My first base hit. I went into the office, the door was not locked. The man behind the desk looked up annoyed.

"Yes?" he snapped.

I showed him my credentials. He was only mildly impressed. He looked at my missing arm.

"Lost it on Iwo-Jima," I told him. "The state don't hold it against me. I'm a real detective."

"Private," he said. "I don't have to tell you anything."

"Unless you want to save the life of one of your program boys," I said.

"Them? Between you and me, mister, they ain't worth saving. Punks, all of them. They takes the job so they can watch the races. Race nuts, all of them. Half the time I finds them up looking at the races instead of selling."

The man was small and red. He had a pet peeve. It was racing and the younger generation. I could see that he hated racing, and hated children. That didn't leave him much to like in his world.

"Talk to me, and I'll take one off your hands," I said. "The name is Olsen. Jo-Jo Olsen. Tall, blond, not bad looking I hear. No telling what he was wearing, and no marks on him. He likes motors. Been here maybe three weeks to a month."

"You just described half of them," the man said. "What the hell's so important about this Olsen anyway?"

It's strange how they always tell you but don't actually get around to saying it. The man had just told me I was still running second.

"Someone else was here?" I said.

"All night I get nuts," the man said.

"How many of them? I mean, how many who asked about Olsen?"

"Two," he said.

"Tell me about them?" I said.

He described the two who had beaten Petey Vitanza. I was running a bad second.

"What did you tell them?" I said.

"What I'm telling you. Listen, so I don't have to say it again. I got no Olsen, the description fits about ten of the punks. I can give you a list, the rest is up to you."

"How long have they got on me?" I asked.

The man looked at the clock on the wall. "Maybe an hour and forty minutes."

They had taken a slower taxi from the airport. I was gaining. I almost laughed at myself. But instead I took the list the man wrote down. He picked the names from a paysheet, and stared up at the hot ceiling as he recalled what his various boys looked like. In the end the list contained eight names.

"I gave them other two ten names, but I figured since that two of them been around town for over two months," the man said.

"Eight is enough," I said.

I looked at the eight names. Somehow I had to cut down the hour and forty minutes lead. It could be the first name or the last. If it was the first name, Jo-Jo

Olsen could be already dead. I read the names: *Diego Juarez, George Hanner, Max Jones, Ted John, Andy Di Sica, Dan Black, Mario Tucci, Tom Addams.*

I looked at the names, and you could take your choice. It could be any of them, or none. In a way I prayed it was none, at least the killers wouldn't find him. I could take the names from the front, and hope to be faster than the two hoods, or take them from the back and hope Jo-Jo was one at the end.

It was bad either way. If I took it from the front, and Jo-Jo was *Tom Addams*, then I lost a good chance to beat them to him. If I took it from the back, and Jo-Jo was *Diego Juarez*, then I lost any chance of reaching him first but maybe in time.

If I started at random, it was pure chance. It was pure chance most of the way. I didn't know the town, the addresses meant nothing so I couldn't map the best route. What I needed was a short cut—some way to go straight to Jo-Jo Olsen. I needed to crack the alias right here and now.

I ruled out *Diego Juarez* with a sigh of relief—too unusual for a tall blond boy, it had to be a real name, it would have drawn attention. I ruled out *Max Jones* and *Ted John* for the opposite reason—too common as aliases. Jo-Jo was a smart boy, Petey Vitanza said. *George* Hanner could be, it sounded a little like *Honda* which was the name of a motorcycle. *Andy Di Sica* and *Mario Tucci* were both good bets—Jo-Jo grew up with a lot of Italians, and he dreamed of Ferrari in Italy. *Tom Addams* was far out, but it sounded a little phony, and Addams is an historical name.

That left *Dan Black*, and I had it!!

I remembered what Packy Wilson had told me about Jo-Jo and the Vikings. I remembered what the experts said about an alias always being connected to a man. I hoped they were right, and that I knew enough. *Dan Black*. The name of a great Viking King, the first of the Norwegian Kings, and one of the names Packy Wilson had mentioned, was—Halfdan The Black! *Dan Black*.

"Call the police," I said to the small man behind the desk, "and get them out to Dan Black's room. What is the address, a motel?"

The man looked at the address and nodded. "A cheap motel about two miles from here. How do I know you …"

"Just call them, and tell them to make it quick. My name is Patrick Kelly, from New York, take my license number."

He took my license number, and I was gone. I was probably in the taxi and half way to the motel before the guy made up his mind he better call the police after all. It didn't matter. What I needed now was luck, not police.

So many cases, so many things in life, turn on luck, fortune, chance. I needed the luck that they had not reached Dan Black yet. I needed the luck that Dan Black was Jo-Jo. I needed luck to go against those two hoodlums, amateurs or not. I needed the luck that Jo-Jo was home. And I would need luck to hold on before the police did arrive.

I got some of the luck right away. The luck I didn't have was something I had not thought about. Jo-Jo Olsen was Dan Black, all right. And he was there. He was in the third cabin of the very cheap motel. The motel had shacks not cabins, the john was outside in a big central building with the showers, and the driveway was dirt.

I was the first one there, because all was quiet and yet normal, and Jo-Jo opened the door. That was all good luck. The bad luck was in his hand. A large .45 automatic aimed at my heart.

It had not occurred to me that Jo-Jo Olsen, alias Dan Black, might not want to be rescued.

HE WAS TALL, blond and good-looking. He was neat and clean and there was a bright look in his eyes. But the automatic was neither neat nor clean-looking, and he did not want help.

"Who asked you, Kelly? Yeh, I know you. Who asked you to butt in? Who asked Pete?"

I didn't answer because I had no answer. Who had asked me and Petey Vitanza?

"How did you find me so easy?" Jo-Jo asked.

He was seated on the single brass bed in the room. The room was as cheap as the motel itself. The walls were paper thin. I could hear every sound outside, every car on the street. I was listening. I expected company any minute.

"Dan Black," I said. "Halfdan The Black. You got a yen for Vikings and history."

I told him what Packy Wilson had told me, and about what the experts say. He seemed interested. I told him about the two boys Roth had sent after him, and about Schmidt being dead, and Petey beaten.

"Roth wouldn't do that," the boy said. "He's my father's cousin."

"You don't believe that," I said. "Roth would kill his mother if he had to."

"I left town. Dad told him we wouldn't talk," Jo-Jo said.

Then I heard his voice clear. Like his father, Swede Olsen, he was talking to himself. Only in his case there was a difference. He wasn't really trying to convince himself that Jake Roth would lay off him, he was telling himself that it did not matter. He was telling himself that this was the way it had to be. I had to be sure.

"All you have to do is talk, and you're safe as a church," I said. "If the cops don't protect you, Andy Pappas will. Talk, and Roth is through, and you don't have a worry. Nobody is going to back a beaten Jake Roth against a live Andy Pappas."

"I'll be okay anyway," Jo-Jo said.

"To protect Jake Roth?" I said. "You're a good kid, you've got ambitions, dreams. And you'll risk your life to save a known killer, a punk?"

"We don't rat," Jo-Jo said, and it sounded dirty when he said it. It is dirty, that code of the underworld.

"But not for Jake Roth," I said. "It's for your father. You want Roth to still do them favors, the favors they live on, your father and mother."

Jo-Jo looked at me steadily. "I owe them that. Dad can't go back to the docks. I can take care of myself."

"He'll be back on the docks anyway when I tell the police what I know," I said.

"You won't tell," Jo-Jo said, the automatic coming up.

"You'll kill me?" I said. "You'll commit murder to save Jake Roth?"

The tall, blond boy flushed, shouted. "NO! Not for Roth, for my family! They depend on him. I owe them. I …"

I lighted a cigarette. When I had it going I leaned back in my sagging old chair. I listened all the time. They would be here sooner or later, and the boy did not have to kill me. He just had to leave me for them.

"What about yourself?" I said. "What about what you owe yourself? You really think your father and mother thought you'd be safe?"

"They did! They do," Jo-Jo cried out, the pistol up again.

"No," I said. "Maybe at first they could fool themselves, but they can't even do that now. If I hadn't chased them down, they'd be sitting up there doing nothing while Roth's boys gun you. They're worrying about themselves!"

"They don't know," Jo-Jo said. "They believe Roth. And so do I."

"Then why did you keep the ticket?" I said.

The automatic wavered in his hand. It was a good hand, strong and clean. His face reddened again, and then became calm. Very calm and set as he looked at me.

"That ticket is insurance," I went on. "You're a good kid, but even good kids learn that kind of play in our neighborhood, right? You've got it stashed, probably. Addressed envelope and all that? You never trusted Roth from the start."

"So?" he said.

"So you knew your folks didn't either, not deep down. They just *wanted* to trust Roth. They wanted to believe it was okay so they could go on living their nice life in comfort. But deep down they knew Roth as well as you do. They tossed you to the wolves, kid."

"They're old," he said. "I owe them."

He was a really nice kid, it was written all over him. A kid with big dreams of a big world. But he was caught. It's always harder for the really good ones. He wanted no part of his father's world, but he had a sense of duty, of responsibility to his father and mother. He knew what his parents were, but he had a code of his own, and he was good enough to stick to it.

He might have made it, keeping his code and still staying alive, if I hadn't come along. I queered the deal. I had them all looking for him. Sooner or later even Pappas would hear about it and begin to wonder. Roth knew that, and so did I. I had ruined his chance, it was up to me to save him.

"How much?" I said. "You owe them, sure, but how much do you owe them, Jo-Jo? You've got a duty to them, sure, but how about your duty to yourself? That's the hard one, Jo-Jo. You got a duty to stay alive."

"It won't come to that," Jo-Jo said, almost whispered, and even he didn't believe it because he added, "I'll keep ahead of them."

I nodded. "All right, let's say you can, and that nobody tells about you. What then, kid? What about all you want to do? What about your dreams? You want to be a race driver, a Viking with cars!"

Jo-Jo's eyes glowed there in the shabby room. I was still listening to the sounds outside. There could not be much more time.

"I'll do it, too!" Jo-Jo said eagerly. "I get the diploma from automotive, and with my record driving, I'll get with Ferrari!"

I hit him with it. "What record? What diploma? You'll never get back to school, and you ain't Jo-Jo Olsen anymore, you're Dan Black. You'll never be Jo-Jo Olsen. You'll be on the run all your life!"

I could see him wince, blink, and I did not let up. In a way I was battling for my own life. If I didn't convince him, there was no telling what would happen when the two bully boys arrived on the scene.

"You got three choices, Jo-Jo, and only three," I said. "You can come back with me, give that ticket to the cops, and let Roth take what's coming to him. Then you can go ahead and live your own life.

"You can try to keep a jump ahead of Roth and his men all your life, and maybe make it. You'll live in shacks like this, you'll never be Jo-Jo Olsen again, and you'll have no past and no future. You'll never be able to set-up a record because you'll be changing your name too often.

"Or you can try to talk to Roth and join him. You can convince Roth you want to play his side of the street and that you're a safe risk. I doubt if he'd go for it, but he might. Maybe you could kill me for openers so Roth knows he's got a hold on you."

I threw in that last one as a shocker. Even if he killed me, I doubted that Roth would trust him. Once Jo-Jo was a full-fledged criminal, it would be too easy for him to get in good with Pappas by telling. But he wasn't dumb, he thought of that. In fact, he was ahead of me.

"There's a fourth way, Mr. Kelly," Jo-Jo said. "I could just go to Mr. Pappas and tell him without telling the police. That should put me in good with him and maybe save my father's job."

I nodded. "Sure, it might even work. But that would be the same as throwing in with Roth. You'd be an accessory to what happened to Roth. You'd be withholding evidence, and that's a crime. Besides, kid, you thought of that from the start, didn't you? That was why you ran and didn't tell your father. You don't want any part of that life or of Pappas."

The boy sat there silent. I had not told him anything he had not thought himself. It was like a psychiatrist. I just made him face it more. His whole world was rising up on him like a tidal wave in a typhoon. He hated his father's way of life, hated what his father had become, wanted to be free and alone, and yet he loved his father.

"Be a real man, Jo-Jo," I said. "Be man enough to take your own dreams, your own way. You want a certain life, you want to do certain things. That's the hardest road, kid. It's easy to do what will please everyone else. It's hard to take your own dream and follow it out of sight over the horizon like the old Vikings did."

Jo-Jo smiled and looked up. It was not a smile of happiness or triumph or any of that. It was a smile of simple recognition.

"They did, didn't they," he said. "My father even lets them call him *Swede* when he takes their favors."

"He lost it somewhere, Jo-Jo," I said. "You've got a chance. It's rough to accept the responsibility of your own dreams, but those old Vikings had to leave the old folks and the weak behind, too. I guess you have to hurt people to be honest with yourself."

"I guess you do," Jo-Jo said.

And that was all. After that it was, as the Limeys say, a piece of cake.

EVEN IF THE TWO bully boys had been pros they would not have had much chance. They expected to find one unsuspecting boy in that motel, and they found two ready-and-waiting men. Two well-armed men waiting for them like bearded Vikings in a cave. The two hoods walked out singing.

The police arrived and we all went down to Headquarters in Daytona Beach. We slept a nice night in the comfort of strong cell bars in case Jake Roth had any ideas of a last-gasp attempt to silence all of us. He didn't try, and the next day we all flew North with lots of friendly guards around.

Gazzo welcomed us with open arms and a secure paddy wagon. Jo-Jo turned over the parking ticket, and the Captain had him locked up safely until Roth was accounted for. Gazzo called in Andy Pappas to identify the license number on the ticket. Pappas looked at it for a long time.

"Yeh, it's the number of my small convertible, a black Mercury. I don't use it much, Captain, I got a lot of cars. I keep the Mercury out in Jersey at my shore place, all the boys use it sometimes," Pappas said very quietly. He looked at Gazzo. "You say Jake used it?"

"It figures that way, Pappas," Gazzo said. "Kelly tells me Bagnio knows that Jake had a losing ticket on a certain horse at Monmouth the day before Myra was killed. You know we found a ticket like that in her place."

Pappas nodded. "Jake always had a temper. Stupid, too. You say the ticket shows the car was on Water Street at five o'clock that day?"

"It does, and Jake hired some boys to find the Olsen kid."

Pappas stood up. "Is that it, Captain?"

"That's it for now. We'll want you again when we pick up Jake Roth," Gazzo said.

Pappas didn't even smile, he was that sad. He looked at Jo-Jo, and then at me, and I almost felt sorry for him. I could see he was thinking about Myra Jones, and all at once he was just another middle-aged man who had lost his woman through a stupid accident and the anger of another man. Only he was Andy Pappas, not just another man, and he had some pain coming.

"Thanks, Patrick," Pappas said. "You did a good job. I'll send you a check. The kid who got beat, too."

"Petey thanks you," I said. "I don't. No checks for me from you, Andy. I made the choice a long time ago."

"Suit yourself, Patrick," Pappas said. He had begun to pull on those white kids gloves he affects now. But his mind wasn't on the gloves.

"Leave Roth to us, Pappas," Gazzo said.

"Sure," Pappas said. As he went out Andy Pappas was smoothing his hand over his suit jacket at the spot where he used to carry his gun.

The two amateur hoodlums Roth had hired to find Jo-Jo sang like *heldentenors* in the last act of *Siegfried*. They told all there was to tell about how Jake Roth had hired them to find Jo-Jo, get the ticket, and kill him. The beating of Petey Vitanza, and the death of old man Schmidt, were just steps down the road to Jo-Jo.

"We never wanted to kill the old man," one of them explained, as if he thought that made it okay, and we could all kiss and make up. "He just kicked-off on us, you know? Jeez, Roth was gonna give us good spots in the organization. Man, that was real opportunity!"

"Book them," Gazzo said.

Both men were indicted on various counts of assault, and one good count of Murder-Second. The DA could have gone for Murder-One, and probably gotten it, but juries are chancy with real guilty ones, and trials cost the state money. The two bums would plead guilty to the lessers counts, all of them, and that would put them away forever.

Jake Roth vanished. When Gazzo and his men went to pick up the tall, skinny killer, Roth was long gone with two of Pappas's lesser men who had always been friends of Roth. Gazzo got a city-wide search going. Then the hunt went state-wide, and, after a time, it got on a national hookup. But Jake Roth kept out of sight and running all the rest of the summer and into the fall.

They were laying odds on Roth in the neighborhood. Joe thought Roth should surrender to the police.

"That ticket and the stub on the Monmouth nag ain't enough to make the Jones killing stick," Joe said. "Besides, it was an accident. Manslaughter-Second at the worst."

"Even the Schmidt killing could be beat with a good shyster," Packy Wilson said. We were in *Packy's Pub* as usual, with the Irish tasting better now that the leaves were beginning to fall if you could find a tree in the district. I had told Packy how he had saved us all with his story on Norwegian history. He was so pleased he was still setting up the drinks for me.

"None of it's enough for the cops to really nail Roth," Joe said.

"It never was," I said, "but it's enough for Pappas. It was always Pappas. If Myra hadn't been Pappas's girl, Roth would have walked in on Gazzo and taken a short one-to-five."

"He'd be smarter to confess to Murder-Two and take twenty-to-life," Packy Wilson said.

"He'd live a week," I said. "In jail Pappas would get him in a week. He'd be a sitting duck."

They both kind of studied their glasses. I tasted the fine Paddy's Irish, and thought about the simple and happy men who had distilled it in the old country and had never heard of Jake Roth or Andy Pappas.

"All Roth's got is a choice of how to die," I said. "He can confess to Murder-One and take the chair. He can let the cops get him and sit in jail waiting for Pappas to give the word. Or he can run and try to stay a jump ahead of everyone."

In the end it was the police who got Roth. On a cold day in October he was cornered in a loft in Duluth. He tried to shoot his way out and was nailed. He had lost fifteen pounds and was all alone when he died. Nobody felt sorry for him.

If this was an uplifting story, I'd probably tell you that Jo-Jo Olsen's decision to accept his duty to himself, his dreams of being a modern Viking, had worked out best for everyone in the end. But it didn't. With Roth gone, and with Pappas knowing that Olsen had tried to help Roth, Olsen is out.

Sometimes, when I've been up all night, I go past the docks and I see Swede Olsen standing in the shape-up. He's old, and Pappas is down on him, so he doesn't get much work even when he goes out and stands there every day waiting to be picked out of the shape. He doesn't drink in the expensive places anymore, he drinks in the cheap waterfront saloons. He's drinking a lot, the last I saw.

Jo-Jo has gone. He never went home. Old Magda Olsen spit on him at the police station. As she said, and meant, they had five kids but only one Jake Roth to make life sweet. After all, Magda Olsen is descended from Vikings, too.

I don't know what happened to Jo-Jo. But I know he'll do something. He finished his schooling, and Petey tells me he's riding his motorcycle on dirt tracks out west. I look for Jo-Jo's name in the papers all the time. Someday I know I'll see it. Maybe even as a member of the Ferrari team, or driving some Limey car to victory at Le Mans. Like I said before, it's all in the background, the air a man breathes, and Jo-Jo goes all the way back to the Vikings. That was what made him run in the first place, and that was what made him come back to finish Jake Roth. His sense of what a man has to do.

Jake Roth didn't have that, and it cost him. Andy Pappas doesn't have it either. Maybe we'll even get Pappas some day.

SOURCES

"If the Whisky Don't, The Women Will." *Mike Shayne Mystery Magazine*, August 1962, as "It's Whiskey or Dames"

"The Dreamer," *Mike Shayne Mystery Magazine*, September 1962

"The Bodyguard," *Mike Shayne Mystery Magazine*, October 1962

"Carrier Pigeon," *Mike Shayne Mystery Magazine*, February 1963

"The Blue Hand," *Mike Shayne Mystery Magazine*, April 1963

"The Price of a Dollar," *Mike Shayne Mystery Magazine*, June 1963

"Even Bartenders Die," *Mike Shayne Mystery Magazine*, August 1963

"Death for Dinner," *Mike Shayne Mystery Magazine*, October 1963

"The Heckler," *Mike Shayne Mystery Magazine*, November 1963

"No Way Out," *Mike Shayne Mystery Magazine*, February 1964

"Winner Pay Off," *Mike Shayne Mystery Magazine*, May 1964

"The Hero," *Mike Shayne Mystery Magazine*, May 1965

"Viking Blood," *Manhunt*, April/May 1966

Slot-Machine Kelly

Slot-Machine Kelly: The Collected Stories of the One-Armed Bandit by Dennis Lynds writing as Michael Collins is set in Garamond (the text) and Bodoni (the chapter titles and running titles), and printed on 60 pound Natural acid-free paper. The introduction is by Robert J. Randisi. The cover is by Tom Roberts based on the Lost Classics design by Deborah Miller. *Slot-Machine Kelly* was published in September 2005 by Crippen & Landru Publishers, Norfolk, Virginia.

CRIPPEN & LANDRU, PUBLISHERS

P. O. Box 9315, Norfolk, VA 23505
E-mail: info@crippenlandru.com; toll-free 877 622-6656
Web: www.crippenlandru.com

ALSO AVAILABLE BY MICHAEL COLLINS

Crippen is privileged to be the publisher of Michael Collins' most-recent collection of Dan Fortune short stories:

Fortune's World. This books contains 15 previously uncollected stories and a complete Dan Fortune checklist. ISBN: 1-885941-46-3. Trade softcover, $16.00.

> "To spin tales as intriguing and thought provoking as these for three decades is a remarkable enough achievement. Even more remarkable is the sustained quality of the pieces – from the earliest, 'Scream All the Way,' a nifty almost-perfect-murder plot, to the most recent, 'Family Values,' a powerful, contemporary puzzle that the prize-winning author wrote for this collection."
>
> Dick Lochte, *Los Angeles Times*

> "Devious puzzle-spinning and a strong social conscience combine to produce powerful and thought-provoking tales."
>
> Jon L. Breen, *Ellery Queen's Mystery Magazine*

LOST CLASSICS

Crippen & Landru is proud to publish a series of *new* short-story collections by great authors who specialized in traditional mysteries. Each book collects stories from crumbling pages of old pulp, digest, and slick magazines, and most of the stories have been "lost" since their first publication. The following books are in print:

The Newtonian Egg and Other Cases of Rolf le Roux by Peter Godfrey, intro-duction by Ronald Godfrey. 2002.

Murder, Mystery and Malone by Craig Rice, edited by Jeffrey A. Marks. 2002.

The Sleuth of Baghdad: The Inspector Chafik Stories by Charles B. Child. 2002.

Hildegarde Withers: Uncollected Riddles by Stuart Palmer, introduction by Mrs. Stuart Palmer. 2002.

The Spotted Cat and Other Mysteries from Inspector Cockrill's Casebook by Christianna Brand, edited by Tony Medawar. 2002.

Marksman and Other Stories by William Campbell Gault, edited by Bill Pronzini; afterword by Shelley Gault. 2003.

Karmesin: The World's Greatest Criminal — Or Most Outrageous Liar by Gerald Kersh, edited by Paul Duncan. 2003.

The Complete Curious Mr. Tarrant by C. Daly King, introduction by Edward D. Hoch. 2003.

The Pleasant Assassin and Other Cases of Dr. Basil Willing by Helen McCloy, introduc-tion by B.A. Pike. 2003.

Murder – All Kinds by William L. DeAndrea, introduction by Jane Haddam. 2003.

The Avenging Chance and Other Mysteries from Roger Sheringham's Casebook by Anthony Berkeley, edited by Tony Medawar and Arthur Robinson. 2004.

Banner Deadlines: The Impossible Files of Senator Brooks U. Banner by Joseph Commings, edited by Robert Adey; memoir by Edward D. Hoch. 2004.

The Danger Zone and Other Stories by Erle Stanley Gardner, edited by Bill Pronzini. 2004.

Dr. Poggioli: Criminologist by T.S. Stribling, edited by Arthur Vidro. 2004.

The Couple Next Door: Collected Short Mysteries by Margaret Millar, edited by Tom Nolan. 2004.

Sleuth's Alchemy: Cases of Mrs. Bradley and Others by Gladys Mitchell, edited by Nicholas Fuller. 2005.

Who Was Guilty? Two Dime Novels by Philip S. Warne/Howard W. Macy, edited by Marlena E. Bremseth. 2005.

Slot-Machine Kelly: The Collected Cases of the One-Armed Bandit by Dennis Lynds writing as Michael Collins, introduction by Robert J. Randisi. 2005.

FORTHCOMING LOST CLASSICS

Rafael Sabatini, *The Evidence of the Sword*, edited by Jesse Knight.

Julian Symons, *The Detections of Francis Quarles*, edited by John Cooper; afterword by Kathleen Symons.

Ellis Peters (Edith Pargeter), *The Trinity Cat and Other Mysteries*, edited by Martin Edwards and Sue Feder.

Erle Stanley Gardner, *The Casebook of Sidney Zoom*, edited by Bill Pronzini.

Lloyd Biggle, Jr., *The Grandfather Rastin Mysteries*, introduction by Kenneth Lloyd Biggle and Donna Biggle Emerson.

Max Brand, *Masquerade: Nine Crime Stories*, edited by William F. Nolan, Jr.

Hugh Pentecost, *The Battles of Jericho*, introduction by S.T. Karnick.

Mignon G. Eberhart, *Dead Yesterday and Other Mysteries*, edited by Rick Cypert and Kirby McCauley.

Victor Canning, *The Minerva Club, The Department of Patterns and Other Stories*, edited by John Higgins.

Elizabeth Ferrars, *The Casebook of Jonas P. Jonas and Others*, edited by John Cooper.

Anthony Boucher and Denis Green, *The Casebook of Gregory Hood*, edited by Joe R. Christopher.

SUBSCRIPTIONS

Crippen & Landru offers discounts to individuals and institutions who place Standing Order Subscriptions for its forthcoming publications, either all the Regular Series or all the Lost Classics or (preferably) both. Collectors can thereby guarantee receiving limited editions, and readers won't miss any favorite stories. Standing Order Subscribers receive a specially commissioned story in a deluxe edition as a gift at the end of the year. Please write or e-mail for more details.

Lost Classics